The Fractured

a novel by
SALLY LOUISE

AUTHOR'S NOTE

This book contains mentions and depictions of anxiety/panic attacks, body image problems, controlling parents, death of a parent/s, child abuse, deportation threat, domestic violence, drug and alcohol use (briefly), mild gore, mild torture, misogyny, PTSD, sexual harassment, sexual themes/content, self-harm, sex scenes, strong language, suicide (implied), trauma-based miscommunication, violence.
Please read at your own discretion.

For Luigi

TEN YEARS AGO
Dean

"You're an embarrassment," Gio Calacoci hissed as we stepped out of the Kings County Criminal Court. His hands remained at his sides in clenched fists, and his dark eyes were glazed with anger, lack of sleep, and traces of his booze fest from last night.

I buried my fists deep in my hoodie pockets and squinted at the afternoon sun reflecting off the sidewalk.

The remnants of my hangover were beginning to fade, but I still felt like shit. I was arrested after being charged with car theft and underage drunk driving last night. At the time, it was tempting to debate that it wasn't theft if the owner had left the car unlocked and I had technically returned it. The parking attempt wasn't great, but they got it back.

I spent the rest of Thursday night and most of Friday in a holding cell, sobering up and nursing a headache before my arraignment in the afternoon.

Gio didn't appreciate getting that call on his day off and having to drive to Downtown Brooklyn to bail me out. He preferred I spend the rest of the weekend locked up, but somehow, Mom talked him out of it.

We rounded the corner of the large stone arches at the building's entrance before he grabbed my arm and pulled me to a stop.

"Wait here. I need the bathroom." His accent was a blend of Italian and New Yorker, the latter of which he had picked up since we moved here.

We had lived in Brooklyn for the past six years. My English was decent enough that I could speak without pausing to find the right word and not worry about making a fool of myself when I said the wrong thing. My accent was changing too. Mom said I had developed a habit of dropping letters when I spoke. Maybe mimicking the speech habits of the locals was my brain's way of trying to fit in with the neighborhood.

Just like Dad...

"You didn't think to use the bathrooms when we passed 'em?" I muttered.

He glared and jabbed a finger at my face. "Don't be a fucking smartass, Deano—"

"Dean."

His nostrils flared. I only deadpanned back.

I could see him contemplating hitting me. The bruises on my ribs from the last time were beginning to turn yellow. It wouldn't surprise me if he refreshed the color again. But I knew he wouldn't hit me in public. The smack upside the head I received as we left the courtroom earlier hadn't counted by his punishment standards.

"Wait here," he repeated with a little more bite before trudging back inside.

I leaned against the exterior wall of the courthouse with a heavy sigh. The guilt of last night's events slowly began to wind through my insides, mixing with the anger and resentment I already had.

The judge had said I only did these things for attention, and I hated that it was partially true. Yes, I wanted my deadbeat father to notice, but only so he could understand how much pain he put us through. What I did was my way of getting back at him. The more he hit, the more I acted up. At least when he was focused on me, Mom was safe.

But I also genuinely enjoyed the thrill of the chase and doing something against the law. It's not like my life was getting better anytime soon, so I may as well enjoy it.

My fingertips skimmed over a lighter and a cigarette wedged in my pocket. The court officers confiscated them before I went to the holding cell, but returned them when I was released. Then Gio took them for himself. While he was busy flirting with the attractive desk clerk, signing me out, I stole them from his back pocket.

I brought the cigarette to my lips, cupping a hand over the end to light it as a breeze kicked up along the sidewalk. I drew back deep, and the smoke burned my lungs in a way that felt good until I coughed, spluttering into the crook of my elbow. I still had to work on my technique.

A city bus pulled up to the stop further to my left, and I watched lazily as several kids got off. Some were my age, others were younger, and all had backpacks and books tucked under their arms.

I forgot today was a school day, but junior year for me was beginning to look like a waste of time anyway. I spent most of my school life in the principal's office, either for talking back, sleeping in class, or fighting other kids.

The latter was always done in defense, more often at the defense of someone else. I never started fights, but would finish them. It was just last month that I defended a kid from a jerk named Scotty Richards.

Scotty was a bully who picked on the weak to boost his ego. So, I bruised his ego and punched him hard enough that he fell back and split his head open on the wall.

He lived and received a half dozen stitches.

The kids getting off the bus looked like they had their lives sorted, or at least fat trust funds to rely on when they fucked up. They were the kind of people whose paths I stayed out of so long as they stayed out of mine. But even staying in my lane, they couldn't help but judge from afar.

Then again, I was also technically judging them.

As they got closer, they held onto their belongings a little tighter, sending sidelong, wary glances my way as they passed.

Because what I want more than anything is to mug a schoolboy for his geometry textbook.

From what I overheard, they were heading to the burger joint down the street.

All except one.

She looked around twelve or thirteen years old, probably only four years younger than me, and wore round glasses that kept sliding off her small, freckled nose. Stray hairs from her messy ponytail clung to her face as she concentrated on her watch, furrowing her eyebrows.

My eyes dropped over the heavy tote bag of books, the art folder tucked under her arm, the violin case in her left hand, and the large backpack on her back. It was a lot for one kid to carry. She also had a small Band-Aid under her arm, peeking out from her short sleeve.

I couldn't help myself when I began anticipating the moment she mistook her next step in her hurry and sent everything flying. It wouldn't be so bad if her violin case knocked the self-absorbed nerd walking a couple of paces in front of her on the back of the head. He had looked at me judgingly one too many times already.

Or I could ask her for the case and whack him anyway.

I focused on the girl again as I drew back on my cigarette.

She wasn't with those other kids. None of them bothered waiting for her, and she showed no sign of following them. Instead, her steps began to slow as she got closer, before her blue doe eyes flicked to me.

I expected to receive the same snobby treatment from her.

She was shy and gentle and offered me a smile. "Hi."

All I could do was blink. I was left stumped by the polite interaction and watched as she took herself into the courthouse.

Suddenly, I wanted to know why she was going to the courthouse and why she bothered saying hello. Did her parents not teach her about stranger danger? At least in the city? Outside a courthouse, of all places? She didn't know me, so why be polite?

No one ever just said hello to me.

She lifted a hand to the door but stopped short when it swung inward, revealing my father on the other side. He plastered an overly generous smile on his oily face as he held the door for her, acting like he was the politest fucking man in the world.

The girl thanked him and then continued on her way.

Gio dropped his smile before he marched for me. Once in reach, he grabbed me by the hood and steered me to wherever his truck was parked. At the same time, he batted the cigarette from my fingers. The gesture came across as a disappointed father giving a shit about his teenage son's health, but Gio only did it out of spite. He wanted to remove even the simplest things that might bring me joy.

The entire two-block walk to the side street consisted of him complaining about how long it took him to find a parking spot and how I was an ungrateful piece of crap. Or how I would never amount to anything, and that prison was my future if I kept going the way I did.

I learned at an early age to stay quiet when he went on these rants.

When we arrived at the truck, Gio grumbled, "I work my fuckin' ass off for this family," but climbed into the front seat before I could hear the rest.

I hesitated outside the passenger door, unable to reach for the handle.

Run for it. Get the bus home. Go anywhere but in the truck.

Gio's voice was a muffled yell from within the cabin as he glared at me with dark brown eyes. "Get in!"

I hated that I did as he said.

My shoulders were tense as I sat there, anticipating his next move. When he shoved the keys into the ignition, I flinched but was beyond prepared for what came next.

The first punch stung my left cheekbone before my head hit the window. I covered myself with my arms as the hits kept coming. Each one was angrier than the last as he spat hate through his teeth. I begged him to stop, but my voice was too quiet — a broken whimper as tears stung my eyes and blood dripped from the split in my cheek.

He grabbed my shoulder and elbow and shoved me against the door as I shielded my face. It was his final bout of frustration before the violence stopped, and he casually turned back to the steering wheel. Smoothing a hand over his black hair, he composed himself and put the truck in drive.

I remained low in my seat for some time, wondering if it was safe to move yet, as if any sudden movements might start him off again. It wasn't until we were halfway into the drive that I carefully tugged my hood up and slowly rose in my seat. Every inch of where his fists had landed throbbed painfully. It felt like they would bruise to the bone this time.

I lowered my head but stared out the windshield. Glassy-eyed and focused on nothing but the thrum of the heartbeat in my ears and his voice echoing through my mind.

You are worthless. You're an embarrassment. You will never amount to anything.

CHAPTER 1
Dean

Present day...

The bounce in my knee hadn't stopped since I sat down in the dimly lit interview room. The blinds were drawn, blocking out the view of the exterior offices, and the clock on the brick wall to my right ticked louder with every passing second.

Car grease stained my jeans and the creases of my hands, but I pulled the latter through my hair, leaving them to rest on the back of my head as I hunched forward in my seat. The cuffs remained on my wrists while I waited and waited. I knew it was a tactic detectives used to make perps sweat, leaving them alone in an interview room to mull over their story, but I also knew I had nothing to hide anymore.

So why is my leg fucking bouncing?

Detective Sergeant Mark Whitmore had made a point of parading me past his organized crime colleagues as we entered the level of their office and headed to the interview room. Not that I was surprised. They were all smug to know they finally had a gang-affiliated member in custody. I was the key that could further their investigations into Antonio Gimello — one of the many Caporegimes in the Genovese family *and* my boss — *if* I chose to cooperate.

Blackmail. Death threats. Murder. It was all stuff I hadn't done, but I was associated with the people who did it.

I dug my fingers into my scalp, tugging my hair at the roots as I stared at the dark gray carpet beneath me. There was no running from this. I was boxed in with two options, and neither of them had great outcomes. The first was to refuse to cooperate, accept that my past had caught up with me, and pack my bags for a lengthy stay in a state prison. The second was to work alongside my girlfriend's dad, feeding him everything I knew about Antonio and maybe, *maybe*, getting some time shaved off my sentence. Either way, I would be going away for a long fucking time.

The door of the interview room opened behind me, and I slowly sat up straighter, choosing to keep my eyes on the empty chair opposite mine.

"Sorry about the wait. I had to organize some paperwork first," Mark said as he closed the door. He then crossed the room, passing me as he loosened his tie, and tossed a thick folder on the table before taking a seat. He retrieved a small silver key from his pocket and motioned for my hands. "Have you had time to consider what I want from you?"

My jaw ticked as I lifted my arms onto the table. "Plenty."

Mark unlocked the handcuffs with a click and a subtly smug expression on his face. I pulled my arms back, rubbing at my wrists.

"So?" he continued. "What are your thoughts?"

"That you should consider a career change." I sat back and folded my arms. "Maybe get into acting. You're a great liar."

He chuckled but ignored my sarcasm as he flipped the folder open and brushed a hand over the top of his graying, dark brown hair. With a casual scan of the first document inside, where my mugshot from several years ago was printed in the top right-hand corner, Mark spoke again. "I can't see a judge being very sympathetic for anything you've done."

I rolled my head to one side, briefly closing my eyes as my neck quietly clicked. "What you're asking me to do, the danger of it, I think I'd rather sit across from a stuck-up judge than put myself or anyone else at risk." My eyes settled and narrowed on him. "If Antonio found out I was working with the cops, he wouldn't only come for me."

"Well, we'll have to ensure he doesn't find out." He smiled briefly as he looked down at the papers and flipped to the next page. With a sigh, he clasped his hands together on top of the papers and looked at me again. "And neither will she."

I scoffed. "Now you want *me* to lie to her?... Great."

"Withholding information isn't lying."

"It's miscommunication."

"That's nothing new for you," he quipped smugly.

"I'm not keeping things from her again." *Things like this, anyway.*

"You will if you want to keep her safe."

The chair creaked beneath me as I leaned forward and braced my bare arms on the table. My voice was low and sharp. "If you wanted her safe, you wouldn't be asking me to get fuckin' intel for you."

Mark's eyebrows rose as he sat back in his seat. "You'd prefer I arrest you and send you to prison?"

"I've been to Rikers before. I was bound to go back eventually."

He tutted, stood, and walked around to the back of his seat. "I probably should've made myself clearer in the drive over... You *will* help us with this whether you want to or not. We can't afford to waste this opportunity."

"You're not listening," I hissed. "This will put Lily in danger. Again."

"Which is why she cannot know." He gripped the back of his chair as he pinned me with a glare. "I want her to remain unaware and unbothered by any of this... Of course, this would be so much easier if you hadn't gotten back together."

I didn't know why I did it; maybe it was the adrenaline coursing through my veins, but my lips curved up as I shook my head in disbelief. "Are you suggesting I break up with her again to make this *easier* for you?"

"You said it," he smirked.

Don't punch your girlfriend's dad because he's making sense...

"And you know I am right," he added.

I gritted my teeth and took a breath through my nose. "No. I love your daughter."

"If you loved her, you'd let her go."

"Yeah? Look at how well that went the first time I did that," I retorted.

"We're getting off-topic... If you're going to stay, you're going to have to get used to lying to her real fast." Mark took a seat again, returning his focus to the folder as he leafed through it. "It shouldn't be too hard for you. You've been lying for most of your adult life."

I could only stare at him as the information stacked up into a giant clusterfuck of problems before me. Then, like the grand cherry on top, Mark pulled out a sheet of paper and slid it across the table to me. Printed across the first line was my mother's name.

I didn't read the rest — couldn't read the rest as anger slowly bubbled up beneath the surface of my skin. Instead, I lifted my gaze to the detective. "What the fuck is this?"

"Are you aware that your mother failed to apply for citizenship? We're aware you and your father had one, but there's nothing for her..."

My fingers curled against the underside of my chair, and there was a subtle pounding in my head with realization. Dad never bothered with one for her. He made sure she rarely left the house. He kept her like a housewife and sucked any joy from her life once we moved to the States on promises he failed to keep.

Mark continued spitefully, "It'd be a shame if immigration were to find out—"

"She's in a fuckin' wheelchair." My jaw clenched so tight I thought my teeth might crack.

He stood and casually collected the papers while I remained still. On the inside, I was thinking of the probable consequences of throwing a detective through a window.

Prison time was on my horizon. What's one more charge of assault gonna change?

While I remained unmoving, my eyes followed Mark's every step as he approached my side of the table. Stopping directly beside me, he leaned against the edge of the table. "I'm guessing she's aware of what you've done too? I would hate to see her face the consequence of that—"

The chair beneath me tipped back with force as I shot to my feet and punched Mark across the face. He staggered sideways, clutching his cheek, before I grabbed the front of his shirt and forced him to stay upright.

I lifted my fist again but hesitated.

"I'd be *very* careful with what you do next, Dean," he smirked as he rubbed his reddening cheekbone.

The interview room door swung open, and several detectives barged in, yelling at me to release the sergeant. But Mark raised a hand to them, silencing them as they halted in the doorway while his eyes never left mine.

He quirked an eyebrow. "What'll it be?"

"Blackmail? Really? That's a little low for you, isn't it?"

"I get what I want, Dean. I will have Antonio locked away for the rest of his life. If it means dragging you through shit to do that, so be it," he muttered.

I shoved him back as I released his shirt. The motion caused the men in the doorway to shift nervously. With nothing else to consider, and my hand now forced, I steadied my breathing and my voice. "I'll do it."

Mark grinned. "Smart man."

I shook my head at myself and combed my fingers through my hair. There were no happy endings with any of this. I had begun to pace as the other detectives left the room. Meanwhile, Mark watched me. Maybe trying to figure out if I was going to explode again.

I stopped. "Now what?"

"You go back to work and then go home to my daughter and tell her how great your day has been." He drew a small, gray business card from his shirt pocket and held it towards me. "When Antonio makes contact, call me."

I took the card and read over it once before looking at him. "He hasn't made contact for a while. I hope you don't mind waiting."

"In the meantime, you can fill me in on all your little adventures with him. We'll schedule you for an appointment later this week for that chat." He stepped forward, dropped a hand on my shoulder, and grinned again, but it didn't reach his eyes. "I trust you won't try to run?"

I faked a smile. "Don't fuckin' touch me."

He tucked his tongue in his cheek as he scoffed in amusement, but dropped his hand and walked to the door.

"You know," he continued as he held the door open for me and prodded at the faint mark on his cheekbone. "I thought you'd punch harder than that, considering you fight for a living."

I pocketed his business card as I strode for the door and the low hum of the office beyond it. Those same detectives from before were watching from their desks.

As I reached Mark in the doorway, I slowed my pace enough to respond to him before I left.

"I was holdin' back."

Several days passed, and so did that appointment with Mark. I revealed most of what I knew or could remember as he took notes, asked questions, and reminded me what was at stake whenever I failed to reveal much else. From every black-market weapon deal to the cocktail parties Antonio hosted in his penthouse, sometimes with the head of the Genovese family.

Another week came and went. I worked at the garage and traveled to and from mine and Lily's. The former visits were spent in denial. I couldn't tell Mom that her citizenship, or lack of one, was hanging by a thread. Then there was the time spent at Lily's apartment, where I pretended life was normal.

Twenty-nine days from the day Mark had blackmailed me, it was Wednesday evening, and Lily's apartment was quiet. The only sound came from the city outside and Kira's *sleep sounds* playing faintly from her bedroom. Tonight, she was listening to the sounds of a thunderstorm. The rumbles conveniently complemented the real rain outside the apartment.

Lily was perched on the kitchen counter, holding up the bottom half of her T-shirt while I gently removed the gauze patches from her skin. Her bullet wounds were healed. All that was left of them were small, twisted scars no bigger than two inches. One on the right side of her stomach, the other on her lower back beside her spine — *too close* to her spine.

The doctor had given her the all-clear today. Wound care was no longer a thing she needed to worry about, and she could return to work, something she seemed indifferent about for some time. Including now. Beneath the surface, hidden within her blue doe eyes, were the slight hints of doubt, nerves, and something else as she stared blankly ahead. Every so often, she winced when the adhesive gauze tugged at her skin.

"Sorry," I muttered.

She didn't say anything.

It was like we had switched roles. She was the one disappearing into her mind.

"Almost done." I angled my head as I carefully peeled off the rest of the gauze on her back. I smoothed my thumb over the redness, and she inhaled sharply.

When the last of the gauze came away from her skin, she dropped the shirt and flattened it down over herself. The uncertainty on her face was quickly hidden by a smile when she caught me watching.

I scrunched up the gauze in my hands as I slowly straightened. "Feel better?"

"I'm going to wash off the stickiness from those patches." She hopped off the counter, but her movements were awkward as she walked between me and the fridge to get to her room. Like she was avoiding being touched.

I turned on the spot as she walked by, then leaned my hip against the counter. "Want company this time?"

She stopped in the doorway, glancing back as she gripped the door frame. The movement caused her short braid of golden-brown hair to fall from her shoulder.

"I think I'll have it alone if that's okay. It'll be quick anyway."

"Yeah, go for it." I crossed my arms loosely before shrugging one shoulder myself. "I was just wonderin'."

Her smile was almost forced, as if to reassure me that whatever I was worried about was nothing before she hurried into her room and closed the door. She couldn't get away fast enough.

I caught myself before I attempted to follow her for answers. She needed time and would talk when she was ready, even if it was killing me to see her like this.

The number for a psychologist, who specialized in treating gunshot survivors, had remained on the fridge since she left the hospital, but that didn't mean Lily wasn't trying. She had dialed the number twice, hung up on the first call, but followed through with the second, only to reschedule it the next day. That was about a week ago, around the same time the touch avoidance began.

CHAPTER 2
Dean

I woke to a strip of light streaming across the room from Lily's bathroom, and her side of the bed empty. Rubbing my tired eyes with the heel of my palm, I slowly sat up as if that might help me understand why she was up so late.

My phone said it was midnight.

Through the gap in the bathroom door, I could see her reflection in the mirror. She stood in front of it wearing an oversized navy-blue T-shirt — one of mine — and light blue checked pajama pants as she lifted the hem of the shirt to examine her scars. She went to touch them, her finger coming within inches of her skin, until she brought her hand back to holding the shirt and pressed her lips together.

I rested on my elbows as her brow furrowed, and she looked at her face in the mirror. She sighed heavily, coming to some unspoken conclusion behind those sad blue eyes as she let the shirt fall over herself and braced her hands against the basin, looking down.

I got out of bed, adjusting the waistband of my sweatpants as I rounded the bottom of the bed and neared the door. The light was bright against my pupils as I half squinted and knocked lightly.

Several seconds passed before she pulled the door all the way open and offered me a small, guilt-ridden smile.

"Did I wake you?"

"No," I lied, brushing a hand over my hair as I forced back a yawn. "You okay?"

Great question, dumbass.

"Mhm." It might've been believable if her voice hadn't gone up an octave.

My eyebrow lifted automatically while my eyes grew accustomed to the light. I leaned against the doorframe. "Are you comin' back to bed?"

"In a minute." Her smile wavered again.

I dropped my head against the frame. "Lily—"

"I won't be long, I promise. Go back to bed." She stepped closer, lifting her hand towards my face.

In my half asleep, but trying to be a fully awake and supportive boyfriend state, I expected her to caress my cheek. It would have been the first time she reached out physically in a week. I missed the feeling of her hands on my skin.

She patted me on the head instead, shared another of her reassuring smiles, and closed the door.

I blinked, processing the interaction.

Grumbling to myself, I went to bed but lay awake, staring at the ceiling in the dark. I was *her* boyfriend and deserved some kind of explanation.

She needed time and would talk when she was ready...

But we also need to communicate.

I was tired of feeling like I was looking in from the outside, waiting for her to crumble. I knew what she was going through and knew what bottling up trauma could do. I never had someone to talk to about mine until her, so it was my turn to return the favor.

So long as I didn't come across as a pushy dickhead.

Lily was in the bathroom for several minutes before quietly entering the room again. Her bed socks scuffed the carpet as she went. She barely jostled the mattress when she climbed in and tucked herself beneath the covers. I wasn't sure she was aware I was awake. She remained on her side with her back to me.

The gap between us felt too far.

I inhaled sharply through my nose and flicked on the lamp beside me. "Yeah, we're not doin' that."

She rolled over, blankets pulled up to her chin as she looked at me with confused, wide eyes. "Doing what?"

"You were worried at one point about what's going on in my head, so now it's my turn." I faced her, resting on my side, and spoke a little softer. "Talk to me."

"I'm not doing it on purpose."

"Okay, so what's wrong?"

Lily sat up slowly, crossing her legs beneath the sheets as she turned to face me. A strand of hair fell from her braid as she glanced down at her hands in her lap. "There's nothing to talk about—I mean, there is, but I can't explain it..."

I was fighting every urge in my body wanting to reach out and touch her, to comfort her. Maybe she didn't want that yet.

"I feel like I'm broken..." she said.

The words came like a punch to my own heart.

Lily frowned at herself. "But I'm confused because I know I should be grateful I didn't die. I should be happy I'm here. With you. And for a little while after the hospital, I was... But then I see myself, and I wonder why you're still here."

I frowned this time as my chest squeezed. "Where else would I be?"

"Anywhere else but with someone who's been nothing but a shell these past couple of months?... I see the way you look at me, like you're worried I'm going to break, and it makes me wonder why you'd bother staying."

"I offered to be here, remember? I wanna be here."

"Are you sure, though? I don't think you've had a good enough look at the scars on my skin to say that. I'm not exactly desirable anymore." She sighed and dropped her face to her hands. "That sounded different in my head."

"Lily."

She looked up, chewing the inside of her cheek.

"What part of me sayin' I love you did you not get?" I carefully reached for her face, and for the first time in a while, she let me touch her, pressing her cheek into my palm. "That includes scars and your overthinkin' brain. I'm not going anywhere."

I shouldn't have said it, but it had slipped out before the thoughts of prison reminded me how much time I had left with her. Sure, there were visiting hours, but that wasn't the same as being with her like this. Just the two of us in the quiet. I also didn't like the idea of her going through metal detectors and body searches only to sit in some seedy visitor's room waiting for me to be led out of a cell.

Lily smiled briefly, despite the sadness in her eyes, and then slowly moved closer.

Her lips were inches from mine, but she paused, looking over my face before gently brushing a strand of my hair away from my forehead.

"I don't deserve you," she whispered.

"Yeah, you do."

My heart backflipped when she brought her soft lips to mine, kissing me so tenderly and slowly. Each kiss was hesitant, but grew hungrier as she melted — her walls were slowly coming down. Without really thinking, my hand drifted to her waist, jostling her shirt enough for my fingertips to skim across her scar.

She tensed, and I quickly removed my hand.

"Sorry—"

"No, it's okay." There was a faint spark of urgency in her eyes. "It's strange being touched there. I half expect it to explode with pain whenever it's bumped."

"Is there pain?" I glanced at her side and then searched her face. Still so close to my own, I could kiss her again.

"No pain." She shook her head. "Just butterflies. *Lots* of butterflies."

"Yeah?"

"I'm nervous. But in a good way."

I was lost for a second, thinking the nerves were from communicating how she felt, until I paid attention to the look she was giving me. I missed that look — the silent invitation within it.

"It's only been a month and a half since the accident," was the first coherent thing to leave my mouth. It was a better choice of words than the, *fuck it, let's go,* that raced through my head.

"I know."

"And you're okay with it? Just a second ago, you weren't exactly—"

"That month and a half has been too long..." Her hands drifted to the hem of her shirt. But then she hesitated. "There is something I should mention... I haven't really shaved since leaving the hospital."

I shook my head. "Not an issue. Ever."

She smiled a little again and returned to lifting her shirt, inhaling as if preparing to step from her comfort zone.

"Wait." I needed to apply logic and not let my dick ignore any potential warning signs — any tells that might say she wasn't fine. "This is what you want?"

"I think, maybe, it might help. Just throw caution to the wind, type of thing. Remind me of what I'm missing." She offered me a faint smile and a raise of her shoulder.

"Should we have a safe word? In case it gets too much for you and you need to..." She slowly peeled the shirt off, and my train of thought went out the window. "...stop."

In the cool air of the bedroom, her breasts peaked as she took a steadying breath beneath my gaze. The scars were there, but were nothing compared to everything else. Her shape, her soft, petite curves, and the way her chest rose and fell with every breath.

My blood rushed south. "Yep. Still desirable."

She huffed a bashful laugh, blushing in the warm lamplight. Her smile alone caused my heart to hammer against my ribs.

"I think stop will be fine." She loosened the braid in her hair until the silken, gold-brown waves hung just below her shoulders.

I raised a brow, slowly lifting my gaze from her body.

"Touch me, Dean."

Goosebumps rose along the back of my neck at the gentle command. My hand drifted to and up her thigh as I rose to kiss her. Every inch of me burned to move faster, but I kept it steady for her, laying her back gently, my lips on hers. Not quite on top of her, I brought a hand to the side of her throat, where her pulse fluttered beneath my palm, and caressed her jaw with my thumb.

She tentatively curled her fingers into the back of my hair and welcomed me deeper, parting her lips and nudging her hips closer.

I guided my mouth to the other side of her throat, where her soft skin burned, and skimmed my hand down her body, just missing the scar. She arched into my hand until I reached her pants.

"Is this okay?" I asked against her skin.

When she didn't respond right away, I pulled back to see her face.

Her gaze was heated, but her lips trembled slightly as she offered me the faintest of smiles. And then shook her head slightly, blinking as her eyes flicked down to where my hand was.

I brought it to her face, trying to meet her eyes again. "Slower?"

"I don't know why I'm so nervous," she said quietly. "My mind is all over the place."

"We can stop."

She watched me a little longer and then inhaled like she was trying to settle herself.

"We could cuddle?" I shrugged.

Lily laughed softly.

I smiled. "What?"

"I don't know why hearing you say cuddle sounds so out of place." Her eyes shone with amusement.

I traced my fingertips along her jaw to her chin. "*Voglio tenerti tra le mie braccia, amore mio.*"

As my thumb caressed her bottom lip, her lashes fluttered. "And what does that mean?"

"Do you trust me?"

"Of course."

"Turn your back to me."

She was a little confused but turned on her side, facing away from me.

"Now scoot back."

It dawned on her what was happening, and she smiled broadly as she backed herself into me. I wrapped my arms around her. She wasn't as hesitant this time and snuggled against me to get comfortable. Soft and warm with her head on my bicep.

"Better?" I murmured.

Lily nodded, finally content as she closed her eyes.

For a moment, it was easy to forget how bad everything was.

CHAPTER 3
Dean

Nine days into October had brought a cool change to most mornings, making getting out of bed harder.

Especially after last night.

I wanted to stay wrapped in the sheets with Lily a little longer, relying on each other's body warmth since the radiator in her room was broken. But she had work, and I wanted to keep up the illusion that everything was still okay.

This was why I started training at a new gym, and running myself ragged on the combined ten miles there and back to Lily's. Running kept my mind busy and, in a way, was my version of self-punishment for getting into this mess.

My chest heaved as I leaned against the back wall of the elevator, wiping sweat from my face using the bottom of my shirt. The numbers above the door slowly ticked to level three, the top floor of this apartment building. I made this elevator trip so many times that it was a habit. It felt normal. Like I had lived here longer. It was only five months ago, during the dark early hours of a Sunday night, Lily had found me in the one-way street outside.

Normally, my cynical self would eye-roll at anyone falling head over heels for someone that fast, especially within five months...but here I was, head over heels and still falling for a woman way out of my league. For me, she was home.

The elevator doors slid open, revealing the hallway leading to Lily's apartment at the other end of the top floor.

Standing right outside Lily's apartment was a woman who was slowly becoming my arch-nemesis — Susan. The nosiest person I had ever met.

She had her back to me and her ear pressed firmly to the door.

You've got to be fucking kidding.

All Susan knew was that Lily needed bed rest. But that obviously wasn't a good enough excuse to keep her nose out of Lily's business.

I approached on steady, quiet steps and managed to get right behind her before I slid my hands into the pockets of my shorts and cleared my throat.

She slapped a hand to her chest as she whirled with a gasp, then slowly drew her eyes up to my face. Her mouth opened and closed as she tried to come up with an excuse.

I cocked a brow.

"You shouldn't sneak up on a person like that. Especially considering my age."

I tilted my head slightly. "Did you forget which door was yours?"

"No, I was going to check on Lily."

I gestured to the door with my thumb. "Through the door?"

"I was going to knock."

"Uh-huh."

Her eyes narrowed spitefully. "You know you can't live here unless you're paying rent, and you seem to be hanging around quite a lot."

"Who says I'm not payin' rent?" I wasn't, but Kira's moms didn't mind me staying for a while.

"People talk."

"Yeah?" I crossed my arms and jerked my chin in a nod. "Who?"

She receded a step, throat bobbing as she fiddled with the thin silver chain around her neck. Her eyes dropped to her watch. "Oh, look at the time! I should be going. I have something in the oven. Not that it is *any* of your business."

"*Really?*"

"Yes." She straightened and walked across the hallway to her apartment. "Tell Lily I hope she feels better soon." She hurried inside.

I folded my arms and settled against the wall, watching Susan's door as I slowly counted to five in my head. At the three-second mark, her door opened enough for her to poke her head out, eager to attempt to eavesdrop again until she saw I hadn't moved.

I flashed her a smile, and she promptly shut the door again, flicking every lock on the other side.

My smile dropped as I pushed away from the wall and let myself into Lily and Kira's apartment using Lily's key.

Lily hadn't hinted she wanted me gone yet, even if she had been emotionally distant. She explained last night, as we lay in bed, that the reason for her distance was only because of her self-consciousness of the scars. She thought I would see her differently once I had a good look at them. *That* was a thought I wanted to make sure never bothered her again.

The smell of toast filled the apartment, and I could hear someone quietly moving around the kitchen as I walked down the short hallway. Coming up on my right was Kira's bedroom door, and seeing as it was still closed, it meant Lily was awake and making breakfast alone.

I walked into the living room, tossing the keys onto the countertop.

Lily, buttering two slices of toast with raspberry jam, looked up and smiled warmly. The way her eyes quickly took in my bare arms didn't go unnoticed either.

"Morning, again," she whispered.

Her eyes were shinier today compared to last night. All of her looked shinier. She was in her work clothes with her hair brushed back into a low bun. Her crisp white button-up top was tucked loosely into a pair of skinny jeans, and she had rolled the sleeves up to sit beneath her elbows, revealing her slender wrists.

There was no use hiding the grin spreading on my face as I walked into the kitchen, stepping in behind her while I eyed her figure in those clothes.

"Morning," I hummed, bracing my hands on the countertop on either side of her.

"I'm guessing the run was good?" She peered over her shoulder, licking jam from the knife she used. The corner of her mouth curved up.

The only response I could muster was to kiss my favorite part of her neck. The soft area above her pulse. When my lips parted and brushed against her skin, she tilted her head, exposing that side of her throat. I held the rest of me away from her, keeping my sweat-soaked shirt off her clean clothes.

"You smell so good," I murmured onto her skin.

She let out a little laugh. "It's just fabric softener."

"You taste good too, but I don't think that's fabric softener," I smiled, leaving lazy kisses wherever my mouth wandered.

Kira's bedroom door clicked open, reminding us we weren't home alone, before she stepped into view. Her fiery red hair was stacked in a messy bun as she yawned and stretched.

I pulled back from Lily, turning down the PDA but keeping my arms on either side of her as I offered Kira a nod in greeting. And briefly glanced down to make sure I wasn't revealing too much beneath the fabric of my black knee-length shorts.

Kira rolled her eyes as she smiled. "You know you don't have to stop doing the cute relationship stuff around me."

"Are you sure? It's not too awkward?" Lily started to move away with her toast, but I gently grabbed her waist to hold her in place. She glanced back with a frown and then pressed her lips together to keep from smiling when she realized why she couldn't move yet.

My body was just a little excited...

Kira hadn't noticed as she continued. "It's a distraction from *he-who-does-not-deserve-to-be-mentioned*." She visibly forced back a shudder.

His name wasn't spoken out loud, but it was enough to subdue the mood.

"And you two are cute together, so don't stop because of me," Kira continued before she swiped a piece of toast from Lily's plate and headed to the couch.

"By all means, help yourself," Lily drawled, lifting the second piece of toast from her plate.

I couldn't help myself when I took a bite, making her suck in a quiet gasp.

The smile in Lily's eyes betrayed her attempt to seem annoyed as she jabbed my stomach lightly with her elbow. "Go have a shower, toast thief."

I chuckled and backed away. "Yes, ma'am."

We pulled up outside the Whitmore real estate agency right before 8 AM, driving slowly along the brown and orange fallen leaves packed into the gutter before I put the Cadillac into park and turned the engine off.

Lily paused, watching as I pulled the keys from the ignition.

"What?" I asked.

"You don't have to come in. It's just work."

I shrugged, tugging the sleeves of my hoodie up my forearms. "It's your first day back."

She smiled as she gathered her bag from the back seat, bringing herself closer. "And I can walk in on my own." She kissed my cheek.

Sue me for feeling a little protective of her. She was finding her feet again, and I wanted her to have a smooth landing when she did.

I rested my wrist on the steering wheel as I watched her and then looked past her shoulder at the office. Through the glass front doors, I could see her mother and the other busybody who worked in reception eyeing the car with scrutiny. Her mother's gaze narrowed with spite when she recognized the loud car was mine.

Still not a fan. Noted.

"I'll be fine, Dean," Lily said, cupping my face in her hands to pull my attention to her. "See you at four o'clock?"

I let out a disgruntled hum in agreement as I read her face. There wasn't a hint of sadness, worry, or fear in her eyes. Like something had clicked into place last night. Or her poker face was better than I thought.

Don't be that guy; trust your girlfriend. And kiss her properly before she leaves—

Lily had already climbed out of the car with a little wave before I jumped out of my door. As I strode around the front of the Cadillac, she watched me curiously from the sidewalk until she realized what I had in mind, and her face lit up with a smile.

"You thought you could get away that easily without a proper goodbye?"

She shook her head. "You're ridiculous."

"I'm in love." I stopped in front of her, cupped her face, and kissed her.

Fuck what people thought about PDA. Fuck what her mom thought too.

Lily's hands curled around my wrists and slid down my forearms as she tilted her head back, kissing me softly until she slowly stopped.

"I should get inside before I change my mind about starting work today," she muttered, eyes lifting from my lips.

I raised an eyebrow.

She looked like she was considering it as she played with the drawstring of my hood, but then she blinked and stepped back. "Nope. No. Don't give me that look."

"What look?"

"You know exactly what look." She lowered her voice to a whisper. "Like you're undressing me with your eyes."

I folded my arms and leaned back on the Cadillac, tilting my head in coy curiosity. "Wasn't aware I could do that... But now that you mention it."

A blush crept to her face, and her lips threatened to curve up. "I'm committed to getting back into a routine, starting today, and I will see you *after* work."

I nodded once, lazily dragging my eyes down in a way that made her fidget on the spot.

"*Oh* my god, okay, bye." She turned and headed for the office, shaking her head to herself before calling back over her shoulder with a smile. "Say hello to Sofia for me."

Mom had texted on the drive over that she needed a lift to a vet appointment with her puppy, Bella, today for vaccinations. Truthfully, like any other time I had visited her, I wasn't looking forward to it; to lying to her face and pretending our life hadn't gone to shit because of my choices.

My thumb drummed faintly on the steering wheel as we drove to a vet in Bensonhurst. I tried to stay present, with Mom in the front seat and Bella on her lap, but my mind was preoccupied. Distant. Mom was talking, but I couldn't concentrate on what she was saying.

How much time do I have before I'm arrested—before Mom has to figure out how she'll do things on her own when I'm gone... Mark is using her situation to blackmail me, but what's stopping him from telling immigration after I've been sent to prison—?

Sound crashed into my thoughts with a blast of a car horn nearby.

"What were you sayin'?" I asked.

"How is Lily?" Mom repeated, scratching the caramel fur on top of Bella's head.

"She's doin' alright."

"Is that all?" She tutted, brushing her thick braid of long black hair from her shoulder when Bella took an interest in chewing the end of it.

I half smiled. "She started work today."

"Oh, good—so when are you moving in?"

My eyebrows shot up as I let out a breath and looked at her. "Cuttin' to the chase, I see."

"You've been there so often already," she shrugged. "Move in together."

"That's very un-Italian of you. Most Italian mothers want their adult sons to stay home." I smirked, knowing that was never her way of thinking. She loved the idea of family staying close, but she always encouraged me to do what made me happy.

"Oh, pfft," she scoffed.

When we arrived at the vet parking lot, my attention was quickly drawn to a gray sedan parked in the only wheelchair access zone.

"Fuck's sake," I muttered.

The driver was leaning against the car door on his phone and showed no signs of needing a wheelchair.

"Language," Mom whispered. She then brushed off the issue with a wave of her hand. "There are other spaces."

"Not for wheelchairs..."

Jaw ticking, I drove on and found an empty spot.

After helping Mom out of the car and into her chair, with Bella waiting in the driver's seat until I scooped her up and plopped her onto my mother's lap, I brought them from the parking lot and along the sidewalk to the clinic doors. Mom checked Bella in at the desk, the woman behind the desk cooed over the excitable puppy, and I stood by the waiting room chairs until Mom was done with the sign-in.

"I'm gonna wait in the car. Text me when you're ready." I began moving to leave, but Mom caught my wrist.

"The parking space we have is fine." Her blue eyes sharpened with a warning. "*Non confrontare quell'uomo.*"

Do not confront that man...

Shouldn't be too hard.

"*Non lo faro.*" I smiled easily, flipping my keys around my finger. Ever the charming, completely well-behaved son...

"Dean," she warned.

"I promise. I won't talk to the guy."

I smiled again and then left the building through the automated doors, stuffing my fists into the pocket of my hoodie as I followed the sidewalk to the parking lot again. At least if my fists were tucked away, there was less risk of me hitting the guy on the way back. It didn't help that I had to walk directly behind his car to get to mine.

He got off his phone as I passed him and strode in the direction of an ATM down the street. I assumed that's where he was going. It was a good four minutes away.

I got to the Cadillac and unlocked the passenger door, and then popped open the glove compartment with one thought in mind.

Four minutes is plenty of time.

Among the things I rummaged through was a bag of Dum Dums, Lily's idea to help me quit smoking. They kept my mouth busy and curbed the cravings whenever I felt the urge to put a cigarette between my lips. Which was exactly what I needed right now.

I grabbed a lollipop, along with the things I was looking for, then straightened from the car and closed the door. Tearing the wrapper open, I retraced my steps through the parking lot and shoved the lollipop into my mouth, flicking the stick to one side as I honed in on the gray sedan.

No one was around as I stepped in beside the driver's side door and began peeling back the rubber lining on the window directly above the door handle. Using my body to block what I was doing from view, I pushed the bent coat hanger wire down into the narrow gap of the door and jimmied it until the lock popped.

I pulled open the door and climbed in, ducking my head for a better view of the underside of the steering column before getting to work on removing it using a screwdriver. The amount of times I had done this in the past, usually in more of a hurry if I was desperate, was something I shouldn't have been proud of, but I couldn't fight the satisfied smirk that spread on my lips when the car's engine started after several taps of the exposed wire ends.

Two short blasts of a horn made me peer up quickly over the dashboard.

A large van, with windows down the side and a wheelchair sticker, had stopped in front of the car as the driver leaned out of her window.

"You know you can't park there, right? At least not without a sticker or sign." Her eyes drifted across the car, looking for those exact things. "I don't mean to be assumptive, but it kinda looks like you don't need the space."

The kid in the back was in an electric wheelchair and holding a teddy up to partially hide their face as they watched.

"I'm just movin' it." It wasn't a lie.

I offered them a half smile and put the gear stick in reverse, resting my arm on the back of the passenger seat as I pressed the accelerator. There were several other spaces nearby that this guy could've taken, so I chose one that was the furthest away. Once the car was off, I fixed the steering column and window to look like they hadn't been tampered with. On the way back, still sucking on the lollipop, I gave a simple nod to the woman of the van now taking up the wheelchair access point.

She was standing at the back of the van, waiting for the kid to slowly reverse down a ramp as she watched me. At first, she sent me a look of gratitude before her brows furrowed in confusion when she watched me climb into the Cadillac. Not long after, the sedan driver returned, shocked at first that his car was gone and then baffled when he found it several minutes later in a completely different spot.

I watched through my mirrors, satisfied, until my attention was pulled to my phone as it buzzed on the dashboard.

My gut instantly twisted at the *Unknown Number* written above the message. It was only his address and a time, but suddenly, the past month of peace was shattered. This simple text would set the ball rolling for what would be the end of my freedom. Work with Detective Whitmore would increase, and everyone I cared for would unknowingly have their lives on the line if I fucked this up.

I picked up the phone and opened my contact list, working my jaw as I reconsidered going through with this. I could lie for a week, or maybe a month, and pretend Antonio never reached out.

And run the risk of Mark finding out, getting annoyed I lied, and then having Mom deported because I didn't cooperate.

I tapped his name and waited as the phone rang on the other end.

"Ah, my favorite person." Mark's sarcasm dripped through the phone. "Have anything good for me?"

"He's made contact."

CHAPTER 4
Lily

Rain pattered against the floor-to-ceiling front windows of the foyer as I shivered behind the front desk.

Candice, the middle-aged receptionist I shared the desk with, insisted on turning the AC to cool when she complained the foyer was stuffy. I think it had more to do with her hot flashes, but I kept my mouth shut, rolled down the sleeves of my white cotton shirt, and focused on work, fighting the urge to shudder again as I glanced at the time on my computer screen.

What felt like forever ago, when Dean had dropped me off, had only been three hours.

He could warm me up. The man was a walking, living heater.

It was almost 11 AM, and, with the foyer growing too cold to sit comfortably in, I decided to do the office drink orders early.

I stood, rubbing my arms for warmth. "Did you want anything from the kitchen, Candice?"

"No, thank you." She glanced at me from over her glasses, noticing the tightness of my shoulders. "Looks like you should've brought a sweater."

I hummed and forced a smile before walking down the hallway.

From every real estate agent's office, as I stopped in their doorways asking if they wanted the usual, I received the same script of questions. They all wondered how I was after so much time away from work and then followed up with a question about why I had "disappeared" in the first place.

As if Mom's explanation of me being unwell wasn't good enough.

Each short conversation only added to the knot of nerves growing in my stomach. Tiny at first, it had started this morning as the usual anxiety I had before starting work, but then pinwheeled as the day went on.

I shut down each question with "I had the flu" and a polite smile before heading to the next office, and then the next, and so on. Skipping the empty one that once belonged to James Henderson, now a temporary storage area, I eventually arrived at Kate Whitmore's office at the end of the hallway.

My mother was on the phone as I peered through the door and mouthed if she wanted anything to drink. She shook her head, so I left for the kitchen.

Making the coffee orders came back like muscle memory, and, without worrying about the unwanted advances of a colleague, it was easier to relax into. It was easy to daydream again as I stirred the coffee, staring at the swirling darkness in the mug until my mind wandered too far.

I felt that dread lingering within the compartmentalized section of my brain. Sometimes, it got through and reminded me of what almost dying felt like.

It was horrible, knowing how easily everything could slip away, but be so peaceful at the same time. And then there were the thoughts that were evenly split, like pros and cons. One reminded me that every single moment alive was precious and should be treasured. The other wondered if it was worth it when death was a promise for everyone...

If I were religious, maybe the thought of death wouldn't feel so dark.

My hand drifted to my side, and I glanced down as I lifted the hem of my top to take a look at the scars. I touched the one above my hip bone, where the bullet had passed through my side, and traced the tip of my finger along the two-inch-long, raised area of skin.

I had to twist to look at the other one beside my spine.

That one was as small as the first but more twisted. A bullet's exit wound was always more gruesome, and mine was no different. Roughly shaped like an X marking a spot, it was where most of my blood poured from. Of course, in the now fuzzy and partially lost memories of when I was bleeding out on Dean's backseat, I thought I was bleeding pretty heavily from both wounds.

All of the past couple of months felt like some strange dream, going by so quickly. The fire at The Den was like a finite closure to one chapter of my life. In turn, ending some friendships...

Dean had mentioned that Terry was working at another of Antonio's clubs. Meanwhile, the old work group chat was mostly quiet now as Jen and Xavier moved on with their lives. They knew of my accident and visited me in the hospital, along with sending me their love in the chat, but sometimes friendships grew apart. I was appreciative of the relationships I had with them at The Den. They taught me a lot in my brief time there.

The last I heard of them was that Jen worked in a tattoo parlour and Xavier was bartending elsewhere.

They had moved on with their lives.

I inhaled deeply to clear my mind and smiled faintly to myself. It was forced, but it briefly tricked my mind into a more positive space.

I'm alive. I have good friends, a family, and a supportive man to be grateful for.

"And coffee orders to finish," I added out loud to myself.

I delivered the coffees two at a time and returned to the cold foyer, having also made a peppermint tea for myself to warm up. I hugged my hands around the mug and held it close as I took a seat at my computer.

"Just going to the ladies' room," Candice said, already on her way out from behind the desk.

As I sipped my tea and enjoyed the silence before I set the mug down to get back to work, two things happened within seconds of each other. The first was Mom walking in behind the front desk and instantly complaining about the cold. I was about to explain to her why the AC was cranked to near Arctic temperatures, but was cut off by a loud bang outside.

The logical part of my brain knew it was only a car backfiring, but it didn't stop my thoughts from racing. Suddenly, I was brought back to Aiden's living room. The gun had gone off, Kira was crying, and I was bleeding. But I couldn't remember the pain.

The human body couldn't remember pain—

"Lily." Mom's voice cut through the memory.

I blinked and turned in my seat, quickly smoothing over my reaction. "Yes, sorry. Candice said it was a little stuffy out here."

Mom rolled her eyes and plucked the AC remote off the wall before bringing the temperature back to something bearable. She then collected what she originally came out for — a folder from her mailbox — and headed back to her office. She was busy for most of the morning and kept her conversations with me brief. But I had a feeling she was giving me a partial silent treatment. Mom was still bitter about me choosing Dean to help while I healed instead of going home to her, but she wouldn't voice her opinions about him anymore, not when he was the reason I was alive.

Candice returned from the bathroom. When she found the AC was turned up, she tutted and turned it back down again with a sideways glance at me.

I couldn't be bothered wasting my energy, telling her it wasn't me, and focused on going through my emails instead. With a soft but heavy sigh, I curled and uncurled my fingers as I reached for the mousepad, trying to gain some control of the faint shake in my hands.

Chapter 5
Kira

"And what do we remind ourselves after every meeting?" asked Libby, the support group leader.

How many times had she heard it all before? The stories of excuses, misplaced forgiveness, and abuse. Libby had listened intently to each of our stories. She made sure we felt heard.

It had taken me two sessions at this Survivors of Domestic Violence support group to open up about my story. After weeks of feeling guilty, ashamed, anxious, and happy, I was free, but sad I was alone — far too many emotions for a person to handle on her own — I plucked up the courage to attend a meeting. I saw the fliers at the hospital while visiting Lily. She had encouraged me to attend these meetings after we made a pact to heal together.

I joined in with the rest of the group as we responded to Libby's question. "We are survivors."

Some, myself included, were more enthusiastic with our responses, while others muttered or remained silent. They still needed to find that confidence again.

For most of the women in our group, showing up was enough.

With a lighter feel to my step after the meeting wrapped up for the day, I followed the others through the corridor to the front exit of an old Williamsburg dance studio, pulling on my new leather jacket as a cool breeze whipped through the exit doors. I inhaled it with a growing sense of closure, freedom, and love for myself again. These group sessions, held once a week for two hours, helped with all of that. The group provided a safe environment to sit, talk, and grow.

A soft tune rang from within my patchwork tote bag, and I quickly pulled out my phone, already smiling at the incoming FaceTime notification on my screen.

I answered quickly. "Hi! Perfect timing. I just left my meeting."

"How was it?" Alex, aka Mom One, asked. Her shoulder-length wavy red hair framed her kind face with feather bangs.

"It was good! I'm feeling more and more like myself again," I said earnestly, and then tilted my head. "Where's Laura?"

"She's finishing with a client on a video call." Alex took a seat on their couch as she propped the phone up on the coffee table. Her attention went to someone off-camera as her smile grew. "Kira's on the phone."

There was an excited "Oh!" before Alex scooted over and Laura, aka Mom Two, took a seat beside her. Laura was the complete opposite of Alex. While Alex was a calm, critical thinker and a high school teacher, Laura was the outgoing, energized, and enthusiastic other half who spent her time as a youth worker. She had blonde hair as wild as my own, sun-kissed skin, and a constant smile in her brown eyes.

They only learned about what I went through with Aiden after I was in the hospital. My guilt over that hadn't quite faded, but they had been nothing but supportive since.

"Hello, baby!" Laura beamed.

I waved to my phone, unable to contain my smile. "I was saying to Mom that these meetings are really working for me."

"That is so good to hear!"

"I still think she should keep a balance. Maybe go to a rage room or something," Alex suggested, raising a brow knowingly. "Just to really get *him* out of your system."

"I would, but I'd look a little silly going on my own," I laughed, stepping out the exit doors onto the stoop outside. That same breeze from before lifted my hair away from my face.

"Bring Lily," Laura shrugged.

"I don't think she's quite ready to make those steps yet. She's doing better, it's just taking longer, considering she's healing from something else."

They nodded in understanding before Laura clicked her fingers. "What about that boy you've been hanging out with? He seems nice."

"Seb?" I spoke his name as if I hadn't been seeing him every week. Or like the mere mention of him had me feeling all warm inside.

"That explains the jacket," Alex nodded, eyeing the leather jacket she could see on my shoulders before she looked up wistfully. "God, I miss my bike..."

"I'm sure he'd be interested in going to a rage room with you." Laura smiled eagerly.

I laughed softly. "I'll have to ask him."

We talked while I waited outside the building, offside to the other women hanging back to chat amongst themselves.

There was a food truck a little way down the sidewalk. For a moment, as my eyes skimmed the line outside the food truck, I caught sight of a young man whose light brown hair was pulled back into a bun. I took a breath, knowing it wasn't him. It would never be him. Not when I knew his jaw was still wired shut, he couldn't walk without crutches, and he no longer had a man bun. This young man in the line had a different face anyway. And wasn't wearing plaid.

And I was moving on.

I said goodbye to my moms when they told me a call from Grandpa was coming through — a call from him was a rare occurrence, considering he despised technology, so Laura was eager to answer it.

I slipped my phone into my bag, right beside where a vintage film camera sat. Photography was very quickly becoming a new hobby of mine. Much like any other hobbies I picked up, this one probably had an expiration date too, but that didn't stop me from pursuing it. Along with the group sessions, photography gave me something else to think about. Every time I focused the lens on a subject, it was like drawing focus to the present instead of the past. A section of my bedroom wall at home was quickly filling with pictures of friends, family, and miscellaneous shots from around the city because of my new hobby.

I secured my unruly hair into a quick braid. Right on time, the sound of an engine, a low sort of hum, pulled my attention to a sleek, matte black motorbike. It stopped at the curb a few cars down on my right. The rider, once he turned the bike off and kicked down the stand, saluted me, and I couldn't fight the smile already spreading to my lips.

One of the women from the group, Fran, a firm but fair kind of lady, nudged my shoulder. "He seems eager every time he's here. Are you sure he isn't stalking you?"

I rolled my eyes, smiling still. "Seb is a good friend."

The flutter in my stomach and the skipping beat of my heart seemed to think otherwise whenever I saw him. I felt a natural pull towards Seb and his carefree, happy attitude. He made me laugh until my sides hurt. Being friends with him was different from what I had with Lily. She was like a sister; we shared so many things and bonded because of it. Seb, however, was the friend who made things simple. I knew I could rely on him to be there when all I needed was a laugh or someone to share an inbox full of memes with.

Fran tutted. "Can't be too cautious."

Fran's husband had abused and stalked her after their divorce. I couldn't blame her for assuming any man eager to spend time with a woman might be suspicious, but Seb was far from being that kind of guy. He didn't have a mean bone in his body. If I had X-ray vision or maybe a third eye, I wouldn't be surprised to find his entire being was made of light and happiness.

I walked over to Seb and his bike as he pulled out the spare helmet we had bought together. Which was around the time I had bought the leather jacket. It felt only right to match his riding vibe. Of course, I added my own little touches. Like the tiny sunflower stickers that trailed down the jawline of my helmet.

Seb lifted his visor, revealing his kind brown eyes, and held my helmet out to me. "Hey, Smiles."

His voice was smooth, leaving me buzzed.

"Hi," I grinned, accepting the helmet and pulling it on. The padding inside muffled the busy sounds of the city and warmed my cheeks.

"You seem happier every time you come out. Or is that because I'm here?" There was a subtle smugness in his eyes, paired with a playful glow.

"It helps to have a friendly face to see afterwards." I climbed on behind him. The closeness to him sent a rush of butterflies through my stomach. Even more so when I wrapped my arms around his middle and leaned into his muscular body.

Seb chuckled, started the engine again, peeled the bike away from the curb, and quickly picked up speed. The bike jolted forward as he shifted gears, and I squealed ecstatically, holding on a little tighter.

We arrived at the apartment, and I invited him inside for lunch — a pretty standard thing for us after my meetings since his apartment was only ten minutes from the old dance hall. It just made sense for him to give me a ride home, according to him.

Like most Thursdays, he talked about his recent job tiling a roof, and I would get ready for my afternoon shift at Green Thumbs Florist and Garden Center.

But today was different.

We walked into the foyer, his bike boots heavy against the linoleum floor.

I was peeling off my jacket as we neared the elevator when he slowed to check the message that came through on his phone.

I paused next to him, jacket halfway down my shoulders. His scent, cedarwood, spearmint, and lemon, lingered in the leather of his clothes and now faintly on me after sitting against him for so long. At 5'5", and Seb six feet tall, my face came level with his shoulder—

Why am I comparing heights right now?

"Damn," Seb muttered as he read the text.

"What is it?"

"New roof maintenance job. One of the guys pulled out, and the boss wants me to take it this afternoon." He tilted his phone so I could read the text too.

"I believe you, Seb," I half smiled.

"I know, but I wanted to make sure you knew I wasn't skipping out on you." There was a happy sparkle in his eyes again.

I pointed to his screen when another message popped up. This one was from an unknown number. "Is that another job?"

Seb's dark eyebrows knitted together as he opened the text in front of me. "Looks like Antonio wants a reunion."

An unknown number, a time for later tonight, and an address. How mysterious of the mob boss.

Also, a little terrifying.

A heaviness settled in the pit of my stomach, numbing the fluttery feeling. I knew what Seb and Dean did for Antonio was dangerous — the fights and the jobs — but somehow, it hadn't really sunk in until now. So much time had passed since their last fight, I had forgotten about that part of Seb's life. And I was worried.

Seb shrugged nonchalantly, seemingly unfazed by the cryptic message, as he pocketed his phone and gave me a lopsided smile. "Sorry, I have to miss lunch."

"No, it's fine. Be safe." I rose to my toes and pecked him on the cheek. And then pulled back quickly, eyes wide as I struggled to find the reason why I kissed his cheek.

Say something cute, chill, easy-going. Anything!

My intention wasn't to test the waters. It was more of a knee-jerk reaction. I guess to make sure he knew I cared for him. As a friend.

Seb's smile only grew wider as he raised his eyebrows. "First base already? You don't mess around, Kira."

I pressed my lips together, despite them wanting to curve upward at the way he made me feel.

Safe. Secure. Unjudged.

I backed away towards the elevator with a slight skip in my step, keeping my smile coy. "You should get going. Don't want to upset the roof tile boss by being late."

He huffed a laugh. "Okay, but maybe we could go for coffee tomorrow?"

The coyness of my smile quickly spread through my body as I tilted my head. "Why?"

"It'd be nice to meet with you somewhere other than outside your SDV meetings."

"Isn't that what our regular lunches are for? To catch up somewhere else besides outside the SDV meetings? And you've seen me outside of those meetings when you visit Dean here."

"Not on your own." He rolled his eyes, his lips twitching as he started backing towards the front doors. "Can we meet for coffee tomorrow, please?"

My façade broke, and I grinned. "Make it bubble tea, and I'm in."

His brow raised. "Bubble tea?"

"It'll blow your mind."

"I'll hold you to that," he chuckled, stepping through the doors.

I felt like I could burst. Overcome by a new thrill as butterflies danced in my stomach.

My smile remained long after Seb left.

Chapter 6
Dean

Antonio Gimello broke his rule about keeping his messages cryptic. Tonight, he had followed up the one containing the address with *"wear something nice"*. Hence, the black button-up shirt I had pulled on before leaving Lily's. I kept the sleeves down and the collar unbuttoned — semi-formal and hiding the little microphone and wire taped to my chest.

Lily didn't know about the wire or the visit I paid to her dad's office after leaving her apartment. But she was aware of the meeting. That much I could tell her.

As we stood in the kitchen, she expressed her concerns about tonight before I left. Worried at first about Antonio resurfacing after months of nothing, concerned that I might be the only one going to this thing, and then curious about why she hadn't gotten a text either, considering she worked at The Den. Her blue doe eyes were perfect windows for me to gauge her entire thought process. When her brows furrowed slightly, I took her hand and brought her knuckles to my lips.

"I'll see you when I get back tonight." I kissed her skin, maintaining eye contact. "I promise. And then maybe we could watch a movie or somethin'."

I wished I could skip to that moment, instead of driving up the curved driveway to Antonio's Bay Ridge mansion.

Several other cars were parked outside Antonio's home, including Seb's matte black Yamaha and Roxy's Aston Martin.

I parked the Cadillac the furthest away and strode for the front stairs that swept out along the front porch, double-checking the wire wasn't visible beneath my shirt before I smoothed my hair back.

I needed to stay calm, which wouldn't be too hard. How many times had I been in the middle of things going to shit and walked out mostly unscathed? A simple meeting was a walk in the park for me.

If I wasn't wearing a wire.

The heavy, stark white front door swung inward as I reached the top of the stairs. Vince, Antonio's right-hand man, stepped out, suited up, and half smiling as his shaved head shone in the overhead porch lights.

"Dean. It's good to see you again." He stepped aside to let me pass.

I didn't bother with the niceties, not when I wanted this over and done with. Vince wasn't the kind of guy to be offended if I didn't say a polite hello. "Am I late?"

Vince shrugged, closing the front door. "Everyone's here."

"Fantastic," I drawled, falling into step with him as we headed down the long hall on our right.

The detectives had taken extra care, and their fucking time, making sure the wires and microphone transmitted to the radios and other devices built into their unmarked van — their unmarked van that tailed me the entire drive here. It was parked out of sight, a few houses down from Antonio's, where they would listen in to whatever unfolded in Antonio's office.

The closer Vince and I got to the doors at the end of the hallway, the more my stomach tensed.

If I were caught wearing a wire, those same detectives would rush to my help. However, based on the way they spoke to me at the office, I knew they would take their sweet time getting here. I imagined I would have a bullet in my head before they breached the gates.

"What's with the sucker?" Vince asked.

My mind was blank for a second before he motioned to my mouth — to the lollipop. Probably my fourth or fifth one today after I received that text. Despite brushing my teeth at Lily's earlier, my mouth was beginning to taste too sweet, and there were faint ridges on the inside of my left cheek from keeping the lollipop in one place for too long.

"Quit smoking." I dropped the lollipop into an ashtray sitting on a wall table.

Vince chuckled. "Yeah? How's that goin'?"

I rubbed my index finger against the front of my teeth to rid them of that furry feeling. "What do you think?"

We reached the double doors of Antonio's office. Vince shouldered one open, and I followed him through.

Everyone was there — everyone meaning the majority of Antonio's best fighters, which was only a handful of us. The boss himself was sitting at his desk, reclined in his black leather chair as he smiled at my entry.

"Now that we're all here..."

Antonio began his usual spiel about the importance of loyalty and family as I edged along the wall and stopped beside Seb in the corner by the window.

He tucked his hands behind his back, lips twitching with a grin as he looked at me side-on.

I rolled my eyes and slipped him the spare lollipop I had in my pocket.

"Where's Joe?" I murmured. I hadn't spotted the old fight announcer in the room.

"Retired," Seb muttered back.

While Seb was busy trying to inconspicuously unwrap the plastic wrapper, I glanced around the room.

There were three other fighters in attendance — *The Viper* and two other guys I hadn't spoken to before.

My eyes landed on Roxy, opposite us, and standing offside to Antonio. She smiled, revealing pearl white teeth behind dark red lips as she winked, crossed her arms across her busty chest, and dropped a hip.

Once upon a time, I would've given in to that look alone. But now? Now I felt nothing towards that woman and everything for the one waiting at home — not quite my home, but close enough. I wanted to ditch this meeting, return to Lily's couch or bed, and wrap myself in her arms.

Antonio was still talking. "As you're all aware, the burning down of The Den wasn't my doing. Not long after it occurred, I received a message, or more of a warning, from my estranged children." The last part looked like it tasted bitter in Antonio's mouth. Meanwhile, the mood in the room changed to subtle shock. "Though they didn't indicate in their message that they were the ones responsible for the fire, I wouldn't be surprised if they did it... They have let me know they are staying for good, which isn't ideal."

I tucked my hands into my pockets and looked around at the scarred and poxy mean faces of the other fighters, watching them process the news of Antonio's other family.

I was one of two in this room who knew about his first family. I hadn't met them — Antonio had them shipped off to Rome with his ex-wife before I started fighting for him. But I knew enough about them, thanks to Vince, to understand Antonio had a good reason for sending them away. Far away. His ex-wife was an alcoholic and tended to blab in her social groups about the things he did. She wasn't so much of a threat these days when she spent most of her time in a luxury villa somewhere in Italy.

And then there were the triplets — two girls and a boy. Each sadistic in their own individual way. They were entitled rich kids, thanks to old money, who had a taste for luxury, revenge, and murder. The latter started with pets when they were kids, and then any enemies with their father when they began working for him. Except they took things too far, made messes, and brought too much attention to Antonio's business deals with their trail of murders.

Antonio eventually cut them off completely. That didn't sit well with them.

Antonio leaned back in his chair, pausing in thought as he steepled his fingers. His white hair was more disheveled tonight. "They have started their own nightclub. And it seems, they have convinced the rest of my fighters to join them."

Another fight club. It explained why there were fewer of us in the room. The guys had dipped for what might be a better offer.

I could picture the detectives in that van listening in with more attention. An opportunity was rising for them to catch not only a mob boss, but his offspring too. Along with everyone else involved.

"I'm sending all of you to this new club, and I expect you to play the part."

Seb cleared his throat. He gave up on opening the lollipop. "What kind of fighting is it? Bare knuckle? Gloves?"

"That's what you'll have to find out," Antonio said. "But you have no affiliation with me anymore, at least that's what we need them to think. Your new representative is Roxanne."

I crossed my arms, unable to hold my tongue any longer. "Why not keep it honest? Go straight to them and end this."

Antonio didn't look too amused by my suggestion, or that I had questioned his overall plans, as he tilted his head and narrowed his eyes. "Because I want to tread lightly while I figure out how to handle them. They won't hesitate to react maliciously if I go directly to them. And I'm sure none of you want that. You all have families. Loved ones."

His calculating stare lingered on me before he looked to the rest of the room. Meanwhile, Seb jabbed me with his elbow.

"Dude," he muttered.

I rubbed my jaw.

Our job was to teach Antonio's kids a lesson, but make sure it wasn't obvious it was coming from their father. Meanwhile, Antonio would be finding a way to get rid of them.

And I would be working undercover while already undercover.

Wonderful.

I needed a cigarette.

"You are to use your fight names only," Antonio added.

The nicotine cravings were making me irate, because I spoke up again. "And if the other fighters–– the ones who know our names and faces and *left* you–– suspect something's off?"

Seb dropped his face to his hands. Even Roxy looked concerned for my well-being.

Antonio's smile was forced as he considered me for a moment. "You're very vocal tonight."

I shrugged a shoulder. "Just concerned for our safety."

"Hm..." He lifted one finger, and I braced myself as Vince stepped away from the door and beelined for me.

"Fuck's sake, Dean," Seb murmured.

"Sorry, bud." Vince half smiled before he slammed his fist into my stomach.

My body wanted to buckle at the sudden strike to my abdomen, but I forced myself to stay upright as I pressed my lips together and hum-coughed through the pain.

Vince patted my shoulder and walked away, removing the golden brass knuckles from his hand as he returned to his position by the door.

The tape on my chest miraculously stayed in place.

"Now," Antonio continued to everyone else. "The other fighters will recognize you. I never suspected they wouldn't. And when they do, you tell them you're there for the same reason they left me; I was an unfit boss, and Roxy, a new owner in the game, offered you a better job and pay when she left me too... Those disloyal fighters won't be around too long."

Meaning he would have them killed for betraying him.

I rubbed at my stomach, nursing the tender area in the center of my abs, but also checking that the microphone wasn't broken.

"None of you are expected to bring me back any information about whatever they have going on. You're there to fight."

And earn him money while his fight club is out of business.

"Roxy will work to get as close to my son to uncover as much as she can." Antonio gave Roxy a soft smile. "So, none of you are to do anything that could sabotage this. Just fight when you're told and keep your head down; play the part."

I waited until I had Roxy's attention again before I raised my eyebrows as if to ask, *And you're okay with that?*

She only shrugged nonchalantly.

"When do we start?" one of the other fighters asked.

"Tonight. That's why I asked you all to dress nicely," Antonio said.

"But, we're fighters. We usually don't meet with the club owners." Seb used a better tone than me.

"I've learned from my sources that my son likes to inspect each of his rivals, including any new fighters." Antonio looked around the room. "When you leave this meeting, make sure you remove anything on your body that they may see as a threat. Any guns or knives..."

Or wires...

"For now, that is all you need to know." Antonio stood. "Roxy will be doing all the talking for you; she knows what to say, so try to remain silent."

That last part was a warning to me after my performance tonight.

Taking it as our cue to leave, we all started for the door.

"A moment, Dean," Antonio said.

I paused by the door as everyone passed me. Seb was the last to leave and shared a concerned look my way before he closed the doors.

I didn't move from where I stopped.

"I hate that I have to ask this," Antonio said, leaning back in his chair. "You wouldn't be talking to Lily's father, would you? He's working on the investigation into me, and he could very easily use you for intel."

Hit the nail right on the fucking head, boss.

"No. We don't exactly get along enough for him to pay me any attention." I decided to play into his obsession with loyalty and family, and flipped the conversation. "Did you *want* me to do somethin'? I could get information on where he is with the investigation."

Please, say no.

"It won't be necessary. As you said, he doesn't pay you much attention. He would think it's out of character for you to suddenly get close."

"Right," I nodded.

"Just focus on the fights for now and keep your head down. You're there as a facade for Roxy. We don't need things getting messy."

I fought the urge to scoff.

Things were already messy.

Seb was waiting for me in the hallway when Vince walked me out.

"What happened?" Seb asked.

"More warnings."

He inhaled through his teeth. "You did bring an attitude tonight."

I clenched my jaw. "I'm tired."

"Well, can you be more careful? You're the only friend I have here."

Vince chuckled from behind us.

"Why not hit me harder next time, Vince? I barely felt that one," I said sarcastically.

"Just wanted to remind you how it felt to be punched. You boys haven't been in the ring for some time."

I huffed in agreement as we crossed the foyer and exited the house, leaving Vince inside.

When we stepped through the front door into the night air, I pulled out my phone. Just as a hand with painted black nails curved around my arm and clung to my bicep.

Roxy's sultry voice floated up to my ears as she fell into step beside me and walked down the porch steps. "You're looking good."

I didn't look at her as I lifted my arm from her hand and focused on my phone and the recent texts I shared with Lily. But it was Seb who spoke up instead.

"He's in a healthy relationship, that's why." He threw her a sarcastic grin.

Roxy hummed. "I wasn't aware I was talking to you too. Are you third-wheeling so much it's become a throuple?"

I glanced up from my phone, slowing my steps as I watched the interaction.

Seb walked to his bike, scoffing, while Roxy gave him a once-over. Tilting her head before she added, "I guess I could accommodate you if you're feeling lonely, *Sebastian*."

"I'm not that desperate, *Roxanne*." Seb faked a smile before he pulled on his helmet.

Roxy flipped him off.

I tuned them out as I walked to my car, lifting the phone to my ear as it rang on the other end.

"Hi." Lily's voice soothed the frustration beating through my head.

"Hi." I climbed into my car and locked the doors, relaxing into the seat as I eyed the others through the side window.

"Is everything okay?"

"Yeah, I'm just—I'm gonna be home a little later." I thumbed the steering wheel, frowning at the lie about to spill from my mouth. "This meeting is going on longer than I thought."

"That's okay... I'm going to read before bed, so maybe I'll be up when you get home?"

I half smiled tiredly, wishing I could sink through the phone to her. "What are you reading?"

Her laugh was soft and scratched something in my brain. "Is that the equivalent of asking about what I'm wearing?"

"I mean, we could talk about that too if you like." The words had left my mouth before I remembered I was still wearing a microphone. Hopefully, they could only hear my end of the conversation. The last thing I needed was Mark overhearing that.

"I wouldn't want to make you uncomfortable in your meeting, but if you really want to know..." There was movement on her end. The rustling of sheets as she climbed into bed. "I'm wearing sweats."

I smiled wider. "Sexy."

"Very."

I opened my mouth to respond, but the other fighters, Seb and Roxy, were ready to leave, all starting their engines before Roxy drove out first. The rest simply followed until it was only me sitting outside Antonio's house.

"I've gotta go... I'll see you soon."

There was a smile in her voice when she told me to stay safe and that she loved me. Her words were sweet and simple, but fed the guilt growing inside me, leaving a bad taste in my mouth as I told her I loved her too.

Hiding shit from her was going to kill me.

CHAPTER 7

Dean

Castello di Vetro, a strip club, was under new management, according to the sign outside the front of the entrance.

I joined the others outside the club in Downtown Brooklyn and cast my eyes across the black glass exterior and flashy, oversized neon sign.

Two oversized knuckle-heads stood guard at the doors.

I rolled my shoulders and pocketed my hands. All too aware of the way the microphone wires, taped to my chest and stomach, tickled my skin. The tape itself was one heated room away from unsticking completely.

Roxy stood in front of our small gathering, adjusting her little black dress and her high ponytail as she looked the club over and lifted her chin.

"Alright, boys," she purred. "Let's do this."

Walking towards the doors and the bouncers stationed at them, Roxy dialled up the sway in her hips while we followed loosely. Once she explained who we were here to see, as she felt up their biceps, the bouncers let us in.

The entrance began with a small, dimly lit foyer with a dark red carpet and black walls. A woman in a tight pink dress with a plunging neckline stood behind a desk that ran along the entire right side of the foyer. She was there to collect hats and coats, but seemed preoccupied with the white lines on the surface of the desk as we entered.

"This is gonna be interesting," Seb muttered as we moved to the next door, where music pounded against it.

I hummed in agreement as I rolled up the sleeves of my shirt. It was warmer inside, and the tape was unsticking already. I casually pressed a hand to my chest, as if I was brushing away lint.

The second Roxy pushed open the door, I was hit with the familiar wave of the club scene. This one was more sophisticated than The Den. The room was wrapped in black mirrors, from the walls to the ceiling, and cast in a pink and blue haze of light that bounced off the scantily dressed dancers and their little stages and poles around the room. Businessmen and preppy college boys filled the place, all ogling the women on show or showering them in cash. Other dancers weaved through the audience, offering lap dances or leading patrons to private rooms for something more. And then there were the aerial performers on black silk ribbons hanging from the ceiling.

One dropped down right beside Seb as we edged through the club. She was upside down, her bare legs wrapped in the thick silk and spread like a capital T as her mouth came to his ear. Whatever she whispered made his eyes pop.

"I'm good, thanks!" He hastily side-stepped her as we moved forward.

Roxy wouldn't let us wait or get distracted, simply because she wasn't stopping. Her eyes were set on the other side of the room. But her determination to meet with Antonio's kids didn't stop the other fighters with us from getting distracted.

It was optimistic to think a group of men could make it across a strip club floor without being tempted.

But somehow, we made it.

Barely.

One fighter had groped a dancer in passing, prompting her to backhand him across the face because of the *no-touching-the-dancers* policy. When he went to go after her, I gripped the back of his neck and shoved him back in line.

At the back of the club, where red velvet sofas lined the black mirror walls, two more bouncers stood by a silver door handle – the only indication that the mirror they guarded was a door. Roxy spoke with them too, and then we were waved forward. But not before both bouncers indicated they needed to check us for concealed weapons.

I clenched my jaw as I went after Roxy, hoping that the microphone wasn't about to get me killed.

The devices whirred as they passed over my chest, back, shoulders, and legs, but neither went off, and I was free to walk through the door and into the top of an all-black stairwell. The only light was the neon blue strip of LEDs along the handrails.

We were all cast in blue as we went, single file, down the narrow stairs.

"There's nothing more uplifting than a black stairwell, don't you think?" Seb's sarcastic tone echoed through the space, joining the sound of our footsteps. "I love the ambience. It's like going on a leisurely stroll down to a torture room. Or a sex dungeon. Maybe both—"

"Shh!" Roxy hissed over her shoulder. "No talking."

I didn't have to listen hard to recognize the sound on the other side of the door at the bottom of the stairs.

I wasn't even fighting tonight, but my body was already preparing itself. My muscles were tense, and my mind was racing through different fight strategies.

To make it all much worse, I was getting warm.

I pressed my hand to my chest again, reapplying the tape as it threatened to peel off.

Roxy pushed the door open, inviting a wave of cheering to rush into the stairwell, and we stepped into a large concrete basement. But it was more than that. Way more.

"Oooh, shiiit," Seb said.

We were all thinking it as our eyes landed on the center of the room.

Surrounded by music, lights, large cargo crates that lined the outer walls, and an audience plied with alcohol from an in-basement bar, was a large glass cube on a raised area of the floor. Inside it were two men, beating the ever living shit out of each other.

"Bare knuckle it is then," Seb muttered.

Roxy led us to the metal staircase on our right. At the top was a mezzanine, where men and women sat at small tables, observing the fight beneath them while they drank and snorted cocaine off tabletops. They were all unbothered by the brutality happening within the cube.

When we reached the back of the mezzanine, where a deep purple, velvet curtain sectioned off a VIP area, Roxy raised her hand, and we slowed to a stop, waiting for further instructions from her. My eyes, however, were on the two men guarding the curtain. Antonio's kids wanted to make themselves known to their father, but they sure as hell were scared if they required this much protection. In the crowd below, I spotted several guys in black suits weaving through the throng. Their eyes were on the exit and every corner of the room.

"Wait here." Roxy sauntered over to the guards and the curtain. Within seconds, she was in, disappearing behind the curtain. As our representative, she had to convince Antonio's kids to let us fight here.

I hoped they declined as I looked at the fighters in that box again, and braced my arms on the mezzanine banister.

Seb joined my side and followed my line of sight. "That's going to be hell..."

"Uh-huh."

"Since when did Antonio start making you wear a wire?"

My head snapped in his direction. "What?"

Seb was frowning at the front of my shirt, and I glanced down quickly. The wire was partially hanging down.

"Fuck," I hissed, trying to reapply the tape only for it to come loose again. I tugged it off instead, unplugging the mic and making sure no one but Seb witnessed when I shoved the wire and microphone into my pants.

Seb raised his eyebrows. "That's one way to do it."

"It's not for Antonio," I murmured.

Seb's eyes popped when he realized who else it would be for. "What?"

I nodded, combing a hand through my hair as I went back to leaning against the banister. "I'll explain later."

"*Fuck*, man—"

The velvet curtain was pulled back again, and Roxy peered out to let us know it was time to meet the owners.

Seb and I were the last to step into the VIP area. Like the club upstairs, everything had a mirrored surface — the coffee table, the couch legs, the fucking ceiling.

Sitting directly across from us, on a dark green sofa and surrounded by bodyguards, were Antonio's triplets.

Lucia Gimello was perched on the arm of the sofa in a black dress, twirling a thick and long lock of auburn hair around her finger as her brown eyes swept over us. Her eyes stopped on me, and she winked. She was the more aloof and carefree of the siblings. Her sister, on the other hand — completely identical but with a harder, more cunning expression — was standing to the side of the sofa. Her brow was set in an arch as she scrutinized us like prey. Her name was Beatrice. She liked to cut off fingers with a cigar cutter for fun, according to Vince's stories. She wore a black tailored suit without a dress shirt beneath.

And then there was Gabriele. He looked exactly like Antonio, just younger, without the stark white hair, and oozing bucket loads of arrogance and pain-in-the-ass.

He was reclined in the middle of the sofa. There was a twisted smirk on his face as he tilted his head. Dark circles clung to his eyes, and a cigar hung from his lips. He too wore a black suit without a shirt beneath. When the suit caught the light, there was a faint purple shine to it.

My attention on the details of the suit was brief. Especially since Lucia casually flipped out a knife and was trailing a finger along the silver blade as she watched me, smiling.

Roxy introduced us by nickname as the triplets listened and considered. We didn't have to talk. Only wait for them to decide if we were worthy of fighting in their club. It wasn't until Roxy had introduced me as Romeo that Gabriele's eyes narrowed slightly.

He combed a hand through the longer section of auburn hair on his head, brushing the cheekbone-length, oily strands back into place. The sides of his hair were buzz-cut short.

He then sat forward, nodding slowly as Roxy finished. The gold bracelet on his wrist and the matching rings on his fingers glinted in the light.

Gabriele may have hated his father but fuck they were similar with their taste of decoration and attire.

Continuing a conversation they had had before the rest of us walked in, Beatrice said with a thick Italian accent, "How do we know this isn't our father's way of planting spies? You all worked for him, no? Why not prove your loyalty to us and fight under our name instead?"

"Tempting as that is," Roxy said. "I like the idea of being the boss for a change. You can surely understand that."

Gabriele hummed in agreement, eyeing Roxy as she continued.

"Anyway, how do you know none of his ex-fighters who joined you aren't already spying on you?"

"We already told them what would happen if they did," Lucia smirked. "We took a finger for their loyalty, and promised to take much more if they betrayed us."

"Maybe I should do something similar," Roxy said, looking to us for a moment before she smiled sweetly. Mostly at Gabriele. "So? What do you think of my fighters? Can they fight here?"

Before he could respond, Lucia leaned forward and muttered into Gabriele's ear with her eyes on me, speaking only Italian. "*Make an offer on that one.*"

I pretended I didn't understand and kept my face blank.

Making offers wasn't part of the plan. We were meant to fight against their men, not for them. And I sure as shit wasn't about to do whatever else Lucia had planned. It didn't help that Lucia's suggestion piqued Beatrice's interest too.

From the stories I heard of these three, I knew anything could change in a second. They were unpredictable — they had gutted a personal driver once simply because he didn't show Lucia the attention she wanted. They were callous, murderous psychopaths who dealt in drug trafficking and weapons as they fought desperately to get back into the Mafia crowd.

And each of them was looking at me like I was a prize.

Chapter 8

Dean

"He looks like he packs a punch." Gabriele's accent was thick. "Are you willing to sell him to me instead?"

Roxy gave him a sultry smirk. "Oh, Romeo is one of my best. Which is why he isn't for sale."

Lucia huffed her disappointment.

"*Romeo.* That is an Italian name." Gabriele stood, his expression calculating as he slowly moved closer. He was several inches shorter than me, but maintained his authority in every movement. Every step. He knew he had the money and reputation to do as he pleased. The oily smirk on his face proved that.

But I also had a reputation. Mostly an issue with people who believed they had more authority over me without proving they earned it.

"My sister seems to have taken a liking to you," Gabriele said. "Do you speak the language?"

"No."

He scoffed and glanced over his shoulder at his sisters, and then spoke Italian. "*He doesn't speak Italian, but this has never stopped you before.*"

Lucia giggled while Beatrice's lips curved into a sadistic grin.

"Just to be clear," Roxy cut in as she positioned herself between me and Gabriele with more sway in her walk. "My fighters are only here for fighting. I figured it was a better place to start fresh. Especially since your father failed us when it came to protecting us from the law... I want to teach Antonio a lesson just as much as you do."

Gabriele smirked at her — mostly at her chest. "I like how you think, *mia cara...*"

Roxy's smile widened. "So, do we have a deal? Can I enter my men in your fights?"

Antonio's only son glanced back at his sisters. They seemed to communicate with that weird triplet connection. Or maybe it's a sibling thing I never understood.

Gabriele turned back to us and lifted his arms out wide, like a proud ringmaster about to start a show.

His smile was cunning. "Welcome to Castello di Vetro."

Seb knew about the investigation and swore to keep his mouth shut after I filled him in on what was going on.

I never doubted he would blab, but with the way the night had gone, I was a little agitated.

Until I stepped through the entrance of Lily's apartment block.

Someone had propped the front door open with a rock. I kicked it out from beside the door once I was inside and then headed upstairs via the elevator.

Getting a key hadn't been something we discussed. Not that we were avoiding it. The conversation just hadn't happened yet.

It was Kira who answered the door when I arrived at it on the third floor.

"Hi, roomie— Should I call you roomie?" She stepped aside to let me in, speaking quietly. "You've practically moved in anyway."

I half smiled as we walked down the short hallway into the living room. "Why are you up so late?"

"Binge-watching trashy TV." She headed to the couch, where she picked up an empty mug, stained with remnants of hot chocolate, and switched off the TV. "Why are you *back* so late?"

"Meetin' with the boss."

"Right. Yes. Seb mentioned you had one..."

We were now standing at opposite ends of the living room — me slowly drifting toward Lily's bedroom door and Kira at hers, hesitating as if she had something to ask.

"Seb is fine," I said.

"Oh, really? Good. That's good... Well. Goodnight." She smiled quickly and then stepped into her bedroom.

Just friends, Seb had told me when I asked him about what was going on between him and Kira.

I half smiled and entered Lily's room.

The lamp was on, and the bed was made, and Lily was fast asleep on the covers with a book closed over her thumb. As she said on the phone earlier tonight, she was in sweats, along with one of my hoodies.

I moved quietly to the left side of the bed, unbuttoning and removing my shirt. Once it was tossed into the wash basket in the corner of the room, I began removing my jeans. They got halfway down my thighs before I remembered what was in them.

"Shit," I hissed, pulling out the thin wire and mic I had haphazardly tucked into my pants at the club. I was meant to return the wire before I got home.

"Why do you have a wire in your pants?" Lily's sleepy voice pulled my attention to her as she propped herself up on her elbow. She yawned and rubbed her eye with the heel of her palm, smiling despite sleep threatening to pull her back under.

"I—Uh..." I glanced down again.

I knew I wanted to tell her, but not like *this*.

In nothing but my briefs and socks. Pants around my ankles.

My hesitation prompted Lily to sit up, her smile quickly fading into a frown.

She asked again, but slower, "Why are you wearing a wire?"

I stepped out of my pants, tossed the device on the bed, and placed my hands on my hips. "You're gonna hate what I say, but fuck it."

Lily simply listened as I went over everything, starting with the day her dad picked me up from work and brought me in for questioning.

The mention of her father deepened her frown.

I was working undercover for her dad, fighting for Antonio again just so Roxy could play boss and get close to Gabriele to figure out what the triplets' plans were, and I was facing prison time. That's if I wasn't caught by the triplets or Antonio before then.

"Everything has gone to shit," I said, trying for sarcasm as I pulled on a pair of gray sweatpants.

Lily was quiet for a moment, processing it all before she spoke again. "But, either way, you'll be going to prison after all of it..."

Suddenly, she looked too lonely on that bed. She worried her bottom lip between her teeth and shook her head in disbelief.

Her voice was quiet. Soft. "Why didn't you tell me sooner?"

"For your safety..."

"My dad told you not to say anything, didn't he?" Her sleepiness was long gone as hints of anger flitted across her expression.

"Yes."

"And you went along with it? Just like that?" She saw right through my casualness of following a detective's orders with ease. She knew there had to be a catch. Something that would force my hand.

"He blackmailed me."

Her eyes sharpened. "What?"

"He threatened to go to immigration about my mother's lack of citizenship *if* I don't work with him. Turns out my dead-beat father failed to hand in her application all those years ago... So long as I do whatever your dad asks, immigration won't find out about Mom's situation— Where are you going?"

She got off the bed, grabbed her phone from the nightstand, and marched to her bag on the dresser opposite the bottom of the bed. A look of determination was on her face as she shoved the phone into her bag and stuffed her feet into a pair of boots.

"I'm going to speak with my dad. He can't get away with this." She grew frustrated when her left boot refused to slide on over her thick bed socks.

"Yeah, he can." I met her in front of the dresser, gently taking her arms so she had no choice but to abandon her plight with the boot.

Her eyes quickly shifted from frustration to sadness as they searched my face. And then she shook her head, coming to terms with it all. "Does your mother know?"

"I haven't told her... I know I should, but I don't think I can."

Lily raised her eyebrows slightly, but she didn't push to ask why. I think because she understood why. Instead, she nodded as she stared at my chest, again processing and coming to a conclusion. "Okay... Okay, well, we'll just deal with this one day at a time, but she needs to know..." Her determination to make sense of it all waned again as she looked up. "Do you know how long it'll be before you are...sent away?"

My heart squeezed.

I shook my head, smoothing my hands down her arms until they interlocked with hers. "Not for a while."

She nodded and removed her hands from mine, only to wrap her arms around my middle. Her head came to rest on my chest while I hugged her back, inhaling her fresh linen and jasmine scent.

"I'll take care of her when the time comes. And we can always visit you."

"Let's not think about it tonight." I pulled away enough to see her face.

With watery eyes, she nodded again.

"Wanna talk about your first day back at work?" This earned me a weak smile and a tired blink.

"I'm mentally exhausted after one day." She wiped her eyes. "I have no idea how I did it daily before. On top of working night shifts at The Den."

I brushed a strand of her hair behind her ear and then pressed my lips to her forehead, smiling gently against her skin. "Bed. Now."

Lily smiled a fraction wider, but out of defeat, and pulled off the one boot she had managed to slip on before she shuffled back to the bed.

CHAPTER 9
Dean

Mark stood behind his chair, arms crossed, as I entered his office. He wasn't impressed as I laid the small microphone and wires on his desk.

"This equipment is expensive," he said tightly. "Not to mention if Lily had seen this—"

"She did." I slid my hands into the pockets of my jeans.

His jaw ticked. "I thought we agreed she wouldn't find out."

"Whoops." I smiled my sarcasm and then jabbed a thumb over my shoulder in the direction of the office door. "If that's all, I've gotta get to work, I ran myself late driving over here—"

"Now that you're here, we can discuss last night."

"Isn't that what the device is for? So I don't have to discuss what was said?"

"Yes, but it'd be helpful to know the layout of Antonio's house, the club, who you saw, and what you saw." He pulled out his chair but gestured to the empty one in front of me. "Take a seat."

"You know some of us aren't rollin' in it, right? We need money to pay bills."

"Doesn't Antonio pay you enough?" He sat down, raising his brow in a way that meant he knew better.

"The Den burned down. I haven't won fight money in months. And he hasn't had any work for me... I'm relyin' on work at the garage and shouldn't be missin' shifts right now. I'll come back later." I turned to leave and got as far as the door.

"Fine by me. It'll give me time to have a chat with immigration."

The only thing Lily shared with this man was the color of her eyes and her curiosity. Except while she paired her curiosity with empathy, Mark's curiosity was driven by the need to find justice regardless of who he dragged down to get it.

My grip was tight on the door handle as I paused, grinding my jaw. There was no escaping this until I had done what was asked. Every little thing, every fucking time. I reluctantly turned around, pulled out the chair with a little too much force, and then dropped into it.

"Good man. Now…" Mark pulled out a notepad and pen. "Tell me about last night."

I told him about Castello di Vetro's interior and the basement below. With each new piece of information Mark heard, he wanted it dissected, asking question after question about where the stairs, exits, and windows were. Or how many people could the club hold compared to its basement. The conversation then shifted to the plans Antonio had for his kids.

"Antonio plans to…teach his kids a lesson?" Mark asked.

I sighed tiredly, rubbing at the subtle ache forming between my eyebrows. We had been talking for a solid two hours, and my phone had several missed calls from my garage boss. "They fucked up a few years back and now they're angry he cut their inheritance. Antonio sees them as a threat."

"And he believes it was his kids who burned down his club?"

My leg was already beginning to bounce with irritation, but I kept my voice calm, disinterested. "Yes… Haven't we talked about this already?"

"Yes, but I want to make sure I have all the facts straight…" He glanced down at his notes again and shook his head as he inhaled. "This is one roundabout way of punishing his kids when he doesn't have all the evidence that it was them."

"That's what Roxy is for. Build some kind of relationship with Gabriele and bring back information to Antonio."

"Maybe we should've gotten her in on our investigation too. Gabriele does have sisters." I could see the plan forming in Mark's eyes.

"Not happenin'."

"Just a thought."

"Are we done now?"

He ignored me. "Has Antonio told you about any of his more detailed plans? Is there anything else we should know about him? Any new weapon deals? Drug trafficking?"

"He plays it close to the chest, and I do what I'm told… He hasn't brought up any other jobs for me other than this one with his kids."

"And if you don't do as you're told?"

"Develop a thick skin?" I pulled my hand through my hair and leaned back in my seat. "Antonio likes makin' examples of people who wrong him. There's always gotta be some *life lesson* with everything he does."

Mark watched me for a beat. "I imagine you've witnessed a few of those life lessons."

I cocked a brow. "Isn't that what I'm facing charges for?"

"I meant directed at you."

I shrugged and rubbed a hand across my stomach where a bruise from Vince's brass knuckles sat. "Sometimes… You learn pretty quickly not to fuck up when you're working for Antonio."

"Right..." He directed his attention to his files.

A thought crossed my mind, and I tilted my head. "How many people are on this case?"

"A handful of the best we have for organized crime. Me included."

"And you trust them?"

Mark sighed and looked up from his notes. "What are you saying? That we'd have a mole?"

"How would you know if you had one or not?"

He scoffed and went back to reading his notes. "They're highly respected detectives, hand-picked by our captain, with spotless records and plenty of loyalty to the badge. None are working for criminals."

"Whatever helps you sleep at night, sarge."

"Moving on... Who were you talking to before you met the Gimello triplets?"

"One of the other fighters." White lies and half-truths were easy.

Evidence of Seb being a fighter was burned with The Den, along with everyone else's photos. In the law's eyes, Seb didn't exist to them, and that was how I planned to keep it.

Mark watched me closely. "He asked about the wire, but then you went quiet."

"The tape got loose, and the wire fell. I put it in my pants before someone else saw. I guess it was unplugged. I told him it was my earphones." My voice remained steady.

He hummed and looked back at his notes. "Are you close with any of the other fighters?"

"No."

"And you aren't saying that to protect a friend?"

I folded my arms loosely across my chest. "None of us are friendly with each other. It's every man for himself in those places."

Mark considered this for a moment, clicking his pen before he continued. "You mentioned life lessons you learned from working with Antonio. I imagine some of those included ways of getting you out of trouble. Maybe dealing with unwanted company?"

I realized too late where he was taking this new line of questioning.

"What happened to your father, Gio Calacoci?"

The mention of his name created tension in my jaw. "Read the death certificate. It was suicide."

"There was no note."

"He wasn't very sentimental."

"It's a little odd, don't you think? Your mother winds up a paraplegic and loses an unborn baby from a domestic dispute, and then five years later, your father kills himself? Quite brutally, may I add."

"What do you want me to say?"

"I'm trying to figure out what kind of man you are."

Guilty people always talked first, so I kept my mouth shut and grew comfortable in the silence drawing out between us.

"Strong, silent type. Got it... Who paid for all your mother's equipment? Like the ramps and the wheelchair."

"Antonio."

"That was generous of him."

"It didn't come free."

"What do you mean by that?"

I rubbed the bridge of my nose. "Why do you think I continued fighting for him?"

"Ah, gotcha." He tapped his temple with his pen and then wrote something down in his notebook. "You know your leg bounces when you're avoiding a topic or irritated?"

"I thought you wanted my help with Antonio. What's with diggin' into *my* past?"

"As I said, trying to figure out what kind of man you are."

CHAPTER 10
Seb

I'm going on a bubble tea date with Kira—It's not a date. Don't get too excited—but I'm already excited. She doesn't want anything. It's too soon after dick face—I should've drawn a dick on his face after cutting his man bun off. All she needs is a friend. Be her friend—Red light!

I hit the brakes hard, and the front wheel of my bike screeched in protest, turning some heads as I came to a halt at the crosswalk. I gave the people watching a small wave.

Nothing could put me in a bad mood right now, not even their unappreciative stares after I had almost run the red light.

When the light turned green, I sped off again en route to Lana's Café nestled in Bay Ridge.

Calm, calm, calm. Be calm.

I spotted Kira's hair first as I pulled up to the curb several shops from the café with its pink umbrellas. The fiery red of her long curls was like a beacon in the crowd and the overcast day.

As she waited at a table, she had that vintage film camera of hers pointed up at the buildings across the street, taking photos of the detailed architecture and the pigeons sitting along the ledges.

It didn't take her long to spot me either.

A breathtaking smile spread on her face as she waved me over. It took everything in me not to run to her. I was taking it slow. She also wasn't aware of the effect she had on me, so it would be weird if I rushed at her.

She was wearing skintight jeans with an oversized olive-green sweater. Two bubble teas were already on the table.

Given the space between us as I left my bike, helmet tucked under my arm, we were in that awkward phase of being unable to say hello yet, but also being aware that we had spotted each other. So, she lifted her camera and aimed the lens at me. I grinned and threw up a peace sign.

As she put the camera away, and I was in earshot, trying to contain my excitement, she gestured to the drinks on the table. "There was a line, and I didn't want to miss out because they have specials on today, so I ordered one I think you'll like."

"Honestly, I'd drink or eat anything you thought I'd like." *Reel it in, moron.*

I knew I wore my heart on my sleeve, but this was ridiculous. She needed a friend, not someone batting their eyelashes at her because she had pretty hair and a smile that might end me.

Kira let out a little laugh, one that wrinkled the bridge of her nose, and I took the seat across from her.

"Okay," she began, pushing one of the drinks in my direction. "Moment of truth; will Sebastian enjoy The Tea?"

I considered the drink, feigning seriousness as I pretended to study its weight, height, and straw closely. Kira grinned as I did.

When I took the first sip, she waited in silence, holding her breath as she raised her eyebrows in anticipation. Me enjoying this drink was important to her. And I did enjoy it. Not just the drink, as the flavors exploded in my mouth, but her company too.

"Consider my mind blown, Kira." I had another mouthful of the drink. "I don't think my taste buds have tasted anything better."

This earned me another smile as she tucked her hair behind her ear. It also brought a light tinge of pink to her face.

I cleared my throat and averted my gaze to the crowded sidewalk. With people milling about or bustling by, the space around our table was quickly disappearing in the hustle. I glanced at Kira to see that she seemed to think the same thing, especially when someone accidentally knocked our table with their laptop bag as they passed.

"Maybe we could walk and talk?" she suggested, already gathering her things and her drink.

"Good idea."

We walked slowly, finishing our drinks with nowhere to get to in a hurry as we talked about anything and everything. Plants, music, hobbies, and fears. Kira loved nature but was weirded out by most things with more than four legs — she was learning to appreciate spiders since discovering jumping spider videos.

She already knew I disliked needles — the tattoo of my niece's initials beneath my bicep was my only exception to facing that fear — but she didn't know about my passion, outside basketball, of gaming and collecting old records.

"You know, I'm surprised, considering what you do for Antonio, needles are the thing that scares you," she teased lightly as we discarded our empty cups into a trash can.

"Well, it's not the only thing. Deep water? No thanks." I shuddered but moved on. "Anyway, he doesn't have me doing that many jobs for him. It was mostly the fighting... Still is."

"I take it that meeting you had last night meant you'd be starting again?"

"Yeah..." I glanced at her and debated how much I should reveal, but my mouth got the better of me, and I let the words flow. I explained the reason we were fighting again — Antonio's twisted plan to get back at his kids for allegedly burning down his club, The Den — and how the loyal fighters who remained with him were now his eyes and ears.

"At least I don't have to wear a wire." The words left my mouth before I could process them. Kira was easy to talk to; she made me feel content, but I had revealed too much. "I wasn't meant to say that."

Kira was perplexed as she frowned. "Who's wearing a wire?"

"Uh—"

"Seb." She lightly jabbed my rib with her elbow. Her eyes lit with curiosity. "Who?"

"It's a police thing— You know what, Imma shut my mouth now."

"It's Dean, isn't it. He's wearing the wire."

I only looked at her, trying to keep my expression neutral.

"It makes sense. Lily's dad is a detective, and Dean has access to Antonio. And Antonio's kids. Dean is the closest source her dad has."

I ran a hand over my head with a sigh. "No one else is supposed to know about it."

She gently gripped my arm, smiling reassuringly. "I won't say anything. I promise. Anyway, I kept Lily's secret pretty well."

My eyebrow lifted. "What secret does she have?"

"If it were still a secret, I wouldn't tell you. But, considering it's mostly out in the open... It was hiding that she worked at The Den and was seeing Dean."

I sighed heavily. "You know, for a second, I thought you meant she was pregnant. Because that would be some secret."

She hummed and looked ahead. "Do you think she's doing okay?"

"Lily? I mean, I guess. You do live with her, though, so you'd know better than me."

"I should, but sometimes I get so caught up in moving forward, getting better... I don't want to leave her behind. And I know she is still healing. We all heal at our own pace, especially after what we've been through..." Kira brought her eyes to me. "I was part of the reason she was shot. If I hadn't texted her that day—"

"Ookay, let's not do that." I stopped walking and faced her. "You aren't doing yourself any favors thinking like that. Look at all the work you've done for yourself in that group. You don't need that going to waste... Lily has got her own thing going on, and yes, you do need to communicate with her that you're concerned, but you also shouldn't blame yourself for what's done and past. It'll drive you crazy." I offered her a faint smile. "And then I'll have to be the one defending the crazy girl because she cared too much."

Kira finally cracked a smile again, and the worried lines between her eyebrows faded. "How do you do that?"

"Do what?"

"Make me feel better so easily." A cool breeze spiraled through the gap between us, catching her hair as it went.

"Good upbringing?" I shrugged.

Something wet dripped onto my cheek. And then again, followed by several more wet drops.

I looked up just as more raindrops fell, covering the sidewalk quickly in a glossy sheen.

Kira and I started in a run for shelter, laughing as we did when the rain soaked through our clothes. The few trees planted along the curb provided little cover, so we aimed for the stoop of an apartment.

In the process of running blind through the sheets of rain pelting our faces, I heard a faint crack and glanced down. My phone had slipped from the pocket of my jacket. Not only had it landed in a puddle, but there was now a fracture right across the screen.

"Oh no!" Kira exclaimed. Her curls hung heavy and damp around her face as she watched me pick up the phone.

"Come on. We're gonna drown in this." I nodded toward the stoop of the closest brownstone, and we headed up the stairs. I leaned against its door, examining my broken phone with my helmet tucked under my arm again. I wouldn't be making any texts or calls for a while if I couldn't turn it on.

"So," Kira began, holding out her hand to catch raindrops. "What's the origin story of how Seb became a fighter?"

I half smiled, putting my phone away.

"Well... It was the easiest and fastest way to make money. The original plan was to save up and be the first of the Cook kids to get to college. Make a single mom proud. *But* that kinda fell through... Are you sure you want the full story?"

Kira looked toward the sky and the rain. "We might be here a while anyway."

"Alright, origin story. Let's see..." I rubbed my jaw in thought. "I never met my dad. I barely finished high school. My first job was mowing lawns and washing cars, and then I worked in a fast-food restaurant until I lost that job for snacking on the job." I glanced at her to check she was still interested in hearing all of this. Sure enough, Kira was listening with her full attention. "One day, I was playing basketball with a few friends when a fight broke out with the other team over something stupid. I'd never liked to resolve things with my fists, but we'd gone past the point of talking it through. Some of Antonio's men happened to be scouting for new fighters at the time and noticed me pretty quickly. I accepted just as fast when I heard of how easy it was to make money. It meant giving my family a secure life for once.

"My mom hated the idea of me fighting, but she'd been a single mom for so long, making ends meet by cleaning houses and working her fingers to the bone, I didn't want her worrying about money anymore. Fighting earned me enough that she wasn't scraping her earnings for bills and food."

"How is she now?"

"She moved out of the city," I half smiled. "She was over the hustle and bustle, and now works as the manager of a nursing home."

"Well done to her," Kira said. "And the roof tiling job? Is that something you got into before or after Antonio?"

"After. He suggested we get day jobs so we had some form of legal money coming in. You know, to keep the IRS off our asses..." I watched her for a second longer. "What's your origin story, Miss Scott?"

"Well," she dusted her hands of the rainwater and stepped back to lean against the door too, her brown eyes sparkling. "I'm an only child to two adoring mothers, I was homeschooled in Warwick until we moved to Brooklyn for Mom's new teaching job; I started high school in Bay Ridge and met Lily; I am a complete nerd when it comes to anything environmental, animals, nature, and biology. And I never went to college. Mostly because I couldn't stand the idea of being in a classroom any longer." She grinned at me. "My life isn't as exciting as yours unless we count the time Lily and I were caught trespassing in an apple orchard during a visit to my grandparents' place in Warwick."

"Badass," I smiled.

"I know. Just living on the edge," she joked. Her eyes lingered on mine for a moment.

Despite being outside, something about being pressed against the door, encased by a wall of rain cascading from the awning above us, suddenly felt more intimate than it should've. We were caught out in the rain, but I wouldn't have wanted to be anywhere else.

The smile on her face softened. "What?"

"You, uh— There's an eyelash," I said quickly before gently brushing my thumb across her cheekbone. Her skin was soft beneath my thumb, and the way her eyes dropped briefly to my mouth hadn't gone unnoticed either.

There was no eyelash.

Too soon.

I took my hand back, pretending to dust the lash away as I plastered on a smile. "Got it."

Kira needed a friend, not a rebound. Not that I would mind if I was her rebound. I was already fighting every urge to ask if I could kiss her. It wasn't helping that she seemed to have moved closer. Or maybe I had.

Her eyes fell to my mouth again. "Seb."

Don't be a dick— Stop thinking with your dick. Be a friend.

"Maybe we shouldn't?" My words cut through the air between us, and suddenly the rain seemed louder.

Kira blinked and stepped back. "Right, sorry. I don't know what I was thinking."

"It's my fault."

"No, it isn't."

"I lied about an eyelash," I admitted. "I'm the one flirting."

Kira smiled. "So am I, Seb..."

That smile of hers was dangerous. Beautiful and heart-stopping, but dangerous when it came to my thought process.

I cleared my throat. "Right."

"Yeah."

We looked at the street where the rain was easing. There was a pleasant kind of awkwardness between us. The kind that might end in laughter if we played it right.

I smiled at her again. "We should go."

The ride back to her apartment was filled with tension of the good kind. The good but dangerous kind that I should avoid if I wanted to be a friend. But her legs in those jeans, on either side of mine as she held me from behind and we sped through the streets, wasn't helping. Neither was the way her hands were placed on my chest as she held on.

How many times had I picked her up from her SDV meetings without reacting like this? My body had suddenly forgotten how to act because of some heavy rain, damp clothes, and a cramped stoop.

It wasn't her fault I couldn't get my emotions or feelings in check.

A thought suddenly had me glancing at my lap. I sighed when there wasn't anything obvious.

Yet.

"Shit," I muttered against the lining of my helmet.

Just get her home, say goodbye, and leave. Easy.

As we pulled up outside her apartment, the rain returned, falling in fat drops across my visor as Kira climbed off the bike.

She pulled up her visor, squinting as the rain got heavier. "I can't let you ride home in this. It's too dangerous."

I pulled up my visor and glanced at the road, now a sleek black surface. "Come up and dry off. I could make us coffee or something."

There was no twisting my arm when it came to her.

"Alright," I shrugged, playing casual as I climbed off the bike and walked it into the one-way street running alongside the apartment building for shelter.

Every inch of us was soaked with rainwater, which caused the walk inside and into the elevator to be full of squeaking shoes and awkward adjustments to our clothes. Kira was the first to laugh about it when we got into the apartment, ringing out her hair over a pot plant as she watched me struggling to pull my jacket off.

"Here," she smiled, coming up behind me in the living room. She took hold of the jacket and tugged firmly while I pulled until the sleeves slowly released my arms.

She hung the jacket over one of the kitchen stools to dry before returning to me.

"Thanks." I rubbed my bare arms, unable to think of anything to say. Me, the guy who could never shut up, had nothing to say to this pretty girl standing in front of me.

When Kira removed her knit sweater, revealing a top that clung to her body the way my T-shirt had done to mine, I suddenly didn't know how to think straight either.

Kira was fit and curvy in all the right places, showcased by the tight wrap of her wet clothes. I knew she did yoga, and the yoga had paid off tenfold.

Why did everything have to look so good wet?

Stop thinking with your dick!

"I have a radiator in my room. We could dry off and get warm." She gestured to her door, sitting on the right side of the living room.

"Yup, sounds good. Radiators are good." *What the fuck?*

Kira half smiled and led the way into her room.

Almost every surface had a plant on it. From the shelf above her headboard to the dresser by the door. Evidence of all her hobbies decorated the room too. There was a crocheted blanket on a chair, macrame plant hangers on the window, colorful origami swans on her nightstand, and a giant collection of photographs on her wall.

Everything about her room was cozy and bright.

The radiator was under the window. She turned the dial on the side, and the heat came quickly. We huddled in front of it with an inch of space between us.

I stole a glance at her, and she instantly redirected her gaze off my wet T-shirt and back down to the radiator, holding out her palms to it to get warm. She had checked me out and was now looking like she was trying to find the right words to say.

I cleared my throat. That line of friendship was beginning to look blurry with every passing second. "Should we take off our shirts?"

"You know, I was just thinking that." She swallowed hard, furrowing her brow. "We'd dry much faster."

I nodded once. "Exactly what I was thinking."

"Yup."

"Great."

"Awesome."

I huffed a laugh, hesitated for a second, and then peeled my shirt off and plopped it on the floor before looking back at her.

She had the hem of her shirt in her hands but had paused to watch me take off mine, and now her eyes were subtly wide as they skimmed over my chest and stomach.

"Sorry," she stammered and blinked before looking away, "I've never seen so much muscle this close."

My lips twitched with a smile. "Did jerk face ever workout?"

A subtle crease appeared between her eyebrows, but it wasn't for the mention of Aiden. She was trying to form a more casual expression without looking at me again. "Um, no. No, he didn't... I'm going to take my shirt off now."

I nodded once, smiling. "Okay."

She hastily tugged the damp fabric off, revealing a deep red bralette that complemented her brown eyes. While I wanted to admire the way the lace hugged her skin, I couldn't help but notice the blaring signs of the past written all over her.

My eyes tracked to the faint yellow marks on her arms and stomach from Aiden.

"Do they still hurt?" I asked.

She shook her head, inhaling shakily while a pink blush crept to her face. "Not anymore."

Our bodies faced the window, but I couldn't stop admiring her from the corner of my eye.

She couldn't stop looking either.

I leaned sideways, brushing my arm against hers as I whispered, "Now what?"

Kira chewed her bottom lip as her eyes darted across every detail of my face.

And then she kissed me.

My eyebrows shot up, but I didn't resist, allowing my eyes to fall shut. She tasted like rainwater and bubble tea as she let me in immediately, tilting her head while I gently took her hips and pulled her closer. Skin to skin.

I was melting and hard all at once. Our friendship was tumbling over the edge, bringing with it every reserved thought. My head was quickly filling with her. The way she tasted and felt. She smelled like magnolia and sweetened lemon, and I needed more.

She suddenly pulled away to take a breath, and I let go of her hips.

It took me a second to open my eyes again.

Her eyes were wide. "I shouldn't have done that. You already said we shouldn't—"

"What if I changed my mind?"

She shook her head but remained close. "I don't want you to think you're a rebound. Because you're not. You mean more to me than that."

"Then I'm not your rebound."

There was a pause as she thought about it and took one step back. "We have seven seconds to figure out what we're doing."

"Why seven seconds?"

"It was the first number that came to my head." She cringed slightly, raising a shoulder.

"Seven seconds is disappearing fast."

"And we haven't moved."

"I don't want to, Kira."

Her pupils were dilated, her hair was a damp mess, and there was a faint curve in the corner of her mouth.

Those lips.

"Fuck it," I muttered and closed the gap, kissing her as she grabbed my face.

My hands went to her thighs, and I hoisted her up to my waist to bring her to the bed.

CHAPTER II
Kira

I hadn't been like this with anyone in so long. Someone gentle and kind who respected boundaries but also encouraged me to do better for myself — to expand my comfort zone and relearn how to accept love. A better kind of love. The kind of love from a good friend.

The way Seb's hands gripped my thighs and the way I rolled my hips against him said he was more than a good friend.

His hands were lightly calloused and strong from working days as a roof tiler, but each touch, full of want for my body to be connected to his, was gentle. Slow. Everywhere he touched burned deep, nourishing the growing ache within me that had been neglected before.

He underestimated how far up the bed he was when he lowered me to it in our hot and heavy frenzy, accidentally knocking the top of my head against the small shelf on the wall above my bed. It was home to several succulents and a newly planted Pothos vine. Their pots rattled slightly at the sudden disturbance, and I clutched the top of my head, giggling.

"Shit, Kira. I'm so sorry," Seb said, resting on his elbows. His dark brown eyes were full of concern as he looked at the top of my head.

I traced my thumb along the fullness of his lips. "Seb, I'm fine. This is okay."

Seb grinned with relief, and then we were kissing again. I found comfort in the weight of his toned body on mine, and smoothed my hands down over his muscular back.

He drew back to his knees, slow and steady as he drank me in with his eyes.

The rain outside eased, and the clouds parted, creating a perfectly timed natural spotlight to illuminate him as he knelt between my legs. All he was doing was making room to remove my jeans, yet every motion sent my heart soaring.

I watched every beautiful inch of him as he unzipped my jeans. When it came to removing them, still damp from the rain, there was a bit of resistance as they clung to my thighs. He tugged them off in length, meaning my legs were up in the air as he stood over me, with both of us laughing as the pants came off.

"Yours too," I said breathlessly, brushing my unruly hair from my face.

He knelt again, hastily undoing his fly until I couldn't resist and pulled him down to kiss him.

"I can't take off my pants if you keep kissing me," he mumbled onto my lips.

My teeth grazed his lip as I smiled, but I let him sit back again.

After rolling onto his back to awkwardly tug his jeans off and toss them across the room, Seb returned to rest between my legs. The bulge in his underwear pressed against me as the kisses grew more intense and the reality of the situation settled around us. But neither of us were stopping. There were no reservations, not when we smiled as we moaned and laughed softly when we discovered how our bodies reacted to each other.

We were living for the moment, forgetting strings and complications, and finally relieving what felt like weeks of tension between us. It crackled beneath my skin, like static ready to burst.

With his mouth inches from my own, as his brown eyes softened, Seb dipped his fingers beneath the waistband of my underwear.

I pushed my hips into his touch.

Heat pulsed through my body at the contact. I forgot what it was like to be pleasured like this from someone other than myself. And Seb was gentle about it, coaxing and teasing each moan and soft sigh.

My lips parted on a breath as he gently stroked my clit.

He smiled softly. "Good?"

I nodded, eyes barely open.

He moved his touch lower and slowly slid his middle fingers into me.

I gripped the sheet in my hands, rocking my hips to the come-hither motion of his fingers.

I reached my hand down between us and dipped my hand under the waistband of his underwear, finding him hard, hot, and straining as I curled my hand around his thick shaft. He immediately rolled into my touch, moaning heavily as he continued to touch and kiss me.

It was way too late to back out now. We had our foot on the accelerator. No brakes.

"Condoms?" I was already imagining how amazing he would feel as my hand slowly slid up and down around him. He wasn't cut and felt gloriously decorated with veins.

"Shit," Seb hissed.

The stroking from both of us slowed to a stop. He looked down between us, his expression filled with guilt. "I didn't bring them 'cause it was just bubble tea. I didn't want you thinking you owed me anything else. But I also didn't think we were coming back here. Also, please don't think that protection isn't a big deal to me, 'cause it is—"

"Seb." My breath was a little labored as I grinned up at him. "Check my drawer."

His eyebrows went up, and his face relaxed. "Wait, really?"

"I hope so."

Unable to contain his smile, he practically leapt off the bed and pulled open the top drawer of the nightstand on our right.

His eyes widened as he peered into the drawer.

I bit my lip in anticipation and watched in amusement as he lifted what he spotted inside.

"Sweet Jesus," he muttered, eyeing the thick, purple vibrator. "Aren't you full of surprises?"

"I dated a boy who never let me finish. It's good to have one handy."

A playfulness came over him. "Did you wanna use it now?"

I laughed and then rolled onto my side, tracing circles into the bed covers with my finger as I looked up at him. "Tempting, but I want you, Seb. Just you."

His smile turned into a smirk as he kept his eyes on me, dropped the vibrator back into the drawer, and fished out a condom. He cocked his head back as he did.

My heart leapt at the subtle shift in the mood, and I started removing my underwear, ready for him as he watched. I waited for nerves to set in, but none came. Everything about this felt right. Unless that was lust talking.

When Seb returned to the bed, he spread my thighs gently. "You're beautiful."

Eyes locked on his, my throat bobbed, and I slowly sat up as he knelt between my legs again.

"So are you." Curling my fingers under his waistband, I edged his underwear down until he sprang free. I gently took the condom from his hand and tore the wrapper with my teeth before rolling the protection onto him. He hummed at the sensation, and it only aroused me more before I leaned forward and pressed slow kisses to his lower abdomen.

Seb tilted my head up with his finger under my chin, and then stooped down to kiss me while I lay back again. In between the messy kisses and him palming my breast through my bralette, he lined himself up with me.

No more hesitation, he kissed me as he pushed in slowly. Pleasurably slow as I grew accustomed to the width, and the subtle ache that faded quickly. The sound I released as he sank deeper was a mix of a cry and a moan. I gripped the shelf above my head and accidentally bumped one of the plants. The pot fell and spilled soil across the pillow beside my head.

Laughter bubbled up from inside me while Seb chuckled and pulled us up.

I straddled his waist and slid onto him completely, gasping at the depth as soil fell from the ends of my hair.

I rolled my hips, adjusting to the feeling of fullness I wasn't used to.

"All good?" Seb asked, holding my waist as he watched my face with half closed eyes.

I hummed my response as I gripped his shoulders. "We made a mess."

Seb's smile was lazy as his hands skimmed down to my hips. "Oops."

I bit my lip as I smiled too, and then slowly drove my hips in a circle, exploring every little sensation it created for us until we found a steady rhythm. Pleasure pulsed through my body with every motion, spreading through my nerves in a rush of heat as I palmed his back.

Seb's hands roamed up between my shoulder blades, warm and comforting, before he unclasped my bralette. Once it fell away, he kissed my throat, and I dropped my head back, releasing a moan as I fell undone.

CHAPTER 12
Lily

My head felt like it was in a cloud. But not a pleasant cloud. It was a crowded cloud of frustration and worry.

The fact that Dean returned to working for Antonio hadn't come as a surprise. It was the fact my father, someone I thought knew better, was sending Dean into criminal meetings with a wire and blackmailing him into revealing everything he knew about Antonio. *That* was what infuriated me.

With my hair damp from the rain outside, I marched down the corridor to the organized crime department. Wet hair and clothes were the least of my concerns as I beelined straight for the seats outside my father's office.

Most of the detectives here knew me and waved or smiled. All I could offer in return was a curt smile of my own before I went back to watching Dad's office door. I crossed one leg over the other as I tapped my foot in the air. And then began picking at the lint balls on the arms of my cream sweater. A single seed of doubt was ready to take root — to tell me that confronting my father was pointless. But at the same time, something in me refused to shake the need to say something. I needed to say something. I just had to figure out how I was going to word it. I even had the photograph he gave me all those months ago. The one of Dean from the basement corkboard. The one my father said would keep Dean safe if it was with me.

The click of his office door pulled my attention, and I moved immediately, hand digging through my purse for the photo as I went.

Dad smiled proudly as he stood in his doorway. "Lily—"

"So, what you said was a lie," I interrupted, holding up the photo for him to see. "That he would be safe from the investigation if this wasn't in evidence."

He guided my hand back down and quickly steered me into his office. "Lily, take a seat."

"No."

"Okay," he sighed, closing the door behind him. He crossed his arms. "You actually just missed him."

The sentence didn't shock me. Of course, I already knew Dean had been here earlier. He dropped off that stupid little recording device.

"You lied to me about protecting him." My voice was surprisingly steady as I stood in the center of his office.

"Things changed. We couldn't risk wasting a good source."

"You blackmailed him, Dad. He is facing possible jail time with potential blackmail charges, and *you* blackmailed *him*."

"He's a criminal, Lily."

"You don't think I'm aware of that?" I could see this conversation was beginning to be a waste of time. I was getting angrier, and my father only looked more assured of himself.

His pause was calculated as he watched me closely before he slid his hands into the pockets of his pants. "Say he wasn't involved in this investigation, but you knew of his past. His crimes. Did you plan on keeping that a secret instead of doing the legal thing, the *right* thing, and reporting it? I'm disappointed in you, Lily."

"That makes two of us."

He inhaled sharply through his nose and took a step closer. "May I remind you, you too can be arrested for what you did?" His voice lowered. "For your involvement with The Den and being aware of what was going on beneath it for so long. The fact you even worked in that basement— You are lucky to have me on your side."

My jaw was tight as I remained silent.

"Now," he straightened, easing the tension in his shoulders. "I've already spent the morning dealing with your boyfriend's attitude towards me, and I need to get back to work. So, unless you need to discuss anything else, can we leave this on a happier note?"

Because it would be so easy to sweep our problems under the rug. Never to be spoken about out in the open...

He took my arm to steer me from his office, hoping I would mirror the smile on his face. I tugged my arm back instead.

"If Dean is caught by Antonio, wearing a wire— If any of Antonio's kids found him wearing a wire—"

"It's no less dangerous than what he's already done. This isn't his first time doing dangerous work, Lily. It's just your first time seeing it happen." He paused, running a hand over his graying dark hair. "He isn't someone who'll ever lead a respectful life. He made that clear with every wrong turn on his record. But you made your choice to live with that, which means dealing with the consequences too. If you're worried about him going to prison, or worse, maybe you should reconsider your relationship."

I scoffed. "I can't believe you."

"He agreed to this."

"Because you threatened to have his mother *deported*!"

He waved his hand to indicate I needed to keep my voice down, hinting that not everyone in the office knew about the citizenship issue. The sharp blue in my father's eyes and the subtle frustration would've once made me back off from a disagreement.

I had never told my father to fuck off before, but I was extremely close to doing it as I stood in his office, heart pounding and fighting the lump in my throat.

"Talking about this is clearly making you upset." He attempted to guide me to his office door, bringing a hand to the small of my back.

"I'm not upset." I stepped out of his reach and lowered my voice as he pulled the door open. "I think you could've done things differently. Or at least helped his mother instead of using her for leverage."

"He was willing to go to prison instead of helping me with the investigation. I needed something to get him to comply." With the door wide open, he knew it would prevent me from raising my voice again. "Does that not say anything about him? He'd rather go to prison than stay with you."

"He knows I won't be threatened with deportation," I hissed.

I was also all too aware that Dean had a self-sacrificing trait. If Dean got his way, he would've gone to prison instead of revealing Antonio's secrets to keep his loved ones safe.

Dad folded his arms, bringing his eyes from me to the office, and smiled casually to his colleagues, pretending our conversation was civilized. "What's done is done, Lily."

"Wow..."

"Is there anything else you wanted to talk about?"

"Not with you." I adjusted the strap of my bag, ready to walk away.

"Before I forget," he added, scanning the room with a show of pride before looking at me. "Tell Dean I need him here on Tuesday morning."

"Why not mention that to him earlier, when he was here? Since you think I should have nothing to do with this," I retorted.

"It was something that came to mind after he left."

"What is it?"

It was worth a shot.

"Confidential to anyone not on the case, sweetie," he smiled, but for a split second, his eyes dropped to my side, where the scars were beneath my clothes. "Just tell him I need to see him Tuesday."

Instinctively, I pulled my arms around my middle. "Fine..."

We parted ways with a begrudged goodbye, and I headed back through the office with less urgency than before. My talk to him hadn't gone anything like how I wanted it to. I wasn't entirely sure how I expected it to go.

While I was feeling defeated by the whole situation, my heart continued to beat faster.

I gripped the strap of my bag and picked up my pace.

Two detectives walked into my path, but I slipped straight in between them with a quick apology. I immediately noted their guns too. Visible beneath their jackets.

A phantom ache pulled at my side and continued tugging as I stepped into the corridor. There seemed to be more detectives and police than I first noticed. And suddenly I was counting each gun I caught a glimpse of.

The corridor to the elevator seemed to stretch on and grow narrower, filled with people coming and going.

Fear quickly rooted itself into my chest and spread, tightening around my lungs and heart until I was suffocating unnoticed.

I needed somewhere quiet and empty, and it came in the form of a cleaning room. I quickly shoved my way inside it, shutting the door behind me and leaning into it with my palms as I looked at the ground.

Inhale, exhale. Inhale, exhale—Why am I panicking?

An image of Aiden and his gun flashed across my mind, but I shook my head and then backed away from the door, pulling my arms tightly around myself.

"He isn't here," I said, shaking my head once more, eyes closed. "He's in rehab, learning how to use his leg again. With an ankle monitor."

That doesn't mean no one else wouldn't use a gun on you.

Panic rose inside me like bile, making it harder to think clearly. Every thought was suddenly too loud, and the single light overhead was too bright. I pressed a hand to my chest and hunched forward, feeling completely helpless. Until I was hastily rolling up one sleeve of my knit sweater.

As a teenager, when everything my parents piled on me got to a boiling point, I used pain. Perfect grades, pressure to fit in and be good, be polite, learn the violin although I hated every second spent with that tutor... I shamefully used pain to cope, and after a while, the panic caused by the pressure grew numb.

Moving out of home made coping with my anxiety easier, but the panic I felt now was inescapable, and was bigger than any I've felt before.

I pinched the underside of my forearm between my nails, forcing down the urge to let go when it hurt too much. It was an anchor I needed and pulled my thoughts into clarity as I shut my eyes and breathed.

As the bad memories receded into their boxes, I slowly released my skin and looked hesitantly at my forearm.

And the blood on my fingernails.

The third-floor hallway was empty as I approached the apartment door. All I could think of, as I pushed the key into the lock and turned the handle, was the welcoming embrace of sleep. I planned to fall into bed and nap until dinner. Except, as I closed the door softly behind me and made my way into the apartment, I paused in the hallway.

Apparently, I had completely missed Seb's bike outside. His helmet sat on the side table beside Kira's bedroom door — her *ajar* bedroom door where the sound of a creaking bed and soft but heavy breathing could be heard.

I quickly exited the apartment, slightly shocked and happily bemused as I stopped in the hallway.

My train of thought was completely derailed.

What do I do?

I started for the elevator and pulled out my phone.

Dean's voice answering my call never failed to cause a faint flutter in my stomach.

"Hey, what's up?" It was paired with a subtle breathlessness and the sounds of the garage in the background.

"I was wondering what time you planned on getting home?" I pressed the elevator button for the ground floor.

"I've gotta run some errands for Mom first, but I should get to yours at five-ish…" The sounds of the garage grew faint. I figured he had stepped outside. "Unless you had something else in mind for right now? Because I could tell the boss there was a family emergency."

My face heated, and I smiled. "I was actually wondering if your mom would mind if I visited? And maybe stay over?"

"We're talkin' about my mother, Lily. She adores you."

Sofia opened the front door with a huge grin on her face. Her long, wavy black hair was pulled away from her face with a claw clip, and her blue eyes sparkled. In her lap was Bella, the caramel chihuahua mix puppy she was gifted so many months ago. The puppy had grown a mere inch since then but was as bouncy as the first time I met her, wriggling from head to white-tipped tail.

"Dean told me you were on your way," Sofia said warmly as I leaned in to hug her. "How are you?"

She knew what I went through, more so than anyone else. Not from retellings but from her own experience of how she came to be in a wheelchair. When I slowly pulled away from the hug, she watched me with a knowing look and a faint smile.

"I'm coping," I said, adjusting the way the strap of my bag sat on my shoulder. I brought my eyes to the rest of the house, noting the sweet smell that drifted in from the kitchen in the back. "Something smells good."

"That is the cannoli. I hope you are hungry." She invited me in with a soft ushering of her hands before wheeling ahead to the kitchen.

I closed the front door behind me and followed, feeling as if the exhaustion from today was left on the porch. I felt better for being here. It was safe, despite my uncertainty on whether Dean had told his mother about his situation.

And the blackmail.

The subject of Sofia's citizenship lingered in the corners of my mind as I helped her prepare the cannoli on a plate, poured two glasses of lemonade, and followed her back into the lounge room. She insisted on showing me a photo album full of memories of her home in Sicily as we ate.

"Would you ever want to visit again? Or move back?" My hands were wrapped firmly around the glass in my hand as I tried to gauge if she was aware of what was going on. Maybe if Sofia took an impromptu trip to Italy, the surprise of deportation wouldn't come so harshly. She could go on her own terms.

"Sometimes. But I do like it here. I have many friends here," she smiled sweetly. "And with how I am, I don't think I could afford traveling back home with my chair." Her eyes lit up. "Maybe you and Dean could go one day."

She didn't know. Not about her citizenship, and definitely not about her son's future.

"A trip there would be nice." I brought my drink to my lips, taking a sip as I eyed the cannoli on the coffee table.

It's not my place to tell her. Change the subject.

"What's in these?" I said, picking up one of the cannoli. "Is it cream cheese?"

Sofia reached over and gently squeezed my knee. When my eyes met hers, she smiled softly, creating faint wrinkles around the edges of her blue eyes. "There is something you are not saying, Lily. You can tell me."

"A lot is going on right now." My attempt to brush off the topic was lost on Sofia. She only watched me closer, waiting for a better response. I put the cannoli down and cleared my throat, dusting crumbs from my lap. "Well, I've only just started work again... My emotions are all over the place." I tried for a laugh, to pretend it was all fine, but that somehow made it worse.

Sofia rested back in her chair with empathy in her eyes and her smile fading. "It took me some time to feel like myself again after my accident. I also lost a little one..."

"I'm sorry. I didn't mean to bring anything up."

"Talking about it helped."

I looked down as that all too familiar lump rose in my throat, causing my voice to come out small. "It doesn't always feel like it works."

Sofia took my hand in my lap, speaking gently with strength in her words. "It takes time to heal something so deep, but I promise you it will get better. You are so young. You will grow from this."

Tears began to blur my vision. When I blinked, one ran quickly down my cheek before I wiped it away, huffing a sombre laugh.

Sofia wheeled herself closer and cupped my face in her soft, warm hands. Her own eyes were watery too as she wiped another tear from my cheek with her thumb.

"You will be okay. I promise."

I wanted to believe her.

CHAPTER 13
Dean

Soft laughter floated through the house as I entered the back door after a long day at the garage, carrying loaded bags of groceries. Bella, like every other time I got home, came bounding through the small kitchen and dining space to greet me with her helicopter tail and chaotic excitement. But it was the sound of Lily's voice and laugh that lifted my mood tenfold.

I ditched the bags on the counter and wandered into the living room, where Lily and Mom were looking through photo albums.

Lily's golden-brown hair was swept up into a claw clip, but several strands had fallen from it, framing her features with a softness that caused my heart to surge within the milliseconds she saw me walk into the room.

She smiled easily. Her blue doe eyes took me in quickly before a subtle knowing smile crept onto her face. Her smile turned cheeky, and had something to do with the images of my childhood laid out in front of her.

"Should I be worried?" I said, pausing at the head of the coffee table.

Lily bit the corner of her bottom lip and turned the album in her lap for me to see.

"Sofia was telling me about how for a very long time you refused to go anywhere without your fire truck red rain boots." She gave me an adoring pout, referring to the two-page spread of toddler me, mostly at the beach, in boots.

"He thought they gave him powers to fight monsters," Mom added, smiling with pride as she wheeled her chair out from behind the coffee table. "I'm getting more food. There are more photos to see, Lily." She wheeled herself towards the kitchen, but left with a warning: "Do not get grease on my couch, *per favore*."

"*Si*." My eyes hadn't strayed from Lily and the way she was watching me with an adoring grin. "What?"

"The reason why you always wear combat boots makes way more sense now." Her eyes traveled south, and she raised a brow in consideration. "It would be interesting to see you in red rain boots, though."

"Nothing but red rain boots?" I quirked a brow, enjoying the way my words made her blush as I leaned in, bracing one hand on the back of the sofa. I planted a soft kiss on the area below the curve of her jaw. "Hi."

She turned her head slightly, her cheek brushing mine.

"No grease on my sofa, Dean," Mom warned, returning from the kitchen.

I reluctantly straightened with an inhale and subtle stretch of my back.

"Why'd you wanna come over? Not that I'm complaining," I asked.

"The apartment was a little occupied." Lily placed the photo album on the coffee table as Mom did the same with the cannoli.

I frowned, picking up one of the desserts and taking a bite. "Occupied how?"

"Seb and Kira," Mom said, sharing a smile with Lily. They had discussed a lot during Lily's visit.

My brow shot up. "That was fast."

"Yep," Lily continued. "I'm happy for them, though. Kira deserves it."

"Yeah, she does." Without thinking, I went to sit beside Lily. My arm was already outstretched to drape across the back of the couch.

"*Dean, the grease!* Go shower and change your clothes," Mom exclaimed, clapping her hands and shooing at me as I paused, halfway to sitting down, while Lily laughed.

I pulled up and half smiled. "*Mamma—*"

Mom shook her head. "*Doccia e cambio.*"

Lily, who had been following the entire conversation with an amused look on her face, shrugged. "You do smell like a garage."

My eyes narrowed on her, and she grinned sweetly.

"Alright, fine. I'm going." I glanced at Mom, finding her attention was on another photo album, and then looked at Lily and tipped my head in the direction of the hallway.

It took her a second to figure out what I was trying to indicate. Her face changed from confused to wide-eyed.

"Thanks for the cannoli, Sofia. They were lovely." She stood and collected her bag.

I backed up to wait in the hallway, hands buried in my pockets. My eyes instinctively traveled over her, drinking in the way she moved with bounce and grace in her steps. Everything she did was careful, like she didn't want to disrupt anything, yet there was still a quiet confidence about it.

She was halfway across the living room, eyes on me with a cute and eager half smile on her lips, when she remembered something and turned on the spot. "Oh, Sofia... Thank you for the conversation earlier too."

Mom smiled softly. "Anytime, Lily."

As we turned into the hallway, I gently nudged her arm. "Everythin' okay?"

Lily inhaled and offered me a content smile from over her shoulder, wrapping her left arm across her stomach to rest her hand on her side. "We were sharing some things. But I'm fine now."

I nodded in understanding.

When we reached the bathroom door, and she mentioned she needed to get a change of clothes from my bedroom, I looped a finger through the belt loop on her pants and slowly pulled her close.

"You stayin' all weekend?" My finger remained in that loop, pinning her in place while I got lost in her eyes waiting for an answer.

Her arms came to rest on my shoulders as she tilted her head back in consideration, grazing her teeth briefly across her pink bottom lip in a way that jolted my pulse.

"I don't think I have a choice now." She rose to her toes to kiss me, simultaneously threading her fingers through the back of my hair.

A deep, involuntary hum vibrated through my throat in reaction to the way she lightly curled her fingers against my scalp. It was my weak spot when it came to her. And probably the fastest way to get me on my knees.

"Dean, I promise it's nothing. I just freaked out a little. That's all," Lily said, sitting cross-legged on the end of my bed in her underwear and my gray hoodie. The sleeves were bunched at her elbows, and the whole thing swam on her. But it was the small mark on her arm, hidden by one of the sleeves, that concerned me.

I spotted it in the shower. And sure, it was just a mark — the smallest cut tucked under her bicep surrounded by a small bruise to match, but it also looked intentional.

When I asked about it, Lily had brushed it off as nothing then too.

I crossed my arms and rested my hip against my dresser opposite the end of the bed.

Lily sighed as she rubbed the bridge of her nose. "I had a panic attack today after speaking with my dad."

I remained where I was but uncrossed my arms and slid my hands into the pockets of my sweatpants. As tempting as it was to cross the room, I knew she still had more to say. I knew I needed her to say more before other temptations got in the way.

"This," she continued, referring to the mark under the hoodie's sleeve, "was something I used to do in high school, whenever I got overwhelmed. I don't know why I did it this time, but I *promise* you it is nothing to worry about. It was a weird one-off thing."

I couldn't help that I deadpanned. It's not that I didn't believe her. It was more that I wondered if she believed herself.

Her lips spread into a smile before she reached back for a pillow and lobbed it at my face.

I caught it in one hand and pushed off the dresser. A smile was already teasing its way onto my lips as I walked to the end of the bed. With her still sitting, the movement caused her head to tilt back to maintain eye contact.

"Stop worrying for five seconds and come to bed," she said softly.

I shook my head and crouched down, bracing my elbows on the edge of the mattress before I took one of her hands.

"I know you were trying to help today by talking to your dad about my involvement with Antonio, and I appreciate it. I really do, but please, and I mean this in the best trying-not-to-be-a-controlling-douchebag way, don't do it again. I don't want you getting overwhelmed... Mom tried once with Antonio years ago. Tried to tell him off for what he got me involved in— It's easier if I do some things on my own."

Lily scoffed. "Dean."

I brought the back of her hand to my lips and watched her from over her knuckles. "While seeing you get protective over me is hot and fucking adorable, I need you taking care of *you*." My eyes briefly went to her side.

"Well, I can't *not* talk to my dad."

"I'm not saying that. I mean, don't get involved with the case."

It was her turn to deadpan.

She took her hand back and pulled her sleeves down, bristling slightly. "You know, he seems to think the same thing. And then he told me to relay a message despite not wanting me involved..."

"Lily."

"He wants to meet with you on Tuesday at his office." She withdrew and scooted off the bed, brushing past me.

I stood, sighing. "Did he say what for?"

"Nope." In one swift movement, she whipped her hair up into a messy bun, pulled back the covers, and climbed into bed.

I'm a douchebag.

"Lily, I didn't mean—"

"Speaking of your mother," she cut in matter-of-factly, "how come you haven't warned her about the whole deportation thing yet? Or is that another thing we shouldn't be involved in?" She pinned me with a sharpness in her eyes as she tucked herself in.

A frown creased my brow, and I shut my eyes briefly. "That's different."

"Is it though?" She pulled her arms around her middle and kept her voice quiet. "What will happen if immigration shows up here to take her away. She'll be blindsided."

I kept my voice low too, and walked around to my side of the bed, closest to the door. "They won't come for her if I work with your dad on this case."

"You could still make it all legal. You could go to immigration and explain her situation. Then maybe they'd grant her that citizenship."

"And if they didn't?" I climbed into bed, albeit a little hesitantly. Lily had daggers in her eyes, and though they weren't aimed at me yet, I felt like I needed to be ready to duck for cover. There was an unwanted edge to my voice, no thanks to the nicotine cravings. "They could deport her on the spot, Lily. Or put her in a detention center."

She let out a breath and glared ahead. But then it eased. "I know being deported isn't ideal, and I'm not saying she should be, but would going back to Sicily be so bad? Her parents are still there. She wouldn't be alone..."

"We lost contact with them. We don't even know if they're still in the same place. Or alive." I rubbed my forehead. "If none of this other crap was happening, I would do it all properly. I'd take her to Sicily myself and help her apply for that citizenship again. And then we'd come back."

"She deserves to know."

"She deserves better than any of this," I muttered sharply.

Silence fell between us, and I hated every second of it. One sidelong glance at Lily instantly hit me in the gut with guilt.

She was chewing her bottom lip, staring ahead with glassy eyes. How many times had I seen Mom with that same look after one of Gio's drunken rampages? *Shit.*

"Hey, look at me." I shifted closer and took her face in my hands. "I'm sorry. I didn't mean to patronize you."

She shook her head and wiped her tears, but kept that eye contact. Those pretty blue doe eyes were another of my weaknesses, and seeing them this sad and torn made me feel like I kicked a puppy.

"I'm a fuckin' prick."

"No, no, you're not. I get what you're saying. I get why you would want to keep her out of all this. I don't even know why I'm crying. Well, I do, obviously, with everything— I'm frustrated because I can't do anything. If it wasn't for my dad, if he'd done as he promised and kept you out of all this." She inhaled shakily. "I could've punched my father in the face today and probably wouldn't have felt bad."

I released her face and brushed a tear from her cheek that she missed. "I already did."

She sniffled and frowned, wondering if she heard me right. "What?"

"The day he brought me in for questioning, when he blackmailed me." I offered her a slightly sheepish smile.

Lily blinked a couple of times, processing as she sat back in silence. Only to start giggling, which flowed into full, breathless laughter.

The corners of my mouth twitched as I watched her, relieved she was okay but slightly confused by the sudden change. "Lily?"

There were happy tears in her eyes this time as she shook her head but continued to laugh, wrapping her arms across her middle again, like before. As her laughter died out with sighs and fading smiles, something crossed her mind, and her attention went to her arms. Her stomach.

Her amusement was quick to fade.

So did mine as I watched her.

"Shit," she groaned, quickly kicking back the covers and jumping out of bed.

I straightened, all amusement gone as I tracked her. She was clutching her lower abdomen as she made the run to the bedroom door. My worst thought was that maybe it was her wounds. Or complications from them. "Lily, what's wrong?"

She reached the door, throwing a grimace over her shoulder right before she left. "I think I got my period early."

Chapter 14

The weekend went by in a haze.

We baked, watched movies together, and received an impromptu dance lesson from Sofia as she instructed us on how to do an informal version of the Viennese waltz in the living room. If I thought I knew how to count, doing so while moving — and trying not to step on Dean's toes as he led me through the steps — showed me a whole new outlook on numbers.

The sad part was that all the while, we were playing pretend in front of Sofia.

On Saturday, the morning after my period made its perfectly timed arrival, Dean began preparing for his upcoming fight at Castello di Vetro. It was on Friday, and while I wasn't thrilled about him walking into another fight — especially since his last one hadn't gone so well with Murphy — my worries were temporarily set aside at the comment he made as he worked out at the end of his bed.

After performing at least two dozen crunches while I sat on the bed in a hoodie munching on a bag of potato chips, Dean rolled onto his front, pushed himself up into a plank, blew at the strands of black hair hanging in his eyes, and muttered, "I'm out of shape."

He proceeded to do several push-ups.

I paused mid-chew and looked him over. "Which part?"

He huffed a laugh and tucked his elbows in closer to his sides to do a different kind of push-up. Every muscle in his core and arms was moving with the motions, somehow becoming more defined than they were seconds ago. His golden-brown skin and the tattoos wrapped around his toned edges began to shine with a light sheen of sweat.

My eyes caught on the muscles rolling in his shoulders, beneath the wings etched there, and I quietly put my bag of potato chips aside and lay down across the end of the bed. Resting my head in my hand, I simply watched.

When that set was done, he sat back on his haunches and smiled so easily at me — so damn handsomely with the little dimple that appeared in his cheek.

"You know you don't have to watch, right?"

"I know."

"But you will anyway?" The smile remained in the corner of his mouth as he brushed his black hair back, steadying his breath.

"One hundred percent. It's like an anatomy study. For drawing."

"Aren't you meant to have the sketchpad and pencil for that?" His right eyebrow lifted, emphasizing the scar there.

I tapped my temple. "I have a good memory. Now, please, continue."

He chuckled and lay down on the floor, tucking his hands behind his head to begin another set of crunches with the waistband of his basketball shorts sitting below his hip bones.

The rest of the weekend was filled with moments like that. Soft and sweet. The kind that should last forever. The kind that were easily taken for granted. I found myself counting each one and storing them in a safe little box, somewhere in my mind for when the inevitable happened.

I had tucked that one away when Kira joined me on our pastel blue couch to begin our impromptu Sunday evening girls' night in — a night that was overdue and needed. With large bowls of popcorn in our laps, red wine, and macarons between us, we were ready to begin our movie marathon of horror and rom-coms.

We started a cult-classic horror first and spent part of it watching from behind pillows as the heroine spoke to the masked killer on the phone.

"Well, don't go outside!" Kira exclaimed, throwing her arms wide at the TV.

"I hate and love cliches," I said from behind the safety of my pillow, waiting for the jump-scare.

Our eyes were glued to the screen in anticipation. My palms were clammy, and Kira was already lifting her pillow as a precaution.

Until Kira's phone buzzed obnoxiously on the coffee table and we screamed.

"Oh my god!" I laughed, sliding off the couch and onto the floor as the buzzing continued.

Kira, perched on the arm of the chair, had a hand pressed to her chest as she quickly paused the movie. "This is why I don't watch scary movies. Jesus Christ."

I let my head flop back on the couch cushion. "Are you going to answer it?"

"You know the rules." She gestured to the TV again. "Don't answer the phone."

"What if it's Seb?" I smiled knowingly.

"Pfft, doubt it..." She glanced at her phone as it buzzed again, and then promptly stepped off the couch and picked it up to answer. "Hello?"

As she took the call, I headed to the kitchen for drink refills, noting the subtle ache in my abdomen as the pain meds wore off. I checked the time for how long had passed since the last two tablets I took. More than enough time had passed, so I reached for the pain meds above the fridge and popped another two. Downing them with a sip of wine, and then another as my eyes settled on the freezer door in front of me, where the business card from that psychologist remained untouched and partially hidden behind bills and several takeaway brochures.

I took another long sip and squared my shoulders.

Tomorrow.

I would call him tomorrow and get it over and done with. Like ripping off that metaphorical Band-Aid, I would make that call tomorrow to begin seeing someone about surviving a gunshot. Even if the idea of talking about it, dredging up all those feelings, was turning my stomach into knots. Everyone else was moving forward from that fateful day, so it was about time I did too.

I mentally shook it off as tomorrow's problem and headed back to the couch with the wine glasses full.

Kira hung up her phone, face indifferent as she plopped onto the couch.

"Not Seb?"

"No. It was someone from work asking if I could cover their shift... Anyway, why would you think I was expecting a call from him?" Her movements to act casually made it all the more obvious.

"I know you slept with him, Kira," I smiled softly.

She couldn't contain her happiness any longer. It burst from her like sun rays as her lips spread into a grin. "I wouldn't exactly call what we did *sleeping*. We did *it*, several times, on Friday afternoon, and then when I woke up that same afternoon, he'd gone. But he did leave a note."

"What did it say?" I was intrigued now, barely containing my smile as I set the glasses down and sat beside her.

Kira pressed her lips together and reached into her back pocket. She pulled out a post-it note and handed it to me to read. On the yellow paper was a simple note.

'Have a good weekend, Smiles.'

I pouted happily. "That is the cutest thing I've ever seen."

"But I don't know what I'm doing," she groaned, dropping her face into her hands while her wild, red hair fell around her shoulders.

"Because of what you had with Aiden?"

She sat up quickly, pulling a face in disgust. "No, definitely not because of him. Without him, I feel wonderful. With Seb, I felt wonderful. I haven't felt this happy in so long. But it feels like it *should* be wrong to dive into something so fast."

"I hate to break it to you, Kira," I placed a hand on her knee, "But slow and steady hasn't ever been your thing."

"Okay, true," she laughed.

"Sooo?" I wagged my eyebrows.

"We just—click. And it feels so easy," she sighed, falling heavily into the back of the couch.

Her happiness was contagious as I grinned. "Have you talked to him about how you feel?"

"No... And it's not because I'm avoiding it," she added quickly when I gave her a look. "Seb dropped his phone when we went for bubble tea, and it broke in a puddle. So, I think he's getting it repaired, which would explain why he hasn't been able to talk to me all weekend... *And* part of me wants to talk to him, because I know how easy it is to talk to him..."

"But?"

"But I also don't want to find out I've read the situation completely wrong and have my heart broken again." Her shoulders slumped slightly, and her smile became more subdued.

"You've had sex, Kira. I don't think you're reading anything wrong."

"What if all he wants is that?"

"Which is why you need to talk to him," I urged, and then frowned slightly. "Obviously, when his phone is fixed. I could always ask Dean to relay a message. They have their fights this Friday."

Kira began nodding slowly as she considered it, but shook her head quickly. "No. No. I don't want to start waiting on a man again... Seb always shows up for my SDV meetings on Thursdays, so I'll talk to him then."

"Even better," I half smiled. "It's not like Seb not to show up. The guy is the definition of loyal."

"Exactly." She nodded in reassurance, more so to herself, before she grabbed her wine glass and took a long gulp. Her brown eyes suddenly widened over the rim of the glass at me, and she lowered it to her lap. "How are you feeling about Friday, though?"

"With the fight?" I hummed nervously and pulled a pillow into my lap. "Not great... It's not like I'm doubting Dean's ability. I know he can handle it."

"Just look at what he did to Aiden," Kira added, lifting her wine glass as if toasting the beating Aiden received that day.

"Right? Handled..." I played with the corner of the pillow.

"It's the investigation, isn't it? All the undercover stuff?"

My eyes shot to her. "How do you know about that?"

"Seb told me everything on our bubble tea date," she winced. "Sorry."

"No, it's fine." I inhaled sharply. "Actually, it's easier now that you know. I have someone else to vent to in case it all goes sideways."

"I'm always here for when shit goes sideways." She grasped my hand. "You know that, right? You can vent to me."

"I appreciate you so much for it."

CHAPTER 15
Lily

I stared at the call button on the office phone, waiting for the number I dialed, the one that would connect me to that psychologist, to ring on its own. I wished it would. That way, I wouldn't have the choice to avoid pressing that button altogether.

The pros of speaking to a professional were that I was getting help, dealing with my trauma healthily.

Cons? Rehashing everything and potentially opening up to more pain before I could work towards feeling normal.

I was chewing at my bottom lip — it was slightly chapped from the cold outside — until I tore at a piece of skin that wasn't as dry.

"Shit," I muttered. It stung like a papercut and pulled me from my thoughts as I instantly brought a finger to it, checking for blood. A tiny red dot marked my fingertip.

As I grabbed a tissue, ignoring the side-long glance from Candice at her computer, Mom stepped into the foyer. Ready for her solo house inspection with her keys in hand and a folder tucked under her arm. She wore a dark blue pantsuit. Ever the professional.

"That can become a nasty habit." She barely glanced at me as she made a quick detour behind the desk, checking her mailbox for anything important. "Also, you know that open house next Wednesday? I want you to attend. It's time you start learning how to conduct an open house." She paused her search and looked over her shoulder at me. "Unless you had *other* plans."

Other plans, as in anything with Dean. I had moved on from believing she would ever change her point of view on him.

I smiled, but not as widely when it caused the cut on my lip to burn beneath the tissue I still held against it. "I'll be there."

Acne cream was blotted across my chin, my hair was in a loose bun, there was a warm wheat bag held to my stomach, and I was in my softest pajamas. It was one of the few times I loathed being a woman as my ovaries went to war with my body.

Kira was to my left as we sat on our pastel blue couch, watching as the host of a cooking show introduced what he deemed the best homemade candy to add to the kids' Halloween baskets this year. All I wanted was for that candy to be at my disposal. Preferably served with chocolate.

For a moment, my eyes slid to Kira as she refreshed her text notifications for the umpteenth time, waiting for that all-important text from Seb. One I doubted would come anytime soon as midnight drew closer. Kira would have to wait until Thursday, after her meeting, to talk to him.

Just like I would have to wait until tomorrow morning to talk to Dean.

So much for not waiting on a man...

Mine had been called in for a job. The kind I hated but knew he didn't have much of a choice with. All I knew was that it involved collecting money and bringing it back to Antonio. All while inconspicuously strapped with a police recording device.

I wasn't fully paying attention to the TV. More staring than anything before a text came through on my phone. My speed of tapping the notification was immediate. Despite knowing a text from Dean during one of these jobs was unlikely, I still half expected his name to be on the screen. Instead, it was a text from my sister, Jane, wondering if I could come to her soccer game this Saturday.

Me: Yeah, of course. Just don't expect me to have any clue of what's going on lol

Jane: It's more that I need your opinion on something.

Me: Why not ask me now for my opinion?

Jane: Because you need to see it in person.

She added a smirking emoji, and I smiled to myself as I responded.

Me: You're weird.

Jane: See you Saturday!

It was past 1 AM as I shuffled back to bed from my bathroom, feeling my way through the dark until I was tucked beneath the covers again. Curling myself

around the wheat bag, I nestled my head into my pillow. As I closed my eyes, the room was illuminated by my phone.

I reached for it and remained beneath the covers as I opened the text from Dean.

Dean: Leaving his house. You probably won't get this until morning, but goodnight x

I smiled faintly and tapped out a response, sending it off with a yawn.

Me: Night x

Dean: You're up late.

Me: Can't sleep. Cramping.

Dean: What do you need?

Me: Snacks and back rubs?

Dean: On my way.

I stared at that message for longer than I meant to, wondering how many more of them I would get before all of this was over. My hormones were making me a little sentimental. An all too familiar lump was forming in my throat before I locked my phone and rolled onto my back.

The days I had with him were limited and disappearing fast with every piece of information Dad was using to build his case.

Half an hour later, as I waited for another text from him to let me know he was downstairs, there was a knock on the apartment door, and I sat up with a frown.

I climbed out of bed and quietly made my way through the apartment, making a mental note to get a spare key made as I felt my way down the short, dark hallway to the front door. Suddenly remembering the acne cream on my chin, I hastily rubbed it in as I pulled the door open.

His sandalwood and leather scent greeted my senses as I found Dean leaning against the door frame. Dressed in a dark, blue-black button-up shirt with the sleeves rolled up, revealing his tattooed forearms, I figured he came from a job that required a more formal setting. His black hair was combed back, except for a few stubborn strands that hung across his brow in the way I loved, and in his hand was a small plastic container.

At first, he was simply gazing towards the elevator as he waited. When the door opened, pulling his attention to me, a soft smile appeared on his face.

"I brought leftover cannoli." He lifted the box for emphasis as he pushed away from the door frame.

I groaned happily as I eyed the box. "Did I mention I love you?"

He huffed a laugh as he considered the box. "They're sort of a peace offering too."

"For what?"

The grimace on his face was subtle. "Our disagreement on the weekend."

"You already apologized for that."

"I know, but it didn't seem like enough. I wasn't fair to you, and you made a good point. So..." When he began lowering himself to one knee in the middle of the corridor, my eyebrows went up in surprise. He half smiled while looking up at me. "Forgive me, Lily. And if I ever speak to you that way again, or raise my voice—"

"You didn't raise your voice," I said gently.

"But if I ever do, with you, please slap me upside the head, alright?"

"Okay, that's a little extreme, but," I took his hand, indicating he could stand, and laughed a little, "You're forgiven... Now come inside before Susan spots us and thinks you're proposing."

Dean raised an eyebrow knowingly while the corner of his mouth twitched. "Since I'm down here already..."

I knew he was joking, but it didn't stop the subtle fluttering in my stomach. My words came out with quiet laughter as I gently tugged on his arm. "Just come inside."

He rose to his feet, handed me the container, and kissed my cheek, smiling as he did.

I led him into the apartment, feeling completely giddy now that he was here. The pain meds were also finally providing some relief. The promise of some sugar-coated cannoli was also helping my mood.

We headed quietly into my room.

"How did you get into the apartment foyer anyway?" I whispered as I shut the bedroom door.

Dean took a seat on the end of my bed. "That guy on the first floor let me in. The one with all the birds."

"Ah," I nodded, approaching the bed as I opened the container. "That's Nigel."

I felt Dean's eyes on me as I sat beside him, deciding which cannoli I would eat first.

He brushed his arm against mine, grabbing my attention.

"By the way, what you said on Friday night, it made me realize I'm a dumbass for keeping Mom in the dark."

"You told her?"

"Everythin'."

"Everything? As in deportation and prison?"

He pressed his lips together and nodded once. "The lot."

I put the container aside and angled myself to face him. "How'd she take it?"

Dean inhaled. His expression was faintly amused. "She cried, ranted about how much she hated it, and called me an idiot for planning on keeping it from her. For not trusting her to keep it a secret like she's done my entire time fighting for Antonio."

"Well," I sighed. "She isn't wrong..."

"You can call me an idiot too, if you like."

I leaned closer. "I'm just happy she's aware... What's the next step for her?"

"Applying for citizenship isn't easy... She said she'll just have to be careful."

"Until we figure something out," I reassured.

"Yes..."

Those gray-blue eyes watched me a second longer, noticing the small cut on my lip from earlier today, before he gently tucked several strands of hair behind my ear and cupped the side of my face. I tilted my head into his touch, searching his face for whatever was on his mind.

"You make me wanna do better."

My heart skipped a beat, and my throat bobbed. That sentimental feeling from before set in quickly. There was a sudden glassiness to my vision.

"The intention wasn't to make you cry." He half smiled out of sympathy, wiping at a tear that tracked its way down my cheek. "Fuck, I'm on a roll this year."

I huffed a laugh and wiped my eyes with the sleeve of my pajama top. "No, it's fine. Let's change the subject before I'm a blubbering mess."

"Good idea." His eyes were still on me, making sure I was, in fact, okay before we continued.

"So," I smiled, sniffling, "how did tonight go?"

That prolonged eye contact of his, still studying me with a calm concern about the tears drying on my cheeks, was enough to make me wish I had skipped this period altogether. He smelled good, looked good, and was actively listening and watching me as if I wasn't dressed like I rolled out of bed.

Dean shook his head. "Boring. Dealing with greedy dicks. Recording the entire thing for your dad." There was a smile in his eyes as he nodded his chin at me. "Tell me about your day."

"Boring," I smiled. "Dealing with greedy dicks — in property. Reporting back to my mom. It's a whole family affair we have going on, huh?"

His smile broadened and dimpled his cheek. "Like a regular mob affiliation."

"You can do anythin', but never go against the family," I said with my best Marlon Brando impersonation, adding hand gestures, a frown, and a pouted bottom lip that made Dean laugh. I continued the butchered impersonation as I picked up the box of cannoli. "Let's eat."

CHAPTER 16
Dean

A photocopier rattled and clicked to a steady rhythm somewhere nearby, and out in the corridor, a New Yorker in cuffs, accent thicker than mine, was voicing his opinions about his arrest as they led him to a holding cell. There was a musty smell of coffee throughout the office, and a low hum of casual office chatter filled the room.

I sat in the plastic seats across from Mark's office with my back to the window as an October wind howled against the glass.

And to my left, the eyes of two men bore into the side of my face.

Detectives Paul Crowley and Dante Riccardo. The former was a beer-bellied, arrogant mouth breather with a bobble-head of some old baseball player sitting on his desk.

Dante Riccardo looked new to the job, but not naïve to the career. He was younger, maybe mid-thirties, and had a near-constant smirk on his face.

I ground my jaw as the watching continued, but kept my eyes forward.

It was the nicotine cravings making me like this. Simply the cravings—

"You know," Crowley finally croaked after a few more seconds of studying the side of my face. "I think he was the kid who stole my police car."

I pretended I didn't hear him as I crossed my arms. My past run-ins with the cops were a blur of running through back streets or climbing walls. I was either too hungover too concussed, or too pissed off at the time to remember those moments as anything significant.

"Yeah, he was probably seventeen. Was in for car theft and took my keys right out from under my nose." Crowley scoffed. "Came from a broken home too."

Don't react. I repeated the two words over and over in my mind, jaw tight as I exhaled.

"Careful," Riccardo said with a hint of sarcasm in his tone. "I think he hears you."

"He can't do anything now anyway. Look at where he is," Crowley said.

From my peripheral I could see he had leaned forward in his seat to speak directly to me.

"Did daddy beat you around a little? Is that why you acted out? If he was my kid, it would've been straight to military school."

"Maybe ease up a bit, Crowley," Riccardo chuckled, talking sense.

"He can't touch us, Riccardo. Wouldn't dare try." Crowley's confidence in himself had begun a subtle roaring in my head. "I bet he got your mother too—"

I straightened in my seat and dragged my eyes to Crowley. The nicotine gum hadn't worked, the patches were pointless, I didn't have any of my lollipops, and this fucker was giving me every reason to slam his head through a window. But I was also surrounded by cops. One misstep and I would be in deeper shit than I already was.

"You wanna hit me, don't you?" A smug little curve appeared on Crowley's mouth.

"Nah." I straightened out my legs and stood, keeping my eyes on Mark's office door before I approached the detective's desk.

Crowley's smile wavered and faded once I stopped in front of him. He leaned back in his chair as if that would create more space between us. But he was cornered between his desk, Riccardo's desk, and a wall. Nowhere to go.

"You're not really worth my time, detective." I casually picked up the bobblehead baseball figure on his desk, looked it over, and then put it down again. Only to pick up the stapler beside it. I turned it over in my hand, weighing it while Crowley and Riccardo watched me carefully.

"Go back to your seat, Moretto," Riccardo drawled, clicking a pen.

I pinned Crowley with a glare. "But talk about my mother again, and I'll staple your dick to the fuckin' desk."

There was a long pause of silence between us until Riccardo chuckled and shook his head. "Jesus Christ, Crowley."

I put the stapler down and went back to my seat, leaving Crowley in silence before the two detectives went back to whatever work they had on their desks, no longer staring or running their mouths. I leaned back in my seat and let my head rest against the window behind me.

Seven minutes later, I walked into Mark's office to discuss more of the same — weapon deals, money laundering, places where Antonio conducts his business, and who his clients are. Hearing every detail leave my mouth, after years of keeping it all a secret, felt like I was having an out-of-body experience, watching myself slowly unravel everything I knew about loyalty.

I wondered if it was even considered loyalty. Maybe it was fear of the repercussions if I stepped out of line that kept my mouth shut for so long. And now all those details were flowing out of me like I had nothing to lose.

Well, not every detail. My father's death was a topic I had locked down.

Mark put down his pen and closed his ever-growing folder of notes. "Lily's chat with me the other day made me rethink the danger of all this a little more."

"You only just realized how dangerous it is?" I lifted an eyebrow.

He didn't respond to my sarcasm. Instead, he steepled his fingers as he stared me down. "How are your gun skills?"

I blinked. "Sorry, what?"

"Don't make me repeat myself because I'll start reconsidering the idea."

"You—" I sat forward and rested my arms on the table. "You want me usin' a gun?"

"I want you to brush up on any skills you may have. Assuming you have used one before?" He inhaled. "It'd be for you and Lily's protection in case I can't get to you in time if Antonio or his children find out what you're doing for me."

I couldn't believe the words coming from his mouth as I stared. "I think I'm havin' an aneurysm."

"You'd attend private supervised sessions at a shooting range with detectives Crowley and Riccardo."

I huffed in disbelief. "No."

"You work for a mob boss, but using a gun is against your morals?"

"Say I agree; I get the gun; I go to target practice with Tweedledee and Tweedledum out there; What's stopping you from saying I was armed when you arrest me?"

"You won't be framed. The gun is only for your protection." He sighed and rubbed his temples. "The team has already called me crazy for suggesting this. Don't make it harder... You can choose to tell Lily you have it or not."

"This is fucked up," I scoffed. "And you're gonna just hand one over? Do you keep spares in lost and found?"

A smile appeared on the edges of his mouth. "You'll get one from Antonio himself."

I sat in complete silence on one of the couches in Lily and Kira's living room as the sunset cast an orange glow across the room from behind Lily. She was on the other couch, adjacent to me, with a book resting in her lap and her eyes on the floor as she processed what I told her. The wheat bag she was holding to her stomach only added to the guilt I felt about making her feel more miserable.

Lily shifted on the spot. "This is a lot to think about... Why would Dad want you to have a gun when you're part of the investigation? What's stopping him from using that against you?"

"That's what I said to him. But he said it's for our protection."

She scoffed, sliding her arms tighter around her middle. Her left hand came to a stop right above her scars as she looked at me with unease.

"Listen." I moved to the coffee table, allowing myself to be directly in front of her as I ducked my head to keep our gaze locked. "If you don't want one in the apartment, it's fine. I'll tell your dad you aren't comfortable."

"No... No, it's okay. The lessons at the shooting range would be a waste of time otherwise. And the protection might be worth it with all things considered..." Her next question was asked carefully. "Have you ever had to use one before?"

"I haven't shot anyone, if that's what you mean," I said gently, edging closer to her. As close as the edge of the coffee table allowed.

She only nodded. Her hands curled against her sides as she remained quiet. "You okay?"

"It's something you have to do. It's not like I haven't been around a gun before. I used to see Dad's gun all the time growing up..." She tried for a smile, but the usual light in her eyes wasn't there.

"If you get uncomfortable, tell me. Please."

"I will." When I challenged that with a slight lift of my brow, she unraveled her arms and took my hand in hers. "I promise. Now, can we talk about something else?"

I sighed and let myself relax a little. With my hand still in hers, my eyes went there instead as I smoothed my thumb along her delicate knuckles. "What'd you have in mind?"

"Well, you have your first fight at Castello di Vetro this Friday."

"Ah-huh."

"Are you nervous?"

I half smiled. "To be honest, I kinda forgot about it for a second. All this other shit has been a little distracting... Are you nervous?"

She huffed a laugh. "A little."

My smile grew more sympathetic as I gently squeezed her hand. "It's nothin' new to me. I know what I'm doin'."

She began to study my hands too. Her eyes lingered on the scars on my knuckles, where the word Game Over was etched into my skin. It was one of my older tattoos. The fine lines of each letter, paired with years of split knuckles and scarring, made it fade faster over time.

"I know you know what you're doing, but the visuals from the last time you fought are still vivid. Like they're burned into my memory..."

Last time, when I was drugged by my opponent Murphy, fighting for Antonio in the basement beneath The Den. Murphy had switched the painkillers from Lily's old medicine cabinet. I could still see the horrified look on her face as she watched me get beaten to a bloody pulp. The drugs, concussion, and deep-rooted habit of pushing people away to protect them caused me to make the dumbest decision of my life that night — breaking up with Lily.

I had been so caught up recently with mending the break I caused between us, I hadn't considered how the fight itself affected Lily. She witnessed something horrible happen to someone she cared about. And I was about to do it again. Except this time she wouldn't be watching, but wondering if I was coming home.

"I also think this is the longest I've seen you without bruises," she continued softly as she traced her fingertips lightly across my forehead, brushing aside the strands of black hair hanging to my eyes.

I wouldn't be able to stop the fights or back out. Promises were all I had.

"I'll do my best not to get any bruises this time." I caught her wrist as she lowered her hand again and pressed a kiss to the heel of her palm, smiling easily as I looked at her. "And then when I come home, you can inspect my entire body to make sure."

"Sounds like a plan," she blushed, unmasking a smile of her own.

CHAPTER 17
Seb

The sun sat directly overhead, warming me through my denim jacket as I lay out the next row of roof tiles. Steadily working from one side of the house to the other, I didn't mind the slow pace. It was careful, basic work that lulled me into a rhythm my mind could focus on.

At least until a bright orange leaf flitted across the rooftop to my right. The same color as Kira's hair.

A smile itched at my lips as I moved on, laying another tile with my gloved hands as I bobbed my head to the music coming through my retro headphones. *Uptown Girl.* A song I loved that also reminded me of her. It took me every ounce of self-control not to blurt out the lyrics in front of the rest of the roof tiling crew working on this Homecrest house.

I tapped my foot instead, peeling off my jacket as the temperature climbed higher with the tiles absorbing all that sun's heat.

"Seb!" The voice was just loud enough to cut through the music.

I planted my feet, removed my headphones, and pivoted at the waist, looking down over the edge of the roof at my boss, Charlie, as he held his phone up and pointed at the screen.

"Your sister is on the phone!"

It wasn't completely unusual for Anita to call me during the day, but it was weird that she called my boss.

She was a busy stay-at-home mom of two kids and ran a very new salon business from the living room of her house. For her to call was usually for something important and never for a chat. But with my phone still at the repair shop since the day I dropped it in a puddle, receiving calls from anyone was difficult.

The concerned look on my boss's face, as I approached him after jumping the last few rungs off the ladder, added to my worry about the call.

"She sounds upset," Charlie added.

My heart rate picked up by a millisecond as I took the phone.

"And get your phone fixed already. I'm not your secretary," he chuckled before walking off.

"Hey, what's up?" I said into the phone.

When Anita spoke, her voice shook. "Seb, hey."

"Is everything alright?" I walked further away from the house to hear her better. One finger in my ear and a frown on my face. "Anita?"

"Not really. Chloe is in the hospital right now after falling from a tree at school. Could you take Mia for a few hours? I know you're at work right now, but Don and I really need to be here."

"I'm on my way."

After Anita told me which hospital they were at, I jogged to my bike across the street. Giving Charlie his phone and the briefest of explanations before I shoved my helmet on, started the motor with a rev as I kicked up the stand and accelerated so fast from the curb, the back tire skidded on the asphalt.

Bunting in the shape of ghosts and carved pumpkins was strung up along the walls of the kids' ward as I rushed the halls to where the nurse said my niece, Chloe Howard, would be. I was looking for a door with a smiling skeleton stuck to it, and when I spotted it, I nearly ran straight past it. I gripped the doorframe and pulled myself into the room, eagerly scanning the two dozen beds inside before a familiar and cheerful, "Uncle Sebby!" was called out from the furthest end of the space.

By a window with a view of a small courtyard outside, my sister's family was gathered around a bed. Chloe was in it, eating an ice cream and grinning from ear to ear as I approached. Her entire leg was in a cast that looked way too big for her.

I clocked the redness of my sister's eyes as she put on a happy façade. She gathered her long box braids over one shoulder, giving me a brief smile in greeting before her dark brown eyes were back on Chloe.

Anita was a hard-working, independent young mom and my calm and collected baby sister. It was because of her maturity, most people thought she was older than me. She always acted like it was that way.

Her doting husband, Don, a guy who was built like a linebacker but worked in IT, was her rock. He was quiet, observant, and one of the best dads I knew. He was everything our dad never was.

He pulled an arm around Anita and kissed her temple. The gesture bumped his glasses as he used his free hand to gently rock one-year-old Mia in her stroller.

"Thanks for coming, Seb," Don said.

"Yeah, of course." I edged along Chloe's bed and gently nudged her cheek with my knuckles. "What happened to you, huh?"

"She was trying to be like her uncle and wanted to check the school's roof," Anita said. There was something else she wasn't saying. Something else neither parent was saying, at least not in front of their girls.

"I almost got to the top, but then a branch snapped, and I fell. I also scratched my elbow," Chloe said, proudly showing off the large bandage on the back of her arm. "It took them a while to find me. Mr. Wilson said it should teach me a lesson."

The last part caused my face to twist with a confused frown as I looked to Don and Anita for an explanation.

"Mama's going to talk with Uncle Seb, okay?" Anita said to Chloe. Don moved to sit in the chair by her bed.

I followed Anita out into the hallway, where she struggled to hold back tears. Angry tears as she shook her head in disbelief.

"She said she was on the ground long after the bell rang. All on her own. When Mr. Wilson finally came out looking for her, he mentioned her friends had said something about her fall, but he didn't do anything about it." She crossed her arms tightly, visibly torn between frustration and being upset. "He's been treating her differently from everyone else for a while, Chloe just didn't tell us. She said he called her a difficult student because she struggles to focus."

My jaw clenched, and I inhaled sharply. "What's Mr. Wilson's first name?"

"Do not do what I think you're planning," Anita said firmly, wiping a tear from her cheek. "The last thing she needs is her uncle getting arrested."

"Fine."

"Seb."

"I won't hurt him, I swear. But he's still a fucking asshole."

Anita released a shaky breath as fresh tears welled in her eyes. Eyes that were on her family as we stood in the hall. "Her leg is completely shattered. And we don't have insurance. We won't have enough to sue him for neglect. Or the school." She passed her hands up over her face before resting them behind her neck, chewing her bottom lip. "And Mia is going to get restless soon and I forgot her fucking bottle."

"That's what I'm here for, remember? I'll babysit for as long as you need." I pulled her into a hug, resting my chin on her head as I held her tight. "I also have some extra work coming up. I can help."

Anita remained in the hug, but her voice steadied. "What kind of work?"

"Not legal," I cringed.

"Christ's sake, Seb." She pulled back. "I thought that was done after the fire?"

I rubbed the back of my head. "You know how it is."

She hummed her disapproval but brought her eyes back to her family.

I slung my arm around her shoulders. "Chloe will be alright. Alright? She's a resilient kid. She's got you for a mom. You're like the Wonder Woman of mothers."

"I am pretty good, aren't I?" she grinned with cheeks still glistening.

"Okay, don't let it go to your head." I curled my arm around her head, smothering her lovingly before she playfully jabbed me in the stomach.

It made her laugh.

"It's disgusting how much I love you," she said.

"Right back at you."

CHAPTER 18
Kira

I liked to think of myself as a pretty resilient person. Yes, I had a habit of leading with my heart instead of thinking things over clearly, but it seemed easier to fall in love with the unknown instead of worrying about the future or the past. That's not to say I ignored whatever happened in the past — the past was what prompted me to go to these SDV meetings, to better prepare myself for what that future held. That future I so badly wanted to enjoy and live to the fullest.

And so, because of my open-hearted resilience and the determination to never let the past drag me down, I found myself sitting in my SDV meeting, unable to focus as I daydreamed about that bubble tea date. Technically not an official date, but it had brought about one of the best afternoons of my life.

My head was in a whirl about it ever since, with questions about what it meant for the friendship between Seb and me.

The friendship we once had…

My daydream faltered slightly at that thought, and I straightened in my seat, pretending to listen to the group.

He still hadn't contacted me. It was the one little worry that frayed my perfect daydream's edges. But it was also Thursday, which meant he would show up to give me a ride home on his bike, and we could talk about what happened. Even if the idea of talking about it sent my heart into a frenzy.

We had sex. Effortless, easy, sex that was everything I never had with Aiden.

Sex with Aiden never brought release. Sure, there may have been one or two orgasms, but with Seb, there was more. There was aftercare and less pressure to be anything more than two adults cuddling in bed. It was nice to just lay in bed and *feel* instead of diving right back into a discussion Aiden had listened to on a podcast.

An involuntary sigh left me before I remembered where I was.

I mentally brushed off my daydream as I looked around to make sure no one had noticed me staring blankly at the wall at the opposite end of the hall.

The group was already wrapping up today's session, with Libby, the group leader, discussing plans for next week's meeting.

As I grabbed my bag and jacket from the back of my seat, Fran approached me and gently nudged my arm. A rare smile played on her lips. "You were out of it that entire meeting."

I grimaced through a smile.

"Thinking of biker boy?"

My smile grew. "Maybe."

Fran rolled her eyes despite the humor in them. "Jesus Christ."

He was ten minutes late.

And then fifteen minutes late.

I kept one eye on the time as I sat on the stone steps of the community hall, watching the hustle and bustle of Williamsburg while I waited for the familiar hum of a motorbike engine to peel through the noise.

It was hard not to overthink why he wouldn't show.

Maybe he changed his mind after all. Maybe he realized he didn't want a girl who was once broken.

Knowing his phone was broken, I tried his number anyway. Only it didn't ring. It beeped a few times and went silent. His phone was definitely still broken. That didn't explain why he wouldn't show up to at least tell me what's going on.

His apartment is ten minutes from here...

"Ugh." I shoved my phone in my bag and stood, scanning the street one last time before I started on a brisk walk to the bakery down the street. "It's fine. This is fine. Don't overthink it. He's probably caught up with work. And we weren't anything serious anyway. It was casual sex."

Telling myself that didn't help the uncomfortable ache in my chest.

As I arrived at the café and joined the line, I pulled out my phone and opened a message notification from Lily. At least it would provide some distraction. She had sent me a funny video of Bella, Sofia's puppy, that she found in her camera roll. It was enough to bring a smile back to my lips again, but I decided to tell her what was going on.

Me: I think Seb stood me up...

Lily: What?

Me: I'm trying not to think the worst, because I know there's a logical explanation.

The line moved up a step as I waited for her response.

Lily: I'm sure he has a really good reason... Are you still outside your meeting?

Me: I'm at a café, ready to gorge myself on pastries and forget my problems. Did you want me to get you anything?

Lily: Ooh yes please! I'll have what you're having. But also, hang tight. Dean said he can come and get you.

Me: Isn't it a little out of the way?

Lily: He said he was picking up clutch covers from Bushwick. He's 20 minutes away...

Lily: Please don't ask me what a clutch cover is. I only know it's a car thing.

Me: lol okay. I would kiss him for giving me a ride home but that might be weird, so I'll get him an éclair.

I slid my phone back into my bag and approached the counter with a smile.

As promised, 20 minutes later, as I finished off my éclair, an emerald-green Cadillac pulled up outside the café, and Dean got out wearing navy blue coveralls with the sleeves tied around his waist. He offered me a casual smile as he walked around the front of the car and opened the passenger door.

"Thank you for doing this," I said as I approached, lifting the paper bag of extra eclairs in his direction. "For compensation."

"Thanks," he chuckled, taking the bag and inspecting the contents. "So. Seb didn't show?"

"I don't suppose you've heard anything?" There was a hopefulness in my voice.

"No, but we have that fight tomorrow night. I'll talk to him then. Get you some answers and maybe ask him why he's being a dick."

"It's out of character, right? I'm not going insane?"

"Not insane." He smiled in reassurance and jerked his chin at the car. "Come on."

I climbed into the front seat, still not feeling any better with the lack of answers.

Chapter 19

Dean

The whole point of the meeting at the shooting range was to test how I handled a gun in case I had to use one to protect Lily and myself — I still didn't have an actual gun, but the idea of keeping one around Lily still didn't sit right with me. Instead, as I stood behind Crowley and Riccardo while they unloaded their guns on the target sheets, I found I was watching something more along the lines of a pissing contest. One that cut thirty minutes into the hour-long session Mark had booked.

I could've walked into one of the other target lanes and started practicing, but I wasn't allowed to use any of the weapons until their eyes were on me.

If I had known it was going to be a waste of time, I would've stayed home after dropping Kira off at the apartment.

Kitted out with earmuffs and protective eyewear, I settled against the cold, gray wall behind me, crossing my arms as I watched their little showboating exercise.

When there was finally a gap between rounds, I cleared my throat.

Riccardo looked over his shoulder. That smirk he carried was getting on my nerves.

"Am I gonna use a gun today, or should I just watch you guys and take notes?"

Crowley shook his head in disappointment and raised his eyebrows in a way that caused his large forehead to wrinkle like an accordion. "Young people these days have no respect for their elders."

"I'll show you respect when you prove you've earned it. Am I usin' a gun today or not?" I pulled off the earmuffs as I waited for their response.

Riccardo chuckled and motioned me over. "Yeah, alright. Come on."

I pushed off the wall and came to stand in between them, bringing the earmuffs to my ears again. I stood taller than both, with Riccardo being the shortest. His short height didn't seem to diminish his arrogant confidence.

Riccardo reloaded the standard-issue Glock 19 and handed it to me before going over a quick lesson on how to hold it and how to stand. But he stopped short when my hand shaped to the weapon without hesitation.

"Still don't think this is a good idea," Crowley muttered.

I hid my satisfaction at the slight unease in his voice and stepped up to the desk that separated us from the target sheet beyond.

"You scared, old man?" I looked at him side-on.

Crowley scowled and narrowed his eyes. "Not at all, smartass."

As the target sheet was reloaded, Riccardo and Crowley took one step back.

When the target was in place, I squared my shoulders and raised the gun in both hands. One cupped under the grip panel, the other with my finger on the trigger. I squeezed it, and the shots came easy. Several of them sliced through the outline of the figure printed on the target sheet ahead, decorating the chest and shoulder region, while a few other shots clipped the edge of the paper and hit the back wall.

I put the gun on the desk and stepped back.

The detectives joined my side, their eyes on the dappled target.

"It's okay. The kickback is a little hard for novices. It's why that sheet looks like Swiss cheese right now," Crowley jeered.

Riccardo huffed a laugh as he folded his arms. "Not gonna lie, I did think you were going to be better at this."

Was I being dragged into their pissing contest? Yes. If I was going to do this, I might as well do it good.

I looked at them blankly for a moment, sighed, and picked up the gun again. This time reloading the magazine with fast efficiency before I stood side-on and lifted the gun in my right hand at a ninety-degree angle. I fired a string of rounds into the target sheet again. This time, shredding a large hole right through the head.

The detectives were silent.

"Better?" I asked, putting the gun down.

Riccardo's smirk had finally disappeared. "Who taught you?"

"Antonio." *In deserted parking lots when I was nineteen, I used abandoned cars for target practice. First the tires, and then the headlights, and then the blinker lights. The smaller the mark, the easier it is to hit something... Or someone.*

I removed the earmuffs and safety glasses and added them to the desk too, before walking by the men.

"We aren't done here," Crowley said firmly.

I stopped and looked at the target sheet. "You sure?"

He stepped forward, ready for a confrontation he wouldn't win. "If you knew you were a good shot, why didn't you say something earlier? You've wasted our fucking time."

"*I* wasted *your* time. *Really?*" I half smiled despite the frustration bubbling under my skin and shook my head as I took one step closer to him. "I'm here because I don't have a choice, regardless of whether I can shoot or not. I'm on borrowed fuckin' time and yet you spent half this session, booked for me, blowing up your sheet for leisure, but you think I'm wasting your time?" My jaw ticked. "And you want respect? From me? How about you remove the self-entitled stick from your fat ass and then we can talk respect. In the meantime, shut the fuck up."

The second the last words left my mouth, I backed off and headed for the door.

White gravel crunched beneath the soles of my boots as I made my way up the long driveway to Antonio's Bay Ridge mansion. I would've parked in the space outside the house, but the boss was hosting a social gathering tonight. Luxury cars took up every inch of the parking zone in front of his house, and others lined the driveway. Meanwhile, mine was several blocks down the street.

The sun was beginning to set as I strode up the porch steps to the large front door. The house was cast in an orange glow because of it.

Inside, I found guests mingling, drinking, chatting; all the usual shit I avoided. They were dressed in clothes that probably cost more than what I earned in a month, and they knew it, casting side-long glances in my direction as I weaved my way through them wearing jeans and a long-sleeved black shirt that had several signs of wear and tear.

I kept my face neutral, paying them no mind as I headed into the large kitchen in the back and stepped through the windowed patio doors into the evening air again. There were more people outside, doing more of the same as the ones inside, but I found at least one familiar face in the form of Vince. He grinned as I approached, and then motioned for me to follow him further into the manicured garden.

We followed a short path to another outdoor seating area off the patio, where Antonio was talking with several acquaintances. His wife, Julia, had her arm looped through his, smiling warmly as she seemed to lead the conversation happening amongst their little social group. Antonio couldn't keep his eyes off her. The expression on his face was one he only had for her.

I understood it; I knew the feeling. Like your heart might explode from holding them, or if the worst were to happen, you would burn the world for them; die for them because there would be nothing worse than living in a world where they didn't exist.

Lily was my heart. My world. She was worth more than everything in this mansion.

Antonio's devotion to his wife brought on the reminder that Julia would also be affected by whatever Mark and his team planned. And Antonio would hate that.

He knew the police were investigating him. It's why he had gone partially underground — partially because hosting a party this big wasn't very subtle for someone laying low — but if he found out I was involved with that investigation...

Poker faces weren't so hard for me. Working for Antonio helped with that. Guilt still gnawed at my insides as I greeted the mob boss and his wife.

Julia smiled. Ever a glamorous woman, as she maintained the appearance of a socialite. Which she was, but she also had a level head and treated everyone the same regardless of social status and money.

"It's good to see you again, Dean." She turned to Antonio. "I'll give you two some privacy."

Antonio lifted the back of her hand to his lips, kissed it, and then watched as Julia left to mingle with the guests. Once she was out of sight, the doting look in his eyes changed to one of consideration when it came to me.

"Follow me." He leaned into his cane as he made a turn, aiming for the pool house to the right of the garden. The limp in his leg was a permanent reminder of his son's retaliation.

Again, the guilt reared its ugly head as I followed him.

This was a guy who helped Mom and me through our toughest time, and I was stabbing him in the back in return.

When we reached the pool house, I pushed my hands into my pockets as Antonio closed the door behind us. It smelled of chlorine, and the space was illuminated by the subtle blue glow of the pool, reflecting bending swirls on the ceiling.

"Something is on your mind." He folded his hands over the golden eagle head on the end of his cane and watched me closely.

My pause was brief, and Antonio didn't seem to notice it as I shook my head, grinding my jaw slightly. "Everything is on my mind, boss..."

"Roxy said the meeting went well with them."

"They didn't suspect anything. We're fighting tomorrow night."

"Good, good..." He rubbed his chin, where gray and white stubble was coming through. "Now, about what you're asking from me..."

Under Mark's advice, I had contacted Vince earlier this week about getting a gun. I hoped maybe he could get me one so I didn't have to have this meeting with Antonio, but here I was anyway.

"It's for protection," I elaborated, leaning my hip against the windowsill. "No offense, but I don't trust your kids."

"You'd be a fool to trust anyone in this line of work. Or any job."

Something shifted in his eyes, and for a second, I wondered if he knew something. He already knew that Lily's dad was investigating him, that his kids were out for revenge, and that his businesses and life could go under at any moment, but could he possibly know more than I thought he did?

"I have a hard time trusting most people anyway," I said.

"Except for Lily."

Something coiled in my gut as I maintained that unbothered demeanor.

"Except for Lily," I repeated in agreement.

"How are things going there?"

"She hasn't said anything to her father, if that's what you mean."

But I have.

He chuckled. "Good to know, but I was asking because last I heard, you had thrown away your relationship, and she was injured."

Antonio wants to chat about my love life?

It threw me off slightly. I was so used to figuring out his angle to keep my guard up, but this topic left me feeling confused.

"We're alright," I said. "She's healed okay too."

"Good. I couldn't imagine how it must've felt to see her like that." He glanced through the windowpane.

I followed his gaze to his wife standing at the center of the party under the warm glow of the fairy lights strung up around the garden.

After a sigh, Antonio continued. "I don't have any spares at the moment, but I'll have Vince track one down for you."

"Thanks, boss." I stepped away from the window, but Antonio made no indication of leaving yet.

"What's going on with Seb? My people can't reach him... He hasn't decided to fight for my children, has he? Because it would be such a shame to lose him."

"No, you haven't lost him..." I rubbed the back of my neck. "He, uh, broke his phone."

Antonio lifted a brow, slightly amused. "That's all?"

"Yep. The repairs are taking longer than he thought. Trust me when I say you aren't the only one wonderin' about his whereabouts."

"Well. Next time you see him, tell him to get a new phone." Antonio's tone was less of a suggestion and more of an order with a gentle warning.

I pressed my lips together and nodded. "Will do, boss."

CHAPTER 20
Dean

"I love you. Be careful. And please come home conscious."

Lily's words had become something of a mini mantra since I arrived at Castello di Vetro, sizing up the large glass box in the center of the club's basement.

It had been a minute since my last fight, and it showed in the bounce in my leg. I had everything to lose now and the more I looked at the large cube with the familiar face waiting inside it, the more I understood how ridiculous this shit was.

I walked onto the platform and stopped before the glass door of the cube as the spectators roared. They weren't cheering for me, not like the crowd at The Den. This was a different crowd. Upper class but just as bloodthirsty as the last ones I had done this in front of. This crowd had no idea who I was, and their cheering was purely for the fight itself.

I glanced up to the VIP section of the mezzanine that wrapped around the basement and spotted Roxy standing right beside Gabriele. She was already working her charm to get him to trust her completely so she could get any information she could about how Antonio's kids ran their little operation. Most of what she discovered was stuff we already figured out; they were here to create disorder. Not only to their dad but to the entire underground.

Fucking overachievers.

Standing beside Roxy and Gabriele were his sisters. Beatrice was watching me like I was a specimen to be examined under a microscope while Lucia was leaning against the banister, twirling a lock of long auburn hair around her finger as she chewed her bottom lip, taking in every inch of me as if she was considering which parts of me she wanted the most.

Reluctantly, I peeled off my hoodie and discarded it on the top of the steps I stood on. The motion caused the audience to grow louder, completely cutting off the sounds of the club above. I refused to look back up at the VIP section.

I wasn't wearing any wires this time. It would've been a death wish if I had. Instead, there were several undercover detectives somewhere in the crowd, blending in and wearing wires of their own.

I steadied my breath and mind before opening the door and stepping inside. The second that door was closed behind me, the noise was reduced. Without the noise, it made fighting seem bearable until I factored in the large overhead lights beaming down through the glass. Standing under them on their own would've been warm enough, but with the added layer of enclosed glass, the air grew thicker. Humid.

The air was still and suffocating. If I won this fight, there wouldn't be a victory until I was out of this fucking cube.

There was no announcer to call the fights. It was a continuous spectacle inside the glass. At the back of the basement, tucked in an alcove, was where the fighters received their instructions on when to go in next. It was also where we would get paid at the end of the night. How much we made depended on how much blood was spilled and how long we lasted — the payments ended up being fuck all anyway based on the rates I saw written on the sign at the payment booth.

$10 per blood spray. $20 for broken bones. $50 if the opponent is knocked out. $100 in the case of *unable to resuscitate*.

These rates only applied to visiting fighters. The triplets paid their own with hefty wages and other club benefits: free drinks, drugs, and women...

My fight was right after Seb's. A splatter of blood remained on the floor in the corner of the cube from when he was punched in the nose, bringing on a nosebleed.

He had barely scraped through his fight because of the heat.

My one advantage was that my opponent was an ex-fighter of Antonio's. I had seen him fight long enough to know his style.

He nodded at me in recognition. His eyes were naturally kinda sad-looking, and he stood with a hunch in his spine despite his muscle tone. He was also older than me by eight-ish years. And on his right hand, where a ring finger should be, was a stump — just as Lucia said, they paid the price for loyalty.

I tipped my head, casting aside the fact that he would be dead within a couple of days once Antonio caught up with him.

And then I lunged.

My right fist connected with his jaw, and his head spun left before I brought up my other fist and knocked his head back in the other direction. The crowd's roar was muffled by the glass. A subtle burn radiated through my knuckles and hand. I briefly readjusted my balled fists and ducked as he swung. He left himself open, so I punched him in the ribcage, knocking him off balance as he gasped and staggered backwards.

Meanwhile, I was already sweating like the fight was over.

The cube was a death trap.

I wiped at my brow and got into position.

Old fighting habits were settling in again, clearing my mind until all that was left was the steady thrum of my heartbeat in my ears. Each punch came from a pattern, urged on by frustration from my past and now. I viewed my opponent as nothing but a walking sack of muscle and meat that was a threat to me. If I didn't knock him out, I would be the one getting pulled unconscious from this place.

I managed to maneuver around him and wrapped my arm around his neck from behind. He gasped and clawed at my arm, but I pulled back, tightening my grip around his throat.

There were no rules here. Nobody cared about what happened so long as there was one winner.

He threw a punch upwards, hitting my cheekbone. In the past, I would've taken it, but the heat under the spotlights, beaming through the glass ceiling, caused me to falter. My arm slipped, giving him enough time to pull forward.

I was flipped onto my back and given barely a second to regroup before he aimed a kick at my head. I rolled aside just in time, only to be punched under the chin.

My teeth clamped down on my tongue, and soon my mouth filled with blood. He gave me enough time to get to my feet, taking a small break for himself while I checked that I still had all my teeth.

I spat the mix of saliva and blood onto the floor and wiped my chin as I faced him again.

The heat was unbearable, sucking out any energy I had left. My shorts and hair were soaked too. If we didn't end the fight soon, we would pass out from heat exhaustion.

I pushed my knuckles against my chin, turning my head enough for my neck to emit a satisfying click, and then rounded on the man standing between me and getting home to Lily.

I prodded the bruise blooming on my left hip as Seb and I made our way to the back of the basement to collect our winnings, joining the line of other fighters also bearing wounds from their fights tonight. I was still spitting blood from the bite on my tongue while Seb had a tissue stuffed up one nostril.

"I think he punched me in the face with my own fist," Seb said as he massaged the bridge of his nose.

I huffed a laugh as I pulled the bottom of my shirt up to wipe more blood from my mouth. "The boss wants you to get a new phone. He's been trying to get a hold of you and his patience is wearin' thin."

Seb grimaced. "Right. Almost forgot about that guy... I swear the repair guy is delaying repairs just to charge me more."

When movement in the line ground to a stop because some guy at the front complained about being underpaid, I opted to lean against the concrete wall of the basement.

Seb didn't join me but instead crossed his arms and shifted on the spot. Like he was struggling to find the right words for what he wanted to say next.

This was the first time in a few days we had a chance to catch up.

"What's going on with you and Kira?" I asked. There wasn't any point dancing around the subject. I was possibly too concussed to use tact.

Seb shrugged and offered me a smile that wasn't very convincing. "Just friends."

I raised an eyebrow. "Just?"

"Yeah, why?"

"Lily told me you guys had sex."

He scoffed. "Since when did you two become a couple of gossips? You're worse than their neighbor Susan."

I waited for a better explanation, deadpanning at him.

Seb's jaw clenched when he realized there was no avoiding the conversation. "I've got some shit going on, and maybe Kira needs to heal first before jumping into anything. Don't get me wrong, I really like her—"

"What kind of shit?"

"Hm?"

"You said you have some shit going on."

Seb paused, watching me carefully.

I rejoined the line as it started moving again. "You really don't wanna tell me?"

"I need your help." He rubbed at the stubble on his jaw. "Anita didn't want me doing anything, but someone hurt my family, and I need to hurt them back."

"Understood." I looked down the line. "What did you have in mind?"

"Coercion."

I nodded once. "Easy enough. When are we doin' this?"

A proud smile twitched in the corners of his mouth as he crossed his arms. "Tonight, if you're up for it."

"Always."

CHAPTER 21

Dean

The motel's underground parking garage was void of people but filled with plenty of cars. It was also dark in places where the fluorescent lights had blown, providing plenty of cover to wait in.

I sat in the car, sucking on a Dum Dums lollipop and casually scanning the parking garage for any sign of movement. The sweet, raspberry flavor of the candy blended with the fading taste of blood on my tongue.

Not too far away from where I was, a biker waited. Dressed in all black and hidden in the shadows with his helmet on and motor off.

Seb and I estimated John Wilson, a kindergarten teacher, would be finishing his poker game with friends in a few minutes. How Seb got that information was a mystery to me.

The exit door to the parking garage stairwell slammed shut. The echo bounced through the dark space, followed closely by the footsteps of Mr. Wilson as he headed to his car — a Prius with a faulty back window and an equally faulty locking system.

I sank low in my seat as John climbed into the car.

His hair was dark and curly with several gray strands, his large glasses sat halfway down his hooked nose, and he was thin. Everything about him screamed fragile ego. Of course, he thought it was okay to mistreat kids. To him, it was how he got power to compensate for being so pathetically weak-looking.

He began searching his glove compartment for something — cigarettes. A pang of jealousy rushed through me as I watched him place one between his lips.

Just as he went to light it, I cleared my throat.

With a yell, he dropped the cigarette and lighter and whipped around with wide eyes, realizing he wasn't alone when he spotted me in his back seat.

I smiled, flicking the lollipop stick to the corner of my mouth. "Hi."

He swallowed hard, adjusting his glasses. "Who—"

"You're Chloe Howard's teacher, right? John Wilson?"

"What happened to her is not my problem." His voice shook as he spoke, no matter how hard he tried to keep it steady.

"Did I mention there was a problem?"

He stammered, but nothing came out.

"Unless you're talkin' about her shattered leg. The one you made her sit with instead of calling for help."

"Here. Is this what you want?" He fumbled with his wallet and tossed it into my lap. "Take it. Please."

I looked down at where it sat, lifted a brow, and then looked back at him.

"Please don't hurt me," he whispered.

"You called her a difficult student. Said she deserved what happened to her. That it should teach her a lesson." I picked up the wallet and leaned forward, slinging my arms over the backs of the front seats and thumping him on the chest with the wallet in hand as I smiled again. "Now let us teach you a lesson."

As predicted, Mr. Wilson chose flight over fight. I had never seen a man jump out of a car so fast, but he did and made a run for the stairwell door.

I climbed out of the car as Seb revved his engine. The bike's headlight shone directly on Mr. Wilson's back as he sprinted in the opposite direction. But the bike was faster.

The matte black Yamaha flew by me first, and then the teacher before Seb swerved and skidded to a halt in front of John, cutting off his initial escape route. When he turned to run the other way, the other way being me, the panic set in, and he backed himself against the back of a parked van.

Seb got off his bike and marched for the teacher.

"We don't wanna hurt you...much," I said as I joined Seb in cornering him. "But we do want somethin' from you."

"Please—" He went to drop to his knees, but I grabbed the collar of his suit jacket and pulled him up again. "I've already said you can take my money."

Seb, with his helmet still on so he wasn't recognized, sniggered. "That's great, but it's not for us."

With his jacket still in my fist, I pinned him against the van. "You're gonna pay for that little girl's hospital bills. Every fuckin' cent. And then you're gonna tell the school what you did."

John went to nod, but he hesitated. His wet eyes darted between Seb and me. "A-and if I don't?"

My brows raised at his audacity before I looked at Seb. "You wanna do it?"

"Nah, go ahead."

"Alright."

I let go of John's jacket and grabbed his wrist instead. Right as he realized what was happening, I took his pinkie finger and jerked it away from the rest of his digits. The sound of it snapping was quickly drowned out by his cry in pain before I pushed a hand over his mouth and stepped into his space.

"It'll be the rest if you don't do as you're fuckin' told. Got it?" I hissed darkly.

John nodded vigorously against my hand.

Just to mess with him, I flashed him a grin and thumped him on the shoulder. He flinched and released a scared whimper as he looked at his mangled finger.

"And remember," Seb added, pointing at the teacher's face, "Don't run off to the cops after this because we'll know. And we have your address." He pulled up the guy's license as proof. "Snitches get stitches, buddy."

I subtly glanced at Seb, raising a brow. When we left Mr. Wilson to drop to his knees in a terrified heap, I muttered under my breath as we approached Seb's bike. "Snitches get stitches?"

"Shut up," Seb mumbled with humor in his voice. He lifted his visor. "I panicked."

I chuckled as I pulled my keys from my back pocket. The Cadillac was right by where Seb had stopped to block the teacher's exit with his bike. Parking it closer to the stairwell was to aid in a getaway where he couldn't memorize my plate since he had passed my car, thinking nothing of it. Meanwhile, Seb had tucked his plate up using a locking hinge under his seat. Not that hiding either plate was necessary. John Wilson had barely given us a second glance before he sprinted to his car and drove off in the other direction.

CHAPTER 22
Dean

It was almost midnight by the time Seb and I got to the apartment. Surprisingly, we were both in good spirits despite the cuts and bruises that littered our faces and bodies from the fights earlier. Somehow, getting revenge for a six-year-old girl outweighed the dull ache in my hip or the bite on my tongue.

With some luck, we managed to get through the foyer doors without having to call Lily or Kira to let us in — someone had left a rock to prop the front door open again.

I kicked the rock aside to let the door close and lock once Seb and I were inside.

What was the point of having a security system if you didn't use it?

The thought didn't linger as we went upstairs, unable to hide the grins on our faces after what we did. So what if we were assholes for finding joy in tormenting a teacher? The prick deserved it.

But we also knew that the girls might not find that as amusing as we did.

Knocking lightly on the apartment door, I tried to mask my smile. And failed miserably.

Lily answered the door, and her expression immediately changed from content to sceptical when Seb turned away to muffle his laugh.

"What did you two do?"

Seb shrugged, still not looking at her, while I stepped forward to greet her with a kiss.

"PTA meeting," I said onto her lips.

She folded her arms and watched me closely. The smallest of smiles was tucked away in the corner of her mouth.

"Had to voice some issues on a teaching method," Seb said as he squeezed by us, heading into the living room.

I nodded in agreement with him, but kept my eyes on her, smiling softly as I brushed a strand of her hair aside. "I'll tell you later."

She lifted a brow and then conceded before nodding to my mouth. "You have a bit of blood on your lip."

"Yup." Instinctively, I wiped my thumb across my bottom lip. "I bit my tongue. But you should've seen the other guy."

Her eyes traveled to my body. She was dressing me down, albeit adorably, as she lifted an eyebrow and dropped a hip. Her arms remained crossed, and her hair was fixed into two buns, which brought my attention to the way her slender neck was on display.

"And the rest of you?" she asked.

I stepped closer, tucking my hands into the pockets of my shorts as I tilted my head to the side and lowered my voice so only she would hear. "Wanna strip search me?"

She lifted the hem of my shirt, her fingers lightly brushing the skin beneath as I continued to look at the details of her face; her freckles, the rosiness of her cheeks, her pretty cupid's bow... When her blue doe eyes found the bruising on my left hip, the little smile she had quickly dropped, and her brow pinched with concern.

"Dean." She ran a whisper-light touch along the bluish-yellow mark peeking out from under my shorts.

I cupped her face, bringing her eyes to mine. "Not as bad as it looks."

"Hm."

"I've broken ribs before, remember? This is nothing."

"That doesn't exactly make me feel better." She paused for a moment. "I'm not used to you fighting again, that's all... When is the next one?"

"Monday night. But remember, this situation is only temporary..." It was temporary because after this came prison. Unless I continued fighting on the inside... I brushed the thought aside and smiled at her. "Tonight, I'm okay."

She inhaled, possibly brushing aside a few thoughts of her own, and then let herself relax. Offering me a happier smile, she took my hand and led me to the living room.

In the short moment Lily and I had remained in the hallway, Seb and Kira had barely struck up a conversation. Instead, it was awkward small talk and plenty of polite smiles on Kira's end when the chat died down. She glanced at her phone.

As I followed Lily to the kitchen, passing Seb where he sat on the end of their pastel blue couch, I nudged his arm. It prompted him to inhale, like he was giving himself a moment to recoup, before his attention was on Kira.

I joined Lily in the kitchen. As she busied herself making tea, I grabbed a bag of frozen peas from the freezer and pressed it to my hip.

"So, Smi—I mean, Kira..." Seb began. Not the strongest of starts, but it was something.

Kira looked up from her phone and waited for the rest of his sentence. The expression on her face was indifferent. "Yes?"

The stirring of the spoon in Lily's teacup slowed.

Seb scratched the back of his head and got to his feet, wiping his palms down his thighs and clasping his hands together. "Mind if we talk?"

Worry flashed across Kira's features, but she stood. "Yeah. Sure. We can talk in my room, if you want."

He nodded. "Sounds good."

Kira led the way.

Once the bedroom door was shut behind them, Lily stopped stirring and looked across at me.

"What *is* going on with Seb?" she whispered.

"Family trouble." I pushed the side of my shorts down to ice the bruising further. Its colors blended with the tattoos that covered my left side. I winced and inhaled. "But we handled it."

"Was that the PTA meeting?"

"His older niece broke her leg at school. And her teacher was a dick about it."

Empathy filled her eyes. "Is she okay?"

"Seb says she's barely fazed," I shrugged. "Probably more excited about getting people to sign her cast."

"Speaking of injuries." She cupped her hands around her tea and brought it closer to her chest. Her eyes fell to my bruise. "Maybe you should see a doctor about that?"

I sighed and crossed the kitchen to her, plopping the frozen bag onto the counter before rolling down the side of my shorts and briefs — and hoping Kira and Seb didn't finish their chat early. I wasn't exactly flashing anything, but enough around the base was showing.

Her eyes drifted across the bruise, as they had earlier, but with the stove light brighter than the dim lighting of the hallway, she could take in more details of it. Examine it as if she were back in The Den's basement. She wasn't a qualified nurse, but still, her role in that place had left a mark. And maybe because she no longer watched me fight, she felt she had to check things over anyway to put her mind at ease.

"It's surface level. No breaks or fractures," I said gently.

Her eyes remained on the bruise, but she nodded. "Okay."

"Hey."

She tilted her head as she studied the bruise, carefully touching my hip and the surrounding skin.

I lifted her chin up and half smiled, finally getting her attention. "Speaking of doctors, I noticed the psychologist's card is gone. Did you call them?"

"Yes. I did. I figured I had procrastinated making an appointment long enough." She cupped her tea once more with her shoulders raised slightly, talking fast. "I start Monday."

"Yeah?"

"Mhm. They seem really nice too..."

"But?"

She shook her head. Eyes wide and innocent. "There's no buts."

I lifted an eyebrow.

"Okay. One but... I'm a little nervous talking about everything. That's all."

"The first few sessions won't be easy, but it's a good step." I cupped her face in my hands again. "I'm proud of you."

She smiled, but her nerves were still there. They made her happiness wane for a moment before she quickly changed the subject.

"Oh! Before I forget." She turned to the counter beside us, putting down her tea as she reached for the designated house key bowl on the furthest side of the counter. When she plucked out a brand-new set of apartment keys and a swipe card, I smiled knowingly.

"These are for you," she beamed, dropping the keys and card into my open hand. "I figured this would make coming and going easier."

They were more than keys. They were the next step. Not quite an invitation to live together, but something to bring what we had closer. The first of these kinds of steps had come in the form of a toothbrush after her stay in the hospital. She was content to have me in her space as I was having her in mine.

I smoothed my hand around to the back of her neck and brought her close to kiss her. She smiled against it and emitted a giggle as her hands lay on my chest.

"I didn't think a set of keys would bring on this reaction."

"I am a simple man."

Her laughter gave me life.

"Well," she continued, smiling, "You might want to pull up your pants because I think they're done."

I glanced down to where my shorts still sat below my hip and readjusted the waistband to cover myself. "Better?"

"Yes," she laughed, turning away from me.

I kissed her on the cheek and went back to icing my hip as Kira's bedroom door opened again.

My ears were pricked as I kept my eyes down, and Lily had lifted her oversized teacup to her lips as she peered over the rim at them entering the room.

Seb was right about Lily and I being as bad as Susan, but we were concerned for our friends. If they didn't reconcile, things would be awkward.

Going off the smiles on their faces and the fact that Kira was scrawling what looked to be her mobile number on a post-it note, everything was good again.

"In case transferring contacts from your old phone doesn't work," Kira said as she handed Seb the note.

"I should get it tattooed on me or something, so I don't forget it," Seb said as they wandered to the couch.

Kira paused with slight amusement in her eyes as she looked at him quickly. "Please, don't do that."

"Right." Seb snapped his fingers in realization. "Dedication tattoos seem to curse relationships."

"Exactly."

Lily casually approached me, bumping her hip into my non-bruised thigh as she offered me a small grin. "He's worried about cursing their relationship," she whispered, containing her excitement as she padded over to the couches.

I grabbed a bag of frozen corn from the freezer, still clutching the frozen peas to my hip, and headed for the living room. Dumping the bag of frozen corn in Seb's lap in passing, which he promptly pressed to his nose with a hum of relief, I dropped into the space beside Lily on the couch and pulled an arm around her.

About an hour later, with the TV on as background noise, I remained on the same couch but this time with my head back while Lily stood behind me. Phone flashlight shining into my mouth, she checked for a broken tooth. All I had done was complain about a dull ache in my mouth from biting my tongue, but she insisted on being diligent.

It was hard not to smile up at her as her brow furrowed.

"Will he survive, Doc?" Seb asked sarcastically.

Lily laughed quietly and flicked the flashlight off. "Definitely just a bitten tongue."

"Told you," I said, still looking up at her.

She leaned down closer, combing her fingers through the back of my hair. "Just making sure," she said as she lightly flicked the tip of my nose.

"I still think they should invest in some mouth guards," Kira added, crossing her legs while she sat on the adjacent couch.

I lifted my head, and Lily slid her arms around my shoulders, hugging me from behind.

"A gold tooth would look pretty cool though," Seb said, tapping his front tooth. "Or imagine a gold-plated grill?"

"Gold teeth come out just as easy as a regular tooth," I noted.

"True... Remember the guy with the dentures?" Seb laughed as he brought up the memory.

Kira and Lily were already laughing as we reminisced.

"You knocked them clean out of his head," I chuckled. "He wasn't even that old."

"Scared the shit out of me when it happened. They flew out looking like those wind-up teeth thingies," Seb added, re-enacting the moment with his hands.

We laughed harder. It hurt to do with a body littered with bruises, but every ounce of the pain was worth it.

Seb was staying the night, invited by Kira, since I was staying too. He originally planned to crash on the couch, but Kira said in more of a passing comment, one that wasn't up for debate, that her bed was fine. She had walked into her bedroom before Seb could refuse.

Lily and I went to bed not long after them.

Showered of any lingering grime from the night, I got ready for bed, tying the drawstring of my sweatpants while Lily dressed in a matching set of pajamas.

I had one thing on my mind: passing out. But those thoughts vanished when I noticed the faint worry etched on Lily's face as she let her hair down.

"When are you getting the gun?" She crawled under the covers, trying to mask the question as something more casual.

"Soon. Antonio didn't really give me a specific date." I climbed in beside her, watching her for any signs of anxiety about the whole thing. There was still a faint frown between her eyebrows.

She nodded in consideration, pausing to think. I was about to ask how she felt, but her mood lightened. Like she simply flipped a switch with a sigh.

"So, Jane has a soccer game tomorrow morning. She wants me to go watch." It was more of a statement than anything.

"Yeah?" I tucked my arm under my head.

"Mom will be there. Keeping up appearances for the PTA stuff." She settled down into the space under my arm, resting her head on my chest.

"You want me to come?" Looking down, I could just make out the way her cheek raised as she smiled at the question.

She traced her fingers lightly across my chest. "Only if you want to."

"I'll be there. I haven't been to a soccer game since I left Sicily."

CHAPTER 23
Lily

I pressed a palm against my stomach, over the scar, as if that might settle my nerves.

Today's a good day... I think.

I wore a long-sleeved, maroon shirt with a wide neck. It was the kind of shirt that sat snug but comfortable, tucked into my high-waist jeans. The only issue was that I hadn't factored in the weather when I dressed for the soccer game this morning. It was cooler, and the thin sleeves of my top were doing nothing to prevent the tiny goosebumps rising on my skin, but I wasn't *cold*, cold. The shivers I was experiencing felt different. It made me feel out of place.

Maybe because I hadn't been out of the house much, other than going to work. It's the nerves from that.

Just nerves.

The crowd didn't seem to help either. Although I knew most of them from the PTA Mom was head of, there were so many of them.

I inhaled deeply, trying to focus on the game instead.

His hoodie-clad arms wrapped around me from behind as we stood along the fence line of the soccer field. In an instant, the shuddering was gone. The warmth was back. I felt safe despite not being in any real danger to begin with.

"I think the ref is blind," Dean muttered from over my shoulder. His gaze was firmly on Jane's soccer game.

I grinned and leaned my head back against his chest. "Maybe you should referee. I'm sure the mothers on the PTA would *love* that."

Those same mothers who hadn't stopped with the uneasy, side-long glances in our direction since we arrived. Once word had spread of my plus-one to the game being someone far outside their social pool, they hadn't stopped muttering or staring. A clear indication that Mom liked to gossip to them about my love life.

"You'd think they'd never seen a tattoo before," I said quietly, offering a polite wave to another mom I saw watching us.

She promptly diverted her attention back to the game and raised her chin.

"I think they might be worried I've corrupted you. And it might spread." His voice was like warm honey down my spine with light hints of humor laced in every word.

Maybe I was corrupted. Dean told me about what he and Seb had gotten up to last night with that teacher, and I had barely batted an eye. Well, I was still shocked, but based on the fact the teacher was a douchebag and the world had shown itself to not be as black and white as I once thought, I wasn't nearly as upset as someone should be if they discovered their boyfriend *gently* threatened a teacher.

And broke the man's finger.

I half smiled, closing my eyes for a second. "I think some of them are a little jealous too."

"Because none of them are in a happy relationship?" He chuckled, and it vibrated through my body.

Our small talk drifted through easy subjects and soft laughter, warmed by the sun and the orange and yellow hues of the trees around the field. It was a moment painted in gold.

"Who's the guy?" Dean asked during halftime as Jane's team gathered on the far end of the field.

My eyes found who he was talking about: a tall, lanky teen handing out water bottles to Jane's team members. And he hadn't taken his eyes off Jane since they started talking during halftime. His smile was broad and unwaning, meanwhile, Jane hadn't stopped twirling her auburn ponytail around her finger.

She never twirled her hair.

"That's what she wanted my opinion on," I said quietly in realization with a smile.

My sister had a crush. Or maybe something more based on the way she was giggling and grinning.

Dean straightened behind me. Arms still around my waist, but a small frown appeared on his face as he watched the interaction.

"Relax. I think he's harmless," I said as the mystery boy hesitated and then awkwardly brushed a strand of Jane's hair behind her ear.

I looked to my right, where Mom was talking with several other moms. Clutching coffees in their hands with buttered bagels, they hadn't noticed the boy interacting with Jane. I doubted Mom knew about him. Any boy she deemed fit for her daughters was paraded and talked about nonstop. She would've talked all about him when we got here earlier, probably around the time she had looked at Dean and said, "Oh, I thought this was a family-only thing."

When halftime was over, Jane jogged back onto the field and noticed us watching. She raised her thumbs as she mouthed, "*What do you think?*"

I smiled and raised both thumbs too.

Mom was none the wiser.

"I could get a job," Jane said, keeping up with our mother's fast stride as we left the field. Her cleats tapped the sidewalk as she went. "That way I can save up for my own car."

Dean and I followed them loosely, hand in hand.

"And if I had my own car, it'd mean you wouldn't have to drive me around everywhere. I'll have more freedom."

"That's what I'm worried about." Mom shook her head in a way that tidied up her shoulder-length hair. "You aren't getting a car, Jane."

"Could I at least get my license?"

Mom remained silent.

Jane rolled her eyes and looked back at me, desperate for backup as she pleaded silently. She had been so happy about her team winning today.

"Dad could teach her," I said. "You'd know she's learning from the best with all his knowledge of the law..." I wanted to cringe at how doting I sounded towards my father. At the moment, I wanted nothing to do with him after the trick he pulled.

"I'll think about it," Mom said. The finality about it really meant no.

Jane's shoulders slumped as we shared a look again.

I mouthed an apology.

"I'll teach her," Dean said, shrugging a shoulder.

Jane spun around, walking backwards with a new skip in her step. "Hell, yes!"

Mom stammered with a scoff. "Definitely not."

Jane's eyes shot to Mom, but her arms gestured wide to the Cadillac parked across the street. "Mom, he drives a *Caddy*. Can you imagine me arriving at school in that thing?"

"It is too big to learn in." Mom's frustration was bubbling beneath the surface. It was evident in the way several strands of hair had dared to stray from her neat hairstyle. "I'd much rather you learn in my Volvo. It's practical. And you'll only be learning from me or your father. No one else."

Despite the sharpness in her tone, indirectly aimed at Dean, it was the fastest I had ever seen her flip on a decision.

The happy gleam on Jane's face only grew brighter. "That's a yes to getting my license?"

"Yes. But don't push it."

Jane squealed with delight and jogged the rest of the way to Mom's car, waving briefly back at us before she climbed in and began frantically texting the good news to her friends. Or maybe mystery boy.

After a curt goodbye from Mom, we headed to Dean's car. Arm in arm as we walked, I leaned into him.

"Did you just use reverse psychology on my mother?" I muttered as we watched Mom's Volvo leave.

"Maybe."

When we got to his car, and he caught my eye again from over the roof, a small smile played in the corner of his mouth.

"How come you never got your license?" he asked.

"Anxiety," I grimaced.

"Fair enough," he nodded, but then tilted his head, squinting in the sunlight. "Would you consider it, though?"

I folded my arms on the roof of the car and smiled. "Are you sick of driving me already?"

"Lily, I'd drive you everywhere for the rest of my life if I could." He mirrored me, leaning on the roof. The happy little glimmer in his blue-gray eyes caused my heart to skip. "But considering where my future is headed, I don't really wanna imagine this thing gathering dust in my garage. So, maybe if you learned to drive, you could take care of it for me."

My eyes widened. "Your car?"

"Why not?"

I laughed in bemusement, running my eyes over the sleek lines of the vintage car. From its glossy, emerald-green exterior to its silver hub caps and detailing. "I don't think you understood what I meant when I said anxiety prevented me from learning to drive. I almost crashed each instructor's car. And my parents' cars."

"Key word being almost." He pulled back from the car, slid on his shades, and flashed a smile as he opened his door. "Get in."

That smile.

Butterflies erupted in my stomach as I grinned wider and climbed into the passenger seat.

CHAPTER 24
Dean

Lily sitting in the driver's seat of my car was one of the best things I had ever witnessed. She was so focused and serious, biting her lip with every turn of the wheel as we cruised around an empty grocery store parking lot, but looked equally beautiful.

I couldn't help but sit closer than I needed to be, with my arm slung along the back of the Cadillac's bench seat as I pointed to the gas and brakes, the gears, and what to look for on the dash. She was a fast learner, and soon my thoughts of teaching her how to drive were drifting to a reward for later.

"That's it. Nice and easy," I commented as she took a left turn.

She blushed but kept her eyes ahead. "You're making it so hard to focus right now."

"I don't know what you're talking about," I said, fighting a smile. She took another wide turn before I spoke in a lower tone. "Good girl."

She shook her head in disbelief, huffing a laugh as she shifted in her seat, and then took a steadying breath. "I think I'm getting the hang of it."

"Great." My attention went to the exit of the parking lot. "Now we try the street."

"What?"

I smirked at her. "You heard me."

Her eyebrows furrowed with worry. "Are you sure?"

"I trust you."

"Ha," she barked nervously, glancing at the street.

I gently took her chin, directing her eyes back to me as I toned down on the nonchalance. "I promise you, nothin' is gonna happen. You've got this. Just do one trip around this block."

Her throat bobbed, but she nodded with determination.

I sat back, giving her space as she checked her mirrors and blind spots, tucked her hair behind her ears, and gently pressed the accelerator. The car moved to the exit, where she stopped to look left and right. The engine rumbled idly beneath us.

"Okay," she breathed. "Okay. This is fine. I'm just going for a drive on the road. In a very large car."

Another breath later, her fingers flicked the turn signal to go right, and she turned the wheel, keeping her head on a swivel and double-checking mirrors as we peeled out onto the mostly empty street. For a moment, we were in complete silence.

She seemed to be anticipating something happening.

I slowly tugged the sleeves of my hoodie up my forearms and rested back in my seat. One arm draped on the back of the seat, and the other angled on the open window while I lightly drummed my fingers on the roof.

Lily stole a glance at me. "I'm doing it."

"You are."

The corners of her lips curved into a radiant smile.

I reached for the dash and flicked the switch to put the top down, which only made her smile more as the sun poured in and a light breeze tugged gently at her hair. Each light brown strand glowed golden in the light.

I rarely used the convertible option with my car. Sometimes, the top jammed, but that didn't matter now. I wanted to watch Lily enjoy a drive with the roof down as we went around the block.

When she parked the car back in the grocery store lot, releasing a heavy but content sigh, the smile on her face remained as she turned in her seat. Tucking one leg under the other, she looked ready to burst with happiness.

"So? How did I do?"

I curled my hand under her bent knee and slid her to me. The motion caused a giggle to pass over her soft lips, right before I claimed them.

"I'll take that as a pass for lesson one," she laughed, taking a breath between kisses. "You will have to teach me a few more things, you know."

I nodded, eyes on her lips again. I couldn't help myself when it came to looking at her.

She blushed, considering something as she chewed her lip. And then she kissed me again. It was tentative and a little teasing. She spaced each kiss like she was figuring something out about them.

Her lips opened wider, letting me in as she leaned into me. Only then did she pull away, a little breathless.

"I think I'm ready," she said.

"Ready for—*Oh*." I cleared my throat and willed myself to move back a fraction more. "Are you sure?"

She nodded quickly. "Mhm. We're going to have sex again anyway, so we may as well start now, right?"

"Okay, fair enough," I chuckled. "But we should only do it if you're comfortable."

"And I am."

I watched her a little longer, trying to find a tell. It wasn't that I didn't believe she was ready. I just needed her to know that there was no rush.

Lily rolled her eyes, took my hand from her thigh, and brought it under her shirt to her scar. The touch caused her stomach to flinch briefly from nerves, but she kept my hand there. Pressed to her smooth skin and the small, rigid scar just above her hip bone.

"I'm ready," she repeated softly. Her pupils had dilated.

Eyes on mine, she guided my hand to her breast.

I could see the outline of my hand beneath her top as she left my hand where it was. Her releasing my wrist invited me to take over.

Pulling her into my lap and holding her body against mine, I turned us horizontally so she lay between my legs, and my head rested against the door. Not the most comfortable angle for my neck, but with a view like the one on top of me, I couldn't complain.

"You really wanna do this in the car?" I followed the familiar curves of her body under the snug fit of her shirt and jeans with my hands.

"Yes, I do." She tucked her bottom lip between her teeth and then kissed me slowly, teasing me each time our lips met until she brought her mouth to my ear. Her cool fingertips skimmed up beneath my shirt.

"If you're going to fuck me in your car," she whispered, sending a shudder down my spine as her bottom lip brushed the shell of my ear, "We should probably close the roof."

"Yes, we should," I said. "There is a switch on the dash to the right of the steering wheel if you wanna just give it a flick."

She smiled and eased herself back, straddling my hips and the bulge in my jeans.

As she investigated where the switch was, I skimmed my hands up her thighs and body and then brought them back down again to her waist.

"Ah-huh," she hummed softly, finding the switch.

There was a quiet grinding in the back of the car, and we both paused to watch as the top unfolded and slowly covered us in again.

And then it stopped halfway.

"For fuck's sake," I groaned, pulling my eyes to her body — where she sat.

"Did I break it?"

"No, it's just somethin' it does... Gimme a second." I started sitting up, and she moved off my lap so I could yank the roof the rest of the way over. As I did, Lily glanced into the back seat and then started climbing into it.

I lowered my arms and raised a brow, watching her as she went over.

God, her ass in those jeans...

"You really wanna do this, huh?" I said, half smiling as I crossed my arms on the back of the seat.

Lily dropped into the back, huffing a strand of hair from her face with a grin. She kicked off her sneakers, maintaining that eagerly excited eye contact, and reached for the button on her fly.

I didn't want to move yet, not when I was enjoying watching her remove her jeans in a cramped space.

"Are you coming back here or what?" She lobbed her jeans at my face teasingly, crossing her bare legs.

My size wasn't making it over the back of the seat.

I stepped out of the car, looking around casually to make sure the parking lot was still empty before I pulled the front seat forward and climbed into the back. Once the door was shut and locked again, and I had put the front seat back in place, Lily's hands snaked around my shoulders and she dragged me on top of her with a laugh.

"It might be easier if I'm sitting," I chuckled, looping my arm around her waist as I rolled us up.

Her knees wedged against the crevice of the seat, and she was flush against me, cradled by my thighs while I spread them for leg room.

It was then that things slowed down a little.

This was the first time we had done anything since the shooting.

Lily seemed to think the same thing as she adjusted herself, breathing a little more shakily. But it wasn't fear that made her apprehensive. She was ready and excited, and equally nervous.

"We're doing this," she said, looping her arms around my neck.

"And we've got nowhere else to be. There's no rush," I added, shaking my head. "You're in charge of where this goes, alright? I'm just here to...provide." I nudged my hips up against her, and it made her smile wider.

She brought her lips closer, kissing me with featherlight curiosity and then opening her mouth for more as her fingers grazed the back of my scalp.

My hands drifted along her thighs, around the curve of her ass, and up beneath the back of her shirt. She was leaving her shirt on, but that didn't stop me from undoing the clasp of her bra.

I pulled my mouth from hers and brought it to her neck as my hands spread across her back and shoulder blades.

Lily pushed herself into me, spreading her legs as she rolled her hips to sit comfortably, but then she moved back a little, bringing her hands and eyes to my fly. Her lips parted as she made quick work of the button and zipper and then lightly trailed a finger along the seam of my briefs, right along the curve of my bulge.

My cock twitched at the faint stroke before she gently released it from its restraint.

Her eyes came to my face, searching as if she wondered if all this was okay with me.

I cocked my head back, half smiling.

It was the one thing she needed before she brought herself closer again, reaching down between us to slip her underwear to one side.

I refused to take my eyes off her face as she tentatively stroked herself against me. Her shoulders relaxed, and her head tilted back as those cautious movements grew heavier with arousal.

She closed her eyes as her hips slid back and forth, finding a slow rhythm and growing wetter and wetter.

I had hardened against her fast and gently pulled her closer as I kissed the front of her throat. A soft moan slipped out from her parted lips, and then she rose to her knees, keeping her body flush with mine.

"I want you in me," she whispered breathlessly.

I nodded lazily, reaching beneath her to hold my cock while she lowered herself to it.

My stomach tensed, and my mouth fell open when she sank onto the tip and then rose off it again. She was edging herself in preparation, and I was loving every fucking second. Each time she pushed down a little further, I was left breathless. And groaning like I had been deprived of sex for years.

Her arousal slid over my fingers at the base of my cock when she lowered herself one more time, taking me in full. I moved my hand so she could go all the way down and sit there for a moment.

There was a faint quaking in her thighs and a look on her face as if she suddenly remembered how it felt — the closeness, the touch, the pleasure.

"You okay?" I asked, bringing my hand up to suck her from my fingers.

"I didn't realize how much I missed...this." She rolled her pelvis forward and up, arching her back so that she slid off me by a few inches before she slid back on.

My mouth twitched with a smile, and I sat forward. The angle made her lean back, resting her shoulders against the back of the front seat. I framed my hands on her hips and then slid my thumb to her clit. The touch made her roll her head back.

I felt her muscles feather around me and kissed the column of her arched neck. "Show me how much you missed this, Lily."

CHAPTER 25

Dean

"Why does it feel like everyone knows what we just did?" Lily had a coy little smile on her face, and her arm looped through mine as we wandered through the streets of Bay Ridge. She held a hot chocolate, loaded with marshmallows. "I mean, logically, they wouldn't. But it still feels like they know something is up."

"Not sure." I took the last swig of my coffee and glanced at her legs. "Are they still shaking?"

She backhanded my chest, forcing back her smile while her cheeks turned a light shade of pink.

I chuckled as I ditched my cup in the next trash can. "I guarantee the majority of people we've passed are probably thinking about sex anyway." I nodded to a guy waiting to cross the street. His hands were fidgeting at his sides, and he had shamelessly checked out multiple women already. "He isn't even hiding it."

Lily screwed up her nose a little as we passed him — thankfully he crossed the street before he could notice her.

"Are men ever not thinking of sex, though?" she asked, sipping her hot chocolate. She knew the answer to that already, based on the look she gave me. Somewhere between deadpan and amusement.

I shook my head. "We're simple creatures."

She pouted up at me and patted my cheek adoringly. "I lucked out. Mine came with emotional intelligence."

I sighed, mocking cockiness as I draped an arm around her shoulders. "I'm the hybrid model, baby."

A soft giggle escaped her, either for the pet name or because we felt like we were on top of the world for a moment. Either way, I didn't think I could develop any more feelings for this woman. She made me feel complete and fucking untouchable.

"By the way, what did you want to do for your birthday?" she said.

"You remembered that, huh?"

"Of course."

"It's not for another two weeks."

"So?" With my arm slung around her shoulders, she brought her hand up to where my hand was and laced her fingers through mine. "What do you usually do for your birthday?"

I shrugged. "Get drunk?"

She rolled her eyes. "Your birthday is literally Halloween."

"Lily, I really don't mind what I do for my birthday. We could sit in my car overlooking the Hudson with burgers and box wine, and I'd be happy."

"I still think you should celebrate it. At least this one, anyway…"

I looked down at her as she cast her eyes to the pavement. The ugly reminder of the investigation was on her mind — my dwindling fucking future was on her mind.

"Alright. I only turn twenty-seven once." I gently squeezed her closer, slowly coaxing another small smile from her as I ducked my head to kiss her cheek. "We won't think about the other shit today."

She inhaled softly as she looked up at me. "Agreed."

We continued, finding small talk in other things until Lily gently tugged my arm away from my body, causing me to slow as she looked at something across the street. A Saturday flea market. It was in a wide side street packed with overflowing stalls, with music and the promise of delicious food.

"Food," was all Lily said.

My stomach rumbled in answer.

While food was the main factor for why two people like us, with a dislike for most crowds, would venture into a bustling flea market, Lily quickly found another reason to go. Barely three stalls in, her steps slowed at a large collection of tables and small shelves all full of second-hand books.

"I'll get the food," I said with a smile and a kiss to her temple before leaving her to peruse alone.

There was a food truck selling hot dogs parked a little way down the packed side street, wedged between a woman selling wooden carvings and a man calling out his fresh produce prices. I ordered two hot dogs and waited back as the food truck attendant got to work.

My eyes drifted casually over the wooden carvings — a hobby I tried once but learned I liked the mechanics of how things worked over how they looked — before I glanced back towards the book stall.

In the bustling crowd, I couldn't see Lily anymore.

She's just deeper in the book stall. Nothing to worry about.

"Foods ready," said the food truck attendant, pulling my attention.

I took the hot dogs and paid. Just as I was pushing my wallet into my back pocket, my ears pricked to the voices of two women speaking fluent Italian.

On the other side of the produce stall, taste-testing cheese, was Beatrice and Lucia Gimello. They hadn't seen me yet, and I wasn't waiting around for them to.

I started for the book stall again, weaving through the crowd. With my height, I could see over everyone and spotted Lily instantly as I beelined for her. The gap between us felt like it was getting wider with every step I took. It didn't help that several strangers chose to walk slowly in front of me, or completely stopped to look around.

We need to fucking leave— I didn't want them to see her— Where was their brother— Fuck!

My stomach dropped.

I found Lily, but I was still nowhere near her.

She was at the back of the stall. A table of books on her left, a shelf to her right, and a young man standing in front of her. Talking to her. He wore too many gold rings and a white shirt unbuttoned to his stomach.

Gabriele combed a hand through his oily black hair as he grinned at her and looked her over like she was an object for him to observe at his leisure.

There was a roaring in my head. I couldn't get to her fast enough. She had no idea who she was talking to.

Why is everyone walking so fucking slow?!

Lily had her arms crossed over several books, holding them close to her chest as she offered Gabriele polite but uncomfortable smiles. When she attempted to end the conversation and move past him, Gabriele cut her off, casually bracing an arm on the table to block her exit and bringing himself closer.

Fuck this.

I stopped weaving, ready to flip a goddamn table if I had to, and someone bounced off my arm as I pushed by.

"Hey, I'm walking—"

"Fuck off," I growled in passing, eyes on Lily and Gabriele as I walked into the stall. The only thought in my head was getting Lily away.

I caught the tail end of their conversation as I approached Lily from behind.

Lily laughed nervously at something Gabriele said. "Oh, no. I'm here with—"

My hand came to her lower back and slid around her waist. "Hey."

"My boyfriend," she finished. The tension visibly left her body as she leaned ever so slightly into my side.

Gabriele's attention slowly drifted from Lily to me, and his demeanor changed from being irritated by the interruption to recognition as he took in my face. A smirk slowly appeared on his lips.

I shouldn't have let him see my face...

"What a coincidence this is," he crooned.

I hummed and looked at Lily. "Ready to go?" I took her hand and plastered an easy smile on my face, hoping to high fuck she would pick up that none of this was good.

"Yep." She instantly stepped away with me. Hand firmly in mine as she offered Gabriele a sympathetic smile.

"*Ciao, piccola cerva.*" Gabriele placed a hand over his heart, feigning heartbreak.

I couldn't give a shit. My heart was racing, but I was trying to act calm.

Once we cleared the book stall, I finally spoke. "Did you give him your name?"

"No. He never got to introductions. Just jumped right into flirting after I bought my books. What happened to the food?" There was a smile in her voice. One of disbelief until she saw whatever was written on my face as we maneuvered the crowds.

I had no fucking clue what happened to the hotdogs.

"Dean, what's wrong? And can we slow down a little? I can't keep up with you." She laughed to ease the tension.

My steps slowed as we came to the adjacent street, and I glanced back to make sure we weren't being followed. There was no sign of the triplets in the crowds nearby, but I kept walking anyway. "That was Gabriele Gimello."

It dawned on her then, and the beautiful happiness that was on her face diminished. "Antonio's—Antonio's son?"

I pressed my lips together and nodded as I scanned the street and every face, car, and shop window. My hand was still wrapped firmly around hers. When we got to my car, I did more of the same searching.

"I don't think he saw where we went..." She didn't sound too sure.

I pulled a hand through my hair as I watched several people walk by. "I wish he never saw you."

"Okay, but I'm not really of interest to him, right?"

I shook my head. "You don't know what this guy is like—the things he's done to people he's met to please his sadistic curiosity—I shouldn't have approached you. Him seeing you with me—Fuck—" I stopped myself and finally looked at her. "Maybe you should stay with your parents."

I've lost my mind if that's the only suggestion I've got.

Her eyes widened. "What? No—Dean... Take a breath." She placed a hand on my chest. "Your heart is beating so fast."

I closed my eyes and did as she said. One deep inhale followed by an exhale as our eyes met again. My heart was still pounding. I wasn't used to feeling this much for someone.

"I don't want to lose you again." The words came out before I could really think them through. Logically, I knew she was safe with me. She also had a father who would put a stop to Gabriele pretty fast if something happened.

Lily took my face in her hands. "You're not going to lose me... But to put you at ease, how about we stay in for the rest of the weekend? Like what we did at yours. We could watch movies, order food, and continue what we did today in the backseat."

The last part made me huff a laugh. She was trying to be positive.

"And Monday?"

"We could have sex on Monday too," she shrugged.

"Good to know, but not what I meant." My hands slid up her forearms, from elbow to wrist, before I moved her hands from my face. I smoothed my thumb over her unmarred knuckles.

"You can't protect me all the time," she said softly. "Everything is okay."

CHAPTER 26
Lily

Nothing was okay at all, but I wanted it to be. I thought saying it out loud to Dean, to reassure him, might change how I felt too, but it hadn't. I only felt worse. My stomach was in knots, and my anxiety was doing a number on the slight ache forming in my temples.

Saturday started so well. Yes, I had general nerves while at Jane's game, but that was a regular feeling for me. I was a naturally anxious person, slowly healing after something traumatic. I even felt okay enough to maybe not go to a psychologist after all. Instead, I had fallen into a false sense of hope — hope that was ripped out from under me the second Dean told me who that man was.

Gabriele Gimello. Another mob boss. Another threat. Another reason for my brain to remind me of what I went through, even if they weren't directly connected.

You're fine. I shuddered as I practiced slow breathing. *Nothing is going to happen. Antonio's kids don't care about me, they have no reason to— They had every reason to if they're as bad as Dean says...*

He hadn't said a lot about them on the way home, I think to not worry me about how dangerous they could be, but it didn't stop my thoughts from conducting worst-case scenarios. Even in the shower, where I had a quick rinse, those thoughts plagued my mind.

I swiped my phone off the coffee table. Not entirely sure why other than to get my mind off everything.

I landed on Pinterest and began doom-scrolling through the main page, scrolling by aesthetically pleasing images of books and art, sunsets and flowers, feel-good quotes and—

An image of blood-covered hands. *Fake* blood.

I shut off my phone and set it aside.

If one image was triggering enough... How was it that I felt like my mind was slowly spiraling out of control, yet I was sitting completely still?

I tried the slow breathing again as I cast my gaze to the kitchen on my left, where Dean was making tea and lunch. He had misplaced the hot dogs on his way back to me at the flea market. Since arriving home, he had also gone extremely quiet.

My hand drifted across to the underside of my arm, where the pinch mark from last week lay beneath the sleeve of my shirt.

It helped last time...

Dean finished in the kitchen.

I moved my hand away from my arm as he joined me on the couch and set down my tea and a large plate of loaded grilled cheese sandwiches. Tomato, ham, and cheese all stuffed into a lightly seasoned bun with charring on the edges. It smelled good, but neither of us made a move to eat any of the slices.

"Might be a little hot." He dropped heavily into the space beside me. "You okay?"

"Are you?" I smiled meekly.

He huffed tiredly and rubbed the heel of his palm against his eye. He didn't have to voice how he felt when it was written on his face.

"It's not every day a gangster flirts with you at a flea market," I continued, trying for humor.

Dean didn't exactly laugh, but he smiled — probably out of sympathy.

I picked up the tea, sipped it, and set it back down before breaking off some of the grilled cheese sandwich. I popped it into my mouth, decided I wasn't so anxious I couldn't eat, and picked up more for a bigger bite.

"I want you to promise me that if you ever see him again, you run the other way." The seriousness in his voice remained from earlier.

I swallowed and brought the plate to my lap. "Trust me, I don't plan on talking to him again."

Dean hummed and then tapped his thigh with his hand. An invite. I lifted my legs across his lap, and he absentmindedly began massaging my calves, thighs, and the bottom of my feet.

Touch was his love language, but I wondered if the extra need for closeness was more to reassure himself that I was fine. That I was there.

"I think we need a distraction." I put the sandwich on the plate and dusted off my fingers.

"What'd you have in mind?" His hand came to a stop on my thigh while he rested his head back, exposing the side of his throat and the moth tattooed across the front of it.

The way he watched me through half closed eyes made my heart flutter as if this was our first kiss.

I returned the plate to the coffee table and then wrapped my hand around his bicep and tugged him closer.

He fell into the kiss easily. With my legs still draped over his lap while he leaned into me, I combed my fingers through the back of his hair.

He hummed against my lips. "This works."

All my previous thoughts were slowly evaporating and quickly being replaced with his presence. His sandalwood and leather cologne filled my senses, and the sensation of his hands on my waist caused my stomach to dip and flutter.

I shifted my hips, aware that at this angle he would feel it.

Dean's stomach growled.

I smiled and pulled away an inch. "Did you want to eat first?"

He shook his head, looking breathless with his kiss-swollen lips and dilated pupils. "I have something else in mind."

I lifted an eyebrow.

Dean grinned, the kind to dimple his cheek, and got off the couch. As I straightened in my seat, watching his every move, he removed his hoodie. It lifted his T-shirt a little before he leaned over me, hands braced on the back of the couch.

He kissed my lips first, and then my jaw, neck, and shoulder as he pulled the neckline of my shirt aside. All as he lowered himself to kneel between my legs.

While I melted under the burning touch of his mouth on my skin, he untucked my shirt from my jeans and slid his hand up beneath it.

"Watchin' you drive my car today." He moved down, skimming his mouth along my shirt above my breasts. His mouth found the bare skin of my stomach while his hands came to the button on my jeans. "Fuckin' irresistible."

"When can we go driving again?" I breathed.

"Soon." He sat back and slowly unzipped and peeled my jeans off.

Once those were discarded on the floor, he brought his mouth to my lower abdomen. He brushed a kiss over my scar, acknowledging it but not lingering, and then trailed several more on a straight route down.

I rolled my head back as his hot breath fanned across my underwear.

God, I hope Kira doesn't come home right now—Maybe she's at the markets too—The triplets might still be there.

The thought was a mistake that sent a barrage of memories from today flooding back. I saw Gabriele's face as he attempted to flirt with me. Now that I knew what he was, I suddenly pictured him with a gun on his hip.

Suddenly, he was Aiden, pointing a gun at me.

My chest tightened until I gasped in pleasure. Thrust back out of my thoughts as Dean kissed me through my underwear.

I focused on what he was doing to stay present.

Running his touch along my thighs, his hands came to my underwear, and he slowly tugged them off and spread my legs.

I thrummed under his gaze as my body relaxed.

He hooked my knees over his shoulders, pulling me down so my ass was on the edge of the couch, and kissed my inner thigh before he gently bit the flesh.

I sucked in a breath, writhing slightly.

"You're also irresistible when you lose control," he continued. Arousal was laced in his deep voice as he lowered his mouth to hover above where I desperately needed him to touch me. With the lightest and slowest lick, he teased my clit with his tongue, sending a shiver through my body.

I whimpered softly.

"And those sounds. They make me so fuckin' hard." He cupped himself through his jeans and simultaneously slid his fingers over my entrance, wetting them. When he slowly plunged two into me and curled them up, I moaned quietly and arched off the couch. A fist full of cushion in one hand and the palm of my other hand against my forehead.

"Just like that." He wrapped his mouth over my clit and sucked gently while he continued pressing up with his fingers, getting me there quickly.

"Oh, fuck," I whispered.

Dean palmed my hips and thighs, dragging his tongue across me as his eyes darkened and sparked with an idea. He took hold of my waist, supporting my weight as he rolled us in one easy motion. I squealed and laughed as I went, finding myself kneeling on the couch while his head remained between my legs.

I held myself up while my hands gripped the back of the couch, panting as the pleasure still pulsed readily through my body.

"What are you doing?"

"Sit down, Lily."

I tucked my hair behind my ears. "I know people do this all the time, but aren't you worried about not breathing? Should I hover?"

"Lily." His voice was husky. "I wanna fuck you with my tongue until all I can taste is you. Breathing can come into the equation later. Sit on my face."

Hot and bothered, I hesitated.

"Sit on my face, please?"

I bit my lip and carefully lowered myself.

Dean brushed his nose against my clit as he half smiled, happy to have gotten his way, before he spread me with his thumbs and proceeded to drive me crazy. A good kind of crazy, as his tongue did things that caused my legs to tremble.

"Huh," I breathed in surprise, smiling in a pleasure-filled daze as my fingers threaded through his hair. My other hand remained on the back of the couch, gripping it tightly as I fought the urge to roll my hips. I didn't want to completely suffocate him, even if he said otherwise. Dean knew this. He gripped my hips and coaxed me into rocking them, nodding with encouragement as he feasted on my pleasure.

I gripped the couch with both hands again and rocked my hips.

My walls tightened, and my body shuddered. I was about to orgasm, all over his face. Then, when I thought I might explode, Dean plunged his fingers into me again, forcing my climax to rush forward.

He wrapped his arm around my quaking thigh and pressed his thumb to my clit.

My eyes rolled back and my mouth fell open, but nothing came out. Instead, I buried my nails into the couch as my orgasm reached its peak, flooding my system with warmth and electricity as it obliterated my worries from earlier.

CHAPTER 27
Kira

I worked at the Green Thumbs Florist and Garden Center, Monday to Friday, from midday to 4 PM.

Being surrounded by so many beautiful plants and given the opportunity to live in my element for a few hours a day always made every weekday so much better.

The plants had provided a distraction during the confusing and brief time Seb stopped talking with me. Now that I knew the reason for that, working with the plants was less of a distraction and more of a pleasant few hours a day again.

Pulling several dried leaves from my ponytail — I had spent the last thirty minutes of my shift removing the dead leaves on several large house plants — I neared the apartment door. Once inside, with my hessian bag slung over my shoulder, I yawned, but then stifled it when I heard heavy breathing.

And then a humming and a thud.

"Lily? Are you home?" She started work at 8 AM and finished at 4 PM, like me, but there was no way she could've gotten home earlier than me. The garden center was closer to our apartment than the Whitmore real estate agency by a few blocks. I had also seen her leave for work this morning.

"Y-Yeah. I'm home," she responded, breathlessly.

I blinked, pausing in the hallway. I couldn't help the smile on my face. "Why do you sound puffed? Are you decent? Should I leave?"

She huffed a laugh. "I'm decent, but struggling."

I continued into the living room and discovered why she was breathless. She was shuffling a brand-new, four-tiered shelf up against the living room window. The frame was an off-white, matching the apartment walls, and the shelves were light brown timber. There was no backing board on it, so once it was up against the window, the sunlight filtered through it and into the living room.

"I thought the plants could use some new shelf space." She dusted off her hands. Her hair was in a bun that was close to falling out, and she wore a baggy T-shirt and a pair of old jeans. She placed her hands on her hips and smiled at me.

I happily walked over to examine the shelf. "It's perfect. But how did you get it up here?"

"It was a self-assemble." She gestured to the mess of spare screws, wooden dowel pieces, and Allen keys on the floor beside a crumpled instruction sheet. "I had it delivered... I'll leave it to you to arrange the plants on it because I'm not sure which ones like more light than the others."

I admired the shelf for a moment before I turned to Lily as she headed into the kitchen. "How was your appointment?"

She was filling up a glass at the sink. "Hm?"

"With the psychologist? You said it was Monday, right?"

"Oh. No, I meant next Monday." She took a few sips of water and then smiled at me. "Don't worry, I haven't forgotten our pact about healing together."

"Right." I shook my head in confusion and went back to looking at the shelf. "Did you go to work today?"

There was a pause before she ran the water again to rinse her glass. "I planned to, but then I didn't get off the bus when it stopped. I wasn't feeling it today."

I turned away from the shelf and approached the kitchen counter. "Is everything okay?"

Dean and Seb would be fighting again tonight. Maybe that's why she seemed off. I was a little nervous about it too.

"Oh, yeah, of course," she said with a nonchalant wave of the hand. "I think I needed a day for myself. Anyway, how was work?"

"It was good. Just the usual..." I knew she was trying to avoid the topic. It was true that she might've needed a day to herself, but I couldn't help but think of what I had told Seb during our first date; Lily didn't seem like herself.

She was shot. Of course, she isn't going to be feeling great just yet...

"Are you excited about this evening?" Lily asked. A knowing smile was on her face as she braced her elbows on the countertop and rested her face in her hands. "With *Seb*."

It shouldn't have distracted me so easily, but the mere mention of him caused my stomach to flutter.

I received a text from Seb over the weekend. It was an out-of-the-blue type of text. The out-of-the-blue aspect tied in well with most of my life events and his general personality anyway, so I wasn't too shocked by it. But the substance of the text introduced a new flutter of butterflies to my stomach.

Seb wanted to know if I would like to meet his family before he had to fight tonight — he figured it was only right for me to meet the people who had had his full attention recently.

Of course, my habit of jumping first and asking questions later had me texting a *Yes!* the second I finished reading the text.

I inhaled shakily, grinning. "I'm feeling *all* the feelings about it."

Lily reached across and squeezed my shoulder. "They're going to love you."

No matter how hard I tried to make things feel normal again, there was some tension between Seb and me. The kind that was filled with awkward smiles as I walked to where he waited on his bike in the street.

He held out his spare helmet and pulled up his visor. "Hey."

I took the helmet with a small smile. "Hi."

"Things are weird, right?" He cringed slightly.

I was glad I wasn't the only one thinking about it. "Yeah. Things are weird."

He huffed. "Okay. How should we make things *un*-weird? I mean, the reason things are weird is because I monumentally fucked up. Like, we had sex—*great* sex by the way—and we never really got to talk about it. The other night didn't really smooth things over."

"No, but at least I know why you disappeared. It was a messy situation to begin with. I think we need to find our groove again." I raised a shoulder. And then inhaled shakily as the evening dawned on me. "I'm about to meet your family."

He pulled his helmet off as he looked ahead. A lopsided grin spread on his lips. "We really don't do things slow, huh?"

"Nope."

"You don't have to meet them if you don't want to. We could go another time. Or never. I don't mind—well, I'd probably mind a little bit if you never wanted to meet them, but right now there's no rush..."

I smiled wider at his rambling and stepped forward, much closer to him, as I leaned in and pecked him on the cheek. His eyes filled with pleasant surprise first, and then changed to adoration as he looked at me.

To witness that change in someone's eyes was far better than the gaze Aiden ever cast in my direction — his gaze was always one looking to control me, or keep me in check.

"I want to meet your family, Seb." I gently squeezed his forearm, staying close to him, before I grabbed his helmet and lifted it onto his head again. Smiling still, I slid my helmet on too and climbed onto the small seat behind him. "Let's go."

"Say less, Smiles," he chuckled, bringing the bike to life beneath us with a flick of his thumb.

I placed my hands on his sides and curled my fingers into his leather riding jacket for something to hold on to. Seb took my hands and pulled them around himself. In turn, pulling me flush against his back.

"Gotta hold on tighter than that."

I laughed and scooted closer to him, finally feeling that familiar comfort from before any of this — the sex and the miscommunication — started. There was something more to the hug too.

Safety. Trust. The L word?

Don't get ahead of yourself, Kira. Try to take some things slowly, at least. Allow your heart some grace before you fall head over heels for this man.

My heart skipped anyway.

Anita and Don's home was a quaint, two-story, cream brick house with a cute little front garden that featured a tree swing and powder blue shutters on the windows. Like all the other homes in the street, they were built close to their neighbors, but each home had its own personality. This one reminded me of something from a storybook. It was cozy and inviting.

Seb and I made our way to the front porch.

The nerves about meeting his family began to sink in properly. They weren't enough to make me change my mind. Instead, they only fed the happy anticipation growing in my chest. I couldn't wait to meet the people he cared so much for. The fact that he was more than happy to introduce me to them made my heart swell.

Before we reached the top of the stairs, the front door was opened by a gorgeous woman I could only assume was Seb's younger sister, Anita.

She smiled radiantly and stepped out to greet us with her arms out wide. The gesture erased any nerves I had, and I hugged her in greeting. She smelled like all things summer and fresh.

"Hi, Kira." She pulled back, holding me at arm's length, and looked at Seb. Her smile fell, and she raised a brow. "You're telling me, you had this fine woman waiting for you to reach out, and you didn't think to go visit her?"

Straight to the point. I loved her already.

I pressed my lips together to keep from smiling.

Seb stammered. "Okay, yes, I was a dumbass for that. But I didn't hear you complaining about me being here to help out."

"Seb, kids sleep. You had plenty of time to go see her. Or invite her here." Anita narrowed her eyes on him. "Treat her that way again and I'll ring your ears."

Seb nodded once. "Noted."

Anita looked at me and smiled sweetly. "It's so nice to finally meet you."

"You too. It's also nice to meet another hugger," I said.

"Oh, we're all about hugs in this house." She kept an arm around my shoulder and led me inside.

"Nice to see you too, sis," Seb said sarcastically as he followed us.

I looked back briefly, catching his smile as he watched the two of us proudly. I think any worries he had about this meeting also faded.

Anita brought us through to the first room on the left, opposite the stairs in the hallway, and I spotted her eldest daughter, Chloe, in a recliner wearing a full leg cast. She was playing a game on her Switch before she looked up. Her face brightened with a smile, much like her mother's, and she waved.

I gave her a small wave back.

Seb went straight to Mia, the chubby baby sitting on the floor playing with colorful blocks. He scooped her up, and she giggled when she realized who he was.

My heart backflipped at the sight of him casually holding a baby in one arm as he walked over to his other niece and kissed the top of her head.

"She looks like a fairy princess," Chloe whispered to Seb after looking me over with eyes full of awe.

I think it was my hair. It was out, and despite wearing a helmet, it managed to look completely windswept. The curls were unruly at best, and today they wanted to be a little extra. I gave up trying to tame them at the apartment earlier, but I was happy someone appreciated them.

"Hi," I smiled at the girl.

"I'm going to assume Seb told you what happened?" Anita asked me, referring to Chloe's leg.

"Oh. Yeah." I frowned. "I'm so sorry that happened to her. And you. I can't begin to imagine how stressful it was—"

"Kira?" Chloe's little voice pulled my attention back to her. She held a purple glitter gel pen in my direction and smiled shyly. "Will you sign my cast, please?"

My mouth fell open in awe, and I hurried over. "Oh my gosh, I thought you'd never ask! It'd be my honor."

Chloe giggled, and I took the pen and signed my name across her shin. I added little flowers too.

Several minutes later, I was introduced to Anita's husband, Don. He was a hulking type of guy who wore glasses and spoke softly, and sported an apron as he came to let us know dinner was ready.

We followed him into the kitchen to lend a hand with plating, while the girls waited in the front room.

There was a large homemade salad, seasoned roast chicken that smelled like paradise on a plate, and fresh bread rolls all laid out on the counter.

"Kira," Anita said as she sliced up an apple and plopped the pieces into a baby bowl with cartoon dogs on the side. "Mind grabbing the ginger beer from the fridge?"

"On it." As I went to collect the drinks, I noticed a large colorful poster on the wall beside the fridge. It was a Haitian language poster.

Seb was picking up the salad bowl, closest to where I was by the fridge, when I turned to join him in walking back to the front room.

"You're Haitian?" It was a question from genuine curiosity.

"On our grandmother's side. Anita wants the girls to learn and embrace their heritage. Their minds are like sponges." We stopped in the doorway separating the kitchen from the living room as Seb chuckled. "My brain, though?" He swiped his hand over the top of his head.

Anita overheard the conversation as she gave little Mia her bowl of apple slices. "He's lazy with his Duolingo lessons."

I laughed and nudged Seb's arm. "We could learn together. Maybe having someone to bounce conversations off could help."

His brows raised, and he placed a hand on his chest. "You'd do that for me?"

I shrugged. "I've always wanted to learn another language. It'll be fun doing it together."

After dinner, Seb and I wandered outside into the lush but simplistic garden at the back of the house. We stopped on the patio as I admired some of the plants growing alongside it.

For a moment, we were in silence, comfortable and content, before it drew out longer than I expected. I even had to check that Seb was still outside with me. He had gone so quiet.

When he was caught watching me, he offered a small smile and looked down, rubbing the back of his head as he hummed. "So, I have a question."

"Okay?" I drifted closer, watching him curiously.

"What do we do after this?"

"With us?"

He nodded, sliding his hands into his pockets as if to stop himself from touching anything. "Well, I wouldn't mind seeing more of you. But I know we're getting things back to normal... I really like you, Kira. Like, *a lot, a lot*." His kind brown eyes settled on me. They had a sort of yearning in them that made my heart skip. "I don't think I can handle being *just* friends with you anymore."

A smile was quick to spread on my face as the butterflies in my stomach amped up tenfold.

He stammered and quickly backtracked. "That made it sound like I wouldn't want to be your friend anymore if you did say no to anything more between us. Because if you did want to be just friends, I'm down with it too. It might take me a little while to get over how I feel, though—you have my heart in a chokehold." He laughed nervously as he continued the rambling. "Or we could try friends with benefits? Honestly, I'm down for whatever you want. You say jump, I'll say *how high*, kinda thing—let me rephrase—"

I grabbed his face in both hands, and his eyebrows shot up.

"Shut up and kiss me, Seb."

CHAPTER 28
Dean

The blue and pink lights of Castello di Vetro cut through the hazy cigarette smoke that lingered in the back area of the strip club. The booths in this spot were black leather and provided a comfortable spot to sit and observe the rest of the room.

Nothing about this meeting was comfortable.

I fought again tonight but wasn't nearly as bruised as last time. There were fresh cuts on my knuckles that stung a little once the sweat got to them, but it wasn't why I was uncomfortable. No, I was uncomfortable because of the person who sat across from me.

Gabriele took one long drag of his cigarette and let the smoke pour from his mouth as he watched me closely. He had asked me to stay back after my fight.

After watching all the other fighters leave earlier, including Seb, an unsettling sensation settled in my gut.

I kept my guard up like always. Face unreadable as if I were uninterested in anything Gabriele had to say.

Beside him, Roxy was playing her part in a tight red turtleneck dress. She had garnered his trust, and they seemed to be closer than the first night they met. She whispered things into his ear or played with the collar of his shirt while he draped his arm around her shoulders.

"You did well tonight. Congratulations." He knocked the ash from his cigarette into an empty glass.

I was temporarily taken over by the urge to ask him for one to settle my already agitated nerves, but I held my tongue.

"You're good. *Very* good."

"Thanks," I said.

"You have a loyalty about you," he continued, gesturing to all of me with his hand. "Like you'd do whatever necessary to protect people you care about."

My jaw tightened.

"He is one of my best." Roxy slid her palm along Gabriele's chest to grab his attention.

His eyes went to her for a moment, and he smiled lazily before his gaze came back to me.

"You know the gentleman you fought on your first night here was found dead the other day?" His smile remained as he drew back on the cigarette again.

I dragged my attention to the room. "That's unfortunate."

Antonio was killing his ex-fighters one by one.

"Hm..." Gabriele sipped the scotch in front of him and made sure to really appreciate its taste. He sucked on his teeth in thought. "You know... My fighters, the ones who used to work for my father, tell me you were his favorite. They say he treated you much better than any of them. Like a son."

Fuck, fuck, fuck—

Gabriele chuckled darkly. "You can see why I might see that as a threat... But they also mentioned he employed you to do jobs for him, *Dean*."

My heart stopped for a second, and I think Roxy's might've too, based on the way she stilled.

Of course, those fighters would tell the triplets what my real name was. We couldn't stay hidden behind fight names forever. But it was the way Gabriele said it that set my mind racing. With my name in their minds, it felt like they had started to chip away at the wall of security I was trying desperately to hold up around anyone I cared about.

This was why I kept my circle small.

"I did." They were the only words I could get out while I tried to remember if there was any moment in my past where my last name might have been spoken inside The Den's basement. Some of those guys, fellow fighters, knew crumbs about my family and what happened to it. What they knew wasn't big enough to be a threat, but—

Who am I kidding? It's a huge fucking threat.

Gabriele's smile was cunning as he watched me process it all. Of all the years working for a mob boss, I had never seen or met someone who could display so much malice in a smile. In that moment, what I wanted more than anything was to smack it right off his face.

Roxy jumped in again, trying to bring Gabriele back on side. "Remember what I said, though? We left Antonio. He wasn't a good boss."

Gabriele scoffed his amusement and rubbed his temples. "Do you think I'm stupid?"

"No, of course not," Roxy cooed, once again sliding a hand up his chest.

Gabriele caught her wrist and held firm.

Roxy's smile grew uncomfortable, but remained on her face as she tried to gently remove his hand. But he wasn't letting up.

I shifted in my seat.

"I know why you're here." Gabriele's eyes tracked along Roxy's body as he spoke. "Collecting information for him because he can't do it himself. He wants to know what more we have planned, yes?"

Roxy's eyes darted to me, and her smile wavered. "No, that's not—"

"Tell me, did he pay you to spy on me as another job for him?" His attention came to me. "Are you recording this conversation? Is he listening now?"

I wasn't wired tonight because of the fight earlier. Detective Whitmore didn't think it was necessary to have undercovers planted in the place tonight either, since he believed I would only be around for a fight. This meeting was unexpected, without warning.

Roxy and I were alone and exposed, surrounded by the enemy.

"Your father underpaid us," Roxy continued, her voice more serious. "When you came to Brooklyn, offering so much more, I couldn't refuse—"

Gabriele grabbed a fistful of her long black hair and tore her head back, exposing her throat as he flipped out a switchblade.

She whimpered, squeezing her eyes shut.

"Put it away," I growled, but didn't move. Not yet.

"I wanna check," Gabriele shrugged, smiling like it was a joke. He dragged Roxy from the booth and, within seconds, tore the front of her dress open. The blade cut clean through the red fabric, nicking her skin before she was left to stand in her underwear. No wires.

My entire body was tense, ready to step in. I wasn't sure how to play this without being shot or stabbed.

Gabriele took a step back and tapped the blade on his chin as he examined Roxy's body from afar, and then said something that made my previous hesitation go out the window.

"*Forse c'è qualcosa in quella biancheria intima.*"

I barged from the booth and stood between them. "We're leaving."

Gabriele chuckled darkly but put the blade away. "I knew you could speak Italian." He took a seat in the booth as he looked over Roxy and me, coming to some conclusion in his head. "I seem to have struck a chord... I'm aware of that sweet little girlfriend you have, but you two? Past lovers?"

I removed my hoodie and passed it to Roxy. She quickly pulled it on.

"You are very protective of the women in your life, I see. It's an admirable trait," Gabriele said. "But it makes me curious too."

I was trying to keep things calm. Move calm, leave calm. Try not to bring any more attention to Lily.

He planted his elbows on the table and balanced his knife horizontally between his fingertips. "What makes them so important to you?"

I could lose it if I wanted to. Beat the shit out of him until his face was a mangled reflection of what it once was, but the consequences would be worse.

I turned around instead, attempting to guide Roxy towards the exit before Gabriele could speak again.

As she snatched the torn remains of her dress from the ground, Gabriele laughed. "Tell my father, he shouldn't send whores to do his work."

Roxy whirled in anger, practically shooting lasers from her eyes. Before I could stop her, she grabbed Gabriele's drink and aimed it, glass too, at his head. While he dodged the glass, the drink within it landed with a splat across his face and chest.

"I'm not a fucking whore!" she snapped, ready to confront Gabriele with another strike before I hooked my arm around her waist and pulled her back.

Gabriele simply stood and dabbed his face with a napkin, at the same time motioning for his men to stand down after they seemed to appear from nowhere to protect him.

I steered Roxy around in front of me and moved us through the club. My eyes were fixed on the exit.

"Don't fucking manhandle me." She smacked my hand away as she attempted to stop.

"Move. Now." My words were clipped.

Despite the glare in her eyes, she listened, walking ahead of me with fury in every step.

When we cleared the front doors, the smallest wave of freedom washed over me, but we weren't in the clear.

"What the fuck was that?" I hissed.

"No one calls me a whore and gets away with it," Roxy spat.

"No one throws a fuckin' drink at a crime boss and gets away with it either, you fuckin' idiot."

She spun around, ready to protest the name-calling, but I cut her off.

"You just put a target on our backs."

"You think I'm supposed to accept being spoken about like that? Does your respect for women only go as far as your mom and girlfriend?"

I inhaled sharply. "No... And no, I just don't wanna stir up shit when we're outnumbered. In a situation like that, when he knows you've been spying on him, you *take* the name-calling and deal with it *later*. Not when you're surrounded by guys who have guns and other intentions."

"Fuck you." She turned on her heel, continuing to where our cars were parked.

I ran a hand through my hair and pulled out my phone. I needed to contact people and at least warn them about what the fuck just happened.

I called Seb first with a brief rundown. He was staying all night at his place with Kira.

With the Cadillac in sight, a few cars away, I called Lily. She didn't answer, and the call went to voicemail. I tried again, fishing out my keys as I reached the car door. At the same time, my bundled-up hoodie hit me in the side of the head and fell across my shoulder.

"Don't want Lily wondering why you're missing a hoodie and getting the wrong idea," Roxy scowled, marching off to her Aston Martin parked behind my car. Unbothered by the fact that she was only in her underwear and heels.

I unlocked the car and ripped my hoodie from my shoulder, dropping into the driver's seat as I threw the hoodie into the backseat and held the phone to my ear.

Out of habit, I pulled out my old lighter. Until I remembered, *I don't fucking smoke anymore.*

Lily still wasn't answering.

"Come on," I said through gritted teeth, dialing again as I started the car. "Pick up."

It went to voicemail again, with Lily politely telling me to leave a message.

"Fuck," I muttered.

I tried Mom instead. She answered after several rings, pleasantly surprised by the call before she started telling me about her evening at bingo.

"Mom, listen. I need you to stay with a friend tonight."

She was quiet for a second and responded with a reserved, "Okay... Do I want to know?"

"Probably best you don't."

"Be careful."

"I will."

I hung up and tossed my phone into the front seat, shoving the gear into drive. Right as I looked ahead, Roxy peeled out onto the street and passed me. I went to follow suit, but my eyes caught on the front door of the club, where Gabriele and several of his men lingered.

His attention came from Roxy's car, and then he looked at mine, drawing back on another cigarette before he tossed it to the sidewalk and snuffed it out with his shoe.

I pulled away from the curb and dragged the steering wheel down to perform a U-turn, heading in the opposite direction to Roxy. It meant taking the long way home to Lily's, but it gave me some control over the situation if he had us followed.

I wasn't sure anything would happen. The prick could just be playing mind games. Regardless, the speed limit was only an option as I gunned the engine.

I let myself into the apartment and went straight to Lily's bedroom, where the lamp was on and even more light was streaming from her bathroom. Her laptop sat open on her bed, playing music, while a small cardboard box with a brightly colored label sat beside it. It was packaging for something round and small, according to the vague images on the side, but I barely processed it as I rushed to the bedside by the window and crouched down.

My hands fumbled for the travel bag under the bed before I took the handle and flipped the bag onto the covers.

"You're back early." Lily stopped in the bathroom doorway, but the pleasant look on her face disappeared as she saw what I was doing.

My thoughts, however, were quickly snagged by what she was wearing: A baby blue, satin lingerie-type dress. The delicate fabric clung to the top of her breasts and hung loosely over her body, yet somehow framed every curve and shape beneath.

And her legs.

Lily might've only been 5'3", but her legs were long for her stature.

If this was any other time— Holy fuck.

Lily wasn't as distracted as me. She frowned at the bag. "What's going on?"

I cleared my throat and moved to her dresser, where I began pulling clothes. Keeping them in their folded state, I shoved them into the bag. "We need to go."

"Why?" Despite her question, she began pulling on an oversized hoodie and leggings, leaving the lingerie on underneath, and whipped her freshly styled, wavy hair into a claw clip.

"Gabriele figured out what Antonio is doing. They know my first name." I zipped the bag. "Somethin' feels off, so I'm takin' you to your parents' place."

"No, wait—how would I be any safer with my parents than I am here? And what about your mom? We should stay at yours." She came around the bottom of the bed to be at my side, and then sat on the covers and crossed her legs.

"She's staying with a friend tonight— He hasn't seen her face, and doesn't know our last name. But you." I stopped what I was doing to look solely at her. "Gabriele knows your face."

Lily's throat bobbed, and the slightest hint of fear settled in her blue eyes.

On the road to her parents, I watched my mirrors to make sure we weren't being followed.

Lily sat quietly in the front seat, playing with the hem of her hoodie as she glanced out the window. Every so often, she would uncross and cross her legs. Or wrap her arms around her middle.

The silence was deafening.

When I glanced at her side-on and noticed that she was chewing the inside of her cheek, I placed a hand on her thigh and squeezed gently. It pulled her attention off whatever was going on in her head, and she smiled faintly, but the worried crease between her eyebrows remained.

CHAPTER 29
Seb

I hung up after the call to Anita, who was less than pleased about staying alert about a potential threat from a gang member. She decided going on an impromptu family road trip to Mom's was a better option than hiding at home, but she had many strongly worded opinions to get off her chest first before our phone call ended.

At the same time, Kira distracted herself by flipping through my record collection under the one window in my tiny apartment — the place consisted of a kitchen, bedroom and living room in the one small space, and a bathroom off the kitchen that was more like a cupboard with a shower head and toilet inside. But it was tidy, unlike the rest of the apartment block, and Kira seemed to like it the second she came through the front door when she exclaimed, "Oh, it's so cute in here!"

That was right before Dean called with the bad news; Gabriele and his sisters were aware of shit and that wasn't good. Everyone was on temporary lockdown, including us.

I tossed my keys and phone on the bed and ran my hands over my shaved head to interlock my fingers behind my neck.

Kira straightened from my record collection and pressed her lips together tightly as she paused by the window. "So."

I half smiled. "Do you regret getting involved with a fighter?"

She shrugged off the comment. "Aiden got me involved."

"Yeah, but he wasn't fighting. Or working for a crime boss." I peeled off my jacket.

"It's scary, yes, but no regrets." She wandered over, unlooping her hessian bag from her shoulder and placing it on the floor by the counter. "Some sleazy, criminal, night club owners aren't going to stop me exploring this." She slung her arms around my shoulders and leaned into me.

My hands went to her waist, and slowly, we began to sway from side to side. "You know it means we have to lay low for some time? Which means maybe staying indoors for more than a few days. Ordering food. Maybe staying in bed more often."

"What a shame." Sarcasm pulled at the corners of her mouth.

"Right? We might have to start running up and down the stairs for exercise."

"If only there was another activity we could do that would have the same results." She tapped her chin in thought. "I think we should think it over in bed."

"Agreed."

She grinned, taking my hand as she backed towards the bed. "We brainstorm so well."

"Oh, I'm gonna brainstorm you so hard it'll blow your mind." I scooped her up, and she squealed with laughter as we tumbled onto the covers.

I held myself above her with one of my thighs planted between her legs as we kissed. When her fingers came to the hem of my shirt, tickling my abdomen beneath, I was more than eager to oblige and helped her tug it off.

There was no hesitation or awkwardness with us. No reservations. It was the easiest whatever-this-was I had ever fallen into, and I had no plans of going back.

Kira's fingernails trailed along my scalp and down the back of my neck before she pulled her mouth from mine.

"Can I be on top this time?" There was a hesitant look in her eyes that made me wonder if she had been told *no* to that question before.

I immediately flipped onto my back and slapped the top of my thighs. "I am so fucking ready for this."

A belly laugh erupted from her before she moved on top of me. With a knee on either side of my waist, she settled down on me and gathered her fiery red hair to one side as she leaned in to kiss me.

My hands drifted up her smooth thighs as I got lost in the taste and smell of her.

Even though we kissed seconds earlier, this one sent a whole new rush through my system. Like a factory reset followed quickly by a system upgrade when she trailed her hands down my front. She followed every dip and edge of my chest and abdomen, like she was memorizing every inch.

My stomach dipped when her hands got lower, and goosebumps raised my skin. My jeans were too tight, and she knew it. Her kisses grew heavier, and she rolled her hips in curious, slow strokes. She straightened away from me, planting a hand on my stomach as she moved.

It was like looking at the human equivalent of the sun — a very sexy, highly aroused sun — and I was completely mesmerized.

I was the moth to her flame.

I shook my head in disbelief. "You are so fucking beautiful."

A half smile came to her lips, right under the blush on her cheeks, before she reached for the hem of her top and peeled it off. Her bra was next, and she removed it tantalizingly slowly before she cast it aside. She then crawled off the bed and put on a show of wriggling free of her jeans.

I tucked my hands under my head to watch, completely dazed by the woman before me. She had curves and subtle hip dips, long legs, and skin decorated with tiny moles. I wanted to play connect the dots with my tongue and each spot on her skin.

There was a playfulness to her movements, and while I had no clue where she was taking this, I enjoyed every second of it.

Her thong was the last thing to come off until she stood naked by the bed. She didn't join me, though, and looked over at the kitchen counter. An idea was brewing in that beautiful mind of hers.

When Kira's attention was on me again, she began to back away from the bed, smiling as she wiggled her finger in a come-hither motion.

I immediately propped up onto my elbows, hard as a rock in my pants, while my throat bobbed. "We aren't brainstorming in bed?"

"Eventually." She practically purred the word as she turned and approached the kitchen, where she walked in behind the small counter area. Her body was hidden from view as she leaned on the linoleum surface. Chin in palm, waiting. "Can you brainstorm outside of the bed too?"

I couldn't remember leaving the bed or grabbing a fistful of condoms from my nightstand drawer, but suddenly I was behind her. With her body flush against mine, I slid my hands down her sides and admired her curves.

She breathed my name like it was her lifeline and reached back to undo my fly.

I took over, unclasping the button and pushing my pants and briefs down. My cock sprung free at full attention, ready for duty.

Kira turned her head with her lips parted, and curled her hand around my shaft before guiding it to her glistening warmth. She slid the tip over her entrance several times as I watched, burning in her grasp while I held her hips firm.

The condoms on the counter, which I had hastily thrown down, were almost becoming an afterthought. Before that could happen, I grabbed one, tore it open, and rolled it on.

She arched her ass back, offering herself as I realigned myself to her and slowly edged forward.

Kira hummed and pushed back onto me.

I was plunged into her core, settling into a depth so right, my eyes rolled back.

Kira let out a breathy laugh, one I hoped was in disbelief or pure ecstasy. She leaned forward, hands sliding along the counter's surface before she gripped its edge. Her red curls slid from her back, exposing the dimples by her spine

— perfect little dents to place my thumbs — and the small sunflower tattoo between her shoulder blades.

The angle she was at opened her up to me and I began pulling out and then sinking all the way back in again, gradually building a pace until every time I thrust my hips flush against her ass, she was moaning.

I revelled in those noises and needed more of them.

I cupped her breast, the soft skin like butter in my palm, and brought the other hand to the front of her throat. All the while, I was thrusting into her hard and slow. I gently applied enough pressure to her throat that it was more of an invitation for her to straighten and bring her mouth to mine than a form of control. I would never want to control her. That untamed, free spirit she had was what I liked the most.

At this angle, each stroke of my cock was right up against *that* precious spot. The one that caused her to moan the loudest until nothing came out. There was a faint smile in the corner of her mouth as it happened. She was enjoying every second, and I loved that it was me who provided it for her.

I brought my hand from her throat and traced it down to her clit. The bundle of nerves was hot to the touch, and she whimpered the second I pressed my finger to it.

"I-I'm going," she panted, splaying her fingers on the countertop, "to c-cum."

I smiled easily. "Already? We haven't even started brainstorming yet."

Who was I to talk? I was ready to burst the second she sat on my crotch.

She whimpered in response, closing her eyes as she shuddered. Her legs started to tremble.

"I want to see your eyes when it happens." I planted an open-mouth kiss on her shoulder and gently pulled out.

Kira turned around, and I hoisted her onto the counter and sank right back into her. This time, the motion made her breasts bob as she lay back on the surface.

"We'll need to find—*oh sweet Jesus*—we'll need to find a place that delivers bubble tea." Her words temporarily blindsided my train of thought.

More like train of dirty thoughts.

She actually wanted to brainstorm our plan to stay indoors.

"Hell yeah, we do," I responded, positioning my hands on her waist. "And movies."

Thrust.

"Lots."

Thrust.

"And Lots."

Thrust.

"Of."

Thrust.

"Movies."

Her thighs squeezed against my sides as she hummed a moan through her lips and dropped her head back. Those red curls cascaded down the other side of the counter. I couldn't see it, but I could picture it. Like a painting in my mind, she was stunning.

And getting close to finishing.

Sweat gleamed on our skin, and suddenly, I didn't care about labels for whatever this was between us. As long as I could spend time with Kira, fucking her or not, I didn't care about anything else.

"Look at me, Kira."

She rose to her elbows. Head tilted to rest on her shoulders, eyes barely open, and brows pinched tightly. At the same time, she was squeezing me from the inside, building towards that final release.

We're more than friends—She's my everything—Don't say I love you *because that'd be weird.*

I bore down, ready to finish, and she brought her fingers to her clit, pleasuring herself too. The sight caused my dick to throb before I smashed my mouth to hers and raced us to that final wall holding everything at bay.

She cried out against my mouth and then came hard, her body quaking.

I think my brain exploded as I followed suit.

Holy shit.

Still deep inside her, I leaned forward and braced my hands on the counter on either side of her body as I caught my breath.

"You good?" Her smile was a mix of exhaustion and pleasure.

I panted as I held up a finger. "One moment."

She laughed, bringing her arms up around my shoulders as she waited patiently.

Once I dredged up enough strength to move, I lifted her from the countertop and brought her back to the bed while kissing her slowly. Relief instantly flooded my muscles the second I was beneath the covers, right beside Kira, who hadn't stopped smiling since we got into bed.

I rolled onto my side to face her, unable to contain my own smile. "What?"

She lifted her hand from under the covers and waited for a high-five. "Great brainstorming."

"You want to high-five us having sex?" I laughed softly.

"Uh, yes. Especially after that. It was a solid team effort."

I squinted slightly, pondering sarcastically. "Um, I'm pretty sure I did most of the work."

She sat up, leaving the covers to fall to her stomach, and poked my chest playfully. "Did you not see the strip tease I put on before? It got you out of bed pretty quickly."

I rolled my eyes, still smiling. "Okay fine. Team effort."

"Hell yeah." She held up her palm again. "Don't leave me hanging, Sebastian."

I laughed and gave her that high-five, only to thread my fingers through hers and pull her close. She rolled over so her back was to my chest, and I wrapped my arms around her.

We were snuggling like we hadn't just fucked like crazy.

"You have no idea how happy I am because of you," Kira whispered. She hugged my arm closer to her chest. "You make me feel whole."

CHAPTER 30
Dean

I eyed every shadow in the street as we walked towards Lily's parents' place, passing the manicured lawn with her travel bag in hand. The windows of the two-story home were glowing gold with light, and unlike most of the other houses in the street, the Whitmores' had gone without Halloween decorations. Which put my nerves at ease. Those decorations made it hard to decipher at first glance what was a ghostly prop and what was someone standing in the shadows.

As we reached the porch, the front door of the suburban home was pulled inward, revealing Kate and Mark on the other side.

Kate was less than pleased to see me, but pulled Lily into a hug and into the house. "Oh, I'm so glad you're home."

I stepped over the threshold as Lily looked at me from over her mother's shoulders, widening her eyes. "It's only temporary, Mom."

At the same time, Mark and I barely acknowledged each other apart from a curt nod. Kate had no clue we were working together, and Mark wanted it to stay that way, so we played the parts of a protective, conservative father and an unwelcome boyfriend.

Pretending we hadn't talked on the phone during the drive over, when I filled him in with what was going on, came easy.

Jane popped her head around the corner at the end of the hallway with a proud grin. "*Salve, Dean.*"

I half smiled. "*Come stanno andando le lezioni?*"

The younger Whitmore paused in thought and cringed with apprehension. "*Bene?* I think? Or is it *Buono?* No, Buono is the greeting—"

"Jane. I think we've heard enough Italian for one night," Kate said, hiding her disdain with a smile as she kept an arm around Lily.

Jane rolled her eyes and walked away.

"So," Kate started, leading us all down the hallway as she kept that arm around Lily. "I suppose I am making up the guest room for *him*?"

"Mom." Lily stepped out from under Kate's arm as we moved into the back of the home, where the large, warm kitchen and dining room overlooked the yard. "He can stay in my room."

Mark cleared his throat. "We have rules here, Lily."

I pushed my hands into my pockets. "Actually, I won't be stayin'."

Lily's attention snapped to me with a small frown and a question on her lips, but she didn't say anything. Meanwhile, Jane, sitting at the kitchen counter on her phone, huffed in disappointment.

Kate looked ready to pop a bottle of champagne. "Oh. What a shame... Anyway, Lily—"

"I need to get my bag upstairs," Lily stated. She turned to me, forcing a smile and an unspoken request; *Can we talk?*

"Yep," I said tightly.

She headed for the stairs, and I followed.

The last time I visited her old bedroom was at her family's BBQ so many months ago, but I hadn't paid attention to the photos on the wall. I was too busy wondering about my feelings towards Lily to notice them. This time, however, as we neared her room, a small picture on a wall table caught my eye.

Lily looked about twelve or thirteen in it. She wore round glasses and held the neck of a violin as she smiled for the camera.

Lily hadn't noticed my pause by the photo as she went into her room at the end of the hall.

I kept moving, bringing her bag with me as I entered the room, and she stopped in the middle of it.

I placed the bag on the bed. "You gonna be okay?"

"Not really." She smiled, but it wavered. "At least I'll save money on public transport while I carpool to work with Mom..."

The situation wasn't ideal, but knowing she was safe here put my mind at ease.

Until I remembered what day it was.

"Holy shit. It's Monday."

"Yes?"

"How was your appointment with the psych?" I raised my eyebrows expectantly as my hands left her face.

"Maybe I should share my calendar with you and Kira— It's next Monday."

"My bad—"

Lily took my hand and spoke quietly. "Please stay."

"They know my car, Lily."

"Okay, but...would they really search the suburbs?" She half smiled, trying to convince me things weren't so serious. Her eyes flicked across my face with a sort of desperation before her feigned happiness dropped. "I'm serious, Dean. You can't leave me here—"

There was a light but abrupt slew of knocks on the doorframe, and Lily suddenly pulled back. Clasping her hands in front of herself, she put on a pleasant, unbothered mask.

I looked over my shoulder to find Kate standing in the doorway.

Her lips were pursed, as if the words she wanted to say tasted sour. "I came to ask if Dean is staying for dinner..."

Lily and I looked at each other briefly. Her gaze reiterated the plea from seconds ago.

When I gave her a small nod, she let out the faintest of sighs and relaxed her shoulders.

"He is," Lily said to her mother. "If that's okay with you?"

Kate painted on another of her fake smiles. I swear I saw her eye twitch too, as the polite response left her mouth. "Why wouldn't it be?"

The tension in the room was minimal, but there. We ate in near silence save for the sound of knives and forks scraping on plates, or the soft *thunk* of a wine glass being set on the table.

Mark was at one end of the table, and Kate the other, while Jane sat opposite Lily and me, my seat being between Lily and her dad's.

After another sip of her wine, Kate set the glass down and turned her attention to Lily. She reached across to her daughter's hair, briefly playing with the ends as she scrutinized the golden-brown waves. "You're growing out your hair?"

I chewed my sirloin steak a little slower and cast my gaze side-on to her end of the table, and then to Lily beside me too, to gauge how she felt about the question.

Lily smiled politely at her mother. "I don't think I want to cut it yet..."

"Oh dear... We should organise a day at the salon to get our hair styled together. Sometime after the open house this Wednesday. Just us girls," Kate beamed.

"What a good idea," Mark threw in.

"Please, god, no," Jane muttered.

Lily brushed her hair behind her ears. "I kind of like it longer—"

"Shorter hair is much tidier," Kate said matter-of-factly, lifting her glass and swirling the white wine within it. "And easier to keep. It also looks more professional. Especially since you are one of the first faces our clients see when they come to the office. I think you should get at least a trim—"

"No!" Lily blurted.

Everyone stopped eating.

Beneath the table, I placed my hand on her thigh to comfort her, despite the fact my jaw ticked with irritation.

Lily took a breath, lowering her tone. "I want to grow it out. It's my hair."

"Well." Kate bristled. "I was only making a suggestion. There was no need to snap…"

"Was it a suggestion, though?" My question flipped everyone's attention to me.

Except for Kate's as she sipped her wine.

"I asked you a question, Kate," I said, keeping the tone in my voice as civil as possible. I doubted my expression matched it.

Lily stayed silent. There was no indication she wanted me to stop — one look from her and I would.

"That's enough," Mark warned.

Kate fiddled with the napkin in her lap, but she still couldn't look at me. "That was a discussion between my daughter and I."

"Seemed more like an ambush."

"The conversation is over." Her eyes were full of loathing when she brought them to me. "If you plan to stay the night, you will respect that."

I smirked, unable to help myself when I gave Kate my full attention, resting my forearm on the table. "Why don't you tell me how you really feel about me being here?"

"How dare you—"

"I said that's enough," Mark repeated.

Lily's hand came to rest on top of mine on her thigh, and I settled back in my seat.

Across the table, Jane promptly stabbed her fork into multiple vegetables until she had a small stack. "If I'm still going to the salon, can I get my hair dyed blue?"

The corner of Lily's mouth twitched before she covered it. At the same time, I looked down and shook my head in amusement.

"No," Kate and Mark stated in unison.

CHAPTER 31
Lily

"I think it's dry," Jane said.

"Sorry?" I blinked, straightening away from where I was trying to eavesdrop beside the kitchen doorway. I looked down at the plate and dishcloth in my hands. "Oh."

"What are they talking about?" Jane whispered as she washed the dishes.

"Dad said he needed to have the *dad talk* with him." I rolled my eyes as I put the plate away.

"Ah, yes, the good ol' parental cock-block—"

"Jane." Mom walked into the kitchen, disposing of a vase of flowers with a frown on her face directed at us. Mostly Jane. "I do not want to hear that word come out of your mouth again, got it? It's vulgar."

"It's only vulgar based on the context." Jane returned her attention to the dishes. Meanwhile, our mother's lips were becoming more pursed by the second. "Anyway, what if I wanted to start referring to roosters as cocks?"

"Jane, that's enough."

"You know there's a type of bird called a Booby? And another one is called a Dickcissel?"

I turned away, fighting a smile as I grabbed another plate to dry.

"My favorite is the Bushtit," Jane said, already smiling.

My attempt to stifle a laugh failed and resulted in me blowing a brief raspberry before I slapped a hand over my mouth. At the same time, right as Mom was about to give Jane another warning, Dad and Dean appeared in the doorway. Both looked equally confused by the conversation they walked in on.

Mom shook her head in disappointment, shock riddling her features. "I should ground you."

"But I already am, so..." Jane put emphasis in her shrug and turned back to the dishes.

In a huff, Mom grabbed several small plates from the cupboard, a premade cheesecake from the fridge, and then marched back into the dining room to prepare for dessert. Dad, on the other hand, only deadpanned at Jane.

"What? I learned it all from David Attenborough," she shrugged innocently.

Dad didn't respond. At least to her. Instead, his attention went to Dean beside him, and his expression grew stern. "I meant what I said, alright?"

"Understood." The smile Dean gave him was one of pure sarcasm.

Dad's eyes narrowed on him slightly — a last-ditch effort to make sure that warning truly sank in — before he left to be with Mom in the other room. She was making an effort to make more noise than was needed while plating dessert.

Dean pushed his hands into the pockets of his jeans and leaned against the doorframe. "What did we walk in on by the way?"

Jane grinned over her shoulder. "The all-important lesson on vulgar bird names."

"It spiraled from cock-block," I explained before looking at Jane. "Why are you grounded?"

"My grades were below average. You know how it is with her... I passed, but not to our mother's standards— You dropped out of school, right?" she asked Dean.

He pulled away from the door frame as he moved to stand by me, resting a hip against the counter as he crossed his arms. There was a faint smile on his face. "Yeah, but I don't recommend doin' it if you're good at school."

Jane groaned and scrubbed the next dish with a little more force. "I can't wait to move out."

I pouted and pulled an arm around her. "You could come live with Kira and me."

"Tempting, but I don't want to be another cock-block for you guys," she mused.

Dean cleared his throat. At first, I wondered if it was because of my sister's insinuation, until he tipped his head to the doorway.

Jane and I looked over our shoulders to where Mom stood, once again shocked by the word she overheard — and possibly the idea of Jane moving out. The expression was brief before she raised her chin.

"Dessert is served." She didn't bother waiting for a response as she left.

"I can already feel that lecture brewing," Jane muttered as she pulled off the gloves.

She left the kitchen first, and we followed her into the hallway. Except while Jane went to the dining room, I slowed to a stop, taking Dean's sleeve to indicate he do the same.

He looked at me quizzically.

"What did you and Dad talk about? Was it the case? Or Antonio? Is he pulling you from this whole thing because Antonio's kids know things?"

A lopsided smile graced his features, and he shook his head. "Not really. Actually, he told me to do as Antonio says. Play by ear, so to speak... What he really wanted to talk about was his rules."

"Wait. He actually gave you *the talk*?"

"While I'm under his roof, I'm not allowed in your room. If he catches me *in* your room, he'll probably shoot me."

"And you're going to be a complete gentleman and not break that rule?"

"You know me well."

I hummed in irritation and crossed my arms.

The plans I had for tonight had already been ruined by one man — Gabriele and his unspoken threats — and any attempt to revive them were just dashed again by my father's slightly misogynistic house rules.

I shaved, for fuck's sake.

Yes, it was disturbing to know the triplets figured out Antonio's oddly avoidant plan and that they were possibly — but hopefully not — planning some type of revenge, but tonight I made the mistake of wearing something extra that was in no way helping my situation. It was drawing my attention to slightly more urgent needs. Pleasurable needs.

Dean raised an eyebrow, smirking. "What *did* you have planned tonight? Because what you're wearing under this is...somethin' else." He brought his fingers to one of the drawstrings on my hoodie and twirled it around his middle finger.

It was hard to stay annoyed when he looked at me like that. "Just...things."

"What things?"

"Distractions."

"Yeah?" He pinched the front of my hoodie and gently pulled me closer, cocking his head back as he looked down at me through hooded eyes.

"Pity you're too much of a gentleman to find out. Considering the rules."

He smiled and ground his jaw a little. "Good point—"

"We're waiting." My mother's voice cut through the moment, and we pulled apart. She stood outside the dining room with a hand on her hip.

"Coming, Mom." I smiled until she left, and then dropped my forehead to Dean's chest with a groan.

He chuckled and pulled me into a hug, resting his chin on my head. "It's just for a couple of days. At least until shit cools down."

"You are severely underestimating my mother's ability to drive me insane."

It was hard to focus on the movie when all I could think about was Dean's hand. Or rather, where it was placed.

We were beside each other on the couch. Dean was sitting casually —
completely unaware of what his touch was doing to me — while I had
my leg, the one closest to him, tucked up against my body with his arm
wrapped around it and his hand placed under my thigh. Every so often,
he massaged the spot absentmindedly — an unintentional caress that was
creating several intentional thoughts in my head.

I wanted him to slide his hand down to find out what he was doing to
me. I wanted him to kiss me against a wall, any wall. I wanted him to spread
me beneath him and press his body to mine. I wanted that distraction
because that way I wouldn't have to worry about staying in this house, or
wondering if my boyfriend was being tracked by a criminal.

Where we sat on the sofa, in front of the living room window, was a
casually strategic choice by Dean. The window behind us faced the street,
and there was a small gap between the curtains that provided enough
viewing space to peer out into the night.

After looking once more through that gap, he brought his attention back
to the living room and caught me watching. He squeezed the underside of
my thigh with a question in his eyes.

"I'm a little warm." I pinched the front of my hoodie and fluffed it out
for emphasis, causing a rush of cool air to skim down beneath the thick
fabric. It danced along the front of my body and the lingerie beneath,
which tickled my skin with the light disturbance.

I'm going to explode.

When Mom stepped into the living room, the feeling waned.

"The guest room is ready for you." The words were directed more to the
room than at Dean.

"Thanks, Mrs. Whitmore."

I frowned at him, slightly amused by his use of formality, and he
shrugged, hiding a smile of his own.

Mom fixed her neat bob with a quick flick of her head. "We also have a
curfew, remember?"

How could anyone forget? The 9:30 PM curfew was a strict rule the
entire family followed to get a good night's rest. At least, that's the excuse
Mom made and Dad agreed to in order to control the whereabouts of Jane
and me. Even though I no longer lived at home, Mom expected me to
continue following that rule while visiting.

"I remember, Mom," I said.

"Jane, that means you too."

Jane, sitting in an armchair and tapping away on her phone, rolled her
eyes and lazily got to her feet. "Aye-aye, Captain."

"I'd appreciate it if you dropped the attitude," Mom said as Jane passed her in the doorway. Her attention then came to Dean and me, and she raised her brow expectantly.

I pressed my lips together as Dean unraveled his arm from around my thigh. "That's our cue," I muttered.

It wasn't until we were on our feet that Mom left the room and headed upstairs to join Dad.

After flicking off the TV, Dean and I eventually made our way to the stairs but paused at the bottom. With the guest room downstairs and at the back of the house, he wouldn't be coming up with me.

I stood one step up from the ground level, almost his height, as I shared a small smile with him.

"See you in the morning," he said quietly as the silence of the house closed in around us.

I hummed, reluctant to move. "Don't be surprised if my mother has forced me into a chastity belt before then."

"I can pick a lock." He winked and made to kiss me. As our lips brushed, the upstairs light went out, blanketing us in darkness. A not-so-subtle hint from my mother, who had been eavesdropping from above.

I exhaled through my nose but brought the subject back to us. Never mind if she was still listening. "You don't have anything to wear for bed."

"Wasn't planning on stayin' the night, remember?" Dean momentarily looked to the top of the stairs and spoke a little louder. "I'll have to go full commando."

A door closed upstairs.

I sighed and reluctantly moved up another step. At least then there was a gap, and I would be less likely to jump into his arms and insist he take me with him. *Maybe.*

I could still jump from here...

"Goodnight," I mumbled.

"Night, Lily."

His voice. It was like my kryptonite. It made me hesitate and resist the urge to groan with irritation when I eventually turned around and climbed the stairs. Passing my parents' closed door, and then Jane's, I got to my room and shut my door with a soft click.

The room was dark save for the moonlight coming through my window.

My hand remained on the doorknob as I pressed my forehead to the cool, white door panel. And then forced myself to step back and go to bed. On the way, I stripped off the hoodie and peeled off the leggings to reveal the crinkled satin lingerie beneath. It was one of two things I had bought today and put on with the plan for Dean to remove them. Instead, I was standing in my old bedroom, with a mound of stuffed bears staring at me from the bay window across the room while I daydreamed about being railed by my boyfriend.

Who was just downstairs!

"Fucking great plan that was, Lily," I grumbled, flopping backwards onto the bed.

I had no intention of going to sleep yet. I was too flustered, overstimulated, and maybe a little desperate for touch as I pressed my thighs together.

Closing my eyes, I let my hand wander down until my phone buzzed on the nightstand.

I swiped it up and quickly opened the text from Dean.

Dean: I don't think I can sleep...

Me: Neither.

I rolled onto my stomach, chewing my bottom lip as I thought of what else to say. Dean was one step ahead, and a call from him quickly flashed across my screen. I answered immediately.

"This is stupid," I whispered.

"I'm surprised they let me stay."

"I'm surprised they haven't tried locking our bedroom doors as a precaution." I rolled onto my back again, causing the lingerie to lift with the twisting motion.

Dean's voice dropped slightly in a way that made my skin prick. "And why would they need to do that, Lily?"

I grinned with mischief. "You tell me."

"To stop me kissing you."

"Is that all?"

"It wouldn't be your mouth."

I pressed the phone to my chest for a second to settle myself before speaking again. "*God*, I wish tonight went differently."

"Now that I'm lyin' here with nothin' on my mind but you and that dress, yeah me too. I'm gonna go insane."

"Hold on," I smiled, and quickly flicked on the lamp by the bed before posing myself for a photo. I wasn't completely nude as I positioned the dress on my body. I wanted to leave something to the imagination as I angled the phone above me and snapped several photos before sending him one. "Did you get it?"

There was a pause as he opened the text, followed by a heavy sigh on his end. "*Fuuuuck.*"

I trailed a finger slowly and lightly down my body and then back up again. "It does not help that I'm wearing kegel balls."

"You're wearin' what now?"

"Kegel balls." I chewed my lip again, smiling at the confusion and curiosity in his voice.

"And...what do they do?"

"Well, Kira recommended them. Part of her meetings is all about embracing sexuality after a bad relationship. And although I'm not in a bad relationship, she said kegel balls strengthen your pelvic floor and improve arousal, which is good for overall healthy sex, etcetera. I bought them today and thought I'd test them before you got home..."

"How do you use them?"

I shifted my hips, squeezing. "Insertion."

"And you didn't get the chance to take them out before we left the apartment." The timber in his voice was giving me heart palpitations.

I groaned softly and whispered, "I am so fucking turned on right now I might actually combust."

There was a smile in his voice when he spoke again. "That explains a lot."

"It does?"

"You've looked hot and bothered all night. I thought it was your anxiety over the whole undercover investigation thing."

"Oh, the anxiety is still there. I'm conflicted." And desperate.

Sex since the shooting seemed to keep any reminders at bay.

"Want me to hang up so you can deal with it?" he teased.

"No, please, don't. I beg you."

"Beggin', huh?"

"I could do it on my knees..." I slid my free hand up beneath the satin of my dress and cupped my breast. "...while I touch myself."

There was rustling on his end of the line, followed by the sound of a zip and a soft grunt.

I grinned. "Are you touching *your*self?"

"Ah-huh." His voice was heavy with arousal. "Are you wet?"

"Very," I breathed.

"And you're still touchin' yourself?"

I slid my fingers down between my legs and felt where the silicone string for the kegel balls was. "It'd be better if it were you."

"This is fuckin' torture," he groaned.

I pictured him slowly stroking himself, and I spread my legs wider. "I've never had phone sex before. What if we tried that?"

He made a noise that sounded like a disagreement. "I wanna be inside you," he almost growled. "The picture is one thing, but knowing you're upstairs..."

"What would you do to me if I was down there?"

"We really doin' this?"

"It'll be interesting to see how long we last."

He huffed a strained laugh. "Trust me when I say I won't last long."
"Wait for me," I said breathlessly, sitting up and straightening out the dress.
"Uh... I'll try?"
"Dad never said anything about me not being allowed in the guest room."

CHAPTER 32
Lily

I hopped out of bed and tiptoed to my door like I was working a spy mission. Opening the door as quietly as possible and then closing it behind me without a peep, I continued into the hallway and kept my ears pricked for any indication of movement in the house.

I passed Jane's room, and then my parents' room, keeping my steps as light and quick as possible while inching towards the staircase. Just as I reached the landing, ready to make the quiet dash down the stairs, I stopped short when I almost ran headfirst into Jane sneaking up the stairs.

With a boy in tow.

The boy from the soccer game.

We all stopped like deer caught in headlights.

I crossed my arms over my chest in sudden awareness of what I was wearing. "Hi?"

"I won't tell if you don't," Jane whispered.

"Deal." I looked at the boy and smiled quickly. "I'm Lily."

"Finn." He gave me an awkward little wave.

"How old are you, Finn?"

"Lily," Jane hissed.

"I'm sixteen," Finn said, paired with a voice break.

"Okay. Just checking. Use protection if you—you know." I spun back around and took to the stairs again.

"*Dude?*" Jane quietly exclaimed.

I threw a grin over my shoulder as I reached the last step, and Jane shook her head. Blushing from head to toe, she took Finn's hand and dragged him quietly to her room.

I would talk to her about it some other time — how they met, what he's like. For now, though, I had one thing on my mind as I hurried through the downstairs in the dark, navigating furniture to avoid a stubbed toe. Only to run my hip into the corner of a side table instead.

I stifled a pained cry as I gripped the table's edge to keep it from rattling everything on top of it. The large lamp was my main concern.

After a beat, and with the guest room door in sight, I kept moving. My heart raced as I got closer to it, as if it were my first time all over again, and I slowed my steps until I was right outside the door.

I knocked lightly and waited.

When Dean didn't answer right away, I wondered if he heard me and made to knock again, except the door swung inwards, revealing a very naked Dean on the other side. His eyes darkened the second they fell on me.

I barely had time to study him in all his tattooed, nude glory — quickly trailing my gaze over every inch of exposed skin and muscle — before he hooked his hand around my back and pulled me into the room.

"You're brave answering the door like this." I fumbled to shut the door until Dean simply pressed me into it.

The door closed with a quiet click as Dean angled his head. "I liked my chances."

Our mouths clashed, moving with passion and heat while I pushed him back, walking him towards the bed. His touch grew with need as he pushed himself against me. With our bodies so close, his semi rested against my stomach and wrinkled my lingerie in the process.

I wrapped my arms around his neck and rose to my tiptoes for more.

His fingers skimmed up my sides, lifting the dress to fall over his wrists as his thumbs brushed over the curve of my breasts. In turn, he devoured the kiss with heavy breaths and grew harder against me.

"We have to be...quiet." I arched my head back as he kissed the column of my throat. "Their bedroom is right above us."

"Ah-huh." He dragged his mouth hungrily along my skin as he slipped one hand down between my legs.

My thighs squeezed around his hand at the touch, and then he found what he was looking for: the silicone string of the two silver kegel balls still inside me. With a gentle and teasing tug from him, they began to slip loose.

The kissing stopped as Dean pulled back inches from my face to watch my reaction. A hint of a smile sat in the corner of his mouth while a faint gasp escaped me.

My body squeezed around the balls, reveling in the way they massaged their way out until they plopped into Dean's palm with a faint click as the metal balls collided.

I thrummed around the subtle emptiness until Dean gently plunged his middle fingers into me, causing my hips to rock forward.

"Better?" he whispered onto my lips.

"Almost." I brought my hand between us and curled my fingers around the tip of his cock. When I began stroking down along his shaft, there was a soft thud nearby as he let the kegels drop to the floor.

His hands slid over the curve of my backside before he effortlessly scooped me up, spreading my legs around his waist so that the tip of his cock brushed against my entrance.

He could've slipped me onto him so easily, but decided to hold off until I was laying on my back, on the bed. He wasted no time giving us what we wanted.

As I sank into the covers, he sank into me with ease and a soft moan.

I needed this— I wanted it. More so than I ever had. It excited and scared me all at once, fluttering my heart and stomach as goosebumps raised my skin where Dean's lips traced my body. Across my neck and shoulders, he took his time as he slowly rolled his hips against me. But I needed more. More until every thrust had knocked every anxiety-filled thought from my brain.

When he brought his mouth to my breast, taking the lingerie fabric and my nipple between his teeth, a guttural moan left my body before I could stop myself.

Dean cupped a hand over my mouth, forcing me to finish the sound into his palm while my eyes rolled back.

"*You* have to be quiet," he smirked down at me.

I nodded against his hand, which he replaced with his mouth as he started thrusting steadily.

A different sound suddenly filled the room; obnoxiously loud creaking, coming from the bed.

He paused, stopping short of filling me completely again.

"Shit," he grunted.

I quickly looked around the room for an alternative, and then pointed at the windowsill seat. "There. Fuck me there, under the window."

"Not the words I ever expected to come from your mouth, but alright." He pulled up and got off the bed. His arm and back muscles rolled with the movements before he held out a hand to me.

His black hair was tousled messily, there was a playful gleam in his eyes, and his body...

My god.

In the darkness of the room, it was the moonlight pouring through the sheer curtain on the windows that outlined the edges of his body in a bluish hue.

I grinned, biting my lip, and placed my hand in his as if he were a gentleman offering me a hand from a cab. And like we weren't about to participate in some debaucherous activity under the moonlight that bordered on pornographic and would leave my legs quaking by the end of the night.

I left my hand in his until I perched myself on the window seat and lay back, spreading my legs for him.

At the other end of the seat was a bath towel to be used by guests in the guestroom bathroom on the other side of the room. Dean picked it up and motioned with his fingers for me to lift my hips. I did so immediately, completely aware of the thoughts running through his mind. It was written on his face too with a knowing smirk; We didn't have a condom, and the pristine, cream cushion cover beneath me was potentially too expensive to rinse in the basin later.

Dean gripped the backs of my knees as he knelt one of his own on the seat. When he brought himself closer, I angled my hips up until the tip of his cock pressed against me. He shifted his hands to my hips, watching what he was doing before he pushed his hips forward. Slowly at first, and then all at once, I was suddenly full again.

A quick gasp came out of me as my eyes wandered over his body. There was a muscle feathering in his lower abdomen as he began to move. Each of his strokes was purposefully slow and controlled.

With my hips raised off the seat, the night gown was jostled to my waist. For a second, my eyes caught on my scar, near white in the moonlight, and everything I hoped to forget quickly came rushing back in.

Dean changed the pace. Whether he noted the shift in my mood or not, he didn't mention it and instead lifted one of my legs to his shoulder. The position opened my hips to pleasure that once again blinded those thoughts. And completely removed the filter between my brain and mouth.

I gripped the edge of the seat. "*Yesss—*"

Dean's hand was over my mouth again as he chuckled breathlessly. "Quiet, remember?"

"*M-m-m—Mhm.*" A tingling took over my body, and I almost squealed.

That climax was coming in hard and fast. I was already dripping for it and fighting the urge to cry out as he hit the right spot every time.

As he moved his hand to my chin, a curious glaze washed over his eyes before he smoothed his fingertips along my bottom lip.

Through half closed eyes, I watched him and parted my lips enough for him to dip his fingers into my mouth. They slid over my tongue until his knuckles brushed my top lip. When his fingers parted, I curled my tongue between them.

It felt strange. I wasn't used to being like this, but it somehow came instinctively. And I liked it.

With my eyes locked on his, I slowly dragged his fingers from my mouth.

His eyes flashed, my leg dropped from his shoulder, and he smashed his mouth to mine, keeping the same rhythm with his hips but thrusting so much firmer. It made my head spin.

He was grappling with control, trying not to lose it. I knew he could go harder if he wanted. Rougher than we had, but he was holding back.

I found myself curious about that kind of pain.

His breathy whimpers and devastatingly addictive moans were what finally brought it to a finish.

I bit my lip to keep quiet. In turn, I raised my hips to meet him before he pulled my legs around his waist.

"Right. There," I gritted.

Dean posted his arms on either side of me. I gripped his biceps as my body arched. That familiar heady pleasure rushed south, and as he drove home the last of the steady rhythm, my body tensed and quivered.

He caught my mouth with his, breathing heavily and barely making a sound as his hips bucked over and over, spilling deep. I thrummed around him with whatever energy I had left, whimpering into our messy kiss and tangling my fingers in his hair.

My thighs trembled at his sides as he slowly rose again. Sweat gleamed on his skin, and I could still feel him finishing, throbbing until there was no more to give.

"Fuck," he panted heavily, glancing at my thighs. The sight of them quivering brought a smile to his mouth. He straightened the towel beneath us and held the base of his cock as he withdrew.

I closed my eyes at the sensation, giving him one last squeeze. Everything down there was completely sensitive to touch, especially when he lightly slid the tip of his cock over my clit. It sent one last orgasmic spasm through my body, and I laughed faintly because of it.

"Tease," I muttered, brushing my hair away from my face as he cleaned up. Me first, and then himself before he folded the towel in a way for me to have a clean side to rest on.

On slightly quaking legs, Dean huffed a laugh, lowered himself to the ground beside the window seat, and rested his head back on my bare thigh. His dark hair was soft against my skin.

"I'm happy you stayed," I said, speaking softly as I rolled onto my side and propped myself up on my elbow. The movement caused the strap of my lingerie to fall from my shoulder.

Dean tracked it with his eyes and raised an eyebrow. Turning in his place on the floor, he slung his arm up on the edge of the seat and placed a hand on my thigh. "Because of the sex?"

I nudged the back of his head with my thigh playfully. "I'm happy you're here with me. You keep me sane when it comes to dealing with my parents and everything else that's been going on."

His eyes softened, and he kissed my thigh. "I'm happy I stayed too. I don't think I would've been able to sleep if I didn't."

"Not that we've done a lot of that yet anyway."

"You're the one who snuck into my room."

"And you're the one who texted first."

"Only because you wanted me to stay."

"Because I knew you wanted to." I leaned closer to his face, screwing up my nose as I smiled.

He mirrored my expression but then kissed the tip of my nose. "Fair enough."

A little smug, I straightened where I sat and yawned.

Dean dropped his head back into my lap, pondering something as he looked ahead.

I couldn't help but admire his eyelashes. Why did guys always have such pretty eyelashes?

"Do you remember heading into the King's County Courthouse ten-ish years ago?"

The question was so random, I stalled before responding. "I guess? I'm not sure about ten years ago, to be exact, but I did go there a lot to meet up with Dad sometimes... Why?"

"I don't suppose you remember a young guy leaning against the wall outside it once? Puffing on a cigarette, thinkin' he was a badass..." He looked up at me. There was a nostalgic light in his gray-blue eyes.

I frowned and shook my head slowly. "No, I don't think so—"

The day of my first violin lesson.

I hated every second of that lesson and every one that followed — my fingers ached, the teacher was mean, and all I wanted to do was read or draw. That same afternoon, I was meeting with my dad at the courthouse after school before going home.

And there was a boy, with black hair, and sad gray-blue eyes, leaning against the building.

My eyes focused on Dean again as he watched me come to the realization. "No way."

All he did was smile up at me.

"That was you?"

"Who'da thought?"

I was happily speechless, until I remembered something else from that day — *someone* else. "Your dad... He held the door for me, didn't he?" The man who had brought so much pain and sadness to Dean and his mother had held the door for me.

And smiled at me.

Dean inhaled as he looked ahead. "Yep..."

I pressed my lips together, hit by a wave of empathy, and guided his head back to rest in my lap again. Providing enough distraction to pull him from those thoughts, I lightly brushed several dark strands of his hair from his forehead.

His eyes slid shut, and his body relaxed against the seat. After a moment, his eyebrows twitched with a thought.

"I've gotta ask..." He turned halfway around and slung his arm on the edge of the seat. It brushed against my thigh. "What happened to the glasses?"

"My eyes improved."

His mouth twitched. "Did you have a lazy eye or somethin'?"

I lightly back-handed his bicep as I laughed quietly. "I had bad headaches, you ass."

"Oh. I'm an ass, am I?" He raised his right eyebrow, putting emphasis on the scar running through it.

I brought my face closer, keeping my mouth inches from his. "Hottest ass around," I muttered, and kissed him.

He angled his head back for better access as my hands smoothed down to his chest.

There was a pattern of short pauses between each slow kiss, along with tongue and nibbling that sent butterflies zooming around my stomach.

Dean's heart thundered beneath my palm as he hummed deeply, and then moved his hand up my thigh, over my hip, and settled it on the side of my waist. When we pulled apart, there was a shadow of the smile from earlier still lingering on his face as he took in every inch of me with his lust-filled gaze.

I looped my fingers under the delicate hem of the lingerie and slowly peeled it up, leaving myself completely naked while my hair fell messily around my shoulders. He continued to watch, turning around to face the seat while I turned too. This time, I rested my back against the curtain — pressing it against the window pane — and parted my legs.

Dean's eyes dropped and he cocked his head back with a sigh as he crawled along the few inches of floor to me.

CHAPTER 33
Dean

The bed sheets rustled softly as I curled my arms further around Lily's naked waist and nuzzled the back of her neck, inhaling that sweet, sweet scent. She was soft and warm in my arms. I could've lived in that moment forever.

Our little revelation last night seemed to bring us closer than we already were.

That and the sex, obviously.

Lily began to stir, humming sleepily as she arched her body with a stretch. She nudged herself flush against me.

I lifted my head to get a better view of her face. I could see every freckle and count almost every one of her eyelashes.

I pressed my lips to her cheek and skimmed my hand up her arm. "You awake?"

She hummed again and turned her head to look back at me through barely open eyes. The corner of her mouth rose in a smile. "I am now."

"Morning." I moved my hand appreciatively down her body, following a familiar path to her hip. The touch wasn't meant to start anything.

Her eyes fluttered shut, and she inhaled slowly as she shifted her thighs, coaxing a reaction from me.

"Oh?" I was already half hard and steadily rising.

"Not what you had in mind?" she asked, glancing over her.

"I can't remember what I had in mind. Please, continue."

Lily rocked her hips slowly back and forth along my growing erection.

My palm skimmed to her breast as my lips formed a kiss on her bare shoulder.

She sighed, lifting one hand to the back of my head while the other went south.

I felt her fingertips touch us both. Then, as she kissed me with gentle hunger, she nudged the tip of my cock into her.

"*Fuck*, I love you," I grunted, my voice heavy with a sleep effected rasp as I prepared to delve deeper.

An abrupt round of sharp knocks rattled through the door, causing Lily to tense and me to jolt halfway into her.

Lily bit the pillow to keep from crying out while I muffled my growl of annoyance into her shoulder, gently biting her skin.

With my cock rock hard and half sheathed in her clenching heat, I mustered up a partially broken, "Y-yeah?"

"I know Lily is in there with you." Kate sounded impatient. "I already tried her room."

Lily pulled the bed sheet over her head with a quiet groan while neither of us dared to move anything below the waist. She emerged after a second. "Yes—Mom?"

"Breakfast is ready, so get up now. I don't want to be late for work."

"Got it," she grimaced, shutting her eyes and pressing her lips together as her legs squeezed.

I felt myself sink deeper, but I couldn't tell if it was a natural reaction or if I was subconsciously doing it, until Lily moved back, slowly drawing me into her.

I hummed softly, fighting the urge that was begging me to move — to fuck her. I couldn't help myself, and slid my hand to her other breast as I sank all the way in. Her nipple was hard against my palm.

Lily bent and raised her knee, creating room between her legs.

"I mean it, Lily. I won't be late."

Lily swallowed hard and masked the pleasure in her voice. "We'll be out in a minute."

Breakfast was a repeat of dinner last night, but with one more person in the room and way more glares coming from the Whitmore parents as they stood in the kitchen, sipping their coffee with disdain as they watched us at the small table by the kitchen island. The glares were aimed at their daughters, me, and Finn, Jane's secret boyfriend. Lily and I were in trouble for working around the rule of me not being allowed in her room; Jane and Finn were in trouble because he was caught trying to sneak out of Jane's room this morning before school.

While Finn and I shared similar situations of being the unwanted boyfriends, I kept an eye on him from across the table. My arms were crossed as I figured out what his intentions with Jane were.

Jane was Lily's little sister. She earned my protection through association. I was always going to be suspicious of any guy who showed interest in her.

Finn gave the impression of another privileged white boy with golden blonde hair. But instead of being boastful like they normally were, he was softly spoken, awkward, and polite.

"Why didn't you get him to climb down the trellis? It's right outside your window," Lily whispered to Jane, scooping cereal onto a spoon.

"Dad removed it after the last time."

Lily's eyes widened. "Last time?"

I shifted in my seat, also interested in hearing the answer with my eyes fixed solely on Finn.

"About a week ago." A smile came to Jane's mouth as she spoke. "Finn was caught going out my window to use the trellis. It got him banned from visiting the house." Her eyes flicked to me. "And nothing happened between us, so calm down, Cujo. We're aware it'd be illegal since we're underage."

I raised an eyebrow but loosened my arms.

Finn relaxed in his seat.

Lily gave her sister and the boy a gentle, sympathetic smile. "It is nice to meet you, Finn. Sorry about our parents."

"It's okay. I guess it's kind of on me for being bad at sneaking. Or climbing." He laughed nervously.

Jane picked up his hand and locked fingers with him. "You have much to learn, young buck."

After breakfast, we were ushered from the house with an unspoken warning: No more overnight stays at the Whitmore house for Finn and me.

When Mark headed for his Ford Mustang Mach-E, and Kate went to her Volvo, where she waited to drive Lily to work, Jane and Finn said their goodbyes while walking to where his bike was hidden beside the house.

Lily didn't move from the porch right away.

I waited beside her and slid on my sunglasses.

The Volvo's horn tooted three times.

"Just a few more nights," I said.

Lily huffed but nodded. "I know... I'll be counting down the days until you come whisk me away."

"Want me to bridal carry you out that door when this has calmed down?"

She smiled easily. "Yes, please."

Another round of impatient toots erupted from the Volvo, causing Lily's smile to fade as she rolled her eyes.

"We should go." She stepped away.

"Hold on." I took her wrist, gently guided her back towards me, and scooped her up in my arms.

I craved the laughter that bubbled out of her and the smile that remained on her lips as I carried her the entire way to the car.

As I set her feet down on the curb beside the Volvo, Mark drove off. I predicted I would get a text in a few minutes about heading to his office to talk about what happened last night — one event from the night would be queried heavily with scrutiny. The other would be about the subtle threat from Gabriele.

After Lily climbed into the car, her mother glared ahead in the front seat while Jane sat in the back, waving at her boyfriend as he rode away.

I closed the car door softly behind Lily, and she rolled down the window, motioning with her finger for me to lean in closer. And I did, bracing my hands on the side of the door as I duck my head into the car and kissed Lily, adding just enough tongue to leave her breathless.

Kate was breathless because she found it offensive, and begin to steer the car away from the curb while I withdrew from the window just in time. Her mother's abrupt exit didn't stop Lily from peering out the window. She grinned at me as the wind whipped through her hair, and blew me a kiss with a wave.

I'm the luckiest man alive, I thought as I watched the car drive from view, unable to wipe my own smile from my face.

Despite her parents being...difficult individuals, I felt a small weight lift from my shoulders. Lily would be safer here. Under her mother's constant watchful eye and her father's strict love for the law, she wouldn't be left unguarded.

CHAPTER 34

Dean

In several red and green cushioned booths, tucked away in the rear of a pizzeria, we all went silent as Antonio addressed us. With his bodyguards surrounding us, and Terry, his old bouncer from The Den, keeping watch at the door, anyone who wandered in for a pizza would think otherwise about staying.

Roxy stood on Antonio's left side wearing a black pantsuit and heels, looking more professional than anyone else here as she kept her chin high.

"After the revelations of last night," Antonio said. "I have decided to pull you all from Castello di Vetro. Especially since my children were so quick to retaliate and took one of our own early this morning."

There was a shift in the room between the other fighters.

Seb was beside me and pivoted his head to see who was missing from the group.

I couldn't remember the faces of the other fighters very well. It was down to pure laziness that I hadn't bothered to get close to any of them besides Seb.

"What happened to him?" another fighter said from the booth behind us. His voice was hoarse.

"Jacob's—or rather, The Viper's head was delivered to my front gates this morning. Along with his girlfriend's." Antonio planted his cane in front of himself and folded his hands over the golden eagle head on the top.

My stomach dropped. Okay, maybe I remembered one other fighter. The Viper was a Russian guy who barely spoke and fought with relentless precision, matching the reputation of the snake tattooed on his scalp. He fought on and off for Antonio, and sometimes versed us after Antonio instructed that we needed to work on our technique. He seemed untouchable until he and his partner had their heads lobbed off this morning.

If someone like him failed to protect his loved one, how the fuck were the rest of us meant to do it?

I crossed my arms while that familiar bounce started in my leg.

"If I am to rebuild another successful fight club, I need you all alive. Some of you will continue doing a few small jobs for me, but other than that, lay low, stay vigilant, and do not go anywhere near Castello di Vetro again."

"Seems easy enough for me," Seb muttered.

"After this meeting tonight, I will only contact you when I really need to. When this is all over, I will see you all here again." He spoke the words as if it was a promise we all had to keep.

Don't die before the next meeting, basically.

Without any further questions, we were free to go and walked out of the pizzeria one by one. I was the last to leave the booths when Vince approached me. Followed closely by Antonio while Roxy lingered nearby.

"The gun you asked for," Antonio said as Vince pulled the weapon from his jacket and offered it to me. A black 9mm with the serial number shaved off.

I took it, weighing it in my hand. Everything about the moment reminded me of the time Antonio handed me the gun I was meant to use the night my father died.

Vince stepped back, giving Antonio room to take his place in front of me. The mob boss put a hand on my shoulder and squeezed.

"I know I say this about all my fighters, that we are family, but you are important to me... You're like the son I never had." His words were meant to inspire something in me, but instead, they only made me hate the situation more.

Antonio implying he never had a son would only make Gabriele's anger worse — their retaliation worse. I couldn't help but think about how the words contradicted Antonio's actions in the past too. Anytime I spoke or stepped out of line in the past, there was a punishment. Those were almost no different from what my father did.

Checking the safety was on, I tucked the gun into the back of my jeans and pulled my T-shirt over it, moving my thoughts on to how I was to present it to Lily. There was nothing romantic about bringing a gun home to your girlfriend.

"Hey, babe. I've got that gun your dad wanted me to get. I know you were shot by one a few months ago, but hey, protection, right?"

Yep. Boyfriend of the fucking year.

None of this was good.

I headed for the exit with Seb and Roxy. For a moment, I was with my thoughts as we walked through the restaurant — I kind of wished I could empty said thoughts into the gutter and drive away. The bad thoughts anyway; the ones that reminded me of my shitty past; the ones that reminded me of my dim future. It was getting harder to stay in the present when my head was being torn in every direction.

"Why'd he give you a gun?" Roxy said, pulling me from my head.

"Protection." I held the door for Seb and her.

"Well, obviously. But why else?" she persisted.

"Can't say."

Seb, knowing exactly what the gun was for, pivoted as we stepped outside and pushed his fists into the pockets of his jacket. A cloud of breath escaped his mouth as he spoke into the cool night air. "Read the situation, Roxy. Maybe we should all get guns, considering how fast everything went south."

Roxy's eyes narrowed, and she curled her top lip. "You better not be blaming me for this."

Seb lifted his hands in defense. "Oh, I wouldn't *dare*."

She scowled at him and hugged her arms around herself to keep warm.

"I'm parked this way so I will see you guys when I see you." Seb tapped my shoulder by way of goodbye, and then sarcastically waved at Roxy as he strode down the sidewalk on our left and rounded the street corner at the end. All the while, casually scanning his surroundings.

It was safe to say we were all on edge.

"It's for Little Miss Goodie-Goodie, isn't it?" Roxy said from where she leaned against the pizzeria windows.

"Don't." I started walking.

She scoffed.

I agreed to walk her to her car after the meeting. That didn't mean we had to speak.

"You're hot when you get all protective over the Goodie—"

I abruptly stopped and deadpanned at her.

She rolled her eyes. "Fine."

I continued forward, keeping an eye on our surroundings. Unlike the night Roxy and I exited Castello di Vetro together, our cars were parked further away from the pizzeria. There were more dark alleys and empty shop fronts, creating plenty of hiding places for an ambush.

Or I was being paranoid.

The purr of a bike engine followed by several beeps pulled our eyes to the road as Seb rode by. He gave us a casual salute, leaned into his bike, and then sped off down the street in a blur of matte black.

Roxy sighed. "Long gone are the days of you fucking me over my kitchen counter, I guess..."

"I'm not even gonna respond to that."

She pulled out a flask from her suit jacket pocket and took a sip. Only to pause when she noticed me watching. "What? Our lives are in danger. May as well fucking live it up while we still can... Want some?"

"I'm good." I pushed my hands deep into my pockets. "Would kill for a cigarette though."

"Ha! I knew old Dean was in there somewhere." She pocketed the flask again and folded her arms, rubbing her hand up and down her biceps. "We were good together, you know... Well, the sex was." She paused to think before she continued. "I still don't understand how it was *her* over me."

"Better morals?" I drawled.

"Ha, fair." Somehow, she thought this conversation was light-hearted.

There wasn't a hint of amusement on my face. "You tried to have Lily killed off by making out she was reporting Antonio to the cops."

"Not my best moment, but you still came back."

"I was drunk and not in the right frame of mind. I thought things with Lily were over..." I looked down at the pavement and scoffed in disbelief. "You said yourself that Lily was good for me."

"You believed what came out of *my* mouth?" she chuckled. "That offer still stands, by the way. Not killing her, but fucking me. If you want something on the side."

"You're unbelievable." I fixed my eyes ahead. All I could think about half the time was getting home to Lily. There was no way in hell my mind could be swayed by another woman.

"You've really got it bad, huh?"

"Yep."

Her silence made me look at her. She was half smiling, considering me as if she was seeing something new before she huffed in amusement. "*God*, people in love are disgusting. Cute, but disgusting."

I half smiled. At least I got one thing in my life right.

Our pace slowed as we reached my car and stepped off the curb.

I paused near the taillight of the Cadillac, fishing out my keys as Roxy crossed the street to her Aston Martin.

The street was eerily quiet.

I could hear the city around us, but something was off.

"Hey, Roxy. Be careful." I don't really know why I said it.

She tossed her long, dark hair over her shoulder as she looked back, strutting across the street in her too-high heels. "Is that a hint of worry I hear? For me?"

"You heard what the boss said. Stay vigilant."

"Dean, I've got this. I'll lay low. Or maybe travel to my family's beach house in Miami." She unlocked the car with a shimmy and climbed into the front seat.

My lips twitched as I shook my head.

And then, for the first time since I met her, Roxy shared a smile that wasn't snarky or smug. It was genuine as she waved at me through the window and turned on the car, triggering a blast so powerful it flung glass and debris in all directions.

One minute I was standing on the road, the next I was thrown backwards. I hit the pointed rim of the taillight first, right on my hip bone, before my head connected with the sidewalk.

Pain rippled through my skull, and my vision blurred.

I couldn't hear or see anything; I couldn't hear anything but the ringing in my ears until everything came back in stages.

The street was vertical when my eyes finally adjusted, and my vision was bordered by blurry, flickering flames. The ringing in my ears grew into a sharp pitch at first, and then gradually faded into the rest of the noises on that street.

The crackle of fire, the pop of glass, the distant shouts, hurried footsteps, and screaming.

Blood curdling, raw screaming.

Roxy.

Gasoline and burning rubber clung to the air, creating a heady daze as I fought to stay conscious.

I sucked in a breath and held it as I rolled over with a broken groan, letting gravity do the rest before I slumped heavily onto my back, wincing as glass crunched beneath me and the gun in my pants pressed against my spine.

Eventually, I let that breath out, slow and steady as I watched the pillar of black smoke rise into the night sky.

CHAPTER 35

Wednesday. The day of my mother's anticipated open house.

Dad left for work this morning before the sun had risen. When I asked Mom about it over breakfast, she said she knew nothing and brushed off the topic as she called for Jane to get out of bed.

The first half hour of being awake felt normal as I sent Dean a text over breakfast, asking how last night went. I didn't think much about him not responding right away until I wondered if Dad's leaving early meant something else.

As I headed upstairs to get ready for work, I called Seb. He was at the meeting too, so he was bound to know if anything happened.

"I haven't heard from him since last night," Seb said, putting the call on loudspeaker so Kira could join. "I could drop by his place if you want?"

"Could you?"

"Maybe he broke his phone," Kira joked gently, referring to Seb's mishap from weeks ago.

I smiled a little but didn't feel completely convinced. "Maybe... I need to get ready for work. Talk soon."

Another hour later, I stood before the bathroom mirror, anxious and overstimulated from being back at my family home — living with Mom again felt like winding back several years of extremely slow confidence building. I was reminded of the reason why I wanted out to begin with. It was suffocating, more so than at work. At work, it was only a few hours of the day where I barely talked to Mom anyway.

But in her house was a whole other level of sanity challenging.

Take the conversation over breakfast about my hair, for example. She was adamant about bringing me to a salon, no matter how many times I said I didn't want it cut shorter.

So, with that discussion adding to my anxiety, I locked myself in the bathroom for a moment of peace.

I stared at myself a second longer and then straightened. "Fuck it."

I yanked open the top drawer below the basin and grabbed a pair of scissors and a comb. I might regret it later, but I needed to do something I could control.

Settling myself with a few breaths, I combed my hair and brought several strands in front of my face. I picked up the scissors next and got to work, snipping the golden-brown waves hanging across my face into soft bangs.

Cutting my hair might not have been the most rebellious act of protest in the history of protests, but it felt great. Possibly better than when I brought Dean to a conservative family barbeque — in hindsight, that was pretty fucking great too.

It was safe to say my mother did not approve of my new hairstyle when I finally emerged from the upstairs bathroom. She spotted me from where she waited in the kitchen, and her mouth dropped open, about to protest my new look before she snapped her mouth shut again and stormed by me on her way to the front door.

Jane walked by next, and she grinned at my hair. "I love it."

"Thanks." I adjusted the freshly cut strands as I stole a glance towards the front door as our mother walked outside. "So begins the silent treatment."

"At least you won't have to talk to her now," Jane shrugged, adjusting the strap of her school bag across her shoulder. Under her arm was a textbook for the Italian classes she was taking — classes Dean had offered to help with before my father intervened with the threat of arrest, prison, and his mother's deportation...

I felt the urge to scream, but opted against it since Jane was still in front of me. Mom would be all too happy to race back into the house and announce that dating a tattooed *bad boy* was the reason why I suddenly *flew off the rails* and cut my hair.

I wouldn't be surprised if she blamed my stomachache on Dean too.

I tried to keep busy, creating small talk with potential clients and handing out fliers as I stood in the kitchen of the recently renovated two-story home in South Bay Ridge. All the while, my mind was on my phone. I kept checking it, expecting a text from Dean, but found none.

At least none from him.

A text from Seb woke my lock screen.

Seb: Sofia said he never came home last night. I'll check in with the garage.

Chewing my nail, I braced my forearms on the stone counter. Its cool surface sent a chill through my body as I opened my phone contacts and tapped Dean's number.

As the call rang out, my eyes drifted to the entry hall of the house, where a large archway opened up the interior. I could see straight to the front door, where my mother was greeting two new potential buyers.

My stomach suddenly dropped at the sight of them. Of *him*.

Gabriele wore a crisp white shirt, unbuttoned at the collar, under a sapphire blue dress vest. Gold jewelry decorated his fingers, wrists, and neck, and his auburn hair was combed back neatly. The closely shaved edges made his features sharper.

He removed his sunglasses as he looked up at the high ceiling that my mother had pointed out. The man beside him, who I'm pretty sure was a bodyguard, did the same. When she encouraged them to look around and pointed them in the direction of the kitchen, I swiped up my things and promptly headed for the stairs. Which meant walking part of the way directly at him, and then making a sharp turn right.

I pretended I was busy looking through the applications on my clipboard as I hurried up the stairs, playing the part of a fussy real estate assistant while I hid my face behind my hair. Maybe the bangs would throw him off. Still, the last thing I needed was him finding out where I worked, in turn discovering my last name.

Just as I reached the landing, I released a breath but faltered when an Italian accented, "Excuse me, *signora*?" followed me up the staircase.

I pretended not to hear him and hurried down the hallway as he took to the stairs.

Shit, shit, shit, shit.

I ducked into the first bedroom on my left and contemplated going out the window, but settled for the conjoining bathroom instead. A great feature for any family home. For now, it was my lifesaver.

Right when I closed the bathroom door, Gabriele stopped at the bedroom door.

He had seen me, barely.

I rushed to the next bedroom, flicked the lock on the second bathroom door, and quietly closed it behind me before hurrying across to the next bedroom's door. I peeked out into the hallway as my heart pounded.

To get back downstairs meant passing the first bedroom again.

When the locked handle on the bathroom door rattled but failed to open, I took off in a quiet jog to the stairs, trying not to roll my ankle as my heeled shoes sank into the plush, cream carpet that lined the hallway.

Once I was downstairs, passing Gabriele's bodyguard, I composed myself and headed straight to Mom.

"I need to charge my phone. In the car," I said quickly and politely, picking up her keys from where they rested on a side table with her bag.

The arrival of more potential clients for her to win over saved me from the *no* forming on her lips, and I escaped the house to go hide in the Volvo.

I wasn't sitting in the car long before Gabriele and his partner stepped out of the house too, reapplying their sunglasses as they scanned the street.

As if the universe wanted to add more to this terrifying coincidence, they started walking directly towards the Volvo.

I shifted lower in my seat, despite the tinted windows hiding me well enough, and quickly opened the camera on my phone. I snapped as many photos as possible as they went by the windshield to cross the street. All the while, they took their time as they discussed something that clearly had nothing to do with the house.

I decided to film them instead.

"...Look into hospital records. Her name could be there if she's lived here long enough," Gabriele said to the man with him.

"Yes, boss."

"We're going to tear his empire apart," Gabriele continued, fishing out his phone as it rang, "Brick by brick, bone by bone, until there is nothing left but the inheritance he owes my sisters and me— *Salve, Lucia.*" His demeanor completely changed from irritated bad guy to a caring young man in an instant after he answered his phone.

I wondered if Lucia was one of the sisters he was talking about.

"Unfortunately, the house isn't really to our taste. Just wait until we get our money. We can shop bigger. Better." His accent rolled rhythmically over every vowel and consonant.

He continued crossing the street, taking the conversation with him.

I stopped recording and instead took photos of his car — a black Chrysler, driven by the man with him. I made sure to get several photos of the license plate too.

Lumping the images and video into one message, I forwarded them to Dad along with a text.

Me: I know I shouldn't get involved, but one of your suspects showed up to work today.

Once the message was loaded, I waited for his reply. Only to be left on read.

"*Really*?" I muttered.

Before long, the open house was wrapped up, and we headed back to the office, signage and leftover applications in hand. The latter only added to my mother's growing irritation as she continued her silent treatment, huffing and muttering to herself about the lack of people showing up to the open house.

Truthfully, I wasn't bothered that she refused to talk to me. I was anxious to speak with Dad, to see if he had any answers about Dean's whereabouts. So, when we got back to the real estate agency and Mom went straight to her office, I didn't stay long.

I let Candice, my fellow receptionist, know where I was going and left without waiting for her response.

When I arrived at the organized crime units building and was told to wait outside my father's office — a familiar scene — I tried not to pay attention to the guns strapped to everyone's hips this time. I was too distracted anyway with questions racing through my head.

I wanted to know who Gabriele was talking about over the phone when he mentioned medical records; I wanted to know why my father hadn't said anything in response to the photos I sent; I wanted to know where the hell Dean was after hearing absolutely nothing from him since yesterday.

It didn't help that the blinds of Dad's office were closed over, making it impossible to see if he was talking to anyone.

"Waiting for Dad, huh?" The gruff voice pulled me from my thoughts, and I looked to my left.

Detective Paul Crowley. I had no opinion on him, but he also didn't seem like the kind of man I wanted to get to know.

"Yep," I said tightly, smiling politely. I wasn't in the mood for small talk.

At a desk beside Crowley's was another detective I hadn't seen before. He was younger, with light brown hair and a near-permanent smirk in the corner of his mouth. Something about him seemed familiar, though.

He gave me a small smile, but instead of introducing himself, he went back to reading whatever was on his computer. Out of the pair, he was the only one to notice I wasn't in the mood for talking while I waited.

Crowley, on the other hand, continued his questions. "Did your dad know you were coming?"

"Ah, no. But what I want to talk to him about is kind of urgent." I shouldn't have said that to a detective. They were naturally curious.

"What kind of urgent? Maybe I could help."

"It's private. But thanks..." I focused on my father's office door, willing it to open already.

When it finally did, I straightened expectantly, readying myself to question him about everything I had worried about over the morning, but that plan was quickly squashed when Dad stepped back to hold the door open for someone in the office with him.

Dean.

He stepped into view with his head down and broad shoulders slumped, moving with a pained sort of stiffness that he masked with a stoic frown. His shirt was covered in black smudges and dried blood spots. Small slices in the material made me realize the blood was his. There were tiny scratches on his skin. They marked his arms too, one of which was wrapped with a bandage.

It wasn't until he looked up that a graze on his cheekbone was revealed, along with more black smudges like the ones on his shirt. As if an artist had smeared his skin with spots of charcoal.

His eyes were almost glazed when they finally came to me, rimmed with red and dark circles. He hadn't slept.

I stood slowly and moved towards him, barely registering when Dad asked me to step into his office.

Dean's eyes were almost empty until he noticed my hair. The faintest of smiles appeared on his lips, and his eyes softened.

"What happened?" I whispered, carefully reaching for his cheekbone where the graze was. My thumb brushed through the black smudge near it, finding it sooty. Like ash.

"Your boyfriend stupidly discharged himself from the hospital too early, is what happened," Dad said.

Dean muttered, "I hate hospitals," right as I said, "Why were you in the hospital?"

"Maybe we should talk about it outside." The soft tone of Dean's voice indicated that not everyone should hear about what happened.

"Okay..." I looped the strap of my bag over my shoulder, eager to leave again.

"Didn't you want to discuss something with me?" Dad said, referring to the images and video I sent.

"Not anymore. Talk it over with your colleagues." My worries about Gabriele had drifted to the back of my mind. I couldn't give a fuck about him, not when Dean looked like he had walked out of a burning house.

Dean and I left, but not before a young officer approached us with Dean's keys in hand. As he handed them over, he said, "Your car is parked at the rear of the building."

"Thanks," was all Dean said. Not a hint of worry about the car's condition or if they drove it carefully. A blank sort of stare was in his eyes, and there was complete disinterest in his voice.

I gently took his hand, trying not to bump any of the cuts in his skin.

Following the officer's direction, we took a back exit that led us down a flight of stairs and opened onto a small parking lot with a tiny area of green space beside it. The Cadillac was parked beside the small garden — if you could call it that, with its single picnic table, one tree, and the evidence of it being used as a smoking area. Instead of heading for the car, Dean led me to that one table.

The clouds in the sky closed over the sun, casting the area in a gray shadow while an icy wind weaved its way through the parking lot.

My gaze fell to the left side of the Cadillac.

"Oh my god…" I breathed, taking in the small dents and scratches that marked the emerald-green exterior.

Dean slowly took a seat at the picnic table, pressing his lips together in a pained grimace. His entire body seemed to ache.

"Dean…" I took a seat beside him. "Were you in an accident?"

He shook his head, still distant as he focused on the car. "No… There was an explosion after the meeting last night—Roxy's car…"

Everything went still, like the city was listening.

I was hesitant to speak as I tried to gauge anything from his face. "Is… Is she okay?"

Dean broke his focus on the car and looked down at his hands. There were no tears in his eyes, just a sort of emptiness. He seemed to be replaying whatever happened in his head. When he spoke again, it was more of an empty statement than anything.

"She's dead."

Something heavy settled in my chest.

"I think it was Antonio's kids… Or at least Gabriele, after he found out she was lying to him to get close." Dean sat forward, resting his elbows on his knees as he looked at his car again. "She was screaming, and I couldn't do a fuckin' thing."

A sickening shiver ran through my body.

"If that was you—" Dean cut himself off, swallowing hard as he rubbed his thumb against his palm. "I couldn't live with myself if something happened to you. Not again."

I knew where this could go if he let his thoughts get the better of him.

"It won't, Dean." I brought my hand to his opposite cheek and turned his head to face me, bringing that blue-gray gaze to mine. "It won't…"

Dean looked at me in silence, and his throat bobbed. Straightening again, he cupped the back of my head and pressed a kiss to my forehead, letting it linger.

When he pulled back, I took his hand. Despite the cold weather, they were warm, unlike mine. On feeling how cold mine were, he grabbed my other hand and wrapped both in his before lifting them to his mouth to breathe warmth onto them.

He inhaled sharply. "Let's get you warm, yeah?"

When we were in the car, with the heat on, we didn't leave right away. As if we needed more time to stew on what happened.

While Roxy wasn't someone I ever imagined being friends with, I couldn't help but feel numb and confused by the news of her death. Several months ago,

Dean went to her on a drunken mistake when we broke up, but I didn't hold any grudges towards her. Roxy became someone I rarely thought of after that.

Suddenly, she was dead.

To be trapped and burned alive. No one deserved a death like that.

CHAPTER 36
Seb

The gloomy weather matched the mood outside the pizzeria.

News reporters were eager to get the best spot as they described the scene that had played out the other night.

They talked about the explosion, and that police were still investigating who was behind it. They also talked about the one victim — the twenty-six-year-old daughter of a celebrity chef. There was the belief that she was senselessly targeted, or that maybe it had something to do with her father's wealth. No one assumed it might've been her connection with a mob boss's estranged son — no one except the few people who knew what she was doing with that son.

All four of us stood across the street, a fair distance away from the scene. Where police tape prevented us from getting closer.

Earlier, Dean mentioned he wanted to see it. Whether it was for closure or to figure out what happened, we didn't ask, but all agreed to go with him once Kira's SDV meeting was done.

The news of Roxy's death came as a shock, and seeing the aftermath left us speechless.

Her car was removed not long after the explosion, but there was a large burn on the curb and asphalt where it happened. Nearby shop fronts were affected by the blast too. Their windows were blown in, and exterior walls were covered in ashy burns, including opposite the street. Where Dean had been standing.

He was lucky to have walked away from it with only scrapes and bruises.

I guess that was part of the reason I was speechless. Knowing my best friend was there that night, and then seeing exactly where he stood when the blast happened, put the whole situation into a surreal reality.

I wanted to suggest we all skip town for a while, but I doubted Lily's dad would like that very much.

Dean had already warned me about coming forward for the investigation. I wanted to give up my name so he wasn't facing this alone, but he reminded me of what I was giving up. And that he needed someone he could trust to be there for Lily and his mom when he couldn't.

Kira, with her arm through mine, was first to break the silence as she kept her eyes ahead. "It could've been either of you."

It was more of a statement than a conversation starter.

I pulled an arm around her shoulders and kissed her temple.

It was getting harder to keep that melancholy sense of our world imploding from getting the better of me. Why did it have to happen when I finally met the girl of my dreams? The potential love of my life?

Dean cleared his throat, keeping his hand in Lily's as he stepped away from the police tape.

"Let's go," he murmured.

None of us were ready to go home yet, but we also weren't ready to return to the shifts we had skipped for this. The girls mentioned they knew of a nearby cafe, several blocks away, and we followed their lead in solemn silence.

We took a seat at a table in the front window of the place, right as rain began to pour heavily on the busy street outside.

"Does anyone want to drink or eat anything?" Kira asked after a moment.

"Not really..." Dean said from across the table, where his back was to the wall and he had a decent view of the entire cafe and the street.

Lily shook her head.

"Me neither," I agreed, trying for a smile.

"I thought I'd check anyway... My appetite is also non-existent right now," Kira said, folding her arms on the table. She rubbed her upper arm as she looked out the window, brown eyes glazed by the overcast light outside. "Everything feels weird."

Lily, playing with the sleeve of her knit sweater, seemed to be looking for something to say to fill the space. I was too. We needed something else to talk about.

"So..." she began, eyes on Kira and me. "Can we talk about what's happening between you two?"

It was a better subject change than mine. I was ready to suggest playing *I-Spy*.

Kira smiled at me from over her shoulder and shrugged. "I don't know. We're just...us."

"What, like friends with benefits?" Dean asked, smiling softly despite the tiredness in his eyes.

"I guess? But we're open to more."

"I know I am," I added, smiling as I leaned back in my seat, planting my hands behind my head.

"It's really about exploring where this takes us," Kira explained. "No pressure. Just fun."

That was an understatement.

Lily smiled a little as she watched us curiously. "And it's exclusively you two?"

"Are you hinting at something, Lil'?" I grinned.

Dean's brow raised as he watched her, also curious about her answer.

Lily's cheeks flushed red. "*No.* I was just wondering."

Dean's mood was slowly lifting as he braced his arms on the table, eyes only on Lily. "I don't like sharing anyway. Unless it's something you're into."

"*Oh my god,*" she laughed, sinking low in her seat.

Kira was grinning from ear to ear. "Now *I'm* curious."

"Dean and I have seen each other naked, if you're still wondering," I shrugged nonchalantly.

Dean didn't deny it when Kira looked at him to confirm. He crossed his arms. "It was a dare."

Kira laughed again while Lily pulled the neck of her sweater up to her eyes, hiding her smile and flushed red cheeks.

"What have I started?" she mumbled.

"Whole can of worms just..." I made a popping sound with my cheek and finger.

When our laughter died down, Kira hummed in thought.

"You know what we should do?" She straightened in her seat, face glowing with a smile. "A rage room."

"Agreed. I went to one for my birthday once, and that shit feels better than therapy—" I stopped myself as I looked at Lily who was apparently starting therapy next Monday. "Not that I've been to therapy to determine what's better than it. I'm sure therapy is really good too."

"It's fine, Seb," she said. "I think a rage room could be fun, though. I've never been."

"It *would* be nice to smash somethin'," Dean admitted.

"Great!" Kira beamed. "We should go this Saturday when we're all free."

I chuckled. "That room won't know what hit it."

CHAPTER 37
Dean

In the two days since Roxy's death, I went to work at the garage on autopilot and took Mom to all her necessary appointments. A physio visit being one to keep her leg muscles moving. She would never walk again, but it prevented muscle atrophy and got her out of the house. Not that her social life was lacking.

When I showed up to drive her to the appointment, she had questions about the cuts on my body. She wanted the truth, all of it, so I gave it to her.

She didn't know Roxy — or about the relationship I once had with her — but Mom mourned her anyway as if she were family.

I didn't inherit that big heart of hers that was capable of loving so many, including people she had never met.

Mom was too good for this world.

Which was why I was sitting on a dining chair in her dark living room, angled beside the front window so I had a perfect view of the street.

I had double-checked every lock in the house after helping her into bed. Most nights she did that herself, but the recent physiotherapy had left her sore and tired. She told me earlier she would be fine alone, but I needed to settle my nerves, and providing her protection gave me some kind of control over a larger, spiraling situation. I knew Lily was safe at her parents' house. This was the least I could do.

On the small side table to my right was the gun from Antonio — the gun I had tucked into the pocket behind the front seat of my car when the cops, paramedics, and Brooklyn fire brigade pulled up after Roxy's car exploded. That was after I managed to drag myself to my feet, crawling through broken glass while my head spun and throbbed.

I was taken to the hospital to be checked over. In hindsight, I knew I should've called Lily while I was there, but at the time I couldn't think straight — being thrown six feet from the road will do that to a person.

Vince had shown up, getting in before the police could get my statement. He was there not out of moral obligation, but to check if one of Antonio's assets was still alive after the explosion happened so close to the meeting.

A few minutes after he left, and while I was struggling to remove my hospital bracelet to get out of the stark white nightmare of an emergency room, two cops showed up. Notebooks in hand and ready for my statement. Before they could say anything, Mark rounded the corner, flashing his badge and saying he would get my statement instead.

It was a save I never thought I would be grateful for.

He told me his team heard the explosion over the mic, which had somehow remained taped to my chest when I was thrown back, but then the signal dropped out.

Mark didn't get my statement. Instead, he insisted I rest before going anywhere. I couldn't remember falling asleep at the hospital, but when I woke up, I checked out as soon as I could. After discovering the police, aka Mark, had organized to have the Cadillac moved — not for investigation, but to be hidden — I had no choice but to go to Mark's office. I spent the morning going over everything with him, right up to the moment Lily showed up. She looked so radiant that afternoon, with the light of the floor-to-ceiling office windows behind her casting a hazy glow around her figure. I almost forgot I was injured.

My phone buzzed on the table beside the gun, pulling me from my thoughts as a call from Lily came through.

I answered mid-ring. "Hey."

She sniffled quietly. "Hi..."

The chair creaked as I slowly straightened in it. "You okay?"

"Not really." She inhaled a shaky breath. "I, um— Things here aren't going great. Mom was sort of badgering me over dinner, and I lost it." Her voice broke with emotion. "I blurted out what James Henderson had been doing to me. I know I wanted to tell them eventually, but not like that—my hands won't stop shaking," she mused nervously. "I just needed to hear your voice to feel sane again..."

Physically, Lily was safe with her parents. Mentally, not so much.

Logic was telling me to tell her it wouldn't be forever, but my emotions were pulling me in the other direction. I needed her with me, in my arms, and as far away from her mother as possible.

I turned in my seat, glancing at the house I knew was secured at every door and window. No one was getting in, but the off chance of being followed back here... My mind was split between two opinions. But one was pulling me towards it faster than the other.

"I'm comin' to get you," I said, rising from my seat as I peeked through the curtain one last time.

"What about the plan to lay low?" she asked, sniffling again.

"Fuck the plan." I held the phone between my cheek and shoulder as I picked up the gun and tucked it into the back of my jeans. "I should've listened to you. I shouldn't have left you there alone."

She let out a soft sigh in relief. It shuddered with the emotion that lingered in her voice. "Thank you."

We ended the call, and I shoved my phone into my pocket, already thinking of several things to say to Kate in the off chance she wanted to confront me when I did show up. I had to remember to keep those words PG.

After collecting my keys from the kitchen's servery window, I headed for the front door. Only to stop in my tracks when I spotted the familiar black Mercedes parked out on the street.

Fuck.

Vince's shaved head rose from behind the car's roof as he stepped out onto the street, casually glancing left and right as he rounded the headlights and made his way up to my house.

Clenching my jaw, I pulled the door shut and locked it.

"Evening, Dean." He stopped at the bottom of the porch steps.

I slowly turned, irritated by the delay in getting to Lily. "What do you want?"

"The boss wants you on a job tonight."

"No text?"

"It's a two birds, one stone kind of evening. Bring the gun."

"If I say no?"

"You got somewhere to be?"

"Did you not see me lock the door?" I gestured back to the house for emphasis. "Yeah, I've got somewhere I need to be."

Vince huffed a laugh, tongue in cheek. "Tell your girlfriend she might have to wait."

I didn't bother asking how he figured I was talking about a girlfriend, so I didn't bother denying it. Instead, I watched as Vince began walking back to the car.

"I don't feel good about leavin' Mom alone right now." I still hadn't moved from the doormat.

Vince stopped and glanced over his shoulder. "This isn't up for debate. Boss wants you to go, so get in the car."

A frustrated exhale blew out of my mouth. "Can I call my girlfriend to let her know?"

"Fine. But be quick." With that, he turned and walked back to the car, pulling out a cigarette as he went.

I could have one of those. Fuck that, I need *one of those.*

I brushed off the idea of asking Vince for one and pulled out my phone again.

The other end rang twice before Lily's hesitant response met my ear. "Hi?"

I rubbed the back of my head, walking slowly to the car while I thought of a way to let her down easy. Which was a bullshit theory anyway. No one was ever let down easy. No matter how gently they were told, they always felt like shit afterwards.

"Somethin's come up," I started.

"You aren't coming?"

"I am... Antonio wants me to do somethin' for him first. Vince is here. I don't have much of a choice..." I slowed my steps at the curb by the car, catching a glimpse of my reflection in the tinted window.

The guy looking back at me needed sleep.

I turned my back to him. "I don't know how long I'll be, but I promise I will come get you."

I was talking into the phone like there was a chance I might slip into the speaker and appear in her room.

Her voice was an emotional whisper. "Okay."

"I love you." My words were met with silence. I checked that the call was connected. And ignored when Vince impatiently tapped on the window from inside the car.

A faint and slow inhale came from the other end of the call. There was a shake in her voice again. She was frustrated because she was stuck; frustrated because of my situation; and maybe frustrated that she was getting upset at all.

It's how I felt anyway.

"I love you too," she whispered.

I waited for her to hang up first, and then cursed under my breath as I pocketed the phone.

Could one fucking thing go our way?

I turned to the Mercedes, scanning the street as a precaution while I got into the front seat. I was leaving Mom home without company — other than a pint-sized dog that couldn't do much against an intruder, except maybe piss on their boot and chew a shoelace.

It wasn't until I settled into the seat that I noticed Vince and I weren't the only ones in the car.

With a soft clearing of his throat, Antonio made himself known in the backseat.

"Boss," I said with a casual tip of my head.

How much of that conversation, and my reluctance to go on this job, had he overheard?

"Sorry for the inconvenience, Dean." It was a genuine apology. For some reason, that felt weirder than when he was planning something with an ulterior motive. "I could have someone send Lily some flowers with an apology. Maybe chocolates?"

"Uh, no, boss. It's fine." I pressed my lips together in an appreciative smile and faced the front. I didn't think Mark would like flowers showing up, addressed to his daughter, from the very man he was investigating.

"Okay, then." Antonio tapped his cane on the floor of the car — a subtle indication for Vince to start driving. "We're in for an interesting night."

The peristyle was a silhouette of pillars against the few yellow lights that illuminated Prospect Park at night. As we approached it, with several of Antonio's other guys flanking us, movement behind the silhouetted pillars made me slow. Not enough to fall behind, but enough for Vince to mutter, "Keep up."

Three figures were waiting for us under the peristyle, also flanked by several men. If it weren't for the street lights on the nearby path, their faces would have remained in shadow. But even then, I would've been able to guess who they were.

Antonio's kids, standing side by side at one end of the structure. All dressed in black and all with revenge and greed written on their faces. They weren't happy with this meeting, and neither was I.

We took up the space opposite them, leaving plenty of room between us and the three psychopaths.

My eyes were locked on Gabriele. Anger simmered deep in my gut at his very existence.

Lily told me about how he showed up to the open house and how he attempted to speak to her despite not recognizing who she was. The knowledge of him being that close to her again made me want to curb-stomp his smug face.

It was obvious he was the reason Roxy was dead, yet he showed up to a house inspection like nothing happened — he tried to approach Lily like nothing happened. The cuts in my skin, from the car explosion, were small reminders of the lengths he would go to get revenge. Whether he killed Roxy because she had used him was debatable. Yes, she had used him, but I couldn't imagine Gabriele being the type to get overly upset over a relationship going bad. Killing someone as a spiteful jab at his father made more sense.

I figured that's what this meeting was about. To try and talk and find a reasonable resolution for everyone attending.

I wasn't sure why I was there until Gabriele spoke.

"Is he our replacement, Father?" He jerked his chin at me.

Lucia, on his right, sent me a small, flirtatious wave.

I stole a glance at Antonio to find his expression indifferent. He wasn't denying that I was a replacement, and soon a faint smirk appeared on his lips.

He was using me, flaunting me as the son he never had. It explained why none of the other fighters were invited along.

"We are here tonight to find neutral ground," Antonio started.

Bullshit.

"And for me to remind you that what you are doing won't be tolerated," he added with a smug air about him.

There it is.

Beatrice smirked at her father. "What we're doing wouldn't be happening if you treated us like family instead of casting us aside."

"You mean reward you with the inheritance you *think* you deserve after the mess you created? There is a reason you were cut from the family business. You conduct your actions too loudly." He tucked a hand into the pocket of his suit pants while he rested the other on his cane. "It brings attention that none of us need... I suggest you go back to Rome and give my love to your mother—"

Lucia bristled. "You don't speak of her—"

"—You don't know what you're getting yourselves into. You have no connections; no strength in numbers like I do. You are fighting a fight you will never win," Antonio said, disregarding Lucia.

It was true what he said. Antonio had the entire Genovese family to fall back on. He was a caporegime.

His kids were nothing but wannabe gangsters.

Unhinged wannabe gangsters.

"At least we are our own boss, Father. We answer to no one," Beatrice smirked, crossing her arms.

"Because you have no one," Antonio responded.

Gabriele raised a hand to silence his sister before she could snap back, offering her a gentle smile as he stepped forward. The motion caused every bodyguard in the vicinity to shift on their feet. "We're aware of what we're getting ourselves into, *padre*. We learned from you, after all. But we also know your game isn't as good as it once was. People are leaving you, your business is falling apart..." He smirked darkly. "Just look at what happened to that little whore you sent for me."

I curled my knuckles, and they emitted a soft crack.

"This is your last chance," Antonio warned calmly. "Hurt one of my own again, and I will see the end of you."

Gabriele's gaze sharpened. Gone was his nonchalant attitude. "We are your own! We're blood!"

Antonio breathed in with a tired sigh, checking his gold watch. "Burning your way through my people and businesses is not how you convince me to change my mind. Neither is screaming at me like a child."

Gabriele's anger faltered as he glanced at his sisters. Each shared similar expressions of confusion and then amusement.

"As much as we love playing with fire, father, we didn't burn down any of your businesses," Beatrice mused.

If this caused Antonio to feel shocked or confused, he didn't show it. Instead, he pondered the information.

I felt eyes on me and glanced towards Vince to find him watching me already.

Squaring my jaw, I casually brought my hands behind my back and focused on the triplets as Antonio spoke again.

"I arranged this meeting to speak reasonably, and thought your agreement to attend meant you felt the same, but clearly that isn't the case." Antonio brushed off the last few minutes like it was lint on his jacket. There was really no love lost when it came to him cutting off loved ones. "We're done here."

The second Antonio turned to leave, we were expected to move with him to show solidarity and respect. And I did move like that for a few paces, until Gabriele chuckled darkly.

"*Manda il mio affetto alla tua piccola cerva, Dean.*"

I saw red. It temporarily blinded logic and common sense as I went to turn back, reaching for the gun tucked in the back of my jeans, but Vince caught my arm and forced me to keep moving.

"Not now," he muttered sharply.

I tore my arm from his grasp as we headed out of the peristyles shelter and stepped into the light mist falling on Prospect Park. Gabriele's taunting laugh seemed to follow me all the way to the car, haunting me as much as his words did.

Send my love to your little doe, Dean.

My hands shook before I shoved them into my pockets. The rage room tomorrow couldn't come soon enough. I needed to hit something, break something, smoke a cigarette. If Gabriele ever went near Lily again, I would put a bullet in his fucking skull.

As we reached Antonio's Mercedes, the boss finally let slip his frustrations. "Find out who the fuck was involved with the fire that burned down The Den. When you do, bring them to me."

Vince briefly glanced at me before he responded. "Yes, boss."

CHAPTER 38
Dean

A crimson dirt bike was parked by the stairs leading to Antonio's grand front door. On its seat was a black helmet. The rider was nowhere in sight.

Neither Vince or Antonio were concerned about the bike sitting there, so I figured I wouldn't worry either and did as they did; get out of the car. And prepare myself for a debrief of the meeting.

It was a two-birds-with-one-stone kind of night...

My eyes landed on the bike again, and I noticed it didn't have plates.

At the bottom of the porch steps, Antonio stopped and motioned between Vince and me, looking depleted. "Send him the address."

Vince pulled out his phone and tapped out a text. A second later, I received it. An address and a small job description: Collect fifty thousand dollars and come straight back.

"Right..." I pocketed my phone.

"This job was meant for Jacob," Antonio explained with a tired sigh. "But that won't be possible for him, seeing as his head was removed..."

I approached the bike, knowing I wouldn't have any other choice but to go, and picked up the helmet, finding a pair of gloves inside. I pulled them on. "You know Seb rides a bike, right? He would've been perfect for this."

The only time I ever rode a bike was when Seb needed his bike serviced.

"I know, which is why you'll meet him at that address... This job needs your expertise and a decoy. Just in case."

I hate just in cases...

Antonio offered me a tight-lipped smile as he turned for the house, relying a little more on his cane than usual. "Get it done."

Vince didn't hang around long either, as he followed the boss inside.

This job would give me a temporary outlet for the anger I felt. Based on what Antonio said, the guy I was meeting was a problem if it was a two-man job.

"Bring on the problem," I muttered, pulling the helmet on and climbing onto the bike.

It was a kickstart and required several of them before the engine finally turned over with a cough of smoke from the exhaust pipe.

A kickstart with issues. Great.

I charged through the screen door at the back of the East Flatbush home and vaulted over the rusted handrail on the stoop. Seb followed close behind, clinging to a duffle bag of cash as he went.

Hearts pounding, we sprinted through the overgrown backyard, dodging a swing set that hadn't been used in a while as we neared the 7-foot-tall back gate.

The last time I scaled anything this tall, I was a nimble 5'8" fifteen-year-old, weighed one hundred and fifty-four pounds, and used a large marble garden statue as leverage to get over a wall. I was a fraction lighter than what I was now.

Seb seemed to be having similar thoughts.

"Ah, shit!" he groaned.

The gap between the gate and us was closing fast, and there wasn't anything to use as a step up. We didn't have time to look for another escape.

I sucked in a breath and made the jump at the same time as Seb, taking two heavy horizontal steps up before I gripped the top of the gate and pulled myself over in a half flip, half fall to the alleyway on the other side. The entire maneuver pulled and twisted at the cuts and bruises all over my body, making me heave a breath as I landed.

We had a second to catch our breath before the Rottweiler that chased us from the house scaled the same gate.

"You've got to be fuckin' kiddin' me!" I said, breathless.

My boots pounded against the uneven, trash-strewn street as the dog gave chase. It gained on us fast, growling and snapping at our heels until the growling morphed into the rumbling of an engine.

I glanced over my shoulder for a second to spot the moment a pickup truck smashed through the gate. The driver was the guy who owed Antonio money. Except he decided he wouldn't hand that money over when Seb and I came knocking.

Admittedly, I probably should have handled the situation better, but I was tired of dealing with entitled assholes and punched him in the face, much to Seb's surprise.

Instead of retaliating with his fists or a weapon, the guy opened the interior door to his garage and introduced us to Rosie the Rottweiler. It prompted Seb to grab the bag as we got the fuck out as fast as possible.

My legs and lungs were burning, but I urged my body to keep moving as the truck's headlights illuminated the alleyway, casting our shadows out in front of us.

Rosie had finally given up the chase, but her owner hadn't. He wanted the cash and would stop at nothing to get it back.

"Give me the bag, Seb!" I called as we ran onto the next street, taking the sidewalk back to the front of the house, where the bikes were parked.

Seb didn't question it and threw the bag at me just as the truck swerved out onto the street. The driver attempted to mount the curb but parked cars and trash cans prevented him from getting closer.

Our bikes were in sight.

I pushed harder, breathing in and out of my nose and mouth. Sure, I ran most mornings but even that didn't prepare me for this fucking shit.

"What's the plan?!" Seb shouted, reaching his bike.

I looped the bag strap across my chest right before I leapfrogged over the tail light of the motorbike, trying not to crush my balls in the process when I landed on the seat. "Split!"

Seb climbed onto his sleek, matte black Yamaha with no issues starting it.

I shoved my helmet on, switched on the bike, cranked the throttle, and pushed down hard on the starter. The bike sputtered beneath me while the truck surged for my ass, drowning us in its headlights again.

"Dude!" Seb yelled, gesturing for me to move.

"Start, you motherfucker!" I kick-started it again, and the engine turned over.

Not waiting another second, I accelerated just as the truck's bumper nudged the back of the bike with a nerve-wracking crunch.

I twisted halfway in my seat and flipped off the driver as I drew out the space between us.

He still gave chase, but at least now we were even.

Seb raced beside me, capable of doing faster speeds on a sports bike.

Mine was built for off-road and awkward turns, but I had a plan.

With an intersection coming up fast, I motioned for Seb to cut behind me. He did, staying close and providing cover before I abruptly swerved, planting my left foot on the ground as I pivoted the bike and pushed the throttle.

Fishtailing onto the opposite side of the road, I aimed for the other direction as Seb sped off with a confused pickup truck driver giving chase.

I still had the duffle bag, but the driver had to slow down to double-check. It bought us time.

The wind ripped at my clothes while I looked for my next escape route. When the sound of screeching tires and sirens met my ears, I hit the brakes enough to pull into another narrow alleyway. It was lined with brick walls and dumpsters, making the path tight.

The sight of a 24/7 gym sign, just visible at the other end of the alley, caused me to slow right down. With no one in sight, I pulled up behind a dumpster and switched the bike off. I was met with silence, apart from the muffled thumping of music in the gym, and I manually wheeled the bike to sit by the brick wall before I got off.

Keys in the ignition, I removed the gloves and helmet and set them on the seat, like a cherry on top of a thief's dream find.

Heading to the adjacent street, I untucked the gun from my jeans and shoved it into the duffle bag of cash. I then removed my hoodie, tied it around my hips, mussed my hair, and dug around in my pockets for an earphone or two. I found one and shoved it in my ear. It had probably been through the wash a few times and most likely didn't work, but no one else knew that.

To the public, I was just another gym-bro coming from a late-night session.

I stepped out of the alley and joined the rest of the late-night community going about their business, all the while minding my own as I began the walk to the subway. I would've called Seb for a ride back to Antonio's, but there was a chance he was still riding, evading police.

I wondered if Lily was still awake.

Hoisting the bag over my shoulder, I pulled my phone out to check subway times.

My steps slowed as I read the temporary track maintenance warning.

"Fuck."

I could book a ride, but it was Friday night, one of the busiest nights of the week, and, going off the line of people waiting on the curb for rides of their own, I doubted I would find one soon.

On a quieter street, illuminated by shop fronts and streetlamps, I crossed into Bensonhurst.

A street cleaner slowly cruised along the curb on the opposite side of the street, and bars were beginning to filter people out.

I already texted Lily, but got no response. I figured she was already asleep. Safe and hopefully finding some peace after the shit-show her parents put her through.

I rolled out my neck as I glanced at my phone again.

The soft beep of a horn brought my attention to the street, where a black Ford Mustang with a fleet number on the back pulled up beside me.

I never thought I would feel relief on seeing *this* car.

The front passenger window rolled down as I approached.

"Evenin', sarge." I rested an arm on the roof of the car as I peered into it.

"Has you walking around this late got anything to do with the description I heard over the radio about a high-speed chase involving a motorbike and a pick-up truck?" Mark asked.

Seb wasn't being investigated, so I wasn't about to bring him up. Mark would be none the wiser, thinking I was the one on that matte black bike.

I smiled. "I thought becoming a detective meant you didn't have to worry about the usual traffic violations. Isn't that below your pay grade?"

He looked at the bag strapped across my body and then rolled his eyes. More so at what he was about to say than anything else. "Get in."

I climbed in without hesitation and dropped the bag on the floor between my feet. "What brings you to Bensonhurst?"

"Work..." He flicked the indicator and waited for a gap in the traffic. "A head was found in a dumpster."

"Huh..." I had a feeling I knew who belonged to that head.

"What brought you to Flatbush?"

"Work." I leaned forward and unzipped the bag to pull up some of its contents. A wad of cash and the gun.

Mark's brow shot up, and he had to double-take before he pulled onto the street. "Jesus fucking Christ— You should've come into the office to get a wire."

I put the cash and gun back in the bag. "It was a last-minute thing."

"You aren't changing your mind about working with us, are you?"

"No... Tonight has been one thing after another." I looked out my window, pausing. "Antonio's kids aren't gonna back off."

"And you know this how?"

"They made it pretty clear in the meeting tonight."

"Great. Something else you weren't wired for— Do you know how crucial this information could be to the investigation?"

"Antonio picked me up directly from my house without warning. It would've been *a little* suspicious if I told him and his driver to stop by your office and wait in the car while I got a wire fitted."

He rolled his eyes but moved on. "What do you do with the bag now?"

"Well," I sighed, "I'm keeping the gun— It's the one you told me to get. But the cash needs to be delivered to Antonio tonight."

Mark scoffed in amused realization. "And I suppose you'll want me to drive you to Antonio's house?"

"If you don't mind."

"Weren't you meant to pick up 50k?" Vince asked after running the wads of cash through the counter, sitting on the glass coffee table.

I stood in the doorway of Antonio's large living room, where the only light came from a standing lamp in the corner of the room. My arms were crossed loosely over my chest. "We didn't have time to count it in between running from a dog and a truck, Vince."

Seb agreed with a hum from the couch. Still in his riding leather with his helmet beside him, he had sunk into the cushions the second we arrived. He had spent an hour getting the cops off his tail until they decided the pickup driver was of more interest and let him go.

Vince sighed, shaking his head as he looked at the cash. "He's 20k short. Antonio is losing respect left, right, and center... You boys go. I'll let him know what happened tonight."

"Awesome," Seb grumbled, lazily getting to his feet.

We left the mansion in silence until we were outside.

"How *did* you get here, by the way?" Seb asked as we approached his bike.

"Lily's dad," I muttered.

Seb released a breath. "You're brave."

I jerked my head towards the driveway and pushed my fists into my pockets. "And he's waiting. So is Lily."

Seb unclicked his plate and got on his bike. "I'm gonna miss this."

"Threatenin' people or runnin' away from crazed drivers?" I knew what he meant, but offered him a smile anyway.

He grinned, but his eyes said enough about what he was thinking. Then he looked down to adjust and readjust the straps on his gloves, hesitating or trying to find the right words for whatever he wanted to say. He didn't have to say it, though.

"Yeah, I know." I scuffed the gravel with my boot.

Seb inhaled and then huffed a laugh before pulling on his helmet. "Go on. Go sweep Lily off her feet."

"Will do."

I walked the two blocks back to where Mark agreed to wait in his car.

He didn't say anything until we were on the road again.

"How'd it go?" he asked, casually checking his rearview mirror.

"I think your investigations are getting to him. He's stressed."

Mark shrugged. "Don't do illegal things, and that won't happen."

I scoffed but didn't answer.

We drove on in silence. With Antonio's mansion located in Bay Ridge, the same suburb as Lily's apartment and her parents' house, I figured he would take me back to his place, where Lily was staying. But then the streets started looking more and more like the ones I drove to get to Lily and Kira's apartment.

It wasn't until we were on their block that I straightened and looked at Mark. "You brought her back here?"

"Things were getting tense at home." He looked at me side-on for a second before focusing on the road. "I think my family is going to have to sit down for a long conversation. But for now, she's here. Lily needed space."

"From your wife."

His hold on the steering wheel shifted. "I don't think you're entitled to comment on it, Dean."

I considered biting my tongue, but the words came out before I could stop them. "I think I am if she's makin' my girlfriend so miserable she has to call me up to organize an escape from her childhood home."

He didn't respond.

"She's meant to feel safe there. Instead, she can't get out of that house fast enough when she has the chance."

"As I said, we will talk about it. As a family..."

"Lily agreed to that? Openly talkin' about her sexual harassment in front of her entire family?"

He was silent again, but I had a feeling this silence was out of guilt for not knowing what his daughter had been through.

I kept my eyes ahead. "Wait until she's ready."

We arrived at the apartment, still not speaking until I spotted the patrol car parked across the street.

Suddenly, the gun was like a branding iron burning in my lap. "Who's that for?"

"Relax. It's protection for Lily while she's here since I doubt she'll want to go back to mine any time soon," Mark said. "I'll organize another car to watch your house too. But for now, go upstairs."

I didn't know what time it was, but it was already Saturday morning. Probably several hours before sunrise. And somehow I didn't feel like sleeping. The night's events had left me wired and wide awake.

I ran a hand through my hair and climbed out of the car, tucking the gun into the back of my jeans as I went.

The cops watched as I entered the building, but then lost interest after receiving a radio call. Probably from Mark.

I rode the elevator to the third floor, slowly feeling the adrenaline from tonight wearing off. My mind was mostly quiet. Much like the apartment.

Apart from the jingling of my keys and the faint hiss of the door scraping along the carpet as I pushed it open, everything was calm inside. Peaceful.

The apartment itself was like a warm hug, inviting me in with the sweet smell of whatever infusers the girls had put in the space.

Apples? Cinnamon? Whatever it was, I didn't suit it. I smelled like the city.

And sweat, I thought as I lifted my arm and grimaced at the smell.

A lamp was on in the living room. The second I stepped into view, Lily jumped off the couch where she was reading. All worry drained from her face as she rounded the corner of the couch and rushed into my arms, regardless of the sweat.

I squeezed her closer, inhaling her strawberry-scented shampoo. "You okay?"

She looked up, resting her chin on my chest. The blue of her eyes was cloudier, and her eyelashes were still wet. "I am now."

CHAPTER 39

Dean

Freshly showered and in sweatpants, I leaned against the counter with my hands in my pockets, watching the soup for bubbles. Behind me on the counter, with her smooth legs on either side of my waist as she drew on my back, Lily waited too, wearing those satin pajama shorts I loved so much with an oversized shirt with a neck hole wide enough to bare one shoulder.

We had the apartment to ourselves.

Lily snaked her hands around my chest and leaned into me with a sigh. Nothing else needed to be said for me to understand what she was feeling; relief I was home, content because she was home, and maybe in a little denial about the gun currently hidden beneath her dresser. Out of sight and out of mind for now.

My eyes went to the clock on the wall to our left, above the counter. It was almost 3 AM.

I should've felt tired, but I wasn't. I was mentally restless. Gabriele's words didn't help with that.

I stared at the soup but placed a hand on Lily's knee.

Any conversation we had since I got home was light-hearted but also a little sombre. Everything that happened tonight was a conversation for tomorrow.

Lily's hand slowly skimmed down over my front, coming close to the hem of my sweatpants before she smoothed it back up again. Whether her touch was intentional or not, I half smiled and looked back over my shoulder, brow raised.

"You good?"

"Just...appreciating." Her breath lightly fanned my left shoulder blade before she kissed it, and then dragged her lips to another area of skin. And another.

She moved her hand south again, following the ridges of muscle on my stomach. Her touch was definitely intentional this time as she continued peppering kisses across my back.

I hummed deeply, rolling my head back as she curled her fingers around the bulge in my sweatpants. She got one stroke in, sliding the fabric up and down along my cock before I turned around.

I cupped the back of her head and the small of her back as I kissed her.

My mouth barely left hers when I asked about her hair. "Why'd you cut it?"

"Needed the change. You don't like it?"

I stopped and braced my hands on either side of her hips to look at her. "I love it."

Lily's cheeks were flushed as she smiled. "If I knew a haircut would get this reaction from you, I would've cut it sooner."

"Baby, you're gonna get this reaction no matter what you do."

The pet name sunk into her in a way that made her melt in my hands. It was evident in the way she bit the corner of her lip and shifted her hips forward in an unspoken invitation. Cradling my bulge against her, she gently rolled her hips up as she watched my face.

Temptation pulled my gaze to where we were touching, where fabric creased and moved. Moved enough so that the leg hole of her pajama shorts was briefly pushed aside. I caught a glimpse of her lack of underwear, and suddenly *I* was melting in *her* hands.

I leaned into my palms. "We're alone all night?"

"I don't think Kira would come home at three in the morning." She rolled her hips harder.

My hand fumbled to grip her hip and slow it down a little. "And, uh, you don't mind what the neighbors hear?"

Lily's eyes darkened, and she bit her lip. "Let them."

"Bedroom?"

"Yes."

In a whirlwind of her hopping off the counter and removing her top, me turning off the stove and moving the soup, and then her dragging me to her bedroom, she closed the door, and I pushed her against the back of it. Our movements were hasty but oh so fucking smooth.

My hands were at her hips as I slipped her shorts over her thighs and kissed her where I could.

At the same time, she tugged the front of my waist band down and I popped up like a fucking jack in the box.

I gripped her thighs and hoisted her up against the door with a thud. The little breath she released once I was flush against her was addictive. I needed more of those sounds, those breathy whimpers, to pour from those lips of hers.

One arm around my shoulders, Lily reached down between us, guided me to her, and gently pushed me in.

Her pretty mouth formed an O, and her eyebrows pinched up as she slid onto me.

Deeper and deeper, her walls squeezed around me like a glove. A welcoming, familiar glove that forced any worry from my mind. It was like magic, the way she easily took up the space in my brain, casting out the bad, making me feel like a fucking god when I was inside her.

That was a thought straight from my cock...

Lily's fingers curled against my scalp when I pulled out halfway, hitching her legs firmly around my waist.

Her free hand came to the back of my head, and when I started thrusting, her fingers curled against my scalp, and her legs locked.

"Remind me to never cut my hair shorter than this," I breathed.

She threw her head back and moaned a response. "Oh?"

I drove my hips forward. "You need somethin' to hold on to."

"In that case," she panted, adjusting her hips. "Give me something to hold on for... Fuck me harder."

"You sure?"

There was a smile in the corner of her mouth. "Fuck me so hard I forget about what happened tonight."

"Lily..."

She shook her head, smiling as she took my head in her hands. "You won't hurt me."

It was hard to think straight when I was still buried inside her.

I adjusted my grip on her thighs, pulled out, and then drove into her a little heavier than I usually would.

She swallowed and combed her fingers through my hair. "Again."

The next thrust had more force and knocked her body against the door.

She tightened but hesitated. Caught between going ahead with this or changing her mind, it was a quick, silent battle in her eyes.

Her body was already quivering in my arms. And she was wet.

So fucking wet.

My control was teetering on the edge.

"Again," she whispered, lips parted and inches from my own.

"Tell me to stop and I will."

"But I don't want you to stop."

With her legs cinched high around my waist, spreading her wide open, I kept going. Obeying her every request to go harder and harder.

The bedroom door began to rattle as her pleasure-filled cries filled the room.

My legs felt like they wanted to give out, but I pushed through the ache, and pushed us to that awaiting climax that made her claw at my back.

I shelved the reservations and gave in to that raw, hot, and hard desire.

And Lily. Oh, Lily. This gorgeous fucking woman in my arms, taking every inch with staggered moans and whimpers. Each one caught in her throat.

She clung to my shoulders and dropped her head against the door, watching me through hooded eyes as her body bobbed with every thrust.

Lily didn't just remind me how badly I enjoyed it, but also how badly I enjoyed it with her.

I kissed her throat and sucked on her skin like I was starved of sex.

She was tightening around me again, and I was seconds from release with her shoulder in my mouth. All thoughts and sense of control were lost on me, save for a steady rhythm that came as second nature. When sweat began to gather on our skin, making my grip on her thighs slip, I hooked my arms under her knees.

Ladies first.

Her body trembled. She was close.

I timed it just right, thrusting deep and staying put as her orgasm rushed through her. It made her entire body convulse, curling her toes and sending a quake through her legs as she gasped. The throb of her walls coaxed me to follow, and soon she was milking everything I had to give.

Lily rested her head on my shoulder, catching her breath while I brought her from the door. I left soft kisses on her shoulder as I went, unable to get enough of her. After the past few days, I was still looking for a distraction. I wanted to worship every inch of her.

I lay her on the covers and slowly pulled out. The gentle sigh that left her lips was a good enough sign that she was happy about what happened, despite how rough.

She tracked me with her eyes as I crawled off her, leaving a trail of kisses down her body. Beginning at her breasts, I gently took her nipple between my teeth. She moaned with a smile, pushing her chest up while she curled her fingers into the covers.

"Do we have any plans in the morning?" I asked, moving my mouth to her other breast to get more of those reactions from her.

Her hips writhed beneath me as I moved further down, arriving at her inner thigh and her hip creases when I widened her legs. I watched her face as I did, determining what she liked and what drove her wild. So far, wherever my mouth went brought her pleasure.

I slowly brushed my bottom lip over her clit. The little bud was hot to the touch.

Lily's body quivered as she found her answer. "N-not in the morning. We do have that rage room thing in the afternoon—"

She was cut off by her own moan when I flicked my tongue over her clit, and then brought my mouth over her peach-pink pussy. I could taste her and myself as I licked her gently, aware of the tenderness while I worked to get her there again.

Her body arched off the bed as she cupped her breasts, and then slung both arms over her eyes. "Why'd you—"

I gently slid my middle finger into her, palm up, as I stroked her from the inside. Her legs knocked against my shoulders as she groaned, slapping her hands to her thighs to claw at her skin.

When I placed my thumb to her clit, barely stroking it clockwise, her hips rocked.

"*Nnnh*—why'd you ask?" she managed.

I replaced my thumb with my mouth, devouring that sweet taste before I lightly blew across her reddening, wet flesh. The cold air caused her to squeal as she bit her bottom lip and lifted her hips. I pinned them back down.

An impatient groan escaped her as she tried to move her hips again, grinding against my face.

I pulled up for a second and considered her nakedness.

"I don't plan on lettin' you sleep much tonight." I kissed her inner thigh and slowly worked my finger in and out. "That's why I asked. I hope you don't mind."

She pulled herself to her elbows, considering me this time as she raised her brow. With her eyes locked on mine, she spread her legs wider with a subtle smirk. "Not at all. Do your worst."

"Alright." I rose to my feet, rock hard under her gaze of anticipation and hunger, before I hooked my hands under her thighs. "Ready?"

Her eyes gleamed with excitement. "Mhm."

Lifting her legs, I flipped her over in one motion.

She let out an unexpected squeal before her knees hit the mattress. Chest down and ass up in full view, she released a chuckle-moan as she curled her fingers into the covers.

I slowly climbed onto the bed to kneel behind her, spreading that glistening pink with the head of my cock as I leaned over her perfect body.

My hand curved around her waist while the other smoothed down her arm to her hand. I threaded my fingers through hers and squeezed.

"Still wanna forget?" I murmured into her ear, grazing the shell of it with my bottom lip.

"Yes." She trembled beneath me, nodding desperately as she started to sink onto my cock again. "Yes, Dean, *please*."

It had been a while since I fucked someone hard. I fell into the belief that I had to keep it gentle every time with Lily — not that I didn't like slow fucking. Slow fucking trumped rough sex any day, but sometimes rough sex worked wonders on the psyche.

And I could see we were missing out.

I slid in with one full thrust. No pauses or edging, just one complete sheathing that knocked a shudder through Lily's body as she groaned loudly and bit the pillow.

Chapter 40

Dean

So maybe fucking the night away wasn't the best idea after spending part of it running from a crazed guy in a truck. Mentally, the sex created a sort of buffer — or a rebalance. Physically, I felt like I woke up in the body of an eighty-year-old man.

It was midday by the time I forced myself out of bed, leaving Lily to continue sleeping.

After a stretch that seemed to crack every vertebrae in my spine, I made my way into the ensuite for a quick shower to soothe my muscles, and then dried myself in front of the bathroom mirror. Only then did I get a good look at what became of my body last night.

Among the healing cuts and bruises from the explosion were fingernail scratches on my chest and back. There was also a faint bite mark on my shoulder.

I half smiled and went back into the room. Not bothered to get dressed yet.

Lily was beginning to stir when her eyes landed on me.

"Hmm-morning." She smiled sleepily and stretched her arms above her head, arching off the bed with a soft groan. It caused the bedsheet across her body to slip from her chest, revealing her perky breasts and the marks I left on her; a hickey on her neck and another lighter one on the curve of her right breast.

I approached the edge of the bed, aware of the way her eyes traveled over my body. "You tore me to shreds last night."

She bit her lip sheepishly, leaving her arms to rest on either side of her head on the pillow. "Oops."

"Last night wasn't too much for you?"

Lily shook her head, smiling easily. "It was fantastic."

I crawled across the covers, making her happiness grow as I came to hover over her. With our bodies separated by the sheet and blanket, I kissed her softly. "Morning, beautiful," I said.

She kissed me more in response, and I lowered my body to hers. Beneath the covers, she slowly began moving against me, pressing her chest to mine and parting her legs.

She was trying to instigate something.

I chuckled against her lips and pulled back. "Breakfast first. We need sustenance."

"Or." She gently pushed my shoulder.

I rolled off her and rested against the headboard while she leaned closer.

Confidence poured from her every move as she traced her nails along my bare thigh and kissed me slowly. She continued that touch along my limp cock. It wasn't limp long, and twitched against my leg as she kissed the side of my throat.

I let out a breath, getting lost in the pleasure the second she curled her hand around my cock and moved to her knees. The rest of the sheet fell from her body, and any thoughts trickled out of my brain.

She moved to straddle my knee and slowly peppered kisses down my body as she stroked her hand up and down, lowering her face to stop beside my cock.

My brows rose when she dragged her tongue along the underside of my shaft, following one thick vein while she fixed her blue doe eyes on me.

A grunt formed in my throat, and I dropped my head back. All the while growing harder in her hand. "Fuck me," I groaned.

She swirled her tongue around the tip and opened her mouth to take the rest, but paused and smiled innocently at me.

Releasing my cock from her hold, she moved to straddle my hips. Barely letting herself touch me as her mouth hovered by mine. "Shower first, then sex, maybe another shower, *and then* breakfast."

I reached for her face, wanting to kiss her again, but she pulled back and happily hopped off the bed to skip to the bathroom.

I watched her bare ass as she went, instinctively sliding a hand down to my erection to give it some attention.

"Are you coming?" she called from the bathroom as she turned the shower on.

I inhaled through my teeth and pulled myself from the bed.

The Smash House Rage Room was located in Coney Island, around twenty minutes from the girls' apartment. Without my car, Lily and I got an Uber and met with Seb and Kira at the front doors of the place.

The warehouse sat a few blocks back from the beach, but the wind pushed the salty sea air right by the door anyway. It ripped at our hair and danced on any exposed skin like cold, sharp knives.

Just as Kira excitedly pulled the front door of the warehouse open, a gust of wind yanked the door from her grip. I went to catch it, Seb caught it, and Lily threw up her hands before the door could hit her.

"Not the smash house trying to smash you," Seb joked, using his body to hold the door open as we went in.

"That would be my luck," Lily said, adjusting the beanie on her head as she smiled. "Pancaked by a door."

Kira wrapped Lily in a side-on hug as they walked ahead of us, approaching the front desk.

The inside of the warehouse was industrial grunge, with graffiti decorating the black walls, metal music playing loud from brightly spray-painted speakers, and a caged ceiling to bring down the actual height of the room but allow for a full view of the old warehouse rafters above.

Seb huffed a laugh, craning his neck to peer up. "I feel like we've walked into your brain, bro."

"Close enough," I agreed, half smiling. "It's missin' the self-loathin' inner monologue."

He shook his head in amusement as we reached the desk.

The guy behind the front desk, with a dark buzzcut and a pierced eyebrow, couldn't take his eyes off Kira and Lily as he talked them through the consent and liability forms he had handed to them on clipboards. Popping a bubble of gum through his lips, he winked at them and then pulled his attention to Seb and I to hand us our clipboards too. Except when his eyes fell on me, he sucked in so hard he choked on his gum.

"Are you okay?" Lily asked empathically.

"Yeah. Fine." His smirk evaporated as he coughed and stammered through a quick run down of our forms, this time avoiding looking at me. "W-When you're done, I'll get you some PPE."

Just as fast as he sucked back the gum, he excused himself to use the restroom.

Kira, excited about getting the day started, glossed over the interaction, called out a "Great, thanks," to the guy as he disappeared around a corner, and then skipped over to the bean bags and hand-shaped armchairs that made up the waiting room to our left. She fell into a giant beanbag.

Lily was less enthusiastic with her movements and gently lowered herself onto a bean bag of her own.

Seb nudged my arm as we wandered over. "You know him?"

I shook my head and took a seat in an armchair. "No idea."

"He definitely knows you..." Seb opted to lean against the wall as he filled out his forms. "His name tag said Scott."

Scott emerged from the bathroom again, glancing at us and then averting his gaze as he sat down at the computer along the back wall behind the desk. With his back to us, I got a clear view of the back of his buzzed head. And the small scar there.

"Scotty motherfuckin' Richards," I muttered. There was no happy nostalgia dedicated to the prick.

"Who?" Seb asked, chuckling.

I leaned back in my seat. "High school bully. He enjoyed picking on the weak until I punched him in the face and slept with his girlfriend a few months after."

"I'm going to pretend I didn't hear that," Lily whispered, looking up at me from her clipboard. She raised an eyebrow.

My smugness faded, and I cringed. "Sorry."

"You mean to tell me, you punched him once and he's still scared of you?" Seb tucked his clipboard under his arm.

"He hit his head and needed some stitches," I shrugged, turning my attention to the forms and signing the bottom. "When he came back to school, I told him it'd be worse if he bullied anyone again."

"We needed someone like you at our school," Kira said.

Seb straightened with a frown. "Who bullied you?"

"No one that matters anymore," she grinned, clambering from the bean bag. "Now fill out your forms so we can get started."

Kira left for the desk to hand her form in, with Seb following close behind, rushing through his forms.

I stood and gave Lily a hand getting out of the beanbag.

"If you ever spot anyone in public who gave you a hard time in school, let me know. I'll thump them on the head. Or hit them with my car," I joked... Sort of.

She laughed quietly. "Who said chivalry was dead?"

After getting our protective gear from Scott, who still refused to look at me, we were directed to the change rooms in the back. Seb and Kira took one, me and Lily took another.

Right up until that moment, Lily and I had done a good job of masking the subtle aches in our bodies. We wore layers that kept us comfortably warm against the cold. But it wasn't until we started getting changed, paired with the unheated air of the change rooms, that those aches felt worse.

Mine was a dull throb in my quads that made pulling on denim coveralls that much more of a challenge. My legs felt like lead.

Lily's soreness was the yellow bruise on her tailbone. She realized after our shower this morning that bending and twisting was a no-go for today.

Unable to bend to lace her borrowed boots, I did them up for her. Sitting on the one bench in our change room, I had her foot planted on the bench space between my legs as I wove the laces around the silver hooks.

"Okay, so maybe doing it against the door wasn't the best idea," she muttered, tucking her hair behind her ears as she watched. She was already wearing the coveralls and helmet, with its built-in face shield and earmuffs. It made her look like a cute construction worker.

"We could rain check." I tapped her calf, indicating for her to switch legs.

"Kira is really looking forward to today, though."

"Yeah, but you'll be in pain the entire time." I tightened the laces firmly and tied them off.

"I'll be fine." She took her foot back with a small smile. "After last night, at my parents' house—"

"Which we've still gotta talk about, by the way—"

"—I think I need to smash something. As do you." She poked the tip of my nose.

She wasn't wrong about that. Gabriele's threat clung to my mind like mold. I would give anything to smash in his teeth for what he said.

And reuniting with an ex-school bully was the cherry on top.

As Lily moved away, I started on my laces, wearing the boots I arrived in. My eyes went to Lily as I secured knots in the laces. She bent to pick up her belongings, but stopped short and pressed a hand to her lower back.

"Ow," she groaned.

I grimaced and stood. "You sure you wanna go through with this?"

"Yep." She smiled stiffly. "I just won't make any sudden movements."

I scooped her things off the floor, along with my stuff. "It's a rage room, Lily."

"And I'll rage carefully." She gave me an uneasy grin and turned for the change room door.

I followed, half smiling. "I think that's the most you thing I've ever heard you say."

As we walked through the door, she jokingly muttered, "At least I can mark getting my back blown out against my bedroom door off this year's bingo card."

I raised a brow. "What else is on this bingo card of yours?"

"What's that about bingo cards?" Kira asked as she stepped out of the change room she shared with Seb. She was tying off the braid in her hair, completely unaware of what we were discussing.

"Nothing," Lily smiled quickly.

I slung an arm around her shoulders.

Seb walked out of the change room next, grinning already and rubbing his hands together excitedly. "Who's ready to smash some shit?"

CHAPTER 41
Dean

"Fore!" Seb called before swinging his golf club into an old flat screen TV. It cracked through the center, glass flying.

I swung next, slamming my metal baseball bat into the TV's side. The frame dented inward, and the screen popped from the front.

At the same time, across the room, Kira was pummeling a row of mannequins with a sledgehammer. It was easy to guess whose face she was picturing on each one.

"This day has been the best decision we've ever had," she exclaimed.

Next to Kira, Lily was smashing vases and dishes against the wall. They were easier to break and caused the least strain on her back when she threw them.

"Take that!" she cried, throwing another plate at the spray-painted target on the wall.

Seb hoisted a glass floor lamp onto our table and didn't hesitate to swing at it. Debris flew out, and I ducked behind my arm, chuckling at the carnage unraveling in the room.

I lifted an old microwave to the table and briefly looked at Lily as I did. I guess it was to see if she was still enjoying herself.

She brought her gloved hand from her neck to check her fingers. A frown was on her face as a tiny line of red bloomed on the side of her throat.

I left the smashing for Seb and approached her with my bat resting on one shoulder.

When she noticed me coming, she smiled quickly. "Just a scratch."

"From what?" I leaned in to get a better look at the cut, gently moving the collar of her coveralls down.

"Part of the plate. What are the odds, right?"

"You're good, though?"

"Of course." Her smile waned, and she jabbed a finger over her shoulder towards the door. "I-I think I might go see if I can track down a Band-Aid."

"Want me to come with you?"

She looked at me seriously, apart from the faint smile in the corner of her mouth, and cupped my face with her hands. "Dean, it's a scratch. I'll live."

I watched her leave and reluctantly returned to smashing some stuff. It wasn't as satisfying when my thoughts were being pulled in Lily's direction.

She was gone for a minute.

The minute turned to five minutes, and I was no longer as interested in smashing whatever was in the room.

Our hired hour was finishing anyway.

"Maybe she needed the bathroom?" Kira said as we headed for the change rooms when the time was up.

"Maybe..." I knocked on the door to the change room we shared, and then opened it enough to poke my head in.

Lily wasn't there.

"Her locker is empty too," Seb noted, motioning to the wall of cabinets. The door to Lily's was open, and her bag and clothes were gone. Her coveralls and PPE sat on a chair nearby.

"I'm checking the bathroom," Kira affirmed, walking down the corridor.

Lily had had time to change, but where was she now?

Send my love to your little doe, Dean.

I strode into the foyer, where Scott sat at the desk, scrolling a website that shouldn't be open at work.

"Hey, pervert," I said firmly, bracing my hands on the desk.

Scott jumped and fumbled to close the desktop window before he spun around. "Y-Yes?"

"Did you happen to see my girlfriend come through here?" My right heel bounced impatiently as I pinned him with a glare.

He stammered over something incoherent.

"Fuck's sake, speak," I ordered.

Seb nudged me aside to take over. I stepped away from the desk and pulled my hands through my hair. All sorts of possibilities were running through my head, but there was one at the forefront: We had been followed, and Gabriele took his chance when she was alone.

"She's about yea high, freckles, really blue eyes," Seb explained.

"Yeah," Scott gulped. "She got a Band-Aid from me and went back to the change rooms—"

"Thanks for that, genius," I muttered through gritted teeth.

Kira emerged from the corridor. When I waited for Lily to follow her out, she shook her head.

My fingers interlocked behind my head as I tried to come up with an explanation for why Lily disappeared.

She hasn't been missing that long. She's fine. She'll show up.

I have too many enemies not to worry about them doing something to her...

I paused when someone outside the glass front doors caught my eye. My heart rate slowed right down as I walked to the doors and stepped outside.

The weather had settled. It was still cold, but the sun had made an appearance.

Lily was sitting on a bench with her back to the building and her hands curled around the edge of the seat. Dressed in what she arrived in, her eyes were closed as the sun warmed her skin.

I quietly took a seat beside her, facing the building.

"What happened?" I asked gently.

She opened her eyes. There was a sort of distant stare about them.

"I got a Band-Aid from the front desk. And then had to explain I wasn't going to sue the place for injury. I went to come back, but then realized our session was up soon, so I figured I'd get changed and wait out here." She motioned to the sky. "The sun was out."

Her intentions were innocent.

I stole a glance at our surroundings, watching as strangers passed us on the sidewalk. "I thought you were gone."

Realization sank into her expression, and her eyes widened. "I'm an idiot. I didn't stop to think about what Gabriele said."

I reached for her hand and curled mine around it, noticing the faint stain of blood on her nails from the cut on her neck. "Maybe I overreacted a little... That prick has made me paranoid."

She lifted her legs over the bench to face the same way as me. With our backs to the sun, she leaned into my side.

"I am sorry." The words were so soft I barely caught them before the doors of the warehouse opened with a squeak.

"You might wanna come in and change," Seb said as he leaned through the gap in the doors. "I think Scotty thinks you're about to steal the coveralls, and he looks like he's dreading that confrontation."

I could see Scotty pacing behind the front desk, looking towards us nervously.

"We'll be right in," Lily said, smiling politely.

Several minutes later, we handed in our PPE and headed out, leaving Scotty to finally relax.

Seb and Kira were still riled up from the rage room, walking ahead of us arm and arm and laughing as they talked. They fed off each other's energy.

Lily and I stayed in a comfortable silence. Mostly enjoying the company.

I looked down at Lily.

She was staring off into the distance as she held my hand, chewing the inside of her cheek.

Lifting the back of her hand to my lips worked to bring her back to reality. It almost startled her back into it, like she suddenly realized where she was.

"Talk to me," I said.

She smiled, shaking her head. "I'm fi—"

Seb suddenly spun around, snapping his fingers. "We should get dinner on the wharf. Watch the sunset." He wagged his eyebrows.

"Oooh yes!" Kira beamed.

Lily hesitated. "I'm kind of tired, but you guys go ahead."

"What? No, you have to come," Kira pleaded, taking Lily's hand.

"I won't be great company. So go on. Have fun." Lily paired her words with a shooing motion.

After a little back and forth of Seb trying to convince Lily to go, the two walked on. When Lily saw I was staying by her side, she nodded towards our friends.

"You can go too, if you want. I'll get an Uber home from here."

"Nah. I'm stickin' with you." I was trying to remain nonchalant as I watched her closely. "Besides, I think I did somethin' to my shoulder."

It was a small white lie, but there were only so many times I could ask what's wrong and receive the same answer.

I paid more attention to her on the way back to mine. Mom wasn't home but had left a note about going out with friends. I left her a note beneath hers letting her know I was staying at Lily's.

We took the Cadillac back to the apartment. The entire drive was quiet. At one point, Lily dozed off, reiterating that her silence might've been from a simple lack of sleep.

So why couldn't I convince myself of that?

I was tired too after last night, but something was off with her.

Lily poured us a glass of red wine and started dinner early, beef stroganoff on rice. She didn't protest when I stepped in to help. She offered me another small smile, sipped her wine, and continued stirring the packet mix sauce into a pan.

Tired was now an understatement, but our stomachs growled hungrily.

She was deep in thought for most of the late afternoon, sometimes offering one-word answers to anything I said as we ate dinner. Half the shit I said was trivial. I wanted her to talk to me about literally anything just to keep the connection open — weather, the new shelves in the living room, her latest read...

She was slowly sinking behind a wall in her mind, disguised in smiles.

"Did you wanna talk about last night? About what went down with your parents?" I asked, dumping our dishes in the soapy water of the kitchen sink.

Lily was pouring us another glass of wine as she leaned against the counter. She shrugged and put the bottle down. "Not really."

I scrubbed at the dishes and rinsed the suds off. "You've got that appointment with the psych on Monday, right?"

Lily hesitated, and I looked over my shoulder.

Another quick smile brushed over her features. "I almost forgot. I'll talk to him about it then, but for now..." She pushed away from the counter and sauntered over to me, sliding her arms around my waist while I faced the sink. "I want to enjoy the weekend with you. We *do* have the apartment to ourselves right now. And the dishes can wait."

I dried my hands on a towel and turned around, leaning on the lip of the counter while she pressed herself against me, smoothing her hands to my chest. "Yeah?"

She hummed, rising to her toes to kiss me.

The sound of a zipper pulled me out of the kiss as she opened my fly.

"What about your back?" I asked, trying not to let pleasure cloud my thoughts yet.

"It doesn't hurt so much anymore." She brought me back into the kiss, one hand clutching the front of my shirt while the other dipped into my pants.

She cupped me through my briefs, and I groaned. "Lily."

Her teeth grazed my bottom lip. "Yes?"

It was a strange feeling to be stuck between wanting sex and the barrage of concern racing through my brain.

I held her jaw gently and reluctantly pulled away.

She removed her hand, allowing clarity to sink into my head.

"We should talk," I breathed.

Her pupils were dilated, and her lips were parted with a question. "About what?"

I dropped my hand. "You."

"Dean, I told you, I'm fine."

"You've been actin' different since you cut your neck... If it's not about the discussion with your parents, is it the gun?"

"No," she sighed.

"Did the blood trigger somethin'?"

"Dean..."

"Was last night too rough? Did I hurt you?"

"No, it's nothing. I'm just overtired and a little restless, that's all." A smirk toyed on her lips, and she reached for the hem of her shirt. "Now, can we continue before Seb and Kira get home—"

I caught her wrists, and her eyes widened. "If you're tired, you need sleep."

"I'm fine."

"I don't think you are," I said softly.

Keys jingled at the front door before Seb and Kira entered the apartment, calling out happy hellos as they walked down the short hallway. They were back early, crushing Lily's plans, but also failed to read the room as they talked about what they did at Coney Island.

I wasn't listening. My eyes were on Lily while I waited for her response.

As our friends entered, Lily withdrew. Not only physically from me, but mentally. I saw the walls in her blank stare, enclosing her firmly in her thoughts as she backed away towards her room.

I followed until the door was shut in my face and locked.

Seb and Kira fell silent.

A second passed as I held the door handle, but didn't try it. I had witnessed my father barge through doors enough to know not to.

I wasn't him.

"What happened?" Seb asked carefully.

I shook my head. "She won't talk to me."

CHAPTER 42

Everyone enjoyed themselves today.

Everyone was moving on.

But I am stuck.

I had been stuck for the past month, trying so badly to act like everything was fine. Being a supportive girlfriend and friend; trying to give the people I love somewhere safe to talk and deal with all the bullshit going on around us.

Meanwhile, I was drowning in fear.

I backed away from the door and sank to the floor at the end of my bed. Every breath was shorter and shorter.

Sex was a coping method. And rough sex, I discovered last night, brought a different meaning to the word pain. Although temporary, it worked to draw me from my head — to reset my brain and bring back some kind of normal.

For Dean to put a stop to it...

The logical part of my brain knew why — we needed to talk — but it couldn't stop the tightening of my chest and the lump in my throat.

Pleasure blocked the darkness. The memories.

It was a small cut, from a broken plate piece, yet my heart raced like it was worse.

It was a small cut, but I couldn't breathe.

I lied about what I really did after leaving the rage room. Yes, I got a Band-Aid and changed my clothes, but I hurried straight to the restroom as soon as I could. I needed a moment to calm down.

I had locked myself in a bathroom stall and pinched my arms until I drew blood. It stained my nails.

Dean thought those stains were from the cut on my neck.

I've been lying to him.

I've been lying to everyone.

I lied to myself.

Nothing is fine—

There was a soft knock on the door.

"Lily?" Kira spoke gently. "Can I come in?"

I covered my mouth to catch a sob and curled my arm around my middle as that dark feeling, horrible and tight, rose through my body like bile, choking off my air supply.

Pinching my arms drew blood, but the pain wasn't nearly enough to take away the pain I felt on the inside.

There was another knock on the door.

Or was that my heart pounding?

The knocks warped into distant gunshots.

I remembered the sharp pain of a bullet passing through my body.

All the blood.

"So much blood," I whimpered, clutching my side as I squeezed my eyes shut. "I'm fine—I'm fine—I'm fine."

Everyone else has moved on. Why can't I?

"Lily." His voice was steady. Calm. "Open the door."

Not a week had gone by since I left the hospital without a single reminder of that one afternoon. Everything triggered that one goddamn memory: loud noises, cars backfiring, Mom's overbearing control of my life, Roxy's death. A fucking broken plate cutting my neck.

And then there was Dean, with the threat of prison looming over his future, while a mob boss and my father split him in two. I wanted to help, but I could barely help myself.

The gun, temporarily tucked under my dresser, was the cherry on top of it all.

"Lily," Dean repeated.

"I can't—" Failing to catch a full breath, I clutched my chest. "I can't breathe."

"Yes, you can, Lily. You can. Just unlock the door. Please." The faint plea in his voice made my heart ache.

I wanted to unlock the door, but couldn't bring myself to move. I was frozen to the floor and staring at the gap beneath my dresser.

There was a gun in my bedroom.

Hushed and quick whispers came from the other side of the door, followed by the soft scraping sound of metal on metal.

My eyes flicked to the door handle as its simple lock clicked and the door swung open.

Dean was crouched on the other side with a bent bobby pin between his fingers. Kira and Seb stood behind him.

All three peered into the room like they expected something far worse, but Dean moved first.

He knelt in front of me, quickly examining my arms but mostly looking at my face — holding my face in his hands while I struggled to exhale.

"What can I do?" he asked.

I shook my head, unable to form a single word. There was a lump in my throat, and tears were forming in my eyes.

"Hey-hey-hey." Dean brushed a thumb across my cheek, wiping a tear. "Breathe with me, Lily. Come on, you've got this."

Just breathe.

I inhaled with him. When he breathed out, mine caught. I forced myself to focus on him, his mouth, his voice, his eyes, the faint scar through his right eyebrow. Anything considered insignificant but simple enough for me to regain control.

We had done this before. At the hospital. It worked then.

I need it to work now.

I tried again with him, following each of his breaths.

"That's it. Nice and slow."

The instant relief of air filling my lungs came quickly before a wave of emotion forced a sob from my chest. The tears came next, falling in giant blobs on the backs of Dean's hands.

Kira quietly stepped into the room holding a glass of water. "Seb and I are going to give you guys some space... Here." She held the glass out for Dean to take and offered me a sympathetic smile. Her eyes were wet too.

As she left quietly with Seb, Dean handed me the glass.

I took slow sips. It hurt my throat at first, and I felt exhausted.

Soon it wasn't fear or trauma that controlled my movements, but the heavy weight of embarrassment about the fact that my friends saw me at my worst. But I also knew they wouldn't hold that against me.

I could deal with embarrassment.

Dean took a seat beside me on the floor, leaning back against the end of my bed with one leg bent and his arm slung over it.

When the apartment fell silent around us, he cleared his throat and pushed his hand through his hair.

I set the glass down, wiping tears from my eyes and breathing shakily.

"You didn't call that doctor," he said with no hint of disappointment in his tone. He was only voicing what was on his mind.

"I tried. And I really wanted to..." I looked down. "I should've told you what was going on."

"Why didn't you?" Again, his voice was steady, no disappointment.

"Everyone was moving forward and dealing with everything better than I was." I pulled my legs up to my chest. "I thought if I pretended to feel normal, maybe I would get better and wouldn't need a doctor after all. But then everything kept piling up. And the gun—"

On hearing the word, Dean moved across to the dresser and reached under it. He blocked the gun from view as he brought it to the kitchen and wrapped it in a hand towel to be left on the counter.

"I'll keep it in my car from now on." He joined me on the floor again.

"But what about the whole protection thing my dad talked about?"

"Don't care. It's stayin' in my car."

I nodded, and my lip trembled as I tucked my hair behind my ears.

Dean brought himself closer, wrapping his arms around me. The gesture was simple, but broke the fragile wall barely holding my tears back.

I cried into his chest, and he pulled me into his lap, stroking the back of my head as he let me crumble.

These tears weren't for anything in particular. I was mentally and emotionally fried. But crying felt strangely better. A weight had been lifted from my chest.

My heart was a fraction lighter.

"I'm sorry you felt like you had to deal with this alone. I'm sorry I was so fuckin' blind." The complete adoration in his eyes, directed at me, was overwhelming and welcoming all at once. No one had ever loved me this much.

He gently lifted my wrist to look at the small pinch marks on my inner arm, where the blood had dried already. With a faint frown, he planted a kiss on my skin.

"You had enough going on," I said quietly.

"Not enough that I can't be here for you. Support goes both ways." He brushed the back of his hand down my cheek. "Promise me you'll call the doctor."

"I promise."

Dean rested his chin on the top of my head. His hand on my upper arm gently squeezed before he rubbed it in thought, huffing a solemn laugh. "I thought we had this communication shit down pat. Turns out, I was very fuckin' wrong."

I wiped my eyes. "I don't think it's necessarily bad. It just needs work... Although I do think rushing into things might've made us *too* comfortable."

That didn't come out how I wanted, and Dean pulled back to look down at me.

His brow furrowed. "Okay..."

"I mean, our relationship happened really fast with everything else going on. We sort of bonded over shared trauma... We didn't have a lot of time to do normal couple things once we were together. Everything stacked up—"

His frown was growing deeper the more he tried to understand what I was saying.

"God, I'm butchering this explanation," I laughed lightly. "I'm trying to say that we got closer faster than any normal couple would because of dangerous situations. But I don't regret any of it... I'd do it all again if I could. Maybe without getting shot."

A flicker of amusement flashed in his eyes, and the frown softened. "I think I get it... You *are* okay with us, though?"

"Oh my gosh—yes, of course! We're in too deep to go back now."

He hooked my hair behind my ear while his expression grew lighter. Even the room seemed less closed in as our moods shifted to something more positive. Open.

"Your turn," I said, turning in his arms so I sat between his legs, resting my back to his chest.

"My turn?"

"What do you want to communicate?"

"Oh, right." He pondered for a second, drawing idly on the top of my thigh with his finger. Then he took a breath, and I watched as his face grew nonchalant, keeping his eyes on where his finger traced the fabric of my jeans. "I started the fire at The Den."

My eyes popped, and I turned sideways in his arms to gauge from him if he was joking or not. But his face was calm. "I'm sorry, you what?"

Dean shrugged. "I was pissed off with myself after I left you, and The Den seemed to be the one place at the time that caused us the most pain. I waited until it was quiet, cut the power so the cameras stopped working, broke in through the back, and sprinkled gasoline through the place. The club itself burned faster than anything in the basement... Burned myself in the process." He lifted his right hand to show me the small scar on the heel of his palm.

I took his hand to look closer as my mouth dropped open. "*Dean*. You told me that was a lighter burn."

He pressed his lips together as he cringed. "Sorry."

"Why didn't you tell me sooner?"

"For the plot?" he joked.

I deadpanned at him, but it only made him smile more.

"There never seemed to be a right time to bring it up. In comparison to everythin' else going on, I didn't care about some casual arson."

"*Casual arson.* Jesus Christ..." I muttered, still mildly shocked as I processed the information. "Does Antonio know?"

"He thought it was his kids until they admitted they didn't. I don't know who he thinks did it now."

"And Dad? He doesn't suspect anything?"

"I don't think so."

"You know if they did find out—"

"Your dad would include *tampering with evidence* on my record, and Antonio would probably kill me."

I breathed in deep, shaking my head. "Am I the only one who knows?"

He nodded once as he studied the end of my hair between his fingertips.

"I'm not sure if I should be concerned that you got away with it or impressed."

"I'm kinda surprised myself," he admitted.

"Well, your secret is safe with me. And from now on, so are any others. Open communication from here on out. Every little worried thought or uncomfortable idea. Or plans to burn down another mob boss establishment." I offered him my hand to shake on it. "Deal?"

The crooked smile on his face created a dimple in his cheek. He took my hand, shook on the decision, and then brought my knuckles to his lips. "Deal."

"Good." I smiled easily, wiping at the remaining wetness of my eyes and cheeks as I sniffled again. "Ugh, I'm all congested now."

"Sexy."

It was harder to deadpan this time when the smile refused to leave my face.

I turned to face him, kneeling between his legs. "I love you."

"Love you too." His mouth twitched. "Snot and all."

I pulled a face and then climbed out of his lap, taking a steadying breath.

CHAPTER 43
Lily

The hem of my sleeve had seen better days before I arrived at the waiting room outside the psychologist's office. The fabric was frayed thanks to my insistent urge to pick at any loose threads. I was one tug away from unraveling more of it before Dean casually took hold of my hand.

He had been waiting for me outside the doctor's office building when I arrived in an Uber. Still in his navy-blue coveralls with the top half folded down to his hips and the sleeves tied around his waist. He had a lollipop in his mouth and wore a backwards baseball cap and white T-shirt, and had smiled at me like there was nothing to worry about. Which was true — my anxiety just wasn't aware of that.

We had been waiting for ten or so minutes since arriving, after I gave my details at the desk. Apart from picking at my sleeve, I spent the time staring at the abstract art hanging on the walls. I wasn't paying attention to the details in the brush strokes. I was too busy thinking about the next chapter of my life. And what this one introduction to therapy was about to change.

The door of the psychologist's office opened, and my heart skipped several beats as I straightened in my seat.

Doctor Hamdan was a stout man with a head of unruly gray curls, a friendly face, and kind brown eyes, but that still didn't settle my nerves. I was about to share parts of my life with him.

"Lily Whitmore?" he asked as he stepped out, addressing the waiting room like Dean and I weren't the only ones in it.

I took a breath and rose, offering the doctor a polite smile while I looped my bag over my shoulder.

"Come on in," Hamdan smiled warmly.

I glanced at Dean.

"I'll be right here. You've got this," he said.

The words were simple but lifted my confidence by a fraction.

I headed for Doctor Hamdan's open door, smiling again at the doctor as he welcomed me into the space.

The First of Many Big Steps, read the poster on the wall in his office.

The streets were busy, but the traffic was flowing.

Halloween was in two days, meaning décor was in full bloom in almost every storefront and business window. Coffee shops sold pumpkin spice lattes and season-themed pastries, and every so often, I would spot a street performer dressed in a ghoulish costume, entertaining a small gathering.

It was all a welcome sight when all I wanted to do was sit and ponder the last hour at Doctor Hamdan's office. For such a small window of time, we discussed a lot in the session. Surface-level stuff that gave the doctor an idea of why I needed help.

He specialized in therapy for gun violence survivors, but he also wanted to help with my general anxiety. Which meant working through the things that triggered it: social gatherings, what James did, my parents...

No more hiding from the problems. I was facing them head-on. Soon, the scars on my body wouldn't be ugly reminders but simply scars.

"Doctor Hamdan said we're going to practice setting boundaries with my parents, which will be fun," I said, breaking the silence.

Dean smiled, eyes on the road. "I'm glad you're doin' this. I'm proud of you."

I took his hand and locked my fingers with his, bringing it to my lips to kiss the snake head tattooed on the back of it.

The corner of his mouth curved up again as he dared to steal his gaze from the road.

I settled our hands in my lap, thinking still as I watched the world go by. "I also want to quit my job. Not right away, but I want to start looking for work again. This time I'd tell Mom, though."

"No more nightclubs?"

"Definitely not." I gave myself a self-deprecating shake of the head. "I want to work somewhere that I'll actually enjoy getting up in the mornings for. Like a bookstore, or maybe an art gallery. Somewhere where I don't feel suffocated."

"I'm all for that." He squeezed my hand gently.

"Are you sure you won't come to a meeting?" Kira pulled away from our embrace, holding me at arm's length from her after she greeted Dean and me in the little hallway entrance of our apartment. "The whole group is *really* supportive."

Dean was already in the living room, talking with Seb.

"I want to settle in with this doctor first." I placed my hand on hers at my shoulder. "But I'll think about it. Maybe it can be part of my next step in therapy."

"Okay, but just know they'll welcome you when you're ready." Her smile broke free as she slung one arm around my shoulder. "And, like, *lots* of cakes and biscuits. Some of the members like to bake."

"That might actually convince me to come sooner," I joked as we headed for the living room.

Five minutes later, we were all seated around the TV. Seb and Kira were in a playful debate as they set up Seb's Switch — the debate was over where and how we would do Halloween.

Dean and I listened from the couch. Well, half listened.

I had picked up a pen from the coffee table and was idly drawing on a scrap of paper before Dean silently offered me his left wrist. I looked at him quizzically, but all he did was shrug. So, I started doodling on his skin instead.

"Don't forget it's Dean's birthday on the thirty-first. He should have a say in where we celebrate," I piped up quietly, keeping my attention on the drawing. Kira and Seb didn't hear, not that it bothered me.

"As long as it's with you," Dean muttered into my ear. "I'm still down for that box wine and burgers by the Hudson, by the way."

"And give up the opportunity to witness us all drunk together?" I mused softly, continuing the drawing.

"I think if we're all drunk, there won't be a lot of witnessin' going on."

I smiled as I added the final touches to the drawing. It was of two small birds flying. The entire thing was no bigger than two inches and sat right below the heel of his palm.

"Why birds?" Dean asked so that only I heard.

"I don't know, but they're sort of flying free in a way. Maybe I'm subconsciously trying to manifest something for you." I huffed a laugh.

Dean took a closer look at the drawing, studying the details with an impressed little smile in the corner of his mouth.

My smile faded. His eventual arrest was going to tear my heart out.

When he looked at me to say something else about the birds, he stopped himself after he saw my face. I tried to smile again, but it didn't work as well as I hoped.

Dean's eyebrows gently rose, and his eyes softened. Without bringing atten-tion to us, he wrapped an arm around my shoulders and pulled me closer. It was a casual enough gesture that Kira and Seb took no notice to ask if something was wrong — I had heard that question enough since the day of my panic attack.

A hug for now was enough.

"I'm not gone yet." The words were barely a whisper.

I nodded and wiped the tears from my eyes before Seb and Kira could see. Their debate had moved from Halloween plans to dinner discussions.

"So," Kira said, getting to her feet. "Chinese or pizza?"

"Pizza sounds good," I said, accepting the distraction.

Kira snapped her fingers and pointed at me. "You read my mind. Pizza it is."

"Do we not get a say?" Seb asked as he linked controllers.

"I'm down for pizza," Dean shrugged.

"You were going to pick pizza anyway, Seb," Kira said as she headed for her phone on the kitchen counter. "You suggested it."

"Eh. Sue me for enjoying banter with you," Seb grinned innocently.

Kira rolled her eyes in amusement before dialing the number for the local pizza place using the menu pinned to the fridge.

She began the order with her preference — gourmet barbecued chicken pizza — and then pointed to Seb for him to say his.

He cupped his hands around his mouth and sang out, "Supreme!"

Kira laughed into the phone. "Did you get that? Okay, cool—" She pointed at Dean next.

"Prosciutto. Extra mozzarella."

Kira nodded once, repeating that into the phone as she looked at me expectantly.

"Hawaiian, please. And garlic bread."

As Kira finished up the order, adding drinks and desserts, Dean hummed in displeasure.

I looked at him. "What?"

Seb took a seat on the arm of the couch. "Now you've done it, Lil."

"Done what?" I laughed a little as I straightened up so I could look at them both.

"This might be our deal breaker." There was a slight hint of sarcasm in Dean's tone. He slung his arm along the back of the couch behind me while he lifted a single brow.

"Pineapple on pizza?" I asked.

"Doesn't go with tomatoes." His eyes were locked on me like we were the only two in the room.

I raised a shoulder. "But it's sweet and salty."

Kira walked over, stopping beside Seb to watch us curiously. "What's going on?"

"They're having their first big argument." Seb wrapped his arm around her waist, but watched Dean and me intently with a goofy smile on his face.

"The sweetness overpowers the rest of the flavors. It ruins the pizza, Lily," Dean continued, lifting a hand for emphasis.

"Oh, god," Seb whispered. "He's starting to use his hands."

It was me who rolled my eyes next. "Okay. It doesn't ruin it, *Dean*. It's also the only time I enjoy pineapple, oddly enough."

Dean ground his jaw as he shook his head, despite the glint of humor in his eyes.

I smiled sweetly at him.

"Dean, you aren't gonna win this. Think of it this way..." Seb stood and walked around to the back of the couch to squeeze Dean's shoulders. "Lily is like the pineapple to your pizza. She's sweet, you're salty. From a distance, no one would guess that it works, but it kinda does." He lowered his head beside Dean's, who sighed as he listened to his friend. "Face it, bro. Accept the pineapple."

"That was the best analogy I've ever heard," I said. "Thank you, Seb."

"He's a pineapple sympathizer," Dean deadpanned. "Of course he'd pick the side of the pineapple."

I feigned a pout and placed a hand on Dean's knee. "I know a good doctor if you need to talk about it."

Dean's brows shot up in surprise while Kira burst into laughter.

"Too soon?" I cringed.

Seb, grinning widely, moved along the back of the couch to wrap his arms around my shoulders instead. "Don't change, Lil'."

CHAPTER 44
Dean

Lily held the slice of Hawaiian pizza up in front of my mouth, smiling sweetly. "One bite?"

I curled my lip slightly at the sight of the pineapple resting amongst the sauce and cheese, but reminded myself that Lily had stepped out of her comfort zone today. I could do the same with pineapple on pizza.

Reluctantly, I took a bite and tried not to cringe too hard when the flavors burst across my tongue.

The face I pulled made Lily laugh. "I'm not changing your mind anytime soon, am I?"

I shook my head, swallowing hard. "Probably not."

"Try the chicken instead," Kira said, gesturing to the box on the table as she handed a Switch remote to Lily.

We were getting ready to play Super Mario Kart when my phone buzzed in my back pocket.

I fished it out and instantly regretted even checking it.

A text from Mark sat on my lock screen like a blaring amber alert.

Mark: Meet me at my office ASAP.

"Everything okay?" I heard.

I pulled my eyes from the screen to Lily.

She was smiling at first until she got a glimpse of the name on my screen. "What does he want?"

I inhaled and pocketed my phone. "It's probably for more information or somethin'."

I stood and kissed her on the forehead, lingering for a second.

"What about the game?" Seb asked, gesturing to the spare controller that was meant to be mine.

"Start without me."

He gasped, feigning shock. "Blasphemy! You're the Luigi to my Mario."

"Yeah, well, this Luigi has a detective to talk to."

Seb clicked his tongue in disappointment and looked at Lily. "Your dad is a killjoy. No offense."

"None taken." Lily masked her concern with a small smile at me. "Come back, okay?"

"Of course. I've gotta maintain my winnin' streak," I winked, gesturing to the game.

"We're reaching the end of our investigations." Mark hit me with the words the second we sat down in his office. He looked as reluctant to say them as I was to accept them. "I thought I'd let you know in advance."

"Right..." I swallowed the information like it was a bitter pill. "When do you plan to start makin' arrests?"

"A little over a week from now."

That was the second blow. It hollowed out my stomach with a sharp slice of reality. Everything was happening so fast.

I looked down, nodding. "Can I let Lily know?"

"Something tells me you will, regardless of what I say." Mark cleared his throat. "Don't forget, your cooperation with the investigation won't go unnoticed. It'll reduce the sentence you get."

"Yeah, but my criminal record won't do me any favors." I huffed a dry laugh. "I probably shoulda thought of that back when I was stealin' cars—"

A knock on the door cut me off, and Mark sat back in his seat, exhaling. "Come in."

It was a young delivery guy with poxy skin and a nervous twitch.

I lowered my head, mostly to mind my own business, as he carried a small box to Mark's desk. But I couldn't help but notice he seemed to watch me more than necessary.

"Little late to be doing delivery runs, isn't it?" Mark asked, taking a box cutter from his desk drawer and sliding the box closer to himself.

The guy shrugged. "Fell beside my seat."

Usually, a normal person would take the end of that sentence as their cue to leave, but this driver hesitated. Which put me on guard.

My attention went back to the box. "Maybe open that tomorrow. Outside."

Mark half smiled, cutting the tape. "It's stationary."

The driver left right before Mark flipped the box open.

I tensed, half expecting fire or shrapnel to fly out of the box like Roxy's car had done. Instead, nothing happened, and I sank back in my seat. "Fuck's sake."

"We have metal detectors at all entrances to the building for that kind of thing," Mark explained, smiling knowingly.

"All this shit is makin' me paranoid," I huffed, combing my fingers through my hair.

Mark hummed, setting aside the box while he brought our conversation back into focus. "So my advice to you from here on out is to lay low. This next week is most likely going to get quite messy, and I don't need you or Lily getting caught in the crossfire... The Gimello siblings don't know about your mother, right?"

"No, I doubt they would. It's Lily I'm worried about."

Mark paused in thought, drumming a finger lightly on the desk. His face looked more drawn than usual. Or maybe I hadn't noticed before how the stress of the situation was affecting him. Hell, we probably all looked like shit to anyone who didn't know what we were dealing with.

"You still have that gun?" he asked.

"Yeah, but I'm keepin' it in my car."

"Not ideal, given you'd need quick access if—"

"She's safe with me even if I don't carry. If it came down to it, I would put myself between her and harm."

"No, you won't. As much as it comforts me that you have her back, I need you alive for her sake." He smiled slightly. "If these were different circumstances—"

"You'd be happy I'm datin' your daughter?" I raised a brow and folded my arms. "No offense, sarge, but if these were different circumstances — and I'm assuming you mean me not being involved with the mob — I'd still be someone you wouldn't approve of."

"Yet my daughter would love you anyway. She has a soft spot for the underdog, it seems."

"Are *you* goin' soft on me?"

Mark chuckled, but he didn't deny it. He went about gathering the paperwork on his desk. "We're done for the night, so I will see you when, well... I'll see you when I see you."

I slowly stood, absentmindedly tracing a finger along a groove in the desk surface. "Do I still have to worry about what'll happen to my mom?"

Mark's frown was subtle as he stood too. "I think we can figure out something for her so she doesn't have to leave." He approached his office door, rubbing at his chin in thought. The frown remained. "I am sorry about the way I handled that. It wasn't my finest moment."

"No shit." I stopped beside him as he opened the door. "But, I've seen Antonio make worse ultimatums for people."

"I bet those people never punched him in the face for it," he mused.

My lips twitched, and I rubbed the back of my head. "Yeah, not my finest moment either."

"You were protecting your mother. I respect that." He placed a hand on my shoulder, and this time I didn't feel the need to ask him to remove it. Maybe I was going soft too. "It was nice getting to know you, Dean."

Sappy moments with a father figure were something I wasn't used to. Even without an immediate threat from Mark, the little voice in my head couldn't help but ask why he was being genuine. My real father created a mindset in me that most fathers were assholes so I kept my guard up, expecting and preparing for violent outcomes. Because of that, I didn't know how to respond.

I gave Mark a simple and subtle nod and then left.

Chapter 45

Dean

Lily flung herself from the bed so fast I thought someone had barged into her room and startled her.

I woke up ready to punch a stranger in the throat. Instead, I watched as she raced into the bathroom and shut the door.

Yawning, I glanced at the curtains. It was morning.

I got out of bed with a sense of déjà vu and made the half asleep walk to the bathroom door, blinking to wake myself up.

The sound of retching, muffled by the door, pulled my thoughts to focus.

"Lily?" I knocked lightly.

"Don't come in here—" More retching cut her off.

"It's nothin' I haven't seen before."

"This is different." She paused, groaning. "If you really want to come in…"

I slowly opened the door to find her hunched over the toilet. She looked up at me, face pale, but then pressed her lips together to force back what was coming up. It didn't work, and she quickly pulled back her hair as she vomited into the toilet again.

I stepped in behind her and gathered her hair in my hands. After a minute, the vomiting eased, and she wiped her mouth with toilet paper as she sat on the floor, still not looking entirely better.

"I could carry you back to bed," I suggested, crouching beside her.

Lily shook her head but smiled faintly. "I can walk. I think the motion of being lifted might set me off again."

"Fair enough." I offered her my hand to help her up. She took it gladly and slowly stood with me. "I'll get you some water—"

She paused suddenly, and I wondered if she needed to vomit again based on the way her eyes had widened, and her hand went to her stomach. Before I could say anything, Lily brushed past me on her way to the bedroom.

I followed and slowed to a stop outside the bathroom as she rummaged through her nightstand and pulled out a planner.

I frowned. My brain was still processing the vomiting. And that I needed to get her water.

Lily started counting back the days as she made her way to me. A faint wrinkle formed between her eyebrows as she frowned, mostly in confusion. Her eyes slowly lifted off the page. "I'm not due for my period yet, but…"

I couldn't help but glance at her stomach.

Mine seemed to drop ten feet.

Her throat bobbed. "You don't think…"

Great. I've knocked up my girlfriend right before I go to prison—

The bedroom door swung open, and Seb rushed through it. Bypassing us, he raced into Lily's bathroom with one hand on his stomach and the other over his mouth.

"Kira's in the other bathroom—We shouldn't have had that chicken pizza," he groaned as he pulled the door shut. "Sorry!"

Lily leaned against the wall, resting her head back. "It's food poisoning… How come you aren't affected?"

"Didn't eat the chicken," I shrugged.

"Smart." She rubbed at her stomach again.

"You good though?"

"I need to sit down. My life just flashed before my eyes… *And* I need to let work know I'm not coming in today."

I chuckled and stepped aside as she made her way back to bed, crawling under the covers like she was about to hibernate for the rest of the year. Until she paused, flung the covers back, and ran into the bathroom again.

The mild food poisoning settled itself early in the afternoon.

Toast, apple juice, scrambled eggs, and water were the only things on the menu for all three of them, and they managed to keep each meal down after their morning of sharing two bathrooms.

Kira and Seb had hunkered down in the living room, with blankets swallowing them into the couch and mugs of green tea waiting on the coffee table as they watched TV. Kira had said green tea was good for stomach problems, so I left the apartment and bought plenty as a precaution. Along with a fresh supply of recovery foods for when they felt up to eating something with more substance.

After putting away the groceries and making the mentioned teas, I went to Lily's room — green tea in hand. She was sitting up in bed on the side closest to the bathroom, sketching in her notebook. There was color in her cheeks again, and her eyes were clearer.

"Did you want anythin' to eat?"

"No, thank you."

I set the tea on the nightstand while she put her notebook aside.

A hesitant look came over her face as she played with the hem of the bed sheet.

I paused, half smiling. "What?"

"I have a question."

"I can see that."

"I'm wondering how to word it."

I shrugged. "Speak your mind?"

She huffed. "Well... Since most couples would have this conversation at some point...to address the elephant in the room..." Her eyes traveled over me in thought before she straightened, clasping her hands together in her lap. "What *is* your stance on kids?"

My brow rose. "Oh."

She pressed her lips together. "Maybe not a conversation we're ready for?"

"No-no-no, I just wasn't expectin' it." I sat on the edge of the bed. "I don't think I'm suited to havin' them."

Well, that sounded a little finite...

I expected her to withdraw, but her eyes remained fixed on me in understanding. That look alone urged me to keep talking.

"My life isn't kid friendly," I reiterated.

"But hypothetically, if it were kid friendly, would you want them?"

My life before Lily consisted of living day to day with no thought of the future. Suddenly, she was casting a light on possibilities I once thought were impossible. Sitting down and picturing myself with kids was something I didn't do, and here I was doing it like I wasn't going to be arrested in a week.

"Maybe. With the right person." The way her eyes were smiling made me continue. We knew realistically it couldn't happen. But this conversation? If talking about happy futures and babies kept that smile on Lily's face, then I would hypothesize for the rest of my free life. "What about you?"

Lily hugged her knees to her chest. The eager gleam in her eyes told me she had thought about it before, maybe more than once.

"I don't know. I think my mother's ideals might have formed the way I think about it. While she's a career woman at heart, she also has strong family values. She expects Jane and me to settle down and have a family of our own...while taking over at the agency when she retires... I *could* easily picture myself with kids, living the typical suburban life that she expects me to have. But I also want to travel and live first..." She stopped herself. "As you said, with the right person, maybe? *But*, if I were to have them, it won't be until I'm at least thirty."

I mocked a frown. "And, uh, who do you plan on havin' these kids with? Because a prison sentence for blackmail alone can put me away for a long time."

Lily's mouth dropped open in shock, but there was a smile hidden at the corners of her lips.

"Too soon?"

"Yes," she laughed, shoving at my bicep.

It barely moved me, so I leaned closer. "There are conjugal visits. Not at Rikers, but other places."

"Oh, how romantic."

I half smiled. "So, hypothetically, you'd have my kids?"

Her cheeks flushed red, and she shrugged. "*Hypothetically.*"

"Even if they inherited my attitude?"

Her smile grew wider. "I'd expect them to have it."

I didn't think I could love this woman any more than I already did.

Lily cast her eyes down. "But who knows? Maybe I'll be living in an apartment full of art, books, and cats by the time I'm thirty. Sending you letters... Maybe the conjugal visits won't be so bad."

I braced my knuckles into the mattress, either side of her thighs, and pressed a kiss to her forehead. When I pulled back, I cocked my head to one side. "If it helps, I don't look too bad in orange."

She fought back a smile until she could no longer.

A couple of hours later, as we lay on her bed watching the sunlight pass through our interlocked fingers, and Lily finished laughing softly at something I said, my phone buzzed on the nightstand.

"Mom. Hey. Everythin' alright?" I answered, holding the phone to my ear while I lay there.

"Everything is fine," Mom responded. "But you have not been home for a while. Have you finally moved in with Lily?"

She knew about my arrest, but she just didn't know it would happen in a week. I hadn't had the chance to tell her yet.

I glanced at Lily. She was listening to my half of the conversation with a faint smile. "No, I haven't."

Mom sighed. I could picture her shaking her head.

"What are your plans for your birthday tomorrow? And please don't say *nothin'*," she mocked.

I didn't not like birthdays. It was the fuss that went into them that made me want to avoid my own. My life was already chaotic enough.

"Work."

"Dean."

Lily sat up and whispered, "Is this about your birthday?"

I nodded and tapped my phone screen. "You're on speaker, Mom. Lily is here."

"Don't worry, Sofia. We're going out for drinks tomorrow night," Lily smiled, leaning against my arm.

I raised a brow at her. "Did you forget you all had food poisoning today?"

Mom gasped. "Food poisoning?"

"It's cleared up now." Lily poked my bicep. "You're not getting out of celebrating this birthday."

"I agree," Mom added.

I pinched the bridge of my nose and huffed a laugh. "I never said I wasn't going."

Probably wasn't the best idea to even be leaving the apartment, considering Mark's warning about laying low, but my birthday coinciding with Halloween had offered up a good cover to hide in plain sight.

"We should go to your mom's on Saturday for lunch too," Lily added.

"Ooh, yes!" Mom exclaimed. "*Grazie, Lily.*"

Lily smiled proudly.

I rolled my eyes, but couldn't stop smiling either. "Did you need anythin' done today, Mom?"

"No, I just wanted to hear from you. But I can't wait to see you both this weekend. I will make cannoli just for you, Lily."

Lily hummed beside me. "I'm already salivating."

Mom laughed. "Well, I will let you go now. Give my love to the others."

"Will do."

"Byeee," Lily sang happily.

"*Vi voglio bene a entrambi.*"

"Love you too, Mom." I waited for her to hang up first before I tossed my phone onto the covers, stretching my arms above my head before loosely draping one around Lily.

After a moment, Lily rolled onto her side to face me.

"Random question: If you're Sicilian, why do you only speak Italian?"

"I know how to say the basics in Sicilian, and how to order a gelato. Mom can speak it fluently." I rested my head back on the headboard with a heavy sigh. "My father only knew Italian. He *was* born Sicilian too, but he grew up in the north before coming to Palermo... He hated the idea that we could hold a conversation he couldn't understand, so he banned us from speaking it."

"Sorry." She gave a self-deprecating shake of her head. "I should've thought before I brought it up."

I gently gripped her chin, turning her face towards me. "All you've brought up is the reminder that maybe I should practice my Sicilian. At least for Mom's sake."

"And I should probably learn Italian for yours," she added with a thoughtful nod.

"You should. That way, during those conjugal visits we can talk without the correctional officers knowing what we're sayin'." I gently squeezed her side, and she let out a half giggle, half squeal before she pulled away to kneel beside me.

"Let's start now."

Was my garage boss pleased that I skipped an entire Thursday to spend time with my girlfriend while she recovered from a mild case of food poisoning? No. There was a backlog of cars that needed attention.

Did I care? Also no.

I would take whatever jobs I could tomorrow, on my birthday. I would also put in my two-week notice and let him know that I wouldn't be coming back for a while. For now, though, something else was on my mind.

I had told the others I had forgotten something at the store, but I had other plans that took about an hour to get done. These plans had a lot to do with the smudged drawing of two small birds on my left wrist and the desire to show Lily some appreciation for her enthusiasm during her lax Italian lesson.

When I returned, it was just Lily in the apartment — Seb had either left for home and taken Kira with him, or they had stepped out for some fresh air. Lily, meanwhile, was in the kitchen as I stepped into the living room.

She was sipping from a glass of water, standing by the counter, when her eyes landed on the second skin plastered on my wrist.

Her welcoming smile spread. "What's that?"

"Oh, this?" I lifted my wrist lazily for emphasis as I moved towards her. "It's just a sketch."

Her eyes sparkled, and she lifted my wrist to get a better look at the fresh tattoo of her two little birds.

I ducked my head to kiss her cheek. "Now I'll have a little piece of your art with me wherever I go."

Her eyebrows pulled up in the middle, and there was a slight pout in her bottom lip.

I cupped her face and kissed her slowly.

She mirrored the action, tilting her head to allow me in.

CHAPTER 46

Lily

Stationed at the kitchen counter with an array of face paint laid out before me, I began dabbing a small sponge of white paint across Seb's face.

"Try not to smile unless you want smile lines included with the costume," I said.

Seb schooled his features as best he could. "Yes, ma'am."

Kira, snapping photos of the process, grinned from behind her camera. "I guarantee he lasts five seconds."

"Shhh, I'm trying to focus," Seb said, a smile already dimpling his cheek.

He was going as a gender bent Harley Quinn. The costume consisted of a red and black dress vest, no shirt beneath, leather pants — one leg red, the other black — big red boots, and black fingerless gloves.

The face paint was the final touch. All white with the plan to paint black diamonds around his eyes and to color his top lip with more black paint that would extend towards his cheeks, giving him a wider, clown-like smile.

Kira was going as Poison Ivy. She had the hair for it and the love for plants. She only had to slip into the skintight, sleeveless, green one-piece and a pair of green, floral, lace leggings, and she was already in character. I added hand-painted, delicate vines and leaves across her collarbones, along her arms, and down one side of her face. Kira did the rest of the makeup, transforming into a costume so gorgeous that Seb was speechless for several minutes when she walked out of her bedroom.

After work earlier today, we had all made a last-minute shop at any dollar stores and thrift stores that sold anything that could be used in our costumes.

My costume was straight from the roaring twenties. The dress was detailed with silver and white, and included a matching sequin shawl and headpiece. I even managed to style my hair to resemble the style of that time with a lot of bobby pins. My makeup was the only thing to have more of a modern twist. Alongside some traditional dark lip and eyeliner, Kira insisted on adding glittering eye shadow and several tiny eye gems to finish the look.

I was sparkling from head to toe.

Literally and figuratively.

The first session with Doctor Hamdan had truly done wonders, and tonight was genuinely something I was looking forward to celebrating, regardless of what would come after. I was focusing on the present.

I glanced over at the reason for the celebration. Sitting on the couch, staring off in content as he twirled a fake hunting knife around his fingers. Dean wore all black — a black long-sleeved shirt that was tight enough to reveal the muscle beneath, black jeans, and big black combat boots. It wasn't very different from his usual attire, except he had a ghostly mask sitting in his lap. He went without the robe, deciding to keep it all minimalistic. And looked absolutely delicious doing it.

Seb chuckled, looking side-on at Dean and keeping his face still for me. "He looks way too comfortable with a knife."

The comment pulled Dean from his stare, and he flashed us a lopsided smile as he gave the knife another twirl for emphasis.

I bit my lip as I smiled and continued with the face paint, this time adding the black lines around Seb's lips and carefully painting the diamonds over his eyes.

The choice not to match my costume with Dean was made out of safety. On the off chance I was recognized by anyone working for the triplets, they wouldn't spot Dean — this was my way of protecting him. His tattoos were mostly covered, and he would be wearing a mask so popular for Halloween, no one would look twice at him. He could move through crowds almost unnoticed.

Tonight was about his 27th birthday, and no one was going to ruin that. Seb and Kira had also found a nightclub in Bushwick that was as far from the triplets and Antonio as possible.

When I was done painting Seb's face, I held up a mirror for him to see. "What do you think?"

The black lines along his cheeks succeeded in making his smile look eerily wider. "I love it."

"Okay, photo time," Kira beamed, hurrying over to the bookshelf by my bedroom door to set up her camera. Seb jumped off his stool to get into a pose on the other side of the living room.

Dean stood, stretched in a way that lifted the hem of his shirt, and then pulled on his mask and slid the fake knife through a belt loop on his jeans. When he noticed me watching, he tilted his head as he approached me, tugging up his sleeves a little.

His new tattoo, the two small birds I drew on his wrist, were still fresh. To think my drawing was now a permanent mark on his skin made my heart flutter. It didn't have the same possessiveness that a name tattoo could hold, but instead showed a type of commitment. And general appreciation for the art.

I grinned. "You're enjoying that costume, aren't you?"

He shrugged, bringing his hands to my waist once I was in reach. "Just a little."

"Guys, come on. Group photo." Seb grabbed Dean's arm and dragged him over to get in the shot.

I followed with a skip in my step while Kira set the timer and jogged over to join us.

We posed in character first, and did a few more casual and funny ones, flexing biceps or pulling faces.

And then, in a flurry of costume touch-ups, grabbing wallets, bags, and keys, and booking an Uber, we made our way from the apartment.

Dean's body warmth thawed out my shivers as we walked along a lively sidewalk in Bushwick. My thin shawl had done nothing against the October cold.

Almost every stranger was dressed in costume, and we passed several people who wore the same mask as Dean. The only thing that gave him away to us was his height and broad shoulders.

Seb and Kira led the way, locked in a quiet discussion about something while also checking their phones and pointing at buildings and street signs.

"Are we lost?" Dean's voice was muffled by his mask.

"*No...*" Seb responded.

"Our Uber dropped us off a little further than necessary," Kira added, throwing a sheepish smile over her shoulder. Her curls bounced with every step.

"You gave him the wrong address, didn't you?" Dean tilted his head, and I could almost see the unimpressed but slightly humored expression through his mask.

Seb held up a finger as he continued checking his phone. "Shush."

"Apart from the cold, it's a nice walk," I offered with a shrug.

Dean tilted his head, definitely deadpanning at me. "Your teeth were chatterin' before."

"*Okay*, but it's still nice to just be here, with you. Regardless of the fact we're freezing our asses off," I smiled, crossing my arms as I looked up at him. "Happy b—"

I staggered as my heel caught in a grate, leading me to hop right out of the shoe with my hand clutching Dean for balance. Without a word, he crouched down and plucked the heel from between the metal and then took the time to guide my foot back into the shoe. His hand rested on my calf until he dared to skim it up behind my knee. A warm, simple but loving caress that sent my heart soaring as he lowered my foot to the ground again. I couldn't see his eyes, but I knew they were on my face the entire time.

It made me blush.

Dean stood and offered his elbow.

I took it gladly, reembracing that warmth. "Why, thank you, sir."

We were three drinks in, and I offered to order the fourth round. I was lightly buzzed by the alcohol and feeling almost untouchable as confidence soaked through my body.

I leaned on the bar as I waited for one of the bartenders. Across the crowded dance floor, where bright colorful lights flashed over dancing strangers in costumes, I could see our mini table, where Dean, Seb, and Kira waited, enjoying the music and atmosphere.

The smile on my face hadn't diminished since the night began, and I doubted anything could make it fade.

Until an arm brushed against mine, followed by the voice of a man leaning in to speak to me as he arrived at the bar.

"Hey, beautiful," he slurred. There was already a drink in his hand. "Watcha doin' sittin' here all alone?"

"I'm here with someone." I focused my attention on the action behind the bar, hoping my lack of interest in him would diminish his interest in me.

It didn't.

He leaned closer with a smirk on his face. "*Sure*, sweetie."

With a quiet sigh, I turned and pointed to the area across the room. The drunk followed the direction of my finger. "See the tall guy in the mask? The one looking this way? That's who I'm here with."

He laughed. "How'd I know you didn't just point out the meanest looking guy here? I think you're playin' hard to get."

"Suit yourself, but I did warn you... You also have *maybe* twenty-ish seconds to move."

To my disgust, he leaned even closer, blanketing my senses with the stench of his breath. "Or what, doll?"

The smile on my face was neither impressed nor genuine. It was pure tipsy confidence and pettiness because I knew this man was not winning tonight.

"Scary boyfriend privilege," I said, nodding in the direction beyond his shoulder.

He rolled his eyes and had another look. The smugness quickly dropped from his expression as he took in the sight of the 6'3" masked man heading straight through the crowd. Never mind the people around him, he was locked in.

The confidence in his stride created goosebumps along my arms and legs. I was about to melt into the bar.

To my mild surprise, Dean wasn't approaching the stranger. He was coming to me.

I turned to face him, leaning back against the bar as he lifted his mask enough to reveal his jawline and lips. The second his boots were planted on either side of my feet, he cupped the back of my head, and kissed me so strongly my heart rate skyrocketed.

There was whiskey on his tongue, cologne on his clothes, and a deep hum from his throat that vibrated softly to my lips. He pulled me closer.

The drunk protested — something along the lines of "hey, fuck off, I was here first" — but was cut off when Dean pressed his palm to the man's face and pushed him away. All while still kissing me.

It was a kiss not meant for public display, but neither of us cared.

He broke first, but only to let us take a breath, and took my chin under his thumb as he lifted his mask a little more. A devilish smile was already on his lips. "Is this the part where I growl and call you mine?"

My knees went weak as I smiled at him, biting the corner of my lip. "You've been reading some of my books, hm?"

He used his thumb to tidy my smudged lipstick. "Just the parts you've annotated the most."

The rest of the night was a happy blur, mostly because of how much we had to drink and how little we paid attention to anything else outside of us.

I vaguely remembered doing shots and possibly licking spilled alcohol from Dean's throat. I also lost my headpiece somewhere in the crowd. And in the car ride home, Dean couldn't keep his hands off me. Then again, neither could I with him.

His mask was off, and his black hair unruly. There was also smudged lipstick on his jaw and mouth from me.

"Whoops," I grinned, trying to wipe it off before he kissed me again. This was before we arrived at the apartment. The Uber driver waited patiently for us to clamber from the car, and then we made our way up to our door, staggering a little, trying to act sober and failing miserably.

"I think," Kira said a tad loudly, carrying her shoes as we walked the long hall to the apartment, "we should have a nightcap."

"Shhh. Don't want to wake *The Neighbor*," I whispered with a wide-eyed nod in the direction of Susan's door.

Dean wrapped his arms around my shoulders from behind. "You sure? I kinda wanna have a chat with her."

I playfully slapped his forearm, and he unraveled both, but not before kissing me on the cheek and walking ahead to lean beside our door. Somehow, despite drinking as much as we had, Dean seemed the most sober — well, apart from the glazed look in his dilated eyes and the nonchalance in his movements.

It was the most I had seen him smile.

God, he has a lovely smile.

Seb rubbed his stomach, rolling his head back. "I want food. Do you girls have food?"

"All the food!" Kira exclaimed.

"Shhh!" I laughed, fishing out my keys as we reached the door.

Once that door was open, Seb jogged ahead to raid the pantry with Kira in tow. I stopped at the kitchen counter, setting my bag down as our friends pulled snack after snack from the shelves. Dean came up behind me with his hand gliding around my waist. Every one of his touches brought a feeling of safety. And even if it was a touch expressing casual appreciation, the alcohol in my system ramped it up to wanting to be careless.

I wanted to peel off every layer of clothing and make drunk love to him, but not in the way I had been doing to cope with trauma. This was different. For the first time in a while, I didn't feel panicked.

And I somehow had to convey this feeling of want to him without Kira and Seb hearing.

Dean's mask was still in his hand, so I gently took it and pulled it over my head to provide cover for how red my cheeks were about to get. He watched me with amusement.

I cleared my throat and addressed everyone first.

"I think I might head to bed." I turned to Dean and continued. "And I want you to...*rimuovi il mio...vestiti?* Did I say that right?"

Dean's eyebrows shot up while Kira and Seb laughed in drunk amazement.

"I think I just fell in love with you again." Dean was thoroughly perplexed but happy as he watched me.

A simultaneous "Awwwww" erupted from Seb and Kira.

I knew my face would be completely red beneath the mask, but I lifted it anyway and spoke softly to Dean. "So?"

"Well, yeah, but only if, you know." He leaned in and whispered. "Only if you're comfortable."

"I promise this is far from being anything like *that*," I whispered back. "I want to be with you and take things slow. *And* continue celebrating your birthday."

Dean's face fell serious — as serious as it could get while under the influence — and he took his mask back, pulled it on, and swiftly bent forward. His shoulder came to my stomach, and his arms wrapped around my thighs before I was lifted from the ground and slung over his shoulder, laughing the entire time. He then headed straight for my bedroom, one arm pinning me in place while his hand rested high on the back of my leg.

"Keep it down now, kids," Kira called out as Dean nudged the door shut with his boot.

He crouched to place my feet on the floor and ever so slowly skimmed his hands up my legs as he stood, lifting the hem of my dress in the process, but not removing it yet.

"*Vuoi che tenga la maschera?*" His voice. The accent. I had no clue what he said but fuck.

Hot and bothered, I shook my head. Throat bobbing. "Sorry?"

He chuckled. "Want me to keep the mask on?"

I paused and blinked. "I—well."

Crossing his arms, he tipped his head back and stepped closer.

Dean was already dripping in self-confidence, but the mask gave him more.

"I've seen the books you read, Lily."

My calves backed into the mattress, and I sat down.

He leaned over me, bringing the mask closer to my face while his fists sank into the mattress beside my hips, locking me in place. His biceps flexed beneath his shirt, and the tone of his voice softened. "We're gonna take this nice and easy, remember? If you get overwhelmed, tell me. If you wanna stop or go—"

"I'll tell you." I lay back on the covers, stretching my arms above my head.

I waited for the panic or feeling of dread to come, but none did. Maybe it was the alcohol, or maybe it was because I knew I finally had a healthy outlet for the bad memories in the form of therapy. For now, in my room, I felt untouchable.

"So, what'll it be?" he asked.

"Keep the mask on."

His fingertips glided lazily along my bare back.

I was on my stomach with my arms crossed under my head. The drunken buzz from earlier was slowly fading, but I was high on something else and unable to wipe the pleased smile from my face.

We had had drunk, ultra-slow sex earlier that seemed to last for eternity before we finally dragged ourselves into the shower.

Beside me, Dean was slowly falling asleep. I could feel it with the way his fingers slowed. He was on his back with the sheets sitting low on his hips.

I rose to my elbows and moved closer to him, admiring his peaceful state before I brought my lips to his collarbone and trailed light, lazy kisses up his throat, to his jaw, and then his cheekbone.

The corner of his mouth curved up until a sleepy smile appeared. His arm, already beneath me, curled around my waist.

"Happy birthday," I whispered, and kissed the corner of his mouth.

He hummed back.

I settled my head on his chest, listening to his heart.

In a week, everything would change, and moments like this would be nothing but memories.

Dean's hand smoothed along my back, and he murmured sleepily. "You are the best thing that has ever happened to me... Which sounds unbelievably fuckin' depressin' now that I've said it out loud...but it's true. I don't know who I would be without you."

CHAPTER 47
Dean

We were hungover.

After a late breakfast of the greasiest things we could find in the kitchen, Seb and Kira stumbled back into bed, armed with aspirin. Lily and I were tempted to do the same, but we had agreed to lunch with Mom.

"We could push it back to dinner with her instead." I pulled on my sunglasses as we left the apartment, trying to nullify the throb in the back of my eyeballs.

"We'll survive," Lily laughed, taking my hand to tow me towards my car. She wore ankle boots, a light purple T-shirt, and skinny jeans that made this hangover only slightly better as long as she stayed in view. "And she's probably already made the food."

"Well, while you eat, I'm takin' a nap." I fished the car keys from my back pocket.

"Okay, old man," she grinned, walking ahead of me, out onto the sidewalk.

Her smile faded when her eyes landed on the front of the Cadillac. She froze.

I followed her gaze.

Placed on the hood of the car was a pristine white lily.

The hangover became a second thought as I scanned the street. There was nothing out of place, and the cop car was still parked across the road fifty feet away.

Lily carefully picked up the flower. "Maybe it was some kids trick or treating..."

I took the flower and marched to the cop car. If it was something as innocent as a joke, maybe it's why they hadn't reacted.

What kids leave flowers on Halloween?

I knocked on the window impatiently with the side of my fist.

The driver lazily rolled down his window. "Can I help—"

"Did you see who left this?" I said.

He looked at the flower with disinterest. "What do you mean?"

Don't drag him through the window.

I gritted my teeth, trying to stay calm. "It was on my car."

"We were told to make sure *she* was safe," he nodded to Lily as she joined my side. "No one said anything about watching your car." He seemed to think this was a joke with the way he chuckled with his partner.

I'm gonna drag him through the window.

"You do realize we're together, right? She travels in my car." My tone was getting sharper. I couldn't help it. "You didn't *think* that maybe those orders to protect her included watchin' for anyone who stops outside the fuckin' apartment block?"

"Watch your tone, Moretto."

My eyebrows lifted, and I stepped forward. "Watch my tone? Are you fuckin' kiddin' me—"

Lily placed a hand on my arm but addressed the officers. "Can you contact my father, Detective Whitmore, please?"

The officers shared a look before the driver sighed and lifted his radio, except right before he went to speak, a report buzzed through about a house fire and gunshots.

He responded to that instead, and I rolled my eyes, moving away from the car.

Lily followed. "It's okay, Dean. We'll take it to my dad after we see your mom—"

An address for the fire was given over the police radio, barely audible over the static but clear enough for Lily and I to stop.

It was my address.

I ditched the flower and ran to my car. Every thought evaporated from my head, and my stomach twisted. "No-no-no—"

Police sirens sounded as the cop car sped by. Lily climbed into the Cadillac as I did. She didn't speak, instead she hastily shoved on her seatbelt while I ripped the gear stick into drive. The flower was on her lap, I guess for evidence later.

I took a shortcut to my house, avoiding more cops as I went way over the speed limit. Lily's hand was pressed against the dashboard.

I need to get home.

I need to get to Mom.

One more street—

Dragging the steering wheel down, I took a hard left onto my street.

The road was blocked with police tape, cop cars, fire trucks, and an ambulance... There was a cop car across from the house with its windshield completely peppered with bullet holes and the front seats covered in blood. That was the police surveillance Mark promised for my mother.

I stopped the car right behind the police tape and climbed out, unable to see the house beyond one of the fire trucks until I rounded the front of it.

Brick was charred, something in the roof continued to smoulder, and the windows all had the same large, splintered hole in their centers.

Police were stationed everywhere.

I ducked under more tape to get closer, but one of the officers stepped in my way.

"What happened?" *I knew what happened.*

"Sir, I need you to get back behind the tape."

I shook my head. "Where is she? Where's my mom?"

Another officer joined, taking hold of my shoulder. "Sir—"

I shoved at his chest. "Get the fuck off me! Where is she?!"

"Dean." Her voice was gentle but firm, and sliced through the tension so easily.

I turned around, ignoring the fact that a few more officers had walked over, and found Lily. Her eyes were wet with tears as she grabbed my wrist and began leading me down the sidewalk. I thought she was pulling me away from causing a scene. Instead, she was bringing me to the ambulance as they brought a stretcher to its back doors.

Mom was on it, covered in foil, and blankets, and bandages, and tubes with an oxygen mask over her face.

I reached them, overhearing the tail end of what the paramedics were discussing.

Patient is a paraplegic.... Burns to 80% of the body, including airways.

I couldn't get to her side. I knew the paramedics were doing their job, but I couldn't get to her side.

"*Sono qui, sono qui, mamma.*" I said urgently.

Her eyelids fluttered and barely opened. Ash and blood caked the side of her head, and her hair, usually so black and beautiful, was matted and wet with more blood.

I needed her to know I was there. That she wasn't alone.

Her eyes found mine as they loaded her into the back of the ambulance.

I went to follow.

"I'm sorry, but we don't have the room," a paramedic said, placing a gentle hand on my arm. "We need to go."

I nodded, backing away from the doors as they said something about a hospital, and closed her in.

Everything seemed to warp and slow. Noises were distant or fading in and out. I couldn't think beyond the buzzing in my head.

Someone gently took my hand, and then their hands were on my face.

I looked down and found Lily, but struggled to speak. "I don't—where—where's Bella?"

"Bella is fine. A neighbor is taking care of her. We need to follow the ambulance."

"I didn't hear what hospital…"

"That's okay. I did." The calmness in her voice provided something to keep me from losing it. "Come on."

CHAPTER 48
Lily

This isn't happening.

The hospital corridor was quiet. Eerily quiet.

I stood by the vending machine, not really hungry or paying attention to what I had picked. I felt like I needed to be doing something. The lingering effects of a hangover weren't making the knots in my stomach feel any better.

This isn't happening.

A doctor marched through the double doors at the end of the corridor, but he walked right by us.

No news is good news, right?

The cold, stark white complexion of the walls and ceiling provided no comfort. Neither did the fluorescent lights or the plastic chairs along the wall.

Dean was sitting on the very last seat, the one closest to the ICU doors. His head was in his hands, his fingers were curled against his scalp, and his right leg bounced.

He hadn't spoken a word since we arrived.

A chocolate bar dropped into the vending machine tray. I fished it out and walked back to Dean with no intention of opening it.

I sat beside him, tucking my arm beneath his and holding it as I rested my chin on his shoulder.

"I should've been there." His voice was barely a whisper. "She was alone."

I held him a little tighter, swallowing the lump in my throat. I couldn't find the right words to make this any better. There was no making this better. It was a nightmare. And I could only imagine how Dean felt.

His home was gone, and his mother...

Sofia survived a tragedy before, and she rebuilt herself to the best of her abilities. At least, that's what I kept reminding myself. She was a strong woman.

I still had so many conversations I wanted to have with her. Like telling her I was finally getting help. I was meant to tell her that over lunch.

Which would've been happening now.

The doors opened again, and this time, the surgeon walking through them spotted us and slowed.

It was hard to gauge what she would say. Her expression gave away nothing.

Dean stood, ringing his hands with anticipation as he approached her. I followed him, hesitantly awaiting the news.

She introduced herself, but I failed to remember her name. She asked for our names, and we responded with quick mutters, trying to get introductions out of the way. She maintained eye contact and invited us to take a seat. She explained the procedures and the injuries. Every second of the conversation refused to take hold in my mind. I couldn't comprehend it, or maybe I didn't want to believe it.

"We did all we could, but her wounds were too severe..."

None of it felt real. The words, the hospital, the fact that Sofia was somewhere beyond those doors...

I muffled a sob with my hand as fresh tears spilled down my cheeks.

Any emotion that was in Dean's eyes slowly glazed over. There were tears and pain within them, but he was suddenly distant as he let the news sink in.

The surgeon recommended speaking with a counselor and asked gently if he wanted to view her later.

Dean backed off without a word, his eyes on the floor, unseeing, while his hands curled at his sides. He shook his head and went to speak, but nothing came.

"Can we—can we have a minute?" The words burned my throat.

The surgeon nodded solemnly and headed back through the doors.

I wrapped my arms around myself as the tears began to flow in heavy blobs, soaking my sleeves when I wiped them away.

Dean was leaning against the wall until he slowly sank to the floor. Tears tracked down his face, but his expression was almost blank.

"Tell me it's not real," he whispered, hugging his knees.

The helplessness of it all pained my heart.

His world had been shattered into a million pieces.

I joined him on the floor, and he took my hand, locking his fingers through mine like he expected to lose me next if he didn't hold on tight enough.

Chapter 49
Dean

For years, I had mastered the art of shoving all the traumatic shit I was exposed to throughout my miserable life down inside me, but this?

Rage and raw emotion leaked through the giant hole carved into my chest.

I needed to focus, but my fucking thoughts — the memories, the what ifs, the last words I said to her — refused to cooperate. I couldn't make them go away.

I couldn't stop these fucking tears.

I was balancing on the edge, holding my shit together because completely losing it in a hospital conference room wouldn't change what happened.

I knew who did it even if they hadn't admitted it yet. It was too similar to Roxy's death. The fire. The explosiveness of it. The damage was so profound that it would send shockwaves through Antonio's business and his people. They didn't care who got hurt along the way.

But I failed her.

"Dad's here," Lily said.

I didn't bother looking away from the floor-to-ceiling window as the detective walked into the room. He organized the room so we had somewhere private to talk. And for him to offer his condolences.

I didn't want to talk.

My eyes were fixed on the gloomy city. The sun was covered by a thick layer of cloud that was heavy with rain. And somewhere out there, Antonio's kids were walking around like nothing happened.

Lily told Mark about the flower and the way it was left on my car, and who we thought left it.

If we had left the apartment earlier, I could've gotten her out.

"Did Gabriele know Lily's name at all?" Mark asked.

"No," I said firmly.

"But the flower obviously meant something." Lily's voice was gentle but edged with emotion.

"It was clearly a message for—" Mark stopped himself. I could feel his eyes on my back. "Do you have any idea when it was put on the car?"

My nostrils flared, and I shut my eyes. This was a fucking waste of time.

"We went out last night, and it wasn't there when we came home, which was around 3 AM," Lily explained.

"You went out." His tone grew sharp, and I knew the next part was directed at me. "I warned you to lay low."

"Dad, please."

"What difference would it have made?" I looked across my shoulder at Mark and turned around, moving away from the window, stalking towards him. "They shot the cops that were meant to protect her."

"You both should've known better than to go out." He shared his disapproving glare evenly between Lily and me. "It was reckless—"

My patience snapped, and I shoved him against the wall with fistfuls of his suit in my hands. The force shook the wall, and a canvas artwork fell from its hook nearby.

Mark raised his hands. "I know you're upset—"

"You wanna talk reckless?" I hissed darkly through my teeth. "You got me involved in your fuckin' investigation through blackmail. You threatened to have my mother deported, and now she's fuckin' dead all because you just couldn't arrest me."

"Dean." The worried tone in Lily's voice pulled my attention to her.

The anger in me, the kind that tempted me to step back behind those walls to keep people out, had nothing against her. She kept me from drifting. Multiple times.

I blinked back the tears in my eyes and released her father, taking a step away. My hands shook at my sides as I looked towards the door, where two cops stood. They saw me shove the detective and were ready to intervene.

I sniffed sharply and wiped my eyes on the back of my hand. Fresh waves of emotion were beginning to rise through my insides, and I felt suffocated. The hospital wasn't helping. Too much bad shit happened in hospitals.

My chest felt tight.

"I need to get out of here."

"Okay, we can do that." Lily stepped towards me, but Mark gently took her arm. His eyes were on me, watching me cautiously.

He thought I would hurt her.

"We still need your statements, and he is in no state to drive. You should both wait here," he said.

"You don't get to tell me what to do right now," I warned.

"Her death was not my fault, Dean."

My jaw tightened as another tear rolled down my cheek. I looked at Lily. "If you wanna stay, it's fine. But I need to go."

"No. I'm going with you." Lily shrugged her father's hand from her arm and spoke clearly. "You can send someone to the apartment to get our statements."

"Lily," he lowered his voice, "I don't want you getting in a car with him."

I rolled my head back out of frustration, stuffing my fists deep in my pockets.

"I don't want him going through this alone," she retorted calmly. "We're going."

We started for the door, and the cops gradually stepped aside to let us pass, but Mark was adamant to get at least one more word in.

"Do not do anything reckless."

The Cadillac rolled to a stop outside the apartment as rain began to patter across the windshield.

I switched off the engine, unable to say a word as we sat still.

It all felt so much darker now.

Lily also looked like she was one trigger away from crying. Her eyes were red, and tears clung to her eyelashes.

"Come upstairs," she said softly.

I gave her a single, subtle nod and waited for her to move first. I needed to clear my head, air my frustrations, and try not to get caught or killed.

In the rearview mirror, a police car pulled into the street. They were some distance away, but I knew they were here for Lily's protection and our statements. There was no way Mark would delay getting those or risk me driving his daughter without a tail. He would want to make sure she got home safe, and with the arrival of the police, they could tell him that.

Lily shut her door. The second she stepped away from the car, I leaned over and manually locked it.

When she realized it was too late, she tried the door handle. "Dean, don't—"

The plea in her voice was cut off as I turned the key over. The engine rumbled deep, and I refused to look at her in case doing so changed my mind.

I shoved the gear stick into drive and pushed down hard on the accelerator, sending the back tires skidding until the car lurched into the street. There were no lights in my rearview, and no sirens to be heard. Even if there was, I doubted I would stop.

Chapter 50
Dean

There was no plan.

I wanted revenge, and I would get it no matter what.

I had no issue avenging her mistreatment three years ago, and would happily do it again.

Taking the gun from the glove compartment of my car, I tucked it into the back of my jeans as I stepped onto the street outside Castello di Vetro.

It was afternoon.

All the clubs along this street were closed until night.

There was no one around, and the rain fell heavier.

"You ready?" Vince asked, tugging his hood and bandana up and pulling on gloves.

I did the same without a response and climbed out of the car.

I approached the front door and didn't hesitate to smash a hole through the black glass with the butt of the gun. Chipping away more glass, I waited for a shout or an alarm. None came, and I reached through, and I unlocked the door.

The foyer was empty. There was no one snorting lines off the front desk this time.

I moved to the next door, gun in hand and my finger hovering over the trigger.

The interior of the club was just as quiet with its lights and music off. There wasn't a single person in sight upstairs, but I kept moving towards the basement entry, passing the black mirrors on the walls. I avoided looking at the reflection.

I knew how I felt. I didn't need to see it either.

The next door was easier to open. I kicked at the lock, and the door swung in, revealing the dark stairwell behind it.

I took to the steps quietly, keeping my breathing in check while I locked in. I couldn't afford to make mistakes.

The apartment's foyer was empty and smelled of cigarettes and cooking oil. I led the way up the stained concrete stairs, eyes fixed on the next landing. And then the next. Each landing had a fluorescent light that either flickered or wasn't working at all. Our stop was on the second floor, where the light was out, shrouding us in much-needed darkness as we closed in on the apartment door to our left.

Vince made quick and quiet work of the lock while my heart thundered against my ribcage.

At the bottom of the stairwell, I kept to the wall and crept towards the basement door directly in front of me. It was ajar, allowing enough of a gap for me to see into the middle of the basement. But it was still a limited view. I needed numbers, and to make sure it matched how many bullets I had.

Fuck it.

I threw the door open and walked in with the gun raised and my head on a swivel, eyeballing every dark corner of the room and the mezzanine above. Without the flashing lights, I could make out several windows along the tops of the high walls.

Apart from the large crates tucked under the mezzanine and the giant glass cube in the center of the basement, there was nothing else here.

I went in first, edging through the gap of the door as my eyes scanned the dark living space. The only light came from an old TV, facing a dirty recliner where a man sat slumped with a beer in hand.

His T-shirt and sweats were stained and worn, and his black hair was long and graying. His eye and cheek were already bruised and swollen, meaning I wasn't the first to speak with him tonight.

Gio Calacoci was too drunk to stand and confront us when he noticed he wasn't alone anymore. Instead, as his eyes lazily scanned Vince and me, he responded with slurred aggression. "The fuck you think you're doin' in my house?"

I ripped the bandana down from my face, tugged my hood back, and then pointed the gun at my father.

Gio lifted his hands, eyes wide on the gun, but he could barely get his vision to focus. "Wait-wait-wait. If you need more money, I can get it. I just need time."

I stepped forward and jammed the gun under his chin. "I don't want your fuckin' money."

"Please-please! Don't kill me! W-we could come to an agreement or somethin'."

I scoffed in realisation. "You have no clue who I am."

Frustrated, I pulled a hand through my hair as I rotated slowly on the spot. Gun in hand and a lump in my throat, I tried to suppress the rage begging to be let out. I needed to save it for them.

But then I recalled the look on Mom's face as they put her in the ambulance. *So much blood.*

The memory changed to the day I found her, after Gio shot her.

So much blood.

I was always too late.

I gripped my scalp this time, squeezing my eyes shut as I pulled at my hair.

I dragged him to his feet and walked him into the filthy bathroom in the back of his tiny apartment. The whole time, Gio whimpered instead of trying to defend himself — no longer the man capable of raping and beating his defenseless wife or abusing his teenage son.

I shoved him into the bathtub.

Vince blocked the bathroom door as I stepped out to the kitchen to hunt down a knife to do the job. Once I did, everything suddenly felt like I wasn't in my body anymore. I was moving on autopilot. Angry but equally calm as I made my way back to Gio and gave him the knife.

"Do it," I said simply, stepping back to lean against the wall.

"Can I write a note? At least for the police to find for my family?"

"You lost your right to a family when you shot your wife and unborn kid."

Gio blinked, and suddenly it dawned on him as he finally looked at me — really *looked at me.*

"Dean?" he whispered. "Son?"

"You don't get to call me that anymore."

Through rage-filled tears, I raised my gun to the giant cube in front of me and fired bullet after bullet into the glass.

"FUUUUCK!" I roared.

Anger and devastation tore through my insides like fire, hot and sickening. I was blinded by fury.

Someone had to pay.

Someone had to die.

I was always too fucking late.

The shots echoed loudly through the basement until the last bullet struck.

There was a loud *crack,* and the entire structure splintered with a spider-web-like fracture. Then it shattered, firing a million shards of glass in every direction. It spilled onto the floor like a giant crystal wave and scattered to my boots.

After the last piece bounced to a stop with a soft *clink,* the basement fell into complete silence.

I stood still, chest heaving.

What have I done?

CHAPTER 51

Lily

The week that followed didn't seem real.

I managed to make the arrangements for a cremation and a small ceremony. After everything Dean had done for me, it was the least I could do.

He had completely closed most people out except for Seb, Kira, and me, but even then, he had barely spoken a word or slept since Saturday.

Everything happened on that Saturday.

What he did at Castello di Vetro *was* careless, but I refused to reprimand him when he was doing it to himself already.

The worry about retaliation lingered in the corners of my mind. An entire week had gone by, and there wasn't a single indication that the Gimello triplets would want revenge for what happened in their club. And that made me nervous. Why hadn't they reacted yet?

There was a moment on Monday night, as I approached my bedroom window to close the blinds before bed, when I spotted something in the dark one-way street below. A figure, but it was hard to tell when it was hidden in the shadows.

I called Dad about it, and he came to check himself, but found nothing.

Maybe I imagined it. I was emotionally drained, so maybe my mind was playing tricks on me. As a precaution, and under strict orders from my father, we stayed inside the apartment. Not that we had much motivation to step outside. The world was a little darker without Sofia in it.

I didn't even want to think about the arrests that would happen in the following week.

I think the one thing that gave us a brief pause was Bella, Sofia's tiny but resilient dog. She wore a small, blue cast on her front leg and needed regular treatment for a small burn on her ear, but she provided a sliver of happiness and comfort when it was hard to find.

At first, Dean wanted nothing to do with her. It wasn't done out of hate but simply because it hurt. Bella was a reminder, yet it was Dean who said he would keep her when his old neighbors asked if they could take her.

As I got ready for the funeral this afternoon, smoothing out the creases in my black, knee-length dress while keeping my emotions in check, Dean sat on the couch with Bella in his lap. He tickled her tummy with a vague stare in his tired eyes and a shadow of a smile on his lips. He wore an all-black suit and had a pair of sunglasses on hand. Both were brand new since most of what he owned, apart from anything he left in my room, was destroyed in the fire.

I watched the time, counting down the seconds until eventually it was time to go. Saying the words felt like the hardest thing to do.

"Dean?" I approached him, hesitant to say the rest. I didn't want to disrupt this rare moment of peace. "It's time."

I didn't know that Sofia's favorite color was purple or that she loved lavender. They were details about her I would've learned in the future if she were still alive. Instead, I heard about it from Dean as we organized the initial preparations for her funeral.

Touches of lavender and purple decorated the coffin, the seats, and the interior of the small crematorium chapel. Everyone in attendance was asked to wear something purple amongst their black attire. Kira had woven friendship bracelets for this reason, in all shades of purple, and gave one to anyone who arrived without a purple item. Dean wore one too and didn't take his eyes off it as the funeral commenced, keeping his head bowed in the front row as the celebrant addressed the room.

What broke my heart the most was that he was the only family member there amongst a sea of friends.

In a way, Sofia had rebuilt her own large family, surrounding herself with love and happiness after what she went through.

I threaded my arm through the crook of Dean's elbow as the eulogies began.

Anyone was invited to speak and share stories that celebrated Sofia's life, and there were plenty. One was about how she saved a young couple's wedding from disaster when the caterer fell through. Another was about the bonds of friendship Sofia nurtured with anyone who got to know her.

Once the last person left the lectern, the celebrant asked if there was anyone else who wanted to speak.

With my heart racing, I stood and approached the lectern as I unfolded the eulogy I had tucked into the pocket of my dress.

My choice to speak came as a surprise to Dean, but the appreciation and relief was evident in his expression. It was the first time he had looked up since the funeral began.

"Sofia was a survivor," I said. "She was a strong, independent woman who faced adversity head-on and managed to remain relentlessly positive every time... I didn't know her for as long as most of you here today, but from the moment I met her, she treated me like we had been friends for years. She welcomed me into the Moretto family without hesitation; with open arms, food, and an ear to listen." I offered Dean a small smile. He returned it with tears in his eyes, in no way helping my effort to keep myself from crying. I huffed a quiet laugh and inhaled shakily as I looked back at my notes. "I think the easiest way to see the effects of her big heart and undying love, and loyalty is to look at her son. The morals he lives by are all a reflection of the woman who raised him." Another look at Dean told me the message was received. He wasn't to blame for any of this and needed to know that. Sofia wouldn't want him to blame himself for any of it.

"Sofia, I will miss you." My hands shook as I folded up the eulogy notes and walked quietly back to my seat. I managed to keep it together, taking a deep breath to still my nerves as Dean took my hand.

"Thank you," he whispered.

The funeral drew to a peaceful end with the celebrant instructing everyone that there would be food and warm beverages in the other room. Slowly, the guests left the chapel a row at a time, heading for the back doors until eventually the chapel was empty save for Dean and me.

I stepped into the aisle, expecting Dean to follow, but he approached the coffin and placed his hand on the lid. A tear streaked down his cheek, but his composure was impenetrable. He unclenched his jaw and spoke softly.

"*Pò ripusari ora.*"

When the day was over, and everyone began to head out, I approached the funeral director and celebrant to thank them, but also to discuss what happened next. It was the kind of conversation that didn't seem real — discussing how long a cremation took and when to pick up the ashes.

They gave me a time frame of three days. I thanked them again, and then I walked away like I still hadn't stepped back into reality yet. Death was one thing, but the preparations afterwards were just as hard. It cemented that she was never coming back.

Outside, the sky was overcast, and there was a wintery chill in the air. I rubbed my arms as I scanned the area for Dean. Friends of Sofia's still lingered for a chat, but it was the short line of people to the left of the door by a garden of roses that helped me spot him.

He was curtly accepting condolences from the guests as they left, keeping his hands buried in his pockets. His face was drawn, and his eyes were hollow, but he managed several small smiles of thanks if someone patted his shoulder or pulled him into a hug.

Once each person had moved on, he would press his lips together and clench his jaw before the next person came along.

He wanted out.

I picked up my pace, also accepting several compliments about the service as I went. I smiled politely at them but kept going until Kira approached. I slowed for her.

"Hey," I breathed.

"Hi." She pulled me into a hug immediately.

"That was harder than I thought," I muttered over her shoulder.

I spotted Seb approaching Dean. The arrival of his friend caused his shoulders to relax.

"You handled it like a boss," Kira said, pulling back. "I would've been a mess."

"I almost was." I lifted my hands to show her the shake that remained.

She half smiled out of sympathy. "I'm still proud of you. Also," she took my hands, "Seb and I might avoid the apartment for a while to give you guys some space."

"Are you sure?"

"Yeah, of course. Funerals are overwhelming, and we figured Dean would like the quiet right now."

"Thank you."

We approached the guys as they waited by the rose bush. Kira offered Dean a hug that was the first of few he was happy to accept, and then our friends left for Seb's bike, hand in hand.

As we watched them leave, Dean slid his hands back into the pockets of his pants, only to withdraw something from within the pocket.

A single cigarette.

He looked at it for a long time, contemplating before he put it between his lips and retrieved his lighter too.

I could've stopped him, but he deserved this one small release.

Who was I to judge when I had used sex to overcome trauma?

His hands shook as he tried over and over to light the end of his cigarette, his frustration growing by the second.

I moved in front of him and gently took the lighter. It was harder than I expected, but I managed to flick the wheel several times before a flame appeared. I cupped a hand around it to protect it from the wind and brought the flame to the end of his cigarette.

The end crackled softly, and he drew back on it long and slow, frowning as he did.

Dean then dropped his head back to breathe out a cloud of smoke, casting his teary gaze to the sky.

A police car was stationed outside the apartment, providing some security to a day that left us emotionally unguarded.

Inside, I slipped off my shoes, fed Bella a dinner of leftover rice because we had forgotten to buy dog food, and drifted into my room where Dean was already sitting on the end of my bed. Head in hands, elbows to knees, he combed his fingers through his black hair. His suit jacket sat beside him, his tie was discarded, and his sleeves were rolled up.

"I didn't think that many people would show," he muttered.

I sat beside him and rested my head on his shoulder. "Your mom touched so many people's hearts; I'm surprised more didn't come."

He threaded his fingers through mine. "Thank you for steppin' up."

I cupped the side of his face with my other hand. The gray-blue of his eyes held so much sorrow. There wasn't a shred of any walls left, only raw emotion and complete trust. We had seen each other at our worst and barely flinched.

"Did you want to lay here a while?" My thumb stroked his cheek.

"Sounds good to me."

We lay on top of the covers, still in our clothes and facing one another with our hands resting in the space between us. There was no talking, only listening to the sounds in my room and the city outside as the sun set.

Eventually, Dean fell into a deep sleep. The first he had had since last weekend.

I stayed beside him for some time, until night fell and the room grew dark; until Kira and Seb arrived home with the quiet click of the front door. They didn't say a word, and I wondered if they went straight to her room.

Bella began to bark frantically.

I frowned at the door. She usually loved Seb and Kira.

Not wanting it to wake Dean, I got out of bed and padded over to the door before slipping out of the room, back first, as I quietly closed the door again.

"Bella," I whispered, turning around to calm the dog and greet our friends. "It's okay. It's just—"

CHAPTER 52
Dean

My body jolted, and I woke up, wondering if the distant scream I heard was part of a dream.

She was still alive in my dreams. That's why I didn't sleep. Seeing her and then waking up only made the loss worse.

I would never get the chance to speak with her again.

I rubbed my eyes, inhaling as I reached out to Lily's side of the bed. But Lily wasn't there, and Bella was barking.

Feeling weary, I pulled myself out of bed and made my way to the door, trying to gain some sense of normal from a day so heavy. I thought I was all out of tears, yet another lump was quick to form in my throat the second I thought about the funeral again.

Focus on the dog.

I dragged the door open. "Bella. Enough... What the fuck?"

I'm dreaming. It has to be a fucking dream.

Lily was on the couch in the dress she wore to the funeral, but there was tape over her mouth, and her arms were bound behind her back as she stared at me with terror in her eyes and a bruise on her cheek.

The barking was coming from Kira's bedroom, but my focus was on Lily as she tried to say something through the tape.

She shook her head frantically and nodded to the kitchen. Her eyes were wide with a warning.

Before I could even think about looking at the kitchen, something solid hit the side of my head.

CHAPTER 53
Kira

I held on to Seb a little tighter on the ride home.

With everything going on, I found solace in him.

After the funeral, we went to the apartment to get my camera, and then we spent the rest of the evening chasing the sunset around Brooklyn to get the best shot. We eventually stopped at the river to watch the final rays dip below the horizon before we headed home.

All in all, it was a pleasant way to end an emotional day. Just us, the sound of waves lapping against the shore, and the sunset as we said goodbye to a woman I never knew.

"I wish I had met her," I said once Seb shut the bike off.

"I wish you did too. She was awesome..." Seb remained seated as he offered me his hand, helping me step off while I was still wearing a dress and heels. He cleared his throat as he pulled off his helmet next, revealing tears in his eyes. "Jesus, I thought I was done crying."

"If you start, I'll start too." I removed my helmet, blinking widely.

"We need a distraction."

I pulled whatever thought popped into my head first. "How about, I want to get my bike license?"

A beautiful smile spread across his lips. "Hell yeah, you should! I could teach you." He reached over and pinched the front of my dress to tug me into him. "But I would miss my backpack."

"We could take turns backpacking."

Seb pressed a hand to his chest while his eyes glistened. "I would be honored to be your backpack."

I stepped back, laughing softly as he got off the bike. His excitement over me getting my bike license continued to bloom.

"And we could go on a road trip to the mountains or something. Ditch the city and travel—We should get those fluffy bunny hoods for our helmets—"

"Seb—"

"And we could make riding videos. Like a vlog of our travels—"

"Seb, pause for a second." I grabbed his arm and pointed to the police car several yards away. "Do they look...okay to you?"

He tilted his head and squinted his eyes.

"Are they asleep?" I whispered.

Seb shrugged and waved wildly at them. "Hello, officers!"

"We aren't meant to interact with them," I laughed.

Neither of the officers responded. They just sat there.

"Kinda rude but okay," Seb frowned.

"I think they *are* asleep."

"On the job? Lily's dad won't be happy." He started for the car with a cheeky grin thrown in my direction while I waited by the bike.

"You're going to get us in trouble," I hissed, unable to remain serious.

Seb reached the window of the driver's side, slinging an arm on the roof and peering in. Right as he went to speak, his radiant smile dropped and was replaced by what I could only describe as dread.

"Seb?" I was hesitant to move but approached him anyway. As I did, the windshield became easier to see through.

The officers' heads were tilted at odd angles.

Seb staggered back from the window, and I stopped in my tracks, still unable to make out what was wrong.

But something was terribly wrong.

"What is—?"

"Get inside." He covered his mouth, forcing down a gag before he walked straight at me and took my hand. Without stopping, he steered me across the street towards the apartment. "We need to get inside—They're dead, like *really* fucking dead."

"*What?*" I kept moving, ripping the swipe key to the building from my bag as we jogged to the doors. I tossed the card at Seb. "You open it, I need to take off these goddamn shoes."

He practically dove at the card reader by the door, impatiently holding the card in front of it until the door beeped and he shoved it open. I trailed behind, half hopping as I kicked off my shoes.

Seb made for the elevator, but I grabbed his arm. "That thing is too slow. Stairs."

We didn't know why we were rushing. We didn't know what we would find. I only hoped we weren't about to have a repeat of last weekend.

I can't lose a best friend.

Every flight of stairs felt longer than the last. My legs burned, but I pushed on. Round and round, up and up until we spilled onto the third floor and sprinted down the hallway.

Nothing looked different.

Nothing was burning or broken.

Seb had my keys and reached for the door handle, only for it to come off in his hand. As if someone had put it back to make it seem untampered with.

My heart rate increased. "Oh, god..."

He cautiously nudged the door open ajar.

"Wait here," he said, taking a step forward.

I gripped his arm. "No. Not happening. We go together."

"Kira—"

There was a soft click, followed by several other clicks. We paused and turned around as Susan, our nosy neighbor, pulled open her door, wearing the glare of someone who had been trying to sleep.

"I should make a complaint to the owners about how many people you've had coming and going from your apartment tonight," she hissed, crossing her arms over her pink dressing gown.

I could've told her my moms owned our apartment, but that wasn't important right now.

"Susan." I stepped towards her. "What people?"

"All men too. You girls should be ashamed of yourselves."

"Are the men still in there?" Seb asked.

Susan raised her eyebrows. "And I suppose you're another one? Shame—"

"Just answer the fucking question," I snapped.

Seb wasn't used to me swearing, and his face briefly expressed that, meanwhile, Susan gasped in offense.

She raised her chin matter-of-factly. "There were a few of them, but it was hard to see, you *rude* girl."

"Did you see them leave?" Seb said firmly.

Susan's eyes narrowed, like she was finally catching on to something. "What's going on?"

"Yes or no, Susan."

Offended again, this time by Seb's curtness, Susan bristled. "Yes, they left."

It was all we needed to hear, and we pushed through our apartment door, leaving Susan to mutter under her breath.

I felt along the wall for the light switch, fumbling through the dark until my knees collided with something solid. But I found the switch.

The second the light came on, I slapped a hand over my mouth and stared in shock at the mess.

The solid thing in front of me was a turned-over kitchen stool, much like most things in the apartment.

Spilled plants, a broken lamp, and miscellaneous items and books from the bookshelf by Lily's bedroom door littered the carpet, mapping out a trail from the living room to the hallway.

It reminded me of Aiden's temper, and I could feel my body wanting to freeze. Everything I had learned in my Thursday meetings was fighting to keep me present.

He's still injured. I'm safe. I'm stronger than before. Seb is here. Aiden isn't.

"Dean? Lily? You here?" Seb moved carefully through the apartment, opening doors and turning on every light as he searched for our friends. But they weren't here. I knew that before he had finished checking.

My eyes were fixed on the blood spots on the floor until Seb pushed open my bedroom door. Bella sprinted out as best she could with a cast on and sat against my foot with her tail between her legs.

I scooped her up, holding her close as she shook. The feeling of her soft fur seemed to regulate my thoughts again, and her shaking eased.

"They aren't here," Seb stated, stopping in the center of the mess. He dragged a hand over the top of his head. "Fuck—what do we do?"

Partially numb, I pulled out my phone.

CHAPTER 54

Dean

Something had dried down the right side of my face, over the dull throb coming from my temple.

I groaned against the tape across my mouth, squinting at the bright lights that hovered above my head as I slowly came to. When I tried to move my arms, I was met with resistance. Restriction. They were strapped to the arms of the chair I was sitting in. I tugged again, but the thick zip ties around my wrists refused to budge.

I blinked a couple of times, forcing the rest of the room to come into focus. Beyond the glow of the bright spotlight above, I saw a mezzanine shrouded in darkness, large wooden crates against the walls, and the lip of the stage I was seated on.

Not a stage, but a platform that once held a glass cube.

Fuck.

I brought my gaze forward, and my stomach dropped.

Lily was on the opposite side of the platform, also tied to a chair with her arms strapped down like mine. There was tape across her mouth too. Unlike me, she was wide awake and visibly shaking. The tears on her cheeks glistened under the light, and she was barefoot in her funeral dress.

I tried the zip ties again, thrashing until it hurt. I didn't know how much time we had before someone returned, and I wasn't going to risk waiting. I was also aware my phone was still in my back pocket.

If I could get one hand loose—

A bang echoed through the room, and we jolted. It was the door opening behind me.

Lily's eyes were fixed on whoever walked into the basement of Castello di Vetro. I could see the flutter of her pulse in her throat as fear gripped her.

They approached me from behind before they gripped my hair and tore my head back.

"Ah, he's awake!" Gabriele grinned. His auburn hair was slicked back, and there was a cut across the bridge of his nose that looked fresh. "You know, I really expected you to be the one to *not* go down without a fight. But no, you went down easy. *Her*, on the other hand," he motioned to Lily, "she almost broke my nose with her head. And managed to kick one of my men in the balls."

He motioned again with his hand, and I realized Lily and I hadn't been alone. A dozen other men were standing in the shadows. One adjusted the front of his pants after what Gabriele said.

"She is...feisty for something so unassuming." The thoughts in his head were written in his smirk as he pulled out his phone. "I am getting off topic... Is this you?"

He tapped play on a video on his phone, showing grainy black and white footage of me breaking in and shattering the cube that was once here. It stopped when I dropped to my knees.

I was so blinded by rage that I didn't even consider cameras.

Gabriele chuckled as he pocketed his phone again. "That was right after your mother died, *si*? My condolences, by the way." He gave my hair another tug before he stepped back. And walked towards Lily.

I strained against the zip ties again.

Gabriele stopped beside her, watching her with his head tilted. "Did you like the flower? The lily flower represents death. We thought leaving one on his car was fitting, considering what happened to his mother, but you can imagine our surprise when we found out about your name, *Lily*."

More footsteps came into the room. These sounded more like high heels than the dress shoes Gabriele wore.

Beatrice and Lucia stepped up onto the platform, the latter approaching me as she reached for my face.

I pulled my head back to avoid her hand, but she caressed my cheek anyway, filling me with disgust and helplessness.

I couldn't fucking move.

I couldn't get Lily away from here.

Lucia gripped my chin as she looked at her siblings, speaking Italian. "*Couldn't I have one moment with him?*"

"*It's not that kind of evening, unfortunately.*" Gabriele stroked Lily's cheek with the back of his finger.

She closed her eyes, throat bobbing.

Lucia huffed her disappointment and stepped aside.

Beatrice, the only sibling not to approach either of us, had her attention on me, trying to figure something out with those calculating dark eyes of hers before she spoke in English. "What makes you so important to our father anyway?"

My attention flicked to Gabriele as he moved behind Lily's chair, lifting a strand of her hair.

"You know the answer already, B. He's the obedient child our father never had…" He lowered his head beside Lily's, smirking when she moved her head away. "I wonder if our father plans to leave all his inheritance to your boyfriend."

My pulse spiked as I watched him bring a hand to her throat.

She was frozen in place, trembling.

All I wanted to do was tear his fucking face off.

Gabriele trailed a finger along her collarbone. "If your boyfriend is dead, though, there isn't really anyone else our father could give it to."

"Except his new wife," Lucia muttered.

Gabriele shrugged and straightened away from Lily. "We can deal with her. Like we did to his mother."

"She didn't see it coming if that makes you feel better," Beatrice said to me. "The fire was meant for you, since you were next on our list of names who worked for our father. But we couldn't help ourselves when we found her all alone at home in her chair… She was paralyzed after being shot while pregnant, yes? How sad," Beatrice mocked.

I shut my eyes.

"Your addresses were so easy to find too. We barely even had to try."

"I recognized Lily at the open house her mother was hosting," Gabriele said, gripping Lily's chin. "Her surname is the business name."

"And then we had her followed, knowing eventually it would lead to you," Beatrice continued. "Then all we did was have you followed. To work, home, Lily's house. Anywhere."

I was racking my brain, trying to remember if there were signs we were being watched.

"I think the best part was finding out you were going behind our father's back and working with the police," Gabriele grinned. "It would shatter his heart to know you betrayed him like that."

The fucking delivery guy.

"We could've told our father this, but then we wouldn't get the joy of ending you ourselves. It's more fun this way," Beatrice said.

Lucia smiled as she reached out to my face again, this time twirling a strand of my hair around her finger. "And I get more time with you now. Since you didn't die in the fire."

"Do you like the setting?" Gabriele asked, spreading his arms wide as he kept his unhinged stare on me. "A stage fit for a fighter's death." He took Lily forcefully by the chin again. "You'll be collateral, though."

I ripped at my restraints, jaw clenched as I cursed against the tape.

"I like him angry," Lucia purred before taking a seat on my lap, resting against my chest. I refused to look at her. "Oh, please let me have one taste of him? At least while you're dealing with the girlfriend."

"If you get time with him, I'll want time with her." Gabriele stroked Lily's hair. "Maybe then I can find out what makes her so important to him."

The zip ties were beginning to cut into my skin as I breathed heavily against the tape.

Lucia chuckled in my lap while Gabriele leaned in close to Lily again. She pulled away as best she could.

Beatrice crossed her arms. "And what am I meant to do?"

"We could share." Lucia stood, turned around, and climbed back onto me so she was straddling my thighs. She brought her face closer — inches closer — chewing her lip while she skimmed her hand to the front of my pants. "That would be fun—"

Her nose cracked under the impact of my forehead, and she toppled backwards off my lap.

Blood poured from her nose before she spat in Italian. "*You bastard!*"

Beatrice laughed, but helped her up. At the same time, Gabriele moved from behind Lily and strode toward me, smirking as he withdrew a switchblade.

"That wasn't very nice," he said.

He flipped the knife and stabbed it through the back of my right hand.

I roared against the tape, curling my body forward as Gabriele twisted the blade. The pain burned white hot, shooting through my nerves as blood pooled and flowed down the leg of the chair.

With manic in his eyes, Gabriele leaned closer. "I'm going to take great pleasure in cutting you up into small pieces and leaving them behind for our father to find."

I groaned in pain, shaking. I could feel the knife against the bone in my hand.

He grabbed my hair, forcing my head back again. "The next fighter we divide into tiny pieces will be that friend of yours. What's his name? Sebastian? My sources tell me he has a pretty girlfriend too."

I dragged my eyes from him to Lily. She was crying behind the tape, pulling at her restraints. Her delicate wrists were red.

"But I'm getting ahead of myself," Gabriele continued. He glanced at her too, and ripped the blade from my hand again.

More blood dripped. My hand was numb and burning at the same time, but it wasn't my priority anymore. Not when Gabriele had started at Lily again.

"We need to deal with you first, little doe."

A new panic set in, and I thrashed in my seat despite how much it hurt.

Beatrice and Lucia were laughing as they watched their brother.

I frantically rubbed my mouth on my shoulder until the tape fell loose. Saliva and sweat helped. "Leave her the fuck alone! We can talk about this. She doesn't need to be here."

Gabriele stood behind her again and lifted her chin to expose her throat. "But Dean, where's the fun in that? All this death will drive our father mad as he watches his empire slowly collapse."

"He's a Capo," I hissed, glaring from under my brow. "He has a boss that'll only come at you harder."

"Let them," he shrugged nonchalantly and angled the blade at Lily's throat. My blood dripped from it and stained her skin. "We take the favorite's lover, and then we take the favorite from our father."

Through the blood dripping from her nose, Lucia hissed, "Do it."

My eyes narrowed. "Fuckin' do it and I'll—"

"You'll what?" Beatrice raised an eyebrow. "You're tied to a chair and will be dead soon anyway."

"Well," Gabriele smiled. "Not soon. Slowly, yes, but maybe dead in a few hours? Her death will be quick, so that provides some comfort, *si*?"

Lily sobbed out of fear when he raised the blade beneath her jaw.

Everything was slipping through my fingers. My entire world was imploding right in front of me and I couldn't do a fucking thing to stop it.

I fixed my eyes solely on Lily, trying to be some kind of comfort for her.

"Hey, Lily." I tried for a smile when her eyes were on me, encouraging her to block out the triplets and their laughter. "We're gonna be okay. It'll be over soon."

At least she wouldn't witness what they had in store for me.

Suddenly, I was seeing every moment we shared. Her smile, her tears, her laughter, her anger. It all flitted through my mind right up until the moment I laid eyes on her the night of my fight, when I spotted her in the crowd.

I was the luckiest man alive to have those moments with her.

And then I remembered the day outside the courthouse.

She said hello to me; she acknowledged me; she gave some no-hope delinquent the time of day to share a smile with.

All those thoughts ran through my head in seconds.

"I love you," I whispered.

CHAPTER 55

Dean

Lily trembled but kept her attention on me, preparing for the inevitable as Gabriele pressed the blade to her skin.

He went to cut, and everything stalled, when suddenly a bang ruptured through the room.

The door.

The blade sliced past her throat as Gabriele jumped back.

I stared at Lily's skin, waiting for blood.

None came.

He missed.

"What?!" Beatrice spat in frustration at whoever barged into the basement.

"Your father is here," the man responded, sounding out of breath.

The triplets shared a look, their faces going pale.

Gabriele snapped his fingers at Lucia. "Check him for a wire."

Lucia hurried over to me, masking her eagerness to get near me again with feigned concern. Her nails curled into the front of my black, button-down shirt and tore it open, unable to contain her smile as she ran her hands over my skin.

I looked away as she did, clenching my jaw and curling my fingers around the arms of the chair. My right hand was completely numb, save for a fluttering of a pulse whenever blood dripped from the wound.

Beatrice began speaking Italian, her voice fast and mildly panicked. *"He wouldn't be wired. You took him from her apartment."*

Gabriele began to pace, also speaking Italian. *"Then how does he know?"*

I rolled my head back, eyes closed. *"Ever heard of a hunch?"*

"Shut up!" he snapped in English.

"Calm down," Beatrice hissed. *"He might be here to tell us he changed his mind. We need to hide them."*

"Fine," Gabriele said in English before barking orders at their men. "Hide them in one of the storage boxes. And tape his mouth shut!" he snapped, jabbing a finger at me.

They moved fast, cutting us from the seats, zip tying our wrists in front of us, and reapplying tape to my mouth. We were dragged off the stage and steered towards the back of the room side by side.

My head spun with every step. I didn't know how much blood I was losing, but it was gradually taking its toll.

Lily looked at me, her eyes riddled with worry, until one of the men shoved her forward, and she fell.

"*Mmphaphkha.*" I grabbed his shirt with my good hand, not entirely sure what my plan was when a dozen guns were suddenly pointed at my head.

The faint sound of popping rang out from upstairs, and the room stilled.

There was distant shouting, more gunshots, and rushed footsteps in the stairwell before a final, much louder bang rang out. Several seconds later, one of the lackeys fell to the bottom of the stairs, spilling into the doorway with a bullet hole through his head.

There was a rush to have all guns on the door as Lily was dragged to her feet.

It was too late to hide us.

Two of the men shoved guns against our temples and pushed us together. At least she was beside me again.

The blood was beginning to drip faster, landing in large splats on my shoe.

Gabriele and Beatrice pulled guns too, but Lucia drew a short, thick knife with a diamante-encrusted handle.

She brought a knife to a gun fight...

I huffed a laugh into the tape.

Heavy footsteps echoed through the stairwell before several men in black suits walked into the basement.

It was like the fucking cavalry arrived.

In the lead was Vince, carrying a 9mm and wearing blood-splattered brass knuckles on one hand. Behind him, Antonio was straightening the lapels of his jacket as he strode in with a gold-tipped cane. His gold watch and rings glinted in that overhead spotlight, and there wasn't a hint of care on his nonchalant expression. The only thing missing was a cigar in his mouth and a martini in his hand.

He looked way too calm for someone interrupting a kidnapping and possible murder.

I did a quick count of how many he brought.

Fourteen, including himself and Vince — he could be considered two men with the way he was built.

Each of Antonio's men likely had two guns on them, which was one gun more than what the triplet's hired twelve men had. It was a pure guess that the triplets had hired these men, but the way they shifted with uncertainty at the arrival of Antonio made me wonder how loyal they were to their bosses. Meanwhile, Antonio's guys were locked in and unflinching, forming a semi-circle around him as he stared down his kids.

"It seems we got here in time to negotiate," Antonio said, adding a curt smile.

I wanted to feel reassured, but the gun poking into my temple wasn't exactly helping.

Gabriele pulled a hand hastily through his hair. The man was anxious. "There will be no negotiations."

"I think you'll find negotiating with me easier than what the police have in store for you."

The confused frown on the triplets' faces matched my own.

"What?" Beatrice said sharply.

Antonio shifted his weight to his cane. "They received a call earlier tonight, alerting them that the daughter of one of their own might've been abducted by someone they were investigating. Now, while they are investigating me, they know I wouldn't kidnap someone. It's not really my style," he continued. "We've arrived before them, but I'm willing to bet they aren't too far away."

Gabriele scoffed. "You're lying."

"You think you're the only ones with the law on your payroll?"

The look he gave me was brief but sent a chill down my spine. Or that was the blood loss… Either way, he knew I worked with the police. He had to.

I wouldn't be surprised if we walked out of this unscathed, only for him to personally shoot me in the head once we were outside.

"We have five or so minutes until they arrive. The only people they plan to let walk out of here alive are Lily and Dean. Everyone else is optional, depending on your reaction. Based on the way you all pulled guns the second we walked in, they won't hesitate to kill you." He spoke like he was reading the terms and conditions of a product. There were no fucks given. "So, unless you want to die, hand them over to me now so we can all clear out before more blood is spilled. Threaten either of them during the handover, and Vince here won't hesitate to shoot."

Vince cocked his head back in acknowledgment of the triplets.

"How do we know this isn't a trap?" Lucia said from behind her hand, nursing her broken nose.

Antonio deadpanned. "If I wanted you dead tonight, you would already be dead. Hand them over and we'll figure something out later."

Gabriele chuckled. "You'll have to forgive me when I say I don't believe you, Father."

"If it's money you want, you'll get it."

The triplets paused and communicated through looks alone before Beatrice nodded to the men with their guns at our heads. "Untie them."

Lucia balked. "What? No."

"Untie them," Beatrice reaffirmed with a glare at her sister.

Gabriele wasn't happy with the plan either, but money seemed to outweigh his hunger for murder, so he agreed and stood by as Lily and I were cut free.

I took Lily's hand as soon as I could and tore the tape from my mouth, aiming for Antonio.

He was on the other side of the room. We had to pass the enemies first, and even as they lowered their guns, there was still tension. Especially in Lucia as she fidgeted on the spot, eyeing me until her eyes dropped to Lily as we walked by.

I swear I saw movement outside the windows that sat high on the basement walls along the mezzanine.

"*Lui è mio*," Lucia scowled.

He's mine.

She lunged, one arm going around Lily's throat as she raised her knife. When Lily's hand slipped from mine, everything seemed to slow right down.

A shot was fired, and Lucia's head snapped back before she had the chance to plunge her blade into Lily's stomach.

As Lucia's body collapsed with a fresh bullet hole between her eyes, Beatrice screamed in agony while Gabriele roared at Vince for shooting their sister.

Gabriele was closer to me, and so was the gun in his hand. But it was Beatrice near Lily, grabbing Lucia's knife to finish the job, that flooded my veins with adrenaline.

Beatrice grabbed Lily, holding the blade to her throat, and I grabbed Gabriele, locking him in a chokehold with my arm as I pressed his gun to his temple.

He gasped for air and clawed at my forearm.

I tightened my grip, leveling Beatrice with a glare. "Don't you fuckin' dare."

Lily's terrified whimpers echoed into the silence of the room. Everyone had a gun on them now, but no one dared to make the first move.

"That was your daughter!" Beatrice screamed at Antonio, pointing the tip of the knife dangerously close to Lily's jugular. The faintest drop of blood slid down her skin.

I began calculating how fast it would take to shoot Gabriele and then Beatrice before she could cut Lily further.

"We're out of time," Antonio said.

Gabriele, barely getting air, choked out, "What?"

There *was* more movement outside those high windows. They were waiting for the right moment, and right now was the best chance with a detective's daughter's life at stake.

Each window was suddenly kicked in before a tactical team dropped in from above, guns ready. They barely reached the ground before the two dozen men beneath them started firing. In turn, they fired back.

I ducked as bullets whizzed past my head, letting go of Gabriele.

He scrambled off somewhere, but before I could attempt to stop him, someone grabbed the back of my shirt and pulled me behind one of the large storage crates.

I stumbled to my ass, thanks to Vince's manhandling, and found Antonio beside me. Phone to his ear — potentially talking to his police source. Or maybe his wife.

"What happened to you?" Vince asked, referring to my hand.

"Small cut."

I peered out from behind the crate, searching the chaos for Lily. My eyes flicked to the stairs leading to the mezzanine as Beatrice made her escape up them.

Lily was in her grasp, pulling against her.

With Gabriele's gun in my hand, I went to go after them, but a bullet clipped the corner of the box before I could step out. When I looked to the stairs again, Lily and Beatrice were nowhere in sight.

"We move to the exit on three," Vince said, already moving to guard Antonio's side.

I shook my head. "I'm not going anywhere without Lily."

"You won't make it across the fuckin' room." He ducked as a bullet ricocheted nearby.

"I'm stayin'..." I addressed Antonio next. "Sorry, boss. For everythin'."

Antonio shook his head, mildly disappointed. "This isn't the time for that conversation. Just survive this."

"If you're gonna do this, go now," Vince barked. "I'll cover you. But then we're gettin' out of here."

I nodded once and crouched behind the corner of the box again, preparing to move.

People were getting shot at or stabbed, and none of the three sides were planning on teaming up any time soon to take down the other. It had become a situation of every person for themselves.

Finally, there was a clear path to the stairs. I made a run for them under Vince's cover, keeping low.

I had already said goodbye to my mother today. I wasn't about to do the same with the woman I loved.

Chapter 56

Lily

Fight, flight, or freeze.

Without a weapon, fighting wasn't an option. With a blade to my throat, neither was fleeing. I was stuck with the third option and did so involuntarily as the surviving Gimello sister shoved me through a deep purple, velvet curtain that blocked off a section of the basement's mezzanine.

I had a cut on my shin from being dragged up the metal staircase, where I banged it. It should've hurt more, but I couldn't feel anything beyond my fear.

"Keep quiet," the woman hissed with a thick Italian accent and a dark glare. "Or I slit your pretty neck."

I didn't dare argue or scream, as she steered me to the middle of the room, scanning it for something. For a moment, she left me standing alone, and I contemplated running, but my body refused to move, and soon she was with me again.

Using a curtain sash, she bound my hands behind my back and tied another one across my mouth. She then pushed me onto one of the plush sofas.

I didn't know if she was Lucia or Beatrice; Dean had only mentioned names, but whichever one she was, she was upset and desperate for an escape. So desperate she began using her sister's knife to peel back sections of the mirrored perspex that lined the back wall, revealing a hidden window.

But I was also desperate to escape and had no intention of going with her.

Heart pounding, I shot off the sofa.

She saw and swiped her hand out in my direction, missing me by inches before I slipped through the velvet fabric again.

And slammed into someone coming the other way.

They gripped my upper arms, their fingertips digging into my skin, and forced me back through the curtain.

The push knocked me off my feet, but I couldn't catch myself with my hands behind my back. I landed on the floor, gasping as the wind was momentarily knocked from my lungs and pain rippled through my hip and elbow. I didn't have time to process if something was broken as Gabriele stepped through the curtain.

Fear lanced through my insides, and I dragged myself backward, helplessly trying to create distance between us.

"A ransom is looking lovely right now," he smirked as he strode closer, looming over me. His eyes went to his sister. "Hurry up, Beatrice!"

"I'm fucking trying!" Beatrice pulled at the rest of the perspex with sheer frustration.

I shook my head as Gabriele got closer.

He nudged my legs apart with his shoes.

I kicked and kicked at him, connecting with his shin once before he grabbed my ankle and dragged me closer. I screamed against the sash in my mouth, ripping my throat raw.

He tutted, fighting to catch my other ankle as I aimed my foot at his crotch. "We're going to have so much time getting to know one another."

My foot slipped from his grasp, and I kicked harder than I had before. It landed where I wanted, right between his legs, and he dropped to his knees as he clutched his groin.

I swiveled on my lower back, using my legs to get up until he grabbed my arm and threw me back down.

I groaned, struggling to breathe in before he flipped me onto my back. His hand was already raised to strike my face as he placed the other on my throat and straddled my stomach.

"You little bi—"

I flinched as a loud bang rang through the room.

Gabriele reeled back with an agonized cry. He reached for his ankle, where the back had exploded in a mess of blood and flesh.

Just as he turned to look at the velvet curtain, another shot rang out.

Warm specks of blood sprayed across my face, and Gabriele fell limp to the floor beside me with a gaping hole in his cheek.

I scooted away from him as Beatrice screamed.

Movement at the curtain pulled my attention off the growing pool of blood around Gabriele's head, and hope swelled in my chest as Dean stepped into the space with a gun already locked on Beatrice. The intention in his eyes was clear.

Beatrice scrambled off the couch and pulled me up.

I tugged against her grasp until she held a gun to my temple and ducked behind me, making me her human shield.

Dean moved steadily, keeping the gun trained on the small parts of Beatrice that weren't hidden by me. Blood continued to drip from his wounded hand, but he didn't care. There was a deadly calm about him.

"Gun down, or she dies," Beatrice demanded. She mentioned something else in Italian. I didn't understand the words, but the feeling behind them was anger and frustration. "Gun down and back away!"

Dean didn't move. His arm was straight, and that gun wasn't lowering any time soon.

I winced as Beatrice dug hers into my skin. "I will fucking kill her!"

"Do you trust me?" His voice was deep and calm.

I dipped my chin, whimpering, and slowly shut my eyes, waiting for the sharp sting of a bullet. I knew how it would feel, but I wasn't prepared.

"I don't have time for your games." Beatrice snapped, right before another gunshot blasted through the air.

My eyes remained shut. I didn't want to look. Not when I felt Beatrice leave my side and heard someone fall.

Suddenly, I was standing alone, shaking and unable to form a full breath as I listened.

She shot him. She shot him. She shot him.

Quiet, slow steps approached me.

I barely had time to flinch before a strong pair of arms pulled me close.

"I've got you, Lily," Dean whispered, cradling the back of my head in his hand. "I've got you."

I shuddered and sobbed, and collapsed against him all at once, opening my eyes as tears flooded my vision.

He quickly removed the sash from my mouth, all the while scanning every inch of the cuts and bruises that must've decorated my face, and then he unbound my wrists.

Before he could discard the sash, I took his wrist and wrapped his hand with it. "So, you don't lose any more blood." My voice felt foreign in a scene so violent.

He cupped my face and kissed my forehead, my cheek, and my lips before he took my hand and led the way through the curtain, mindful of the broken glass from the shattered windows above.

The noise in the basement, a continuous cluster of bangs and yelling, seemed to come back into focus now that the threat of kidnapping no longer hung above my life. It was as if I had blocked it out earlier, and suddenly it had all rushed back.

Dean ducked behind the mezzanine handrail, and I followed, squatting right beside him. It was then that I noticed the sweat on his brow and slightly labored breaths as he focused on a plan to get out without being shot.

"We're gonna go straight down the stairs and to the exit. Stay low and close to me, alright?" He pressed his good hand to my cheek. "You're gonna see some things—"

"I know," I said with a nod, taking his wrist. "Low and close. We've got this."

His half smile was tired but adoring, and then we were moving, quick and steady, down the stairs.

Men shouted at each other, while other voices were cut short by another round of bullets.

I kept my eyes on the stairs and the exit, while Dean kept an eye on the others until the door was mere inches away and he steered me in front of him.

I tried not to pay too much attention to the body in the doorway as I stepped over it hastily, avoiding the blood as the cold floor bit into my feet.

A bullet pinged off the door frame above us, cascading drywall across Dean's hair right as we escaped into the stairwell.

Almost there.

We went up the stairs together, but Dean stumbled and caught himself, closing his eyes for a second as he hung his head. The purple sash on his hand was already covered in blood.

"Shit," he breathed.

"Dean, come on." I looped his arm around my shoulder, took the gun from him, and held his waist. "I'm going to support you as much as I can, but I still need some help. We have to keep moving."

"I'm pretty sure you're meant to sit still when you're bleeding out," he muttered sarcastically.

Good. Sarcasm was a good sign.

"Yes, but you aren't bleeding out." I was in denial, but still, I pulled him to the next step. And the next flight of stairs.

He managed the climb to the top, but the way he swayed on his feet wasn't exactly reassuring.

We passed two more bodies at the door that went into the strip club. This door was propped open, revealing a darkened room on the other side where glass from the black mirrors littered the floor.

"Careful," Dean said, nodding to my feet. "I would carry you but—"

A pair of bright lights suddenly flashed in our faces, and we stopped inside the door.

"Put the weapon down!" shouted a man, followed by the click of a gun.

Police.

"We were the hostages, you dumb fucks," Dean muttered sharply.

I hastily put the gun down anyway as the officers lowered their flashlights and guns. They didn't quite apologize for the mistake, but they were quick to escort us out, carefully guiding me around the broken glass that littered the entire floor. It caught the light of the flashlights like a floor of diamonds.

Antonio's men had come in earlier with their guns blazing, and it showed. Every mirror was broken, and the front windows were smashed in.

Outside, the street was cordoned off and filled with flashing red and blue lights. Police vehicles, two large black vans, and ambulances were parked a safe distance from the club's entrance in case the fight spilled onto the street, but still close enough that Dean and I were whisked away to the paramedics. Well away from the front line of it all.

Dean was seen first. Initially, he refused and told them to check me first, but when he stumbled, they guided him quickly to sit in the back of the ambulance.

They checked me over too, but all of my injuries were bruises and superficial cuts that would heal on their own.

I *was* suspected of having a concussion, not that I could recall when or how it happened.

Wrapped in one of the blankets from the ambulance, I stood beside Dean as they cleaned and treated his hand. I could feel the adrenaline subsiding as I came to terms with what happened.

"Lily!"

I turned, searching the sea of police cars for the owner of that familiar voice, and found Dad walking right to us. With his arms out wide, I could see the bulletproof vest under his coat before he wrapped me in a tight hug.

He noted the blood on my clothes and in my hair, glanced at Dean, and then held me at arm's length for a better look.

"How did you know to come?" I asked.

"Kira called us from your apartment. She said it looked like you'd been robbed. There were also reports of multiple gunshots in this area. So when we tracked Dean's phone here, we knew something was off. And since the triplets figured out who Dean was a few weeks ago, I thought it was odd he might willingly come here again on the day of his mother's funeral..." He glanced at Dean, who was doing his best to look like he wasn't listening as he watched the paramedic begin wrapping his hand in gauze. "I'm just happy you're both safe."

"You know Antonio's down there," Dean said.

Dad pressed his lips together. "I do... The entire investigation has been shot to pieces."

The realization that I might not ever see Antonio again struck me harder than I thought it would.

"Someone tipped him off," Dean added.

The paramedic finished wrapping his hand and began strapping it across his chest to keep it elevated. Dean's eyes remained on Dad, who had paused to process what he was saying. He looked like he was reevaluating who on his team he could trust.

Dad didn't share these concerns out loud. Instead, he inhaled and put his arm around me.

"You two should get to the hospital. I will feel a lot better once I know you're both as far away from this place as possible. And *he* needs to have that looked at properly." He pointed at Dean's hand.

Dean gave him a lazy, two-fingered salute with his other hand. "Yes, sarge."

With Dean taking the stretcher, under strict instruction by the paramedic in case he felt dizzy from the blood loss, I sat in the spare seat beside him in the back of the ambulance.

I allowed myself to relax in the seat. My body was tired and ached all over, but I was alive.

Dean reached across and squeezed my knee gently to get my attention, half smiling.

We were alive.

Chapter 57

Dean

For the first time in fuck knows how long, being in the hospital didn't bother me. I still hated the place but with the amount of blood I lost, and with how much shit we went through, I was happy laying in a hospital bed for a night, processing and recovering.

In a fresh change of clothes, thanks to Kira and Seb visiting earlier, and finally free of the blood and debris of the basement, we shared the bed. Lily was asleep, tucked against my side under my arm and bandaged hand, with her head on my shoulder.

I never wanted to let her go again.

At least for the next twenty-four hours.

Three hours ago, Lily had given her statement to the police while I got my hand sewn back together and checked for nerve damage — my middle finger was the only one I couldn't feel. While I was getting stitches in the emergency room, chaos exploded as paramedic after paramedic wheeled several stretchers in.

Survivors of the shooting — police and criminals.

No sign of Antonio. Or Vince.

It was way past midnight, officially Saturday morning. And a whole week since Mom's death. It was a bitter pill to swallow, accepting how fast the week had gone without her.

I waited for the tears; the lump in my throat, but there was nothing. Maybe my emotions were worn out. My life had been blown apart, and I was too exhausted to think. I guess that's why, two hours ago, when Mark arrived with news that there were no more survivors from the shooting, I just stared blankly.

Antonio's body was found where I left him and Vince. They were men I had shared most of my early adult life with, making it hell but also providing me a fucked up form of job stability, and I felt...indifferent by their passing. There was no love lost there, but there was a loss of something.

Lily stirred with a small stretch. Her eyelashes fluttered open, and those pretty blue eyes sleepily took in the room. She seemed to remember where we were before she sighed and closed her eyes again.

"You okay?" I mumbled.

She smiled softly and nodded, keeping her eyes closed. "*I* am. You're the one who was stabbed."

I huffed a laugh. "Fair enough."

"My therapist will hear all about it, though." She snuggled against my chest, placing a hand on my stomach.

"I thought he was a psychologist?"

"Tomato, tomato."

My lips twitched, and I kissed the top of her head, savoring her scent. She smelled of fresh linen and jasmine again. It lingered in her clothes from home and the soap Kira had brought. I never wanted to forget that smell.

This scene was a stark contrast to the one when we first arrived. That one was filled with questions from doctors, worried friends, and detectives. But the most intense interaction came from Lily's mom.

I had forgotten that she was none the wiser about anything Lily and I were involved in from day one. Kate thought I was just a tattooed petty criminal. When she found out Lily was at the hospital after a hostage situation, and Mark gave her a rundown of *everything*, she exploded in a fit of rage. Mostly aimed at me, in the form of a misaimed water bottle and a pillow, until Mark led her from the room before she could scream the hospital down.

Jane was with them, understandably shocked to find out what else I did for a living. I hoped it didn't change how she saw me.

Kate had every right to be mad. If I were in her shoes, I would also want to smother whoever put my loved ones in danger with a pillow.

Since that moment, Lily and I had found some peace for the night.

Lily slid her hand to my chest, leaving her head on my shoulder as she lightly traced invisible shapes into the front of my hoodie. Her voice was quiet. "How long before they take you away?"

Our attention went to my left arm. There were cords and needles, replenishing my fluids and blood, but it was my wrist, cuffed to the side of the hospital bed, that prompted the question.

Outside the doors, two cops were stationed in the hallway in case I tried to escape.

Mark had warned me about the arrests. It hadn't come as a surprise when some of his colleagues strolled in to read out the charges, and my rights, and slap the cuffs on me. At the end of the day, I was what they had written on paper — an unofficial member of Antonio's soldiers and an illegal fighter. A criminal. I worked for him and saw things that any law-abiding citizen would go to the police for. I enabled his crimes, I was an accessory, I blackmailed, stole, and threatened violence...

The only thing that didn't come up was the forced suicide of Gio Calacoci.

"Twenty-four hours," I responded.
She hugged me tighter.

CHAPTER 58
Lily

Five months later...

The bus ride over the girder bridge had become part of my weekly routine. It was the only road in and out of the island, and I went over it every Wednesday like clockwork. Starting in the borough of Queens, with only a handful of other people making the same journey to Rikers Island.

I hadn't missed a single visit.

After the bus ride, we were shuffled off to the visitor's center at Robert N. Davoren Complex, or RNDC, where we signed in and had our belongings and bodies searched. It was an unpleasant process. I always zoned out and focused on the reason I was there in the first place.

Today was no different, and once everything came up clear, our belongings were signed in at the desk, and they checked everyone was wearing suitable clothing, an officer escorted us down a long grayish-green hallway to the visiting room.

I wore white sneakers and a white T-shirt tucked in at the waistband of my skinny jeans. The rules were no clothes showing too much skin or cleavage, but also nothing so baggy it could conceal something. I wore the same style of outfit every visit, just to guarantee I wasn't turned away at the front desk.

I trailed along at the end of the single-file line, following the corridor to the next set of doors. No matter how many times I did this walk, I couldn't ever subdue the barrage of butterflies fluttering around my stomach. Or get control of the excited shivers that spread goosebumps along my skin. It felt like the anticipation before Christmas morning, only it was better than Christmas.

My heart felt like it was ready to lurch from my chest as we walked through the doors.

The visiting room wasn't exactly something spectacular, or at all comforting. The paint on its walls was cracked and chipped in places, and the windows on the right-hand side of the room were fitted with bars. There were also cameras in every corner.

Three correctional officers slowly paced the room, weaving around the tables and chairs that were bolted to the floor.

Bleach was the first thing I smelled as I walked to an empty table.

I perched on the edge of my seat, anxiously looking around the room as I clasped my hands together. The waiting was the hardest part, but not the worst.

A distant but loud buzzing echoed from somewhere beyond the doors on the other side of the room, indicating a prison door opening. This was followed by another echo of the same door slamming shut, another buzzing alarm, and then the distinct sound of footsteps. Many of them.

We all watched those doors.

I crossed my legs and cradled my chin in my hand as I leaned on the table, trying to at least look composed.

It's only been a week...

A long week.

My heart skipped a beat when those doors finally opened, and another officer walked in. Behind him was a line of inmates in orange jumpsuits.

The first inmate beelined to a waiting family, grinning eagerly. The second inmate was an older man who approached a younger man at another table — likely father and son based on how similar they looked. And the rest did more of the same, dispersing to the awaiting visitors.

The last inmate entered the room with his head cocked back and an arch in his brows that gave him a sort of nonchalant expression.

I couldn't contain my smile any longer, and when he spotted me sitting alone, his own lopsided grin finally cracked through that façade.

Five months in Rikers hadn't changed Dean much, but there were subtle differences. He was working out a lot more than he ever did on the outside; his face was only a fraction gaunter, and the back and sides of his black hair were kept short, giving him a much sharper look.

I wasn't allowed to stand until he got to my table, so I sat on my hands with my legs bouncing as I watched him walk over.

There was a small, fading cut on his bottom lip. Something he got last week after a brawl broke out in the prison cafeteria. For the most part, Dean steered clear of fights — it helped with the trial — but that didn't stop others from attempting to fight him. The cut on his lip was from another inmate who had punched him for being a bystander.

The bruises on his knuckles, also from last week, were fading too.

"Hey, baby." Love dripped from every syllable in his calm, deep, Brooklyn-accented voice.

I jumped from my seat the second he was beside the table and flung myself at him so hard, a small, surprised huff was knocked out of him, followed by a chuckle as he wrapped his arms around my middle, breathing in my scent while I melted against him.

He left a kiss on the side of my neck before an officer cleared his throat.

The rules were that we had to be seated for the visit, so we did just that. Another rule was that we had to sit across from each other instead of beside.

Hand holding was permitted, so long as it was done above the table.

Dean threaded his fingers through mine, drinking me in with his gray-blue eyes.

I noted the scar on the back of his right hand, a single raised line right through the middle of the crown tattooed on his hand. There was an almost identical scar on his palm from Gabriele's blade.

We only had an hour. Don't waste it thinking about Gabriele.

An hour a week, every week for five months — I had gotten good at summarizing life events into small portions for him to hear something good. He needed something to distract him from waiting for the trial to be over.

He had already missed so much because of it.

Seb's 27th birthday, Christmas and New Year's, my 23rd birthday, Kira getting her bike license, and me starting my new job as a receptionist in an indie art gallery.

We rarely talked about the trial either, coming to an unspoken agreement not to discuss it much when he already would with his lawyer. He also didn't like talking about his daily life in prison. The excuse was that it wasn't interesting, but I think he was protecting me from hearing what went on behind those walls.

"Did you receive the books I sent?" I sent him six every two weeks.

He smoothed his thumb over my knuckles, following the motion with a smile in his eyes. "You're turning me into a bookworm. Now I get why cliffhangers drive you nuts."

"I promise not to send you an incomplete series next time," I laughed softly, remembering the phone call I got from him a few weeks ago. "But maybe by the end of next week, you'll be able to walk into a bookstore and buy as many books as you like."

He hummed. "Maybe..."

Everything was riding on next week. The trial was wrapping up, and Dean would find out his fate. The possibility of him walking into a bookstore might've been extremely optimistic on my part, given what he was on trial for, but one of us had to stay positive.

"Five minutes." The officer's voice cut through the room like a cold knife.

Already?

Dean's hand squeezed mine as he searched for something more to say. Anything to make those five minutes last.

"Seb taught Bella to dance." Random, yes, but I panicked.

His eyebrows shot up as he huffed a laugh. "Oh?"

"Well, it's more hopping on her back legs with her paws up, but she only does it to Get Low."

"By Lil Jon?"

"Yes."

Dean chuckled as he rubbed the bridge of his nose. "Of course he would."

The remaining minutes of the visit fell away too quickly. Soon, the inmates were being told to line up at the door again as friends and family waved from their tables.

Dean didn't move right away. He leaned across the table, took my chin in his hand, and kissed me.

He kissed like how he made love, putting so much pressure, warmth and passion behind each clash of our mouths, that it left me breathless. He didn't care if people watched as he cupped the back of my neck and angled his head.

"Move it, Moretto," the officer nearby drawled.

We stood and met each other at the edge of the table for a hug. He was now the only inmate at a table as the others walked out of the room.

With his hands on the sides of my neck, he kissed me over and over again.

"I love you. I miss you. I'll see you soon," he said between each rushed kiss.

I could already feel that familiar ache beginning to burn in my chest.

I didn't want to let go yet.

From the corner of my eye, I could see the officer coming over. "Visiting hours are finished, *Romeo*. Wrap it up."

Dean planted one more lingering kiss on my forehead, holding the back of my head with a gentle strength, and then reluctantly backed away.

I took a seat again, wiping at my eyes as I watched him leave.

That was always the worst part.

CHAPTER 59
Dean

The suit was a rental and smelled like one too. It was the first time in a long time I was wearing something other than orange.

I lowered my head to my hands and hunched forward, sitting on a bench in a quiet holding cell in the back of the courthouse. My only company was the clinking sound coming from the lightbulb outside the cell.

I was the only one of Antonio's fighters who went on trial. None of the others were ever caught because there was little evidence of others being involved.

Many of his other men, associates above my pay grade, were also on trial for crimes worse than mine in much bigger court cases with media present and a multitude of lawyers on their sides. Their arrests had created a giant void in Antonio's usual business dealings.

His death was another reason everything halted.

In a way, his kids' wish for his empire to crumble had worked, but it hadn't been their doing.

I didn't know why I was giving them headspace. They were gone and I had my own shit to deal with.

The jury had all the information they needed and spent the past half hour discussing it.

All I could do, besides thinking about my ex-boss, was replay what happened in court earlier today to ease the tension in my head.

Aiden Miller was terrible at playing the victim.

He wore a brace on his leg and used a crutch to get around. There were also scars on his jaw from the reconstruction surgery, and his dirty blonde hair was shaved into a buzz cut.

When he was called to the stand, he pulled on a façade so pathetic I was ready to risk life in prison just to break his leg again right in front of everyone present in the courtroom. Instead, I looked to the back of the room where Lily, Kira, and Seb sat in the furthest row, each wearing their own masks of hate directed at Aiden.

He was there as a witness to my "violent death threats" and to show what I had done to him, painting him as an innocent in all of this until my lawyer, DA Anna Davis — hired by Antonio's widow, Julia — started asking him questions too.

"You mentioned in your statement that my client was capable of doing those things to you because of his alleged involvement in illegal fighting. Is that true?" Ms. Davis began.

"Yes."

"How do you know about these alleged fights, Mr. Miller?"

Aiden hesitated. "I heard about them."

"So, you weren't there, gambling illegally, to witness my client participating in any fights?"

"N-no—"

"Meaning you can't be certain that he was involved in those fights beneath The Den?"

"I heard about it from a friend." Aiden's face was bright red.

"But you never witnessed or participated in the illegal gambling on these fights yourself?"

"No—I told you, I heard—"

"Is it true that you were charged with the domestic assault of your partner and the use of a firearm on her friend on August 16th of last year?" She flipped casually through her notes to double-check. "Which is what you are on probation for?"

Aiden went to respond but was cut off by the other lawyer. "Objection; relevance?"

The judge, sitting back in his seat, nodded once. "I'll allow it."

"Yes." Aiden's throat bobbed nervously. He was squirming like a fucking bug. "But he did this to me. I think that's proof enough that he's an illegal fighter."

"Mr. Miller," she placed a hand on her hip. "Getting your ass handed to you by someone good at fighting doesn't make them an illegal fighter."

Hushed giggles and laughter flitted around the courtroom while Seb barked a laugh.

I looked down, pressing my lips together as I fought hard not to smile.

"Order," the judge drawled. "Ms. Davis, please refrain from using derogatory language in my courtroom."

Anna smiled. "Yes, your honor. My apologies... Mr. Miller, is it possible you are only here because you seek revenge for what my client did to you?"

"No. He is an illegal fighter."

"How can you prove that when you said yourself you never went to one of these fights where illegal gambling took place? Just a reminder, you're under oath."

"I saw him—I mean, I heard about—"

"That's all, your honor," Ms. Davis said simply before taking a seat, leaving Aiden dumbfounded.

I massaged my thumb into my right palm, where a thick, long knife scar remained. Sometimes the nerves in my hand played up and created a tingling numbness in my fingers. Massaging and flexing my hand temporarily relieved it, but the sensation was forever.

My eyes tracked to the small tattoo of two birds on my left wrist. They were a positive reminder not to give up hope because maybe Ms. Davis's closing statement would be enough.

She had reminded the jury of all the mitigating factors surrounding the charges I was facing. My past with an alcoholic and abusive father; my father's suicide that provided no closure to a hellish upbringing (I didn't mention that his death did, in fact, give me plenty of closure); caring for my mother; my willingness to help with the police investigation and the threats that brought on my own life; the loss of my home and Mom.

I hated that even in death, she was used as leverage to fix my problem. *At least she wasn't here to see all of this.*

Footsteps echoed in the hall outside the cell, and I stood expectantly.

The courtroom officers came into view. One unlocked the door, and the other walked into the cell to cuff my wrists before they escorted me back to the courtroom. My heart was in my throat the entire time.

Ms. Davis stood at our table as I entered the room. The look on her face gave away nothing about how she felt about my chances. Her track record of getting Antonio out of sticky situations in the past had never failed. It's why Julia, his wife, had suggested I accept the lawyer for myself.

"Breathe," she muttered once I reached the desk. "You look tense."

"Can you blame me?" I waited for the officer to remove the cuffs and leave. "This isn't gonna be good..."

"You don't know that."

I inhaled slowly, remaining on my feet as the judge entered the room. It didn't take him long to call up the jury foreman.

My heart was no longer in my throat. It seemed to have stopped completely. I wouldn't be surprised if I looked down and found it on the floor. Alongside my stomach.

I looked down and closed my eyes, trying to think of something else to focus on. Lily was the first and only thing that came to my mind. That woman had saved my life in her own small way. She had given me something to fight and live for.

The judge's voice interrupted my thoughts. "How do you find?"

"For the charges of aggravated harassment in the second degree, we find the defendant guilty."

That verdict wasn't a surprise. It covered everything on record of me intimidating someone. From threatening a cop to Aiden's assault.

I took the hit with my jaw clenched, nodding faintly as I prepared for the next one.

Ms. Davis briefly placed a hand on my shoulder in reassurance.

"For all charges related to Mr. Moretto's involvement with Mr. Gimello's fighting ring and the illegal work outside of that fighting ring, we, the jury, find the defendant not guilty."

There was a silent shift in the room. And a few disgruntled murmurs from the opposing side.

I paused and fought hard to keep any look of shock from my face as I glanced at Ms. Davis to make sure I heard correctly.

She gave me the subtlest of winks and fixed her attention forward.

I wasn't sure if I imagined it. Had they heard what was said in every testimony? Did they even consider my record?

The judge finalized the moment with my punishment regarding the aggravated harassment charge — twenty-four months under house arrest, a one-thousand-dollar fine, and community service. For aggravated assault. What I did should've gotten me at least a year in prison, not house arrest.

I was struggling to believe any of it was real as I took a seat again, breathing a heavy sigh before I looked at the judge.

Based on his expression, he didn't exactly believe the verdict either, but he tapped the anvil anyway.

I pushed open the door of the small and empty room, tugging my tie loose and unbuttoning my collar as I went. "What the fuck just happened?"

Ms. Davis, ever calm and professional, strode in behind me with her black briefcase in hand and a look of confidence on her face. "Antonio protected his assets." She closed the door and sent me a knowing look.

It took me a second to realize what she meant.

"The jury. They were—"

"Smart people. Just don't mention it to anyone."

"I'm free because of another crime."

"They believed you were remorseful, and that you're a decent young man." She shrugged her shoulders and made to leave again. "Take the win, Dean."

I rubbed at my forehead, unsure of how to feel until she opened the door to three very eager people on the other side. It was hard to stay perplexed when a smile pulled at my lips at the sight of them. Of *her*.

Lily grinned and hurried past Ms. Davis with a skip in her step. She collided with my body, and I wrapped her in my arms, lifting her high off the ground.

She cupped my face and kissed me from above.

It was Seb thumping my shoulder with the energy of an excited kid that pulled us apart again. I set her on the ground before he tackled me with a hug of his own, knocking the wind from my lungs as he held on tight.

"Holy fuck, man. What the fuck?" He made the gesture of his mind being blown as he stepped back. "I am thoroughly flabbergasted."

"Congratulations!" Kira beamed, offering me a slightly less suffocating hug.

"I'm not sure if I should be congratulated." I glanced at Ms. Davis as she closed the door on her way out.

Lily slid her arm around my waist. "Why?"

"Antonio pulled some strings beyond the grave."

"Spooky," Seb said, wiggling his eyebrows.

"Do I want to know how that happened?" Mark muttered after casually approaching me in the large courthouse hallway.

The others were nearby, talking excitedly amongst themselves over plans for the rest of the day. From the sounds of things, drinks at a bar to celebrate my trial outcome was becoming a definite in their plans.

I slid my hands into my pockets. "Probably not."

Despite it bothering him, Mark accepted the outcome with a curt nod before he clapped my shoulder. "Use this second chance wisely."

"I will."

I watched him leave until Lily filled the spot where he had been and took my hand.

"What do you do now?" she asked.

"I need to get a bracelet fitted and a fixed address."

Lily's expression turned deadpan with a small smile as she tilted her head. "You know you can use mine..." She trailed off as her gaze drifted to something she spotted behind me. Her face softened. "I think she wants to talk."

I frowned and followed her line of sight to the corner of a corridor off the main hallway, where Julia Ricci, Antonio's widowed wife, stood. Dressed in a designer black dress with her hair slicked back into a bun and sunglasses on.

When she caught my attention, she calmly turned and disappeared around the corner. Whether or not it was an invitation to approach her, we did anyway.

Falling right back into old habits, I scanned the many faces of people walking by as we reached the secluded corridor, looking for familiar faces. There were none, but my guard stayed up anyway.

Julia waited a few feet from the corner with her hands folded over her clutch. She offered us a small smile as we stopped beside her.

"Julia," I said, glancing beyond her to the end of the corridor.

"Relax. I'm not going to ambush you." Julia was one of the good ones, but.

Lily was more forgiving with a response. "You can understand why we might be a little on edge..."

"Of course. And I don't blame you for it. I'm only here as a messenger."

My guard was still firmly in place. "From who?"

"Antonio."

"Antonio is dead."

"Well, I hope so. It would be unfortunate if he were buried alive at the funeral," she said with mild sarcasm.

"Sorry for your loss," Lily said gently, smiling slightly at Julia's dark humor.

"Thank you, hon."

I tried to relax. And tried Lily's approach of being more understanding. "How are you? With everything?"

"I'm coping. Antonio left behind a lot of unfinished business, which is the reason I'm here." She seemed to brace herself for what she had to say next. "Antonio had plans in place for if the worst should happen to him. He left me in charge, but he also wanted me to have a trusted business partner... The only person he ever truly trusted was you, Dean."

I had betrayed Antonio's trust by working with the cops — he knew this because of his mystery informant — but he was okay with that?

"He always said you reminded him a lot of himself — putting your loved ones first above all else. He respected that about you, despite what you did... I have made some changes to his plans, though. While he didn't leave it open for discussion, I want you to know you have a choice in this; take the offer and pick up where Antonio left off, or leave it."

When the initial shock wore off, I looked at Lily. There was a fine crease between her eyebrows, and she was subtly picking at her fingernails. Her eyes came to me and were filled with uncertainty.

She had been seeing Doctor Hamdan for the past five months, and slowly but surely, it was working for her trauma. If I went back to that life, what would it do to her?

The decision was easy.

"No."

The crease between Lily's eyebrows faded.

I pulled my attention off her as I continued. "Today was the last favor from him. I'm out."

Julia's smile was almost proud before she joked, "I don't think anyone ever truly leaves *the family*, but I respect your decision... Which is why I also have this. Not a bribe but a gift."

She popped open her clutch and pulled out an envelope, handing it to me.

I hesitated but tore the envelope open and tipped the contents into my palm: a key and a bank check.

"Antonio wanted to give you that after your mother's funeral, but that wasn't possible," Julia explained.

"That's a check for a million dollars," Lily whispered with her eyes on the piece of paper.

"*That's* how much Antonio made off Dean's fights," Julia grinned. "And then some."

I scoffed in amazement. "That's more than some... But what's the key for?"

"Address is in the letter in the envelope." She sighed to herself, before that warm smile was back. "I should get a move on. My brother is waiting... Good luck, you two."

The fact that I didn't know she had a brother was the least of my worries as we watched her walk down the secluded corridor to a back exit, where a man stepped out from an alcove and greeted Julia with a smile.

He wore sunglasses, casual clothes, and a baseball cap, but I recognized him immediately from my many visits to Mark's office.

Detective Dante Riccardo.

Or Dante Ricci, Julia's brother.

It was easy to figure out who Antonio's new informant had been.

He pushed the exit door open for his sister, sending one last look our way before they left the building, bringing with them the weight that once sat on my shoulders.

My attention drifted to the envelope again, and I pulled out the letter within it while Lily watched.

True to Antonio's style, there wasn't much detail. Just an address for a place in Park Slope, Brooklyn, scrawled neatly across the middle of the page.

Chapter 60

Dean

I was meant to go straight from the courthouse to get an ankle monitor fitted, but DA Anna Davis said she would buy me time — maybe an hour or two — when I showed her the contents of the envelope. She knew nothing about it, at least that's what she said.

Shortly after that, Lily and I found Seb and Kira, waiting out in the courthouse foyer scanning the menu for the in-building café. We were just about to tell them about the envelope when Kira spotted someone in the swarm of people moving through the building. Her smile dropped, and then so did ours as we watched Aiden approaching on his crutch. Waiting nearby was his probation officer.

"He's got a fuckin' death wish." I moved myself in front of Lily, partially blocking her from view.

"If he's coming over here with some *I need to get your forgiveness as part of my anger management therapy* bullshit, I'm gonna hit him with the menu board," Seb said, rolling his shoulders, until Kira took his hand. His attention went to her and she smiled as she placed a hand on his cheek.

"I have a better idea," she said before kissing Seb. As she did, she raised two middle fingers in Aiden's direction.

Seb pulled his arms further around Kira's waist, completely enveloped in her as he smiled onto her lips.

Whatever Aiden's intentions had been, he seemed to forget. He stopped in his tracks, watching as the woman he broke put on a show of adoration and love for the man who had helped pick up her broken pieces.

Aiden miraculously got the hint, glowering a little and flushing red from embarrassment as he limped back to his probation officer.

Lily's hand slid into mine, and the tension left my body as I looked at her. She had just finished her own sigh of relief when she said, "We should get going."

"You know, we could leave right now," I said with my arm around Lily's shoulders in the backseat of the cab.

"You mean run away and breach your conditions?" She raised an eyebrow. "I don't think so. I just got you back, and I'm not letting you become a..." She lowered her voice to a whisper, "fugitive."

"I'm pretty sure I'm breachin' those conditions now," I whispered back, smiling.

"Bending the rules. Anna gave us two hours."

I brought my lips to her ear. "There's a lot we can do in two hours."

"Focus," she giggled.

As the drive went on, more and more Brownstone houses with tree-lined streets came into view. Eventually, the cab slowed in front of one of the few homes with a long, narrow driveway down its left side, leading to a garage and maybe a small courtyard garden in the back.

I leaned across Lily's lap to get a better view of the place through the window.

It was two stories high — three including the basement beneath — and built with red brick and black trimmings. Everything about it was elegant but cozy, right down to its dark green front door.

"Are you gettin' out or what?" the driver drawled.

"Yes, right, sorry." Lily quickly paid and we climbed out of the cab.

Long after the cab had left, we stood on the sidewalk looking at the place.

"I'm assuming this is yours," Lily said in awe.

"One way to find out." I fished out the key from my back pocket and made my way up to the stoop. There were several potted plants at the top of the stairs, and ivy clung to the corner of the house, creating a green wall that stretched the length of the driveway.

The door unlocked, and I let it swing inwards while we remained on the stoop, peering inside.

There was no furniture, and it smelled of fresh paint and wood. Expensive wood, based on the original timber floors that were polished to the point I could almost see my reflection.

A hallway stretched out before us, with living rooms on either side and a bright kitchen and dining room in the back. A grand staircase with white carpet and black metal rails ran along the hallway, leading to the next level.

"Is this real?" I asked, taking a step over the threshold.

Lily took a few steps ahead of me to peer into the living room on the right. Her smile only widened, and she turned around. "There is an entire wall of empty shelves in there."

My lips curved up.

She bit her lip and took another step into the room while I drifted towards the stairs.

"And a fireplace," she added.

I investigated the living room on the left from its doorway. It also had a fireplace.

"Jesus Christ," I muttered, pulling my gaze up to the top of the stairs. There was shelving up there too, inside an alcove that would make for a perfect reading nook.

While Lily got lost exploring downstairs, I went up, finding three large bedrooms, two of which had bathrooms. The master bedroom was at the end of the landing, around the corner of that book nook. Its windows invited the afternoon sun to shine down directly onto the carpet, warming the space. As I walked over to the windows, more of the courtyard at the back of the house came into view.

There's a fucking greenhouse.

I heard Lily come up the stairs, followed by a quiet gasp as she discovered the second floor too.

"There is a bathtub in here!" she exclaimed from one of the bathrooms. "With jets!"

I chuckled, more so in disbelief as I turned slowly on the spot, locking my fingers behind my head.

When Lily walked into the bedroom, her eyes lit up, and she approached the window.

"What do you think?" I asked.

"It doesn't matter what I think. Antonio left you a house. This is all yours." She looked at the carpet, where the sun was shining. "Though I think that might be my favorite spot."

With that, I lowered myself to the floor with a smile on my face and took her hand to guide her down with me. She happily obliged and took up the space between my legs, resting back against my chest as the sun shone down on us.

I rested my chin on her shoulder and pulled my arms around her. "I wanna run somethin' by you."

She tilted her head back, eyes closed, as the sun danced along her skin. "Hm?"

"When this house arrest is done, I wanna bring Mom's ashes home, and I was wonderin' if you'd wanna go with me."

"To Palermo?" She half turned in my arms to look at me.

I nodded, already lost in that blue sparkle of her eyes.

"Of course, yes," she beamed softly.

My fingertips tucked her hair behind her ear, and then smoothed along her jaw. "One more thing."

The look she was giving me, like she was falling for me all over again, jump-started a barrage of butterflies in my gut. I never got butterflies. A little nervous, maybe, but not this fluttering feeling.

"Move in with me." Technically, we were living together before the trial, but this was different. "It's a big place for just me and a small dog. And considering I'm gonna have a curfew for the next twenty-four months, which means no sleepovers at yours…"

Lily laughed. "That is a very polite way of asking me to be your in-house booty call."

"Okay, so I worded it wrong. What I meant was, I wanna share this with you."

She was beginning to blush. "I'd have to talk to Kira first."

"Of course."

"And I'd have to bring my furniture. Not that I have a lot to fill this place. It'd be whatever is in my room. And my books. *And* maybe the pastel blue couch."

"We'll buy stuff with that million," I shrugged. "But I want you to decorate. One, because I'm shit at it, and two, because you'll make it feel like home. You're already doin' that by being here."

Lily got to her knees but remained between my legs as she brought her hands to the sides of my face and leaned in, smiling as she spoke. "Okay."

She kissed me like it was a signature, making the move-in official.

I lay back, bringing her with me to keep her lips on mine. She moved her legs to straddle my hips, devouring a groan that left my body as my hands roamed over her.

No sex for five months had left me itching to touch her again.

We were definitely about to have sex on the carpet regardless of any deadlines to be elsewhere. There was still an hour and a half to kill, and five months of love to catch up on. Plus, the carpet was invitingly soft.

When Lily pulled back slightly, the sun coming through the window created a warm glow around her.

"Ignoring the fact you have to wear an ankle bracelet *and* stick to a curfew," she said. "How does freedom feel?"

I brought my hand behind her head and kissed her slowly.

We were in our own little slice of paradise with a lifetime of memories ahead of us.

"A lot like this."

Acknowledgements

Thank you, the reader, for your patience and love you share with these brain babies of mine. Readers are the reason I write (well, I would still write even if no one read my books, but this awesome audience of mine gives me the boost I need to pursue this hobby and career). You're awesome and I will be forever grateful to you for giving my books a chance!

To my betas, this was the first time I ever enlisted beta readers for a book and you made the entire process easy. If it wasn't for you guys, Dean would probably be speaking with a few accidental Australian terms, and there would be plenty of car parks and garbage bins hanging around, so I thank you for your eagle eyes, awesome feedback, and abundance of support!

To AJ, for answering any of the little questions I had about editors, publishing tips, and just any bookish advice. You're the Pandora's box of indie author advice despite being a newbie to it all like me. And I will forever be grateful to you for introducing me to the world of book boxes!

To Madi. My soulmate an entire ocean away. You're f*cking awesome. We've been through it these past couple of years, and expelled some toxicity, but we came out on the other side ready to fight god (and our ovaries) with flaming dump trucks and the right amount of spite and petty attitude. And now we're both kicking goals with our dream jobs, so f*ck yeah to that! You have the kindest soul and biggest heart, and your opinion is one of the few I listen to — I literally only write the spicy stuff if it is to your standards. Thank you for sharing all the spicy art, all the Pedro Pascal thirst traps, and all the unhinged videos and memes. Love you!

To Charlie, my goofiest of goofs, you may be a dog but your antics, big butt, and understanding eyes keep me sane regardless of if I'm writing or not.

And to Mum. You aren't much of a reader, so you might not ever see this, but thank you for putting up with all of my rantings and ravings about characters, writing, editing, plot holes, and publishing. And even if you have no clue what happens in my books, you still tell your friends (or anyone who will listen) all about them. When I said I wanted to be an author, which feels like a hundred years ago now, you didn't discourage that choice, or push me into doing something I didn't want to do. Instead you let me explore the passion and see where it took me (that also goes for my reading and drawing obsession). Thank you for being my biggest support.